Usurper

Peter Darman

Contents

List of characters

Those marked with an asterisk * are Companions – individuals who fought with Spartacus in Italy and who travelled back to Parthia with Pacorus.

Those marked with a dagger † are known to history.

The Kingdom of Dura

Aaron: Jew, royal treasurer at Dura Europos

*Alcaeus: Greek chief physician in Dura's army

Azad: commander of Dura's cataphracts

*Byrd: Cappadocian businessman resident at Palmyra, formerly chief scout in Dura's army

Chrestus: commander of Dura's army

Claudia: daughter of Pacorus and Gallia, princess of Dura

Eszter: daughter of Pacorus and Gallia, princess of Dura

*Gallia: Gaul, Queen of Dura Europos

Isabella: daughter of Pacorus and Gallia, princess of Dura

Kewab: Egyptian, deputy commander of cataphracts in Dura's army

Marcus Sutonius: Roman, quartermaster general of Dura's Army

*Pacorus: Parthian, King of Dura Europos

Rsan: Parthian, governor of Dura Europos

Sporaces: commander of Dura's horse archers

Talib: Agraci, chief scout in Dura's army

The Kingdom of Hatra

*Diana: former Roman slave, now the wife of Gafarn and Queen of Hatra

*Gafarn: former Bedouin slave of Pacorus, now King of Hatra

Pacorus: Prince of Hatra, son of Gafarn and Diana

Other Parthians

Khosrou: King of Margiana

*Nergal: Hatran soldier and former commander of Dura's horse archers, now the King of Mesene

Peroz: King of Sakastan

†Phraates: King of Kings of the Parthian Empire

*Praxima: Spaniard, former Roman slave and now the wife of Nergal and Queen of Mesene

Roxanne: Queen of Sakastan

Salar: prince of Sakastan

Silaces: King of Elymais

Non-Parthians

†Kujula: Emperor of the Kushans

Malik: King of the Agraci

Noora: Agraci wife of Byrd

Rana: Kushan, queen and Kujula's sister

Rasha: Agraci, Queen of Gordyene

Spartacus: adopted son of Gafarn and Diana, King of Gordyene

Chapter 1

'It looks brand new, as though it has just been carved.'

The man who had escorted my daughter Isabella from the eastern edge of the empire stroked the limestone.

'It is magnificent and looks like it has been created by one of the gods.'

I laughed when I thought of the man who had carved the griffin standing guard over the city of Dura by day and night.

'The stonemason was a barrel-chested Greek by the name of Demetrius,' I told him, 'who had a foul temper, irreverent manner and treated me like one of his apprentices. But he knew how to create a masterpiece from a slab of rock.'

'The princess told me your kingdom is safe as long as the griffin stays here, majesty, though your sorceress once told her that one day it might fly away to the mountains in the far north.'

He was talking of Dobbai who had been dead for eighteen years but who still cast a long shadow over Dura and its king. I thought back to the encounter with the old woman in black at Lake Urmia during the campaign against Mark Antony. It was she, I know it was, but as the weeks passed the meeting became more and more like a dream. Perhaps it was a dream?

'Majesty?'

I snapped out of my daydreaming to smile at Agbar, the commander of King Peroz's bodyguard from far-away Sakastan. He and two hundred of his men had arrived three weeks ago along with my daughter. Isabella had spent many months in Sakastan and it would have made sense for her to stay there while the guests to her wedding, which included her parents, made their way to Sigal,

Sakastan's capital. But Gallia had wanted all her daughters to be reunited at Dura one last time and insisted she and I accompany Isabella to the wedding. And so Isabella had returned to Dura to prepare for the journey to her betrothed's city and their marriage bed. Gallia was delighted. I thought it a complete waste of time that Agbar and his men had been dragged across the breadth of the empire for no reason at all.

'Would you like to inspect the legionary camp?' I asked.

'That would be a great honour, majesty.'

Tramping round a dusty, sun-baked camp was not everyone's choice but since his arrival Agbar had shown a keen interest in Dura and its army. I had no idea if he was genuinely interested or was being the perfect guest but he had made a favourable impression with his impeccable manners and generous sense of honour. We walked down the stone steps in one of the towers flanking the griffin that stood above the Palmyrene Gate, mounted our horses and rode to the camp half a mile to the west. As usual the entrance to the city was a mad press of people, carts, spitting camels and flustered guards trying to keep a semblance of order, but we managed to thread a way through the throng to ride the short journey to where the Exiles and Durans were based. Both legions were on an extended training exercise though a skeleton garrison had been left behind to guard the mud-brick wall perimeter, stores and the Staff of Victory. The griffin and lion standards always marched with the legions but the staff stayed behind under heavy guard.

Because the camp was mostly empty it was mercifully free of dust but not the heat beating down from an angry sun in a cloudless sky. We rode to the commander's large tent, though Chrestus was away leading his men in the desert to the west and would not return for ten days. Agbar, wearing his open-faced helmet but not his cuirass of overlapping polished square steel scales, dismounted and looked around at the neat rows of tents accommodating the legionaries, almost all empty. Among them were larger granary tents, a hospital, stabling blocks and workshops.

'What do your soldiers sleep in when they are away, majesty?'

'In tents exactly the same as the ones here in camp. But because these tents stand in the open for months until they are replaced, tents used for campaigns and exercises are held in warehouses in the city.'

I nodded at the nearest block of tents. 'These are replaced on a regular basis though in truth they are very hardy.'

'They are Roman?' he asked.

'They are based on those used by the Romans, yes, but are produced by the city's tannery.'

'I would like to visit it, majesty.'

I thought of the stench of urine hanging over it at all times, a consequence of the need to employ piss in the manufacture of hides, which is why it was located well away from the city.

'If we have time I should be delighted to take you there.'

Legionaries took our horses and those of our escort to the stables near Chrestus' grand headquarters tent but what Agbar really wanted to see was the Staff of Victory. There were three tall, square tents positioned immediately behind Chrestus' living quarters, all usually heavily guarded but today only one of them ringed by legionaries. The other two normally housed the golden griffin and silver lion but they marched with the legions. The remaining occupied tent was where the Staff of Victory resided. We walked over to it, the duty centurion with his white transverse crest eyeing warily the tall man beside me wearing a yellow silk tunic, yellow leggings and red leather boots. But he and his men snapped to attention as we passed, though he held out his vine cane to prevent the escort – yellow-clad soldiers from Sakastan – from entering.

'You lot stay here,' he growled, menace in his voice.

A frown spread across Agbar's clean-shaven face.

'We only allow a limited number into the tent at any one time,' I said apologetically. 'When we have finished your men can take turns to see the Staff of Victory.'

It sounded grand but in truth it was an ordinary wooden pole topped with a silver horse's head, the brainchild of Lucius Domitus. The silver discs fixed to the staff, each one bearing a unique design, had value in themselves but it was what they represented that made the Staff of Victory priceless. Inside the tent Agbar stood admiring the discs, each one created to commemorate a victory won by the army of Dura. The army that had never tasted the bitterness of defeat, albeit one that had come close on several occasions. There were discs saluting the victories of Surkh, Susa, Uruk, Carrhae and Persepolis. I tried to maintain a kingly demeanour when Agbar's eyes rested on the disc showing a dying elephant being speared by legionaries – my defeat of King Porus of Sakastan. That triumph really belonged to Domitus and a herd of swine and I hoped Agbar would not question me about it.

The atmosphere inside the tent was oppressive, not only due to the heat but also because each legionary present stood with his hand on the hilt of his *gladius* , ready to pull it should the foreign stranger attempt to steal the Staff of Victory. If in a moment of madness he tried such a ruse my presence would not prevent him from being hacked to pieces.

9

'It should be in more appropriate surroundings,' said Agbar at length.

'A marble hall, perhaps?' I suggested. 'I have thought about it but this has been its only home and over the years the army has come to regard its presence in camp as a lucky mascot. And with each victory the idea that to move it would anger the gods took root. So it stays here.'

'So many victories, majesty,' he said admiringly.

I smiled politely but as the years passed all I saw was the loss of friends and the earth drenched in blood. The moment of victory was sweet indeed but glory commanded a high price; perhaps too high.

We rode back to the city after an inspection of the camp, which must have disappointed Agbar somewhat on account of it being largely deserted. When we arrived at the Citadel an agitated Rsan was waiting for me. *Tegha* and the other horses were taken to the stables to be rubbed down and unsaddled. Agbar and his men returned to barracks to refresh themselves before Sporaces, the commander of my horse archers, gave Agbar a tour of the armouries beyond the Citadel's walls.

Rsan bowed his head. 'May I have a word with you, majesty?'

He held a rolled papyrus scroll in his hand and I suspected that more than one word would pass between us.

'Of course,' I replied, 'come to the terrace.'

We walked across the cobbled courtyard to the palace steps. Near us carts were unloading supplies at the bakery and granary along the northern wall, and the sound of hammers working metal on anvils came from the workshops in the northwest corner. Rsan said nothing as we walked through the porch into the high-ceilinged hall leading to the throne room. But I could tell by the frown he wore he was far from happy. Now in his seventies, unlike most of us his skin was not dark and weather beaten, a result of him purposely staying out of the sun. The first day I set eyes on him he was wearing a spotless flowing white gown and today was no different, though now his steps were a little stiff and his shoulder-length hair thinning.

We passed the guards on each side of the dais and made our way to the palace terrace accessed via a corridor to the rear of the throne room. The head steward reported to me on the terrace as we settled under a white canvas awning in wicker chairs stuffed with cushions. Below were the blue waters of the Euphrates and beyond the river the lands of my brother, King Gafarn of Hatra. I ordered refreshments to be brought, though I knew most would be sent back to the kitchens. Rsan was abstemious at the best of times and more so when he was troubled.

'How can I help you?' I asked him.

He smiled politely and unrolled the scroll.

'We are all delighted that Princess Isabella is back in the city, majesty, albeit only for a short time. I remember when she was a young, carefree girl and now she is to marry. How the years pass in the blink of an eye.'

I too smiled politely and held up a hand.

'I'm sure you did not want to speak to me to reminisce about my daughter's childhood.'

Rsan said nothing as servants placed a table between us and loaded it with dishes of olives, pastries, bread, cheese and a jug of water, pouring the liquid into two cups. The governor waved them away but took no refreshment as I sipped at the water. He held up the scroll.

'This is a list of people who will be accompanying the princess back to Sakastan in a few weeks.'

He perused the list. 'You and the queen, naturally, the princesses Claudia and Eszter, Lord Byrd and his wife, the king and queen of Hatra.'

'I am acquainted with who will be travelling with us to Sakastan, Rsan. What of it?'

He cleared his throat. 'May I draw your attention to King Malik and Queen Jamal, majesty?'

I picked up a pastry and took a bite. 'You should try one of these, they are delicious. What of Malik and Jamal attending Isabella's wedding? She has known Malik since she was a child.'

'Can I assume King Malik will be accompanied by a bodyguard, majesty?'

I finished the pastry and picked up another. 'Two thousand warriors will be accompanying the Agraci king and queen, the same number that will be escorting each of the monarchs of Dura, Mesene, Hatra and Gordyene.'

'Is it wise for so many Agraci warriors to be crossing the Euphrates in light of King of Kings Phraates' policy, majesty?'

'You mean his ludicrous Parthian purity policy?' I answered, finishing the second pastry. 'Please, try one, they melt on the tongue.'

Rsan picked up a pastry and nibbled the end. 'Most appetising. But to return to the Agraci problem.'

'There is no Agraci problem, Rsan,' I told him. 'Isabella wants Malik and Jamal at the wedding, Gallia and I want them there and it would be entirely inappropriate for a king to travel anywhere without an escort. As a stickler for rules and regulations I would have thought you would be the first to acknowledge this.'

Rsan put down the pastry. 'Such a gesture will arouse the ire of the high king, majesty.'

I picked up an olive. 'It may, though I'm sure the high king is mindful he is only high king and not a Roman puppet due to the armies of Dura, Mesene, Elymais, Hatra and Gordyene in the recent campaign. Like a pair of finely balanced scales he will find that his annoyance over a party of Agraci travelling from the Euphrates to the Indus will be offset by the recognition that he owes his crown to those traveling with King Malik and Queen Jamal.'

'A most interesting analogy, majesty,' said Rsan without enthusiasm.

I had received no word from the high king since the return of the army from Persis after the campaign to kill Prince Alexander, the second son of my dead friend King Atrax and my very much alive and embittered sister Queen Aliyeh. Alexander had indeed been killed and Dura's army had marched back to its homeland, soon after another silver disc being added to the Staff of Victory. I had no doubt Aliyeh and the new King of Media, King Darius, had petitioned Phraates long and hard about mounting a campaign against my kingdom but the high king had been content to stay at Ctesiphon. The son of Orodes and Axsen had inherited few of his parents' good qualities but he was the rightful heir to the high throne and for the sake of continuity I had lobbied hard for his coronation. His reign and indeed the empire had faced an immediate challenge when Mark Antony had invaded Parthia at the head of over one hundred thousand Roman and Armenian soldiers. But we had chased Antony back to Armenia in a campaign that had cost him a third of his army and left the rest demoralised and without weapons and equipment. Phraates had been present throughout most of the campaign, though had taken little direct control of actual operations. Nevertheless, his presence had reinforced his credibility and afterwards the scribes and priests at Ctesiphon had been working tirelessly to create an image of the young high king as a military genius who had inflicted defeat after defeat on the Romans.

'To allay your fears, Rsan, I have given much thought to how we may proceed without provoking the high king into taking any action he may later regret.'

'I do not understand, majesty.'

I finished off another olive. 'The clarification will be arriving shortly.'

King Silaces arrived three days later. The ruler of Elymais was now in his early sixties and had always had a world-weary look but the recent campaign in the north, during which he had lost Valak who had been like a son to him, had deepened the worry lines on his face. It had also made him more embittered. He arrived at the head of a hundred horse archers who were quartered in the Citadel along with the yellow-uniformed soldiers of Agbar.

I stood on the palace steps with Gallia when Silaces and his men rode into the courtyard, squires running to assist the king from his saddle, only to be waved away.

'I'm not a cripple yet,' he bellowed, easing himself to the ground.

Rsan walked forward and bowed. 'Welcome, majesty, quarters have been prepared for you and your men. You will want to rest and refresh yourself, I assume.'

Silaces gave him a withering look. 'Why? Do you need to rest? You are after all older than me.'

Gallia walked over and embraced Silaces, planting a kiss on his cheek.

'Don't bully my governor, how are you?'

'In need of a drink,' he replied.

She linked her arm in his and together they walked back to the palace. I slapped my friend on the shoulder and walked beside them into the porch, Rsan issuing orders to the duty centurion regarding the billeting of the riders from Elymais. Silaces stopped when he spotted two soldiers in bright yellow tunics and leggings across the courtyard.

'Soldiers from Sakastan, part of Isabella's bodyguard,' I told him.

'When you travel to her wedding make sure you have a big bodyguard,' he said, 'I don't trust that bastard Phraates.'

He used that word to describe the high king a lot. Silaces was never a man to curb his tongue but since the loss of Valak his utterances towards Phraates had become coarser. Among friends it did not matter but I worried that his disparaging words would reach the ears of the high king, who might march against Elymais.

Later, after he had washed and dressed in fresh clothes, Silaces questioned me concerning my request for him to travel to Dura. We sat on the terrace as the sun was dropping in the west to turn the desert pink and the waters of the Euphrates orange. The King of Elymais stood at the stone balustrade holding a silver cup filled with wine and stared at the river below. I joined him and we stood in silence for a while, drinking in the majestic and serene view.

He took a large gulp of wine. 'You know what I think?'

'I am eager to learn.'

'If I lived here I would never leave the palace. I would stay here with my family and ensure a constant stream of friends visited me so I could enjoy days filled with fine wine, good conversation and peaceful vistas.'

He turned away from the river. 'Why did you ask me here?'

I nodded to a waiting servant who refilled Silaces' cup and walked back to the table where other servants were placing serviettes and silver dishes. According to etiquette a royal family should eat its meals in the banqueting hall but Gallia and I preferred the terrace, which was more intimate and relaxed. Tonight she wore her hair loose and sported a beautiful white dress that clung to her still shapely figure, her arms bare. She gave Silaces a dazzling smile when she appeared from our private apartments and took her place at the table. He smiled back, the first time he had done so since his arrival as my queen beckoned him over to sit next to her.

At that moment Claudia walked on to the terrace and Silaces froze. It was the first time he had seen her since the murder of Valak and her terrible ordeal and I saw the surprise in his eyes. Claudia still had her mother's cheekbones and thick long hair, though hers was light brown instead of blond, but the old Claudia had long gone. In her place was a serious, studious woman who always wore black and was older than her years in many respects.

Silaces bowed his head. 'Princess. I hope you are well.'

'The gods have been kind, lord. And you?'

'I'll be better after a few more cups of wine,' he said.

She nodded and took her seat at the table on the other side of Gallia. Claudia was the only one of our daughters in residence, Eszter being at Hatra and Isabella having travelled with Talib and his men to

Palmyra. The last to arrive was Rsan, the governor bowing solemnly to me, Gallia, Claudia and Silaces before taking his seat.

Food was ferried from the kitchens – roasted chicken and lamb and cooked fish, accompanied by pickled radishes, almonds, garlic, raisins, bread and mustard – all washed down with wine, fruit juice and water. As the wine flowed Silaces' mood lightened and he and Gallia chatted and laughed about past times, though I noticed that the king frequently glanced at the sombre figure of Claudia engaging in polite conversation with Rsan. Her formality and distance ironically put my governor at ease, unused as he was to sharing informal occasions with his king and queen.

It was dark, the terrace lit by oil lamps, when I informed Silaces of my reasons for requesting his presence at Dura.

'For one thing it has been too long since you visited us, my friend,' I told him. 'And I also want to ask you a favour.'

'Name it and it shall be yours,' he said, his speech slightly slurred.

'Soon we will be travelling east to Sakastan,' I said, 'and I want you to command the armies of those kings who will be travelling with us. I have been in discussion with Gafarn, Spartacus and Nergal and they agree with me that in our absence you should lead their combined armies, plus the army of Dura.'

Silaces frowned. 'Lead them against whom?'

I placed my cup on the table. Of those present only Gallia knew of my plan.

'I shall write to Phraates informing him of my intention to escort Isabella to her marriage with Prince Salar. The rulers of Hatra, Mesene and Gordyene will likewise inform the high king of their intention to journey to Sakastan. He will appreciate the courtesy.'

'You hope,' said Claudia, 'though someone will have to explain to him the notion of courtesy first.'

Silaces laughed and banged the table with his fist, much to Rsan's chagrin.

'Be that as it may,' I continued, 'I shall also be informing Phraates that in our absence King Silaces has been granted full authority to command the armies of Hatra, Mesene, Gordyene and Dura, along with any auxiliary forces that said kingdoms may raise. This is both to preserve the western frontier of the empire and the territorial integrity of the aforementioned kingdoms.'

Claudia was nodding in approval, Rsan appeared uncomfortable and Silaces none the wiser.

'You think the Romans are planning another invasion?' he asked.

'Highly unlikely,' I replied, 'but in our absence I do not want Phraates to be tempted to take any unwise actions, the more so because I have no doubt that my sister is still pouring poison into his ears. One hundred and thirty thousand men should curb his avarice.'

Silaces grinned. 'Ah, I see. Clever, Pacorus, very clever.'

But Rsan was horrified. 'You would threaten the high king, majesty?'

'I do not threaten him, Rsan, I merely remind him that the armies of the western kingdoms stand ready to battle their enemies.'

'Of course, he will see straight through the ruse,' said Claudia. 'Phraates has a malicious mind, father. He will seek to strike at you but not in a manner you expect.'

Everyone stopped their eating and looked at her, the princess who was now part of the secretive, semi-mystical Scythian Sisterhood that operated in the shadows. Like most people I knew very little about them, only that Dobbai was their high priestess, though she had been dead for many years.

'But you know?' queried Gallia.

Claudia picked up a date and nibbled at it. 'Why should I know, mother, I am not privy to Phraates' schemes?'

'He should have been strangled at birth,' grumbled Silaces, causing Rsan to nearly choke on his wine. 'You should have been high king, Pacorus.'

Gallia placed a hand on Silaces' and smiled warmly at him but Claudia would have none of it.

'Father is entirely unsuited for the role of high king,' she announced. 'His sense of honour and loyalty to his friends would wreck any chance of maintaining peace within the empire.'

'How so?' I asked.

Claudia finished the date. 'Imagine a dispute between King Nergal of Mesene and the ruler of the adjacent Kingdom of Babylon. You would naturally side with your friend, notwithstanding the merits of the king of Babylon's case.'

I held up a hand. 'Nergal would never try to encroach upon another king's realm.'

Claudia threw back her head and laughed. 'Oh, father, you are so predictable and in a single sentence reveal that you would never side against your friends. In any case I said nothing about a territorial dispute. Let us theorise that King Nergal had taken a liking to the queen of Babylon.'

Now I was angry. 'Impossible. I have known Nergal for more years than you have been on this earth and he would never be unfaithful to Praxima.'

'He's right, princess,' agreed Silaces.

'I have always found King Nergal to be a most conscientious monarch,' stated Rsan.

'You have all proved my point,' said Claudia. 'Notions such as conscience, loyalty and friendship mean little to Phraates. I doubt he has any friends and I'm sure he does not care. But such an individual is well suited to the role of high king. It is probably the loneliest position in the whole world.'

'He's still an arrogant bastard,' spat Silaces unapologetically.

'He's content playing with his silver eagles, I have no doubt,' I opined, thinking of the two captured Roman eagles that were presented to him by Claudia and Rasha after our victory at Lake Urmia.

'A case in point,' said Claudia. 'You all remember how Phraates was promoting his ludicrous Parthian purity doctrine, which was instantly cast aside when Rasha presented him with the Roman eagles.'

'How can anyone trust such a man?' asked Silaces.

'They cannot and would be foolish to do so,' said Claudia, 'but such pragmatism, allied to ruthlessness, will ensure that the empire holds together, which is what we all want.'

What *I* wanted was to attend my daughter's wedding in peace instead of having to worry about the Romans, Armenians, the politics at Ctesiphon or the hostility of my sister Aliyeh. My other sister Adeleh, a member of the Sisters of Shamash, remained at Hatra and did not journey with Eszter, Gafarn and Diana to Dura in preparation for the grand procession east. A tent city sprang up on the eastern bank of the Euphrates, opposite the escarpment on which the Citadel perched, as the kings and queens began to arrive. Soon the red griffin banner that fluttered from the Citadel was joined by the white horse of Hatra, the double-headed lion sceptre crossed with a sword of Mesene, the silver lion of Gordyene and the black flag of the Agraci. The latter made Rsan wince every time he looked up at the standards but the Agraci had been visitors to Dura and its palace for many years and no one batted an eyelid when black-robed riders appeared out of the shimmering heat haze to trot through Dura's gates. Indeed, Malik had a large house in the city so frequent were his visits to Dura. He came with Jamal, Byrd, Noora, Talib and his scouts and two thousand warriors, plus a host of camels carrying tents, food, weapons and a thousand goats.

'Goats?'

'The Agraci's wedding gift to Isabella,' Malik announced proudly as he walked with me to the palace after dismounting, Gallia and Jamal deep in conversation behind us.

'That is most generous, my friend,' I said, wondering how we would be able to herd a thousand goats from Dura to Sakastan.

For the pre-journey feast Gallia had insisted that all the guests be lodged in the palace, notwithstanding Malik's property in the city. It was now rare for the many bedrooms in the palace to be occupied all at once but for a brief time they would be filled and the corridors would echo to the sound of laughter and conversation.

We had not gone a few steps when Eszter ran down the stone steps and flung herself at Malik, laughing, hugging him and planting kisses on his tattooed cheeks. Ignoring all protocol, she then embraced Jamal and kissed her too. Gallia laughed but I raised my eyes to the heavens. It was our fault that Eszter had spent too much time at Palmyra with the Agraci, learning their ways and becoming a wild child of the desert. With her dark brown eyes and even darker complexion she looked like one of the desert people and, too late, we

21

had packed her off to Hatra to soften her hard edges and become a Parthian princess. But a wild animal is never truly tamed and so it was with Eszter.

'Try to remember you are a princess,' I scolded her.

She kissed me on the cheek, grinned at the Agraci king and queen and bounded back up the steps.

'It so good to be back at Dura,' she squealed before disappearing into the palace.

'I had hoped that she would find a suitor in Hatra,' I lamented, 'but alas the young nobles have no desire to marry a wildcat.'

'She is a credit to you both,' smiled Malik. 'There are many men at Palmyra who would love to tame such a beauty.'

'We love having Eszter at Palmyra,' said Jamal.

I looked up at the blue sky and swore I could hear the gods laughing. Of my three daughters one had become a mystic, another was seemingly fated to marry an Agraci warrior, which would ensure she would be forever banished from Parthian society, and the other was to marry a prince of a kingdom at the eastern edge of the empire. What had I done to deserve such a brood?

'What are you looking at?' asked Gallia.

'Nothing.'

Isabella was the most orthodox of the three, though she too had been a frequent guest of the Agraci. It was a stroke of good fortune that Peroz had found his way to Dura in his youth because when he ascended to Sakastan's throne, he and his son Salar were frequent visitors to my kingdom. Isabella and Salar first became friends, then besotted with each other and so it was decided they should marry. It was an unusual occurrence for a union between

Parthian kingdoms because both parties were extremely happy about the arrangement.

At the feast that evening she certainly looked like a queen in the making with her unblemished skin, thick, softly curling brown hair and large brown eyes. Her slender but shapely frame was wrapped in a shimmering blue dress that would have complemented the blue sapphire ring that Salar had given her but it had gone missing during the journey from Sakastan. Isabella had been distraught so I had told her I would find a jeweller to replicate it. She had told me that was not the point. But she hid her disappointment as she sipped wine from a silver rhyton and talked politely to Gafarn seated next to her.

It was like the old days with the dining hall filled with guests and the drink flowing freely. Kalet and his lords sat at one table, gorging themselves on huge chunks of roasted meat, on another Malik's warlords trying their best to out-consume them. Dura's nobles and their ladies sat at other tables, ignoring the ruckus. If this had been any other Parthian city there would been outrage and indignation at the behaviour of the 'barbarians', but this was Dura, a frontier city where people were judged on their character and not by which social stratum or race they belonged to. They knew that the lords who lived in the desert around the city were wild and uncouth. But they had spilt much blood in defence of the city and its kingdom. Likewise with the Agraci, once feared foes but now valuable allies responsible for safeguarding the lifeblood of the kingdom. That lifeblood was the camel caravans that came from China carrying silk bound for Parthia, Egypt and Rome. The customs dues paid by the caravans poured into the treasury and made Dura rich.

I sat between Nergal and Gafarn on the top table, basking in the company of my family and friends. Gallia was laughing and joking with Diana and Praxima, three of the original Amazons, while Eszter was teasing Spartacus, the strapping ruler of Gordyene and the husband of Rasha, his Agraci wife. Sitting aloof from the revelry was Prince Pacorus of Hatra.

I tipped my rhyton at him. 'Is the prince unhappy?'

'Not as far as I know,' replied Gafarn. 'I think he finds Dura's frontier atmosphere strange. His wife is expecting their first child. That might also be on his mind.'

'Excellent news,' I said loudly. 'When is she due?'

'In six months, give or take,' replied Gafarn.

'You are to be a grandfather again,' smiled Nergal, 'I salute you.'

I slapped the King of Mesene on the back. He and Praxima had never been blessed with children on account of the hard usage his wife had been subjected to when she had been a slave in a Roman whorehouse. Dobbai had once told me Praxima would never bear children and although Nergal never mentioned the topic, I'm sure the absence of an heir weighed heavily on them both.

'Why so glum, then?' I asked.

Gafarn grinned. 'He is worried he may be summoned to Ctesiphon. As a result of him covering himself with glory in the campaign against Mark Antony the high king believes he has the qualities to be his chief military adviser.'

He gave us both sideways glances. 'Those of us who also took part in said campaign being beyond the pale as far as Phraates is concerned. How long do you think we will be away for?'

I shrugged. 'Four months, give or take. Surely Pacorus could stay at Hatra if he is worried about missing the birth.'

Gafarn shook his head. 'Hatra's Royal Bodyguard is going to Sakastan and where it goes, its commander goes. You know what a stickler for rules my son is.'

He was being sarcastic but I could still hear the pride in his voice. Pacorus was a fine young man, the heir to Hatra's throne who was accepted by all the noble families of the city as being suitably qualified to rule them. Gafarn's other son, the strapping King of Gordyene, was also a source of pride to his parents though it was as well that he ruled the wild kingdom of the north. Being the natural son of the slave Spartacus was bad enough but the fact he had taken an Agraci wife meant he would never have been acceptable to Hatra's nobles. But fate had been kind to young Spartacus: he had a striking wife, three sons and a kingdom reflecting his character.

'Where did you find it?'

Isabella was beaming with delight at the sight of her sapphire ring placed on the table before her.

'In your tent, lady.'

I immediately stood and pointed at the woman who faced my daughter.

'Arrest her.'

Guards walked briskly from their stations behind the top table with swords drawn as Isabella picked up the ring and looked quizzically at the tall, striking woman with hair as black as night.

All chatter died away as the guards circled the woman, standing her ground and fixing Gallia with her piercing brown eyes. Two guards seized her arms and bundled her away, her voice filling the chamber.

25

'I would have words with you, Queen Gallia, before you have me murdered, just as you did my brother.'

'Stop,' Gallia told the guards. 'Bring her here.'

The raven-haired woman smiled in triumph as she was shoved in front of the now standing Gallia, people mumbling to each other and pointing at the strange woman surrounded by legionaries.

'Search her for weapons,' said the duty centurion.

'I am not armed,' stated the woman, 'I am not an assassin like those who live in this city.'

'Shut her up', 'get her out of here', the guests demanded angrily, while Kalet spat out a piece of meat and shouted, 'I'll slit her throat for you, princess'. His lords banged their fists on the table to signal their support. I walked behind those at the top table to stand beside my wife. The rough search of the prisoner revealed her to possess no weapons.

'As I told you,' said the mysterious woman to the centurion, 'did you enjoy fondling my body?'

'Enough!' I commanded. 'You will provide me with your name.'

The women bowed her head. 'Indira, sister to Spada, commander of the army of Persis who was basely murdered by your wife, Queen Gallia, during an agreed parley.'

There were gasps around the hall, Gallia's stern expression showing no emotion, but out of the corner of my eye I saw my namesake's head drop. He knew the truth and so did I: Spada had been lured to a conference where Dura's desert lords, on the orders of my wife, killed him and his commanders.

'What do you want?' demanded Gallia. 'Compensation for your dead brother?'

'If you were indeed his sister,' I added.

Indira looked unconcerned. 'I do not lie, unlike your wife.'

More astonished gasps greeted her words. She was either totally fearless or completely mad. Either way this charade had to be brought to a speedy conclusion.

'Take her away,' I told the guards, 'she will answer to the law for trespassing on this feast.'

'Kill me and you and your guests will not reach Sakastan, King Pacorus, for just as I easily took your daughter's ring so will the warriors of Persis exact their revenge for the murder of their leader. But your wife can guarantee the safety of your family and guests, King Pacorus.'

'How?' demanded Gallia.

'In a trial by combat, Queen Gallia. Let Verethragna judge which of us should live.'

'Who?' belched Kalet.

'The Persian God of War,' answered Claudia, 'who has ten incarnations.'

This Indira was clearly mad. 'Take her away.'

But Gallia had other ideas and walked from her place to stand before her accuser.

'I accept your challenge.'

My jaw dropped as the hall was filled with wild cheers from Kalet, his lords and the Agraci warlords, while everyone else sat in stunned silence.

Chapter 2

'You are forbidden to fight her.'

I paced the terrace, pointing and issuing orders to Gallia who sat eating her breakfast in the company of our daughters. The feast had ended abruptly after Gallia had accepted Indira's challenge because I had ordered everyone to leave. I had toyed with the idea of having the unwanted guest strangled and her body thrown into the Euphrates, but Gallia had her escorted under armed guard to Malik's home just beyond the Citadel's walls, having received permission to do so from the bemused Agraci king. She then specifically forbade me to harm even a hair on the woman's attractive head.

'I am not one of your officers to order about,' she replied calmly.

'You are my wife,' I exclaimed.

'Just chop off her head,' offered Eszter.

'She should be flogged at least,' added Isabella, staring at her sapphire ring.

'What do you say?' I asked Claudia, hoping for some pearl of wisdom that would dissuade Gallia from fighting Indira.

'Verethragna punishes evil done by men and demons,' she answered. 'Was this Spada murdered?'

Gallia dipped a wafer in a pot of yoghurt. 'He was a casualty of war, nothing more, nothing less.'

Claudia wore a deadly serious expression. 'I interpret that as an admission that you murdered him, which would explain why this Indira woman was able to enter the Citadel so easily.'

'Lax sentries, more like,' I said.

Claudia gave me a pitying look. 'You could have ringed the Citadel with thousands of men and she would have still entered the Citadel easily. When you have the aid of the gods, soldiers are useless.'

'Just kill her and have done with it,' said Eszter.

'I thank you all for your advice,' replied Gallia, 'but she challenged me in front of my family, my friends, the lords of the kingdom and the nobles of the city. You are right, Claudia, I did kill Spada and I will do the same to his sister. The topic is now closed for discussion.'

I pleaded with her, her friends implored her not to fight, and every Companion still living begged her not to battle Indira, all to no avail. Gallia had the bit between her teeth and fire in her eyes. I knew it was hopeless to try to change her mind. I told her that Indira was at least fifteen years younger than her and reminded her it had been a long time since she had used a sword in anger.

She cut the air with a sideways slash. 'Nonsense, I use it every day.'

We were on the training field outside the city, the Amazons having just finished their early morning target practice on the shooting ranges and were now wrenching arrows from the straw targets. Zenobia, their commander, was holding the reins of Gallia's horse and those of *Tegha* as my wife swung her sword.

'You use it here, on the training field, but when was the last time you used it on the battlefield? In Italy?'

She stopped and faced me. 'Draw your sword, then, and let us see who is more adept with a blade.'

'This is ridiculous. I will not fight my own wife. I ask you one last time. Will you abandon this ludicrous duel?'

'I will not.'

'Then I will have her executed.'

She spun around and held the point of her sword at my throat.

'Do that and I will never forgive you for you will have betrayed me.'

I held up my hands. 'Very well, have it your way. Why are you so adamant about this?'

She lowered her sword and sheathed it before walking over to her horse, uncorking the water bottle strapped to the saddle and taking a long drink. It was still early but the heat was beginning to rise. It would be another hot and dusty day at Dura.

She replaced the cork in the top of her water bottle. 'When I was a child my father, King Ambiorix, was the arbiter in a dispute between two of his lords, Brennus and Cerethrius. Their disagreement concerned the ownership of a fertile valley adjacent to both their lands. Brennus was a great warlord, brave, fearless and the leader of a mighty war band. He had three sons who were as brave and formidable as their father. Cerethrius was very different. Older and wiser, he had three daughters but no sons, but was respected for his wisdom and fairness throughout the lands of the Senones.'

The Amazons had completed their arrow gathering and began to gather in a semi-circle around their queen. Instances of Gallia speaking of her time with the Gauls were rare and they listened intently, as did I.

'My father, true to his cunning nature, did not want to rule against either man, Brennus because he could have been a rival to the throne, and Cerethrius because of the high esteem in which he was held in my father's kingdom. So the matter was handed over to the chief druid. Both Brennus and Cerethrius presented their cases to the holy man, Brennus stating that he should be given the valley because his many warriors needed land to farm, and in any case his claim was stronger because he had three sons, whereas Cerethrius had only daughters and an insignificant number of warriors.

'Cerethrius stated that it was true that Brennus had a large retinue and three sons, but pledged that should he be granted the valley, then in gratitude he would give the druids half its annual crop yield in perpetuity. The druid awarded the valley to Cerethrius, which outraged Brennus. Soon after Cerethrius was found murdered after having been lured to a meeting by an unknown party. Soon one of Brennus' sons was boasting that he had killed Cerethrius on his father's orders but when the dead man's daughters petitioned my father, he washed his hands of the whole affair and awarded the valley to Brennus.'

There was absolute silence as Gallia continued her tale, and I too was spellbound.

'But the year after, when the crops were being sowed, flocks of ravens descended on Brennus' new valley and devoured the seeds. Thereafter misfortune befell his sons. One fell off his horse and broke his neck, another drowned and the third choked on a chicken bone. Eyewitnesses reported seeing ravens at each of these instances and the druids told the people that it was the work of the Goddess Morrigan, who often took the shape of a raven and is the Gauls' deity of revenge.

'I have no desire to bear witness to the deaths of my own daughters, Pacorus. I take full responsibility for my actions and I will honour the gods. That is why I will meet Indira in combat and that is why no harm will come to her beforehand.'

Indira looked calm and refreshed the next morning when she was escorted into the Citadel's courtyard by a score of legionaries led by Chrestus, the shaven-headed commander of the army. He had a face that looked like thunder as he left the guards and stomped over to where we were standing at the top of the palace steps. Gallia, hair braided down her back and dressed in leggings and a loose-fitting white tunic, nodded to him.

'Commander. I hope the prisoner has not been molested in any way.'

'If I had my way her head would be mounted on a spike on these walls by now, majesty. But no, she has not been harmed.'

He turned and nodded to the duty centurion who instructed two of his men to close the gates, other legionaries ensuring the doors of the buildings facing the courtyard were also closed. I had commanded all the clerks in the headquarters building to stay at home, though the servants, stable hands, farriers, blacksmiths and apprentices were still in residence to keep the palace and its garrison functioning. But they had been told to stay indoors, leaving the courtyard strangely quiet.

Gallia unfastened her sword belt and drew her weapon, a *spatha* similar to the one I carried. She handed me the scabbard and belt. I grabbed her forearm.

'It's not too late.'

She smiled kindly. 'The die is cast, my beloved. It is in the hands of the gods now.'

She turned to Chrestus. 'It is time, commander.'

He nodded again to the centurion who blew his whistle. Two centuries of Durans in full battle array marched from the barracks and formed the outside of a square in the middle of the courtyard.

Gallia smiled at our daughters and began walking down the steps with Chrestus, only to halt after a couple of steps. My heart soared and I beamed with delight. She had seen sense and decided not to fight this strange, sultry woman from Persis, if that is where she was from. My wife handed Chrestus her sword and marched over to Gafarn, who was holding a bow. She pointed at it.

'Why is the King of Hatra carrying his bow in my Citadel.'

'A Parthian is never far from his bow, Gallia,' he replied, straight faced.

She looked at him and then at me and sighed.

'You are Bedouin, not Parthian. Give me it.'

'I will not,' Gafarn insisted.

'Do you have so little confidence in my abilities, Gafarn, that you readily agreed to shoot my opponent? Let me guess. Pacorus begged you to kill her if I got in trouble, for he and I both know that you are the best shot in the whole empire and only you could guarantee that the arrow would hit the right target.'

Gafarn's mask of self-assurance began to crumble as he eyes darted from me to Gallia. She held out her hand. 'If you have any respect for me at all, give me the bow.'

Diana was going to try to reason with her friend but thought better of it, as did Praxima. So Gafarn handed Gallia his bow and my ruse failed. She handed the bow to Chrestus and they recommenced their journey down the steps to the waiting Indira, who was holding a dagger in each hand. I saw the *spatha* in Gallia's hand and was heartened. She was clearly mad if she thought two daggers could defeat an Amazon with a long sword.

Gallia faced Indira as the legionaries formed an enclosed wall using their shields facing inwards, half of them kneeling to place their shields on the cobbles, the other half holding their shields directly above those below. Two hundred men thus created a makeshift fighting arena so the two combatants could do battle. Chrestus withdrew and the fight began.

Gallia attacked immediately, lunging forward to thrust the point of her sword into Indira's chest. But the Persian side-stepped right and parried the blade with one of her daggers, using the other to slash at my wife's belly. Gallia stepped back but then attacked again with a flurry of overhead scything blows, which Indira beat away with her daggers, the blades becoming silver blurs in her hands. Gallia's blade was also moving fast, forcing Indira back towards the locked shields. I clenched my fist as my wife flicked her wrist to deceive her opponent who brought a dagger up to block an overhead strike but instead saw the sword blade sweep low to slash her belly. But Indira was lithe and sucking in her belly fell back into the shield wall, which buckled slightly.

'Hold!' bellowed Chrestus from the top of the steps.

Indira recovered and darted left to take herself away from Gallia, slashing my wife's leg with the dagger held in her right hand. There was a collective groan from those around me as Indira grinned in triumph and red began to show on my wife's leggings.

The wound did not seem to bother Gallia who again mounted a withering series of strikes against Indira, which were all parried. Gallia appeared tired and let her sword drop, Indira grinned but was then almost decapitated when my wife whipped her blade upwards in a lightning-fast strike. The edge of her sword missed Indira's neck by inches.

Now Indira attacked, using both her daggers to cut at Gallia from left and right. Deft sword positioning fended off all the blows

34

but as Indira spun away she whipped one of her daggers back and cut my wife's left arm. Diana shrieked in alarm and I felt sick to my stomach. Around me our friends stood open mouthed and ashen faced as Indira danced around Gallia, who seemed incapable of inflicting a scratch on her opponent. And then it happened.

Gallia deflected a dagger strike with a downward cut of her sword, only for Indira to jab the other knife into my wife's right hand, causing her to drop her sword. The blade clattered on the cobblestones a second after Gallia gave a shriek when Indira plunged the other dagger into her side. The right side of my wife's tunic began to turn red and Diana wailed and nearly collapsed. Isabella was praying and Eszter crying but Claudia was strangely calm as a smile crept over her face. I was about to throw up in panic when Gallia took advantage of a gloating Indira to grab the two dagger blades, gripping them firmly as she sprang forward to head-butt the Persian, splitting her nose and sending her sprawling.

'Yes,' shouted Chrestus in triumph.

Indira staggered to her feet but collapsed as blood poured from her broken nose. She was nauseous, disorientated and had blurred vision but could see well enough to appreciate the cold steel being pressed to her neck. Gallia had retrieved her sword and held it with her bloodied hand against Indira's throat.

'I give you your life,' said Gallia forcefully, 'do you yield?'

'I yield,' said Indira faintly.

We cheered and Gallia staggered.

'Defend your queen,' shouted Chrestus.

The shield wall dissolved and a circle of legionaries formed around Gallia, who had gone down on one knee. I rushed down the steps to cradle her in my arms, blood oozing from the wound in her side. She gave me a half-smile.

'The gods are appeased, Pacorus. Our daughters are safe.'

Gallia winced as the dog licked the wound in her side, Claudia holding up her mother's bloodstained tunic so the canine could use its tongue to maximum effect. The mutt had already licked the wounds to Gallia's arm and hand and was now lapping up her lifeblood with gusto. Claudia watched it carefully; a mangy flea-bitten dog that she insisted was beloved of the gods. Gallia rolled her eyes, Isabella was disgusted and Eszter bemused as Claudia encouraged the beast to finish its task.

'What in the name of the gods is going on here?'

Alcaeus, Companion, friend, and head of the army's medical corps, rushed over to Gallia and shouted at the dog to get away. His reward was the dog growling and baring its teeth at the Greek physician. Claudia led it away and used soothing words to calm it before ordering a servant to take it to her quarters. The young woman glanced nervously at the beast and then at Claudia.

'He won't harm you,' she assured the girl, 'he only likes to bite Greeks.'

I laughed but Alcaeus stopped rummaging through his bag and rounded on me.

'First you allow your wife to take part in a ludicrous duel and now you allow your daughter to indulge her mysticism on your injured wife, injured as a result of your folly.'

'He did not allow me to do anything,' said Gallia in a low tone, 'I do as I wish.'

Alcaeus probed the side wound with a finger.

36

'You are to be congratulated. It looks clean enough and probably won't need stitches. You were lucky.'

'Nonsense,' said Claudia, 'luck had nothing to do with it. Mother appeased the gods and they gave her victory over a far superior opponent.'

'You are too kind,' said Gallia sarcastically.

Alcaeus fished out a jar of ointment and began applying it to Gallia's wounds.

'You won't need that,' insisted Claudia, 'mother will heal quickly.'

Alcaeus finished applying the ointment and took a bandage from his bag.

'Now who's talking nonsense?'

Behind them the servant was leading a well-behaved dog from the terrace, though it gave our Greek friend a sneering departing glance. Alcaeus held up the ointment jar.

'This ointment is made from yarrow, which stops bleeding, combined with comfrey and calendula, both of which assist healing.'

Claudia pointed at the dog. 'Have you heard of the Goddess Gula, Alcaeus?'

The Greek racked his brains. 'I cannot say I have.'

Claudia gave a triumphant grin. 'I thought not. You have an enquiring mind so I will indulge you.'

Alcaeus began bandaging Claudia's wounds. 'You are too kind.'

'Gula is a goddess of healing, indeed she is called "the great healer",' stated Claudia, her sisters listening with fascination, 'who often appears to mortals as a dog.'

Alcaeus stopped his bandaging. 'That was a goddess? I have been remiss. Please get the servant to bring the dog back so I can throw myself at its paws in submission.'

Isabella and Eszter roared with laughter but Claudia's eyes narrowed.

'I did not say the dog was an incarnation of the goddess, I stated that she is closely associated with dogs. That particular dog appeared in the city's temple, the high priest informing me it has licked several worshippers suffering from a number of afflictions.'

Alcaeus was horrified. 'You should get Rsan to instruct his officials to round up the city's stray dogs, Pacorus. They appear to be infesting temples now.'

'The afflictions disappeared,' said Claudia smugly. 'Just as mother's injuries will heal quickly without your potions.'

Alcaeus tied off the bandage. 'Says the high priest.'

'Meaning?' snapped Claudia.

Alcaeus smiled at Gallia. 'Meaning a temple that possesses a healing animal sent by the gods will make a lot of money in a short period of time.'

'Rather cynical of you, Alcaeus,' I said.

'Have it your own way,' mocked Claudia, 'I have heard the Greeks are a godless lot.'

'You sound more like Dobbai by the day,' the Greek shot back. 'What are you going to do with the woman from Persis after we have patched her up?' he asked me.

'How is her nose?' asked Gallia.

'Broken,' replied Alcaeus.

'She should be flogged,' offered Eszter.

'After she has healed she will be free to go,' stated Gallia.

'She is dangerous,' I cautioned. 'Remember she spirited herself into Isabella's tent and stole her ring. There is no guarantee she will not seek to avenge her defeat.'

'I murdered her brother and now I have repaid the debt I owed her and the gods,' shrugged Gallia. 'We will not hear from Indira again.'

How wrong she was but she was not to be dissuaded and so Indira lived like a lady in Malik's mansion while he and Jamal slept in one of the palace bedrooms. Her nose healed, she did not cause any more trouble and so she left Dura on a horse gifted to her by Gallia. In return Indira sent the daggers she had used in the duel to the Citadel as a gift for my wife. Attached to them was a note from the Persian.

From one enemy to another. In recognition of your decision to face me in combat I did not lace the blades with poison before our match.

The kings and their entourages stayed at Dura for another two weeks while Gallia's wounds healed, during which time Gafarn humiliated me in an archery competition, Nergal had a fine time hunting gazelle in the desert with Malik, and Spartacus spent much time at the armouries enquiring about the cost of mail armour, cataphract tubular armour and the sword blades carried by my heavy horsemen. Each cataphract was armed with a sword forged from ukku steel, the strange ore that came from the lands east of the Indus. When made, each ukku sword had a blade containing strange swirling patterns that gave it an odd appearance. However, appearances are deceptive and an ukku sword was not only light but could cut through the blades of other swords with ease. But ukku blades were no longer forged at Dura because each ingot used to create a sword had cost the kingdom a gold bar.

I knew Spartacus was making his capital Vanadzor a centre of weapons production and was eager to learn how he could source ukku. I stood with him in one of the hot, bone-dry armouries watching big men with huge forearms and wearing leather aprons beating and shaping red-hot metal on anvils.

'I wish to equip my horsemen with ukku swords, uncle.'

'An ambitious project. Can Gordyene afford such an outlay?'

'Gordyene cannot afford not to be strong,' he shot back, which was hardly an answer.

'The war is over, nephew,' I told him.

We had to shout to hear ourselves above the din of hammers striking metal, the constant bellows feeding the fires of the forges and the incessant tapping of armour being fixed and smiths barking orders at sweating apprentices. I grabbed his elbow and led him outside the inferno where panting, sweating workers quenched their thirst at a water fountain that brought cool liquid from the Euphrates.

'You are in luck,' I told him, 'once we are in Sakastan I will send a letter to Patanjali Simuka enquiring as to the current price of ukku ingots.'

Spartacus wiped his sweating brow and neck with a cloth. It was a blisteringly hot day.

'Who?'

'A great lord of the Satavahana Empire, a great power to the east of the Indus. It was he who brought the ingots to Dura all those years ago. He might be dead, of course, but I'm sure King Peroz has contacts with the peoples east of the Indus. Do you have a thousand gold bars?'

He smirked. 'No.'

'Then how do you intend to pay for the ukku? As far as I know it is a strictly gold on delivery purchase.'

He picked up a newly made javelin that was standing in a rack near to a finishing shed to examine the soft metal shaft and point more closely.

'Put that down.'

The gruff armourer was fifty paces away but his thundering voice made everyone turn and stare in his direction. Spartacus looked at him.

'Yes, you,' bellowed the armourer, pointing at him, 'put it back.'

'Better do as you're told,' I advised, 'my armourers are very protective of their weapons.'

Spartacus did so and we walked back towards the entrance to the walled compound located to the west of the Citadel.

'Gordyene has little wealth but has an army that can take it from its enemies,'

I frowned in alarm. 'What enemies?'

'The Armenians,' replied Spartacus.

I sought to allay him. 'Having been defeated along with Mark Antony, I doubt the Armenians are in any state to threaten Gordyene.'

Our escort deployed around us as we walked from the armouries into the street.

'You are lucky, uncle. Dura is surrounded by allies and friends but I have to watch my northern border constantly and Media to the south is no friend of the son of a slave and his Agraci wife.'

'Your friends and allies are gathered here, Spartacus,' I told him, 'an attack on Gordyene will be viewed as an attack on all of our kingdoms and will be met with force against any aggressor.'

That seemed to please him. 'You are very kind, uncle. Will Dura join Gordyene if it decides to implement preventative action against Armenia?'

'You mean will I support you if you invade your northern neighbour on a whim? No.'

His cold, dark eyes regarded me and for a second I thought I was back in Italy being interrogated by his father.

'I do nothing on a whim, uncle. But the current peace is only a cessation of hostilities. When the Romans have recovered, they will strike at Parthia once again.'

'Perhaps you are right,' I said, 'but if you invade Armenia you will give them an excuse to wage war against us.'

'Do the Romans need an excuse to wage war? In any case, there are some who look to us to free them of Rome's tyranny.'

'Who?'

'It does not matter,' he answered evasively, 'but Gordyene will always support those who fight for freedom.'

I stopped to face him. 'Did I ever tell you of a man called Afranius?'

He gave me a blank stare. 'No.'

'He was like you, though about six inches shorter. A stocky Spaniard who had short hair and an even shorter temper. Following the death of your natural father he believed he could defeat the

Romans and capture Rome itself. He overestimated his abilities and underestimated the Romans and ended up nailed to a cross on the Appian Way, or so I heard. And whereas I do not believe you overestimate the strength of Gordyene's army, I do believe that you think taking Armenia would be as easy as picking a ripe apple. Raiding is not the same as conquering.'

He raised an eyebrow and fell silent but I knew that Lord Spadines and his Aorsi brigands were laying waste the borderlands of Armenia, under orders from Spartacus who encouraged their depredations.

'You are playing a dangerous game, Spartacus, and if you are not careful Gordyene and other Parthian kingdoms will be dragged into an unwanted war. I hope you will not use the absence of the kings of the western kingdoms to incite war with Rome.'

'Have no fear, uncle, Gordyene's army is a disciplined force that will not fight anyone without its king and queen leading it.'

'And the Aorsi?'

He shrugged. 'The Aorsi are a free people independent of Gordyene. I have no say in any course of action they may or may not take.'

'Of course not.'

Alcaeus declared his intention to accompany the wedding party to keep an eye on Gallia, who insisted she was fully healed.

'Nevertheless, I should attend you just in case your wounds reopen.'

'They are fully healed,' Gallia insisted.

The temperature inside the Headquarters Building was stifling and everyone was drinking liberal quantities of water in a vain attempt to quench their thirst. It was the weekly council meeting, the last one before we departed for Sakastan.

'You are welcome to come with us, Alcaeus,' I smiled, 'I know you have always wanted to see the eastern parts of the empire and this is an ideal opportunity for you to do so.'

'I must confess I have always wanted to see the Indus,' said the Greek.

'It's a river,' grunted Chrestus. 'You can see one just like it a few hundred yards from this very room.'

'I will not dignify that with an answer,' replied Alcaeus.

I looked at Kewab, freshly returned from the north of the kingdom.

'What news from Syria?'

He made to stand but I gestured for him to remain seated.

'The gossip from across the border is that after his defeat Mark Antony is busy trying to rebuild his army, majesty, assisted by Queen Cleopatra. But it will take many months before he is able to take the field once again. He and his queen are more concerned with their Roman enemies than with Parthia.'

I wiped my sweating neck with a cloth. 'Good, that is one less thing to worry about. Syria was denuded of soldiers to swell Mark Antony's army so I do not envisage any trouble from the north or east.'

'Thank the gods,' said Rsan.

I suppressed a smile but Chrestus was grinning like a fool. Poor old Rsan, he always imagined that a mighty army of Romans was waiting in Syria, poised to attack Dura the moment its king left the city, even though no enemy soldier had been before its walls in seventeen years.

'Rsan, you will rule in my stead while I am away.'

'In *our* stead,' stressed Gallia.

'And Aaron will be your deputy,' I continued. 'Chrestus will remain here with the army with Sporaces as his deputy. Azad will accompany us with the cataphracts and you, Kewab, will command the horse archers.'

Chrestus raised his eyebrows. 'You will take the whole dragon, majesty?'

'Isabella is my daughter and I wish to impress the people of Sakastan. A thousand cataphracts will do that. Besides, their presence will draw attention away from Kalet and his warriors, who despite my best efforts insist they are coming.'

'Of course they are coming,' said Gallia, 'Isabella views Kalet as a surrogate uncle. She wants him to be there when she is married.'

Alarm spread across Rsan's face. 'If Kalet and the lords depart, Dura will be defenceless.'

'I'm glad you have so much faith in me,' grumbled Chrestus.

'Only a thousand men will accompany Kalet,' I told Rsan, 'the rest will be staying to guard the western frontier.'

Rsan looked at Chrestus, who was bored and now irritable.

'I trust you will not be taking the army on manoeuvres while the king and queen are away, general. The citizens of Dura must know the army is ever vigilant.'

Chrestus gave him a malevolent grin. 'Actually, the army will be marching to Elymais to be at the disposal of King Silaces. Every horse archer, legionary and remaining desert lord will be coming with me.'

Rsan began shaking. 'Who will defend the city?'

'This is most irregular,' agreed Aaron.

Chrestus maintained a straight face. 'The replacement cohort will stay to protect your and your clerks, Lord Rsan.'

Rsan blanched. 'Untried new recruits and their instructors?'

'I have a gift for you, governor,' said Chrestus, pulling his *gladius* from its scabbard and placing it on the table in front of Rsan.

Rsan looked at it as though it was a poisonous snake.

'For you, governor, in case the enemy breaches the walls of the city.'

'Enough,' I commanded. 'The general is joking with you, Rsan, although his attempt at humour is in bad taste. He and the army will be staying at Dura.'

'Unless King Silaces demands its presence elsewhere,' added Chrestus.

'It is true that Dura's army will be at the disposal of Silaces while we are away,' I admitted, 'but the chances of him summoning it are slim.'

Rsan heaved a huge sigh of relief and after the meeting I recalled Chrestus after everyone had left.

'Don't prey on Rsan while I am away.'

Chrestus looked hurt. 'Me? I am just a soldier.'

'Very droll, but I am serious. Rsan is elderly now and deserves some peace in his dotage. I do not want to return to find he has died of a heart attack.'

'Perhaps he should retire.'

'Perhaps he should,' I said. 'But he has served this city and me well and he will be removed from his position only when he himself desires it. There are few men in the world like Rsan.'

Chrestus laughed. 'That is true enough, majesty.'

He looked out of the open window into the courtyard below.

46

'I wish I was coming with you. A route march of a thousand miles would be worth attempting.'

Now it was my turn to laugh. 'The tanners would have to produce ten thousand hobnailed sandals to re-shoe the legions when they returned. Aaron would not be happy.'

'Accountants and clerks do not keep this kingdom safe.'

I nodded. 'They do not, but they ensure those who do have excellent weapons and enough food and supplies to perform their duties. Anyway, we are not marching to war but to my daughter's wedding.'

On the day of our departure, the sky overhead was blue and cloudless, a pleasing breeze ruffling my banner held by Zenobia. In the Citadel's courtyard, Gallia was in an emotional state. While our friends descended the steps to mount their horses that had been brought from the stables, she gathered our daughters together and hugged them. There were tears in her eyes when she spoke.

'The occasions when we are all together like this will become much rarer now. It seems like only yesterday when you were small children running through the palace corridors. And now here you are, all grown up and strong women in your own right. Pacorus come here.'

I did as I was told, *Tegha* waited and I put an arm around Eszter and Isabella's waists.

'Whatever happens in the future,' said Gallia, 'wherever you are in the world, remember that Dura will always be your home, will always be a place that will never abandon you.'

'We are going to my wedding, mother,' said Isabella, 'not to our doom.'

Gallia wiped a tear from her cheek. 'Never yield to anyone, believe in yourselves and hold true to what you have learned here. All of you are individuals in your own right, beholden to no one and no husband's chattel.'

She kissed each of our daughters on the cheek and gripped their hands. There were tears in Isabella's eyes and a mask of proud defiance on Eszter's, while Claudia seemed strangely reflective.

'Come, my daughters,' said Gallia, 'it is time for the women of Dura to ride east.'

I embraced my daughters and caught Gallia's hand.

'Are you all right?'

She snatched it away. 'Of course, don't be a fool.'

The kings and queens of Hatra, Mesene, Gordyene and the Agraci, plus the King of Elymais, were our escort as we rode from the Citadel to the Palmyrene Gate. Durans and Exiles lined the street down to the gate, behind them cheering crowds of citizens bidding farewell to one of their princesses. The occasion may have been tinged with sadness but Isabella beamed with delight as people threw thistles, iris and Jericho roses onto the road to create a carpet of foliage for her to ride on.

When we exited the Palmyrene Gate everyone halted their horses to stare in wonder at the Durans and Exiles standing in full battle array with their standards. Either side of them were Sporaces and his horse archers and Azad's mounted cataphracts – thousands of men in mail and steel armour and helmets, saluting their departing princess. I rode to where Chrestus stood with his senior officers, leaned down and shook his hand, raising my hand to his commanders in recognition of their thoughtfulness.

The soldiers of the other kings had crossed over the Euphrates earlier to accompany their lords for our plan was to travel down the left bank of the river for four hundred miles before crossing the river adjacent to Uruk. Then we would ride through Nergal's kingdom to head for the city of Elymais and on to Sakastan. But firstly, we rode into the desert a short distance to avoid trampling crops and date palm groves.

I had worked hard to restore the agricultural lands of my kingdom, which spread south from the city of Dura for a hundred miles. Peace with the Agraci meant farmers could grow their crops free from the threat of being attacked by desert raiders. The garrisons of the mud-brick forts spaced at five-mile intervals along the length of the Euphrates throughout the kingdom assisted the farmers in constructing irrigation channels bringing water from the river to their fields. The western bank of the Euphrates was now blossoming and I did not want thousands of camels and horses to trample crops and scatter livestock. Nor did I want the more unruly elements of our force – Kalet and his lords – grazing their animals on farmers' crops.

In appearance there was little difference between the lords and their warriors and Malik's men. Both sides wore loose-fitting black robes with *shemaghs* as head and face protection. Like all of us they applied antimony powder around their eyes to alleviate the damage caused by squinting in the sun. All of us had adopted the Agraci goats' hair tents, which in the inferno of summer were very hot to touch on the outside but which remained pleasant inside in extremes of heat. Of course, those who lived on the other side of the Euphrates denounced those who inhabited Dura as semi-barbarians and half-breeds who intermarried with the Agraci and other races. It was true, but the Parthian Empire also contained many different races and peoples that had intermarried over the centuries, making a mockery of Phraates' policy of Parthian purity.

Our column kicked up a huge amount of dust as it wound its way south across the barren, scorched landscape, a small army comprising over eleven thousand warriors and soldiers, seven thousand camels and three thousand squires. Gafarn had brought Hatra's Royal Bodyguard, its members drawn from the cream of the city's nobility. On the battlefield their steel armour and helmets glinted in the sun and their white horses were encased in scale armour, but today the armour for men and horses was stored on camels led by squires, their masters riding in leggings, tunics and floppy hats. Two squires served each cataphract, each one leading a camel that carried armour, food, tents, spare weapons, clothing and fodder for their horses. The horse archers, considered the poor relations of the mounted arm, were supplied by the camel train, which also carried an adequate quantity of replacement arrows. As we were not marching to war, however, we were not equipped with a dedicated ammunition supply train.

We maintained a steady rate of travel, riding for two hours and dismounting to give our horses a rest before recommencing our riding for another two hours, and so on. In this way, we covered forty miles a day, halting in the early evening to pitch camp and prepare an evening meal, though the horses were unsaddled, rubbed down, watered and fed before we partook of our own food. Our sustenance, if it can be called that, consisted of hard biscuit, dates, cured meat and water. We ate well at Dura and would do so again when we reached Uruk, but I saw no point in bringing along a small army of servants, barrels of wine and animals to be slaughtered for an evening meal.

Prince Pacorus made a face as he chewed on a piece of cured goat.

'This is not Hatra's palace, alas,' I said.

We had all gathered to eat our evening meal in my tent, where we sat at a table on the carpet-covered floor.

'You should have asked to borrow Phraates' pavilion,' Gafarn told me, 'that is how a king should travel. Purple and crimson rugs underfoot and rich curtains decorated with animal patterns in gold and silver. It even has guy ropes made of silk.'

'Completely useless,' said Silaces, biting off a chunk of dry meat, 'like its owner.'

'Let's not spend an evening listing Phraates' shortcomings,' I pleaded.

'Why not?' asked Silaces, 'he has so many, as you yourself recognise, Pacorus. After all, you would not be gifting me command of your army if you did not feel he needs restraining.'

He looked at Spartacus, Gafarn and Nergal. 'You all feel the same, do you not?'

They nodded but Diana wanted to change the subject.

'Let us not speak of Phraates, he is so hateful. Let us hope maturity will come with age.'

'Tell us of Sakastan,' requested Rasha of Isabella.

My daughter had a wistful look as she described her adopted homeland.

'It is a land of great beauty, one dominated by towering mountains and forbidding desert but one where you will find lush forests of larch, aspen and juniper. The rivers feed irrigation ditches that water flat plains filled with wheat and vines, while swampy terraces are abundant in delicious rice.'

'Sounds idyllic,' opined Nergal.

Isabella sighed. 'It is.'

I smiled as she waxed lyrical about Sakastan, its topography and people, painting a picture of a land of milk and honey. When you are in love everything seems rosy and free from blemishes, but I remember Peroz painting a more realistic picture of his kingdom during one of his visits to Dura. He told me of hot, dry summers and cold winters, of a land that could be lashed by severe dust storms and spring floods when melt water came from the mountains. It suffered plagues and pestilence like all other kingdoms and its people worshipped the gods and prayed for a better life. But I was more interested in Sakastan's current relations with Carmania.

Agbar and his men were never far from Isabella during the journey, guarding her tent at night and surrounding her during the daylight hours. The commander of her bodyguard was mortified that Indira had spirited herself into my daughter's tent on the journey to Dura but Claudia had criticised him for reproaching himself.

'The knifewoman had the help of the gods, commander, no security measure would have made the slightest difference.'

'Why would the gods assist an assassin, princess?' asked Agbar, his yellow attire in sharp contrast to the black robes worn by Claudia.

She shrugged. 'Perhaps Spada was beloved of the gods and they were angry that my mother had robbed them of his life. Or perhaps they thought Indira and my mother would make a good match and wanted to discover which one would triumph.'

Agbar was relieved that what might be viewed as a dereliction of duty was absolved by divine intervention. I liked the honest and forthright Saka who was very forthcoming when it came to the king of the Carmanians.

'King Phanes has continually tried to provoke his brother, my master, into starting a war, majesty.'

I had heard the same from Khosrou of Margiana but wanted to hear the story from a new source.

'He sends raiding parties across the border to rape and pillage.'

'And yet Peroz does not retaliate?' I queried.

'He is too noble to sink to his brother's level,' stated Isabella. 'If it wasn't for the queen mother the two brothers would have reconciled long ago.'

I was curious. 'The queen mother?'

'Queen Hamide, majesty,' Agbar informed me, 'the woman who casts a long shadow over the kingdoms of Sakastan and Carmania.'

Chapter 3

We travelled through the passes of the Zagros Mountains to reach the city of Elymais, the capital of the kingdom of the same name that was positioned in the foothills of the mountains. It was a pleasant, clean city freshened by cool mountain breezes and fed by clear water from the highlands. The mountains themselves although bleak and imposing contained large, fertile plains providing fodder for herds of wild horses, the most famous being the Nisean that mounted Parthian horse archers and cataphracts. Elymais supplied horses to the other kingdoms in the empire and even to the Chinese emperor. This made its kings and merchants rich, the more so because the Silk Road passed through their territory. The caravans used to be prey to the semi-nomadic tribes that infested the Zagros range – the Uxians, Baktiari, Quashqui and Kamsa – but the rulers of the kingdom had used bribery and repression to keep the roads free of bandits, as well as recruiting the young men of the tribes to fight in their armies. I myself had recruited Zagros tribesmen to fight the Romans in Judea many years before.

The soldiers and their horses and camels pitched camp outside the city walls, the kings and queens being lodged in Silaces' palace, an impressive structure constructed on a stone terrace and containing a throne hall, stables, temples, stone columns and walls decorated with friezes of mythical creatures. It was also filled with slaves who attended to the wishes and whims of their guests.

At Dura councils of war were held in a room in the Headquarters Building but at Elymais they were conducted in the War Hall, a square structure surrounded by stone columns. It had a marble floor, cedar doors and a huge hide map of the Parthian

Empire on the wall facing the couches on which we sat, white-robed slaves serving us fresh fruit juice and pastries. Silaces pointed at the map, slapping the backside of a striking female slave with raven-black hair down her back and sultry brown eyes.

'Persis is under the rule of a new satrap, one of Phraates' lackeys by the name of Osrow. He's a little toad by all accounts but you should know that he and Phanes are allies, or kindred spirits might be a better name.'

I was alarmed. 'Peroz's list of enemies grows.'

'What about Drangiana and Aria?' asked Spartacus.

Those two kingdoms lay north of Sakastan and I had to confess I knew next to nothing about either. Silaces winked at the slave who beamed back at him. Clearly the King of Elymais did not sleep alone when back in his homeland.

'Aria is ruled by Tiridates the Younger, the son of the now deceased Tiridates the Elder, and Drangiana is ruled by King Antiochus. Both monarchs are more interested in what is happening to the east rather than the squabbling between Phanes and Peroz.'

'And what is happening to the east?' asked Gafarn.

Silaces walked over to the map and pointed at the lands beyond the empire's eastern frontier.

'They are concerned about the Kushans, a warlike people who a generation ago were unknown but who now lie across the Indus.'

'Where did they come from?' asked Nergal.

Silaces walked back to his silver rhyton. 'From somewhere in the east. The point is they are looking for new lands to conquer and the Indus is broad but shallow.'

'Then what keeps them on the other side of it?' said Spartacus.

'We do,' smiled Silaces, 'or at least us and the other kings of the empire. The Kushans know that the Parthian high king can raise a mighty army to come to the aid of the eastern kingdoms, so Kujula is wary of starting a war with the empire, for the moment.'

I was intrigued. 'Kujula?'

'The leader of the Kushans,' he told me.

'What else do you know of him?' asked Gafarn.

'He's got a big army,' stated Silaces.

I emptied my rhyton. 'It is as I have always believed. *If* the empire stays united and strong it can repulse its external enemies. That is why it is important for all of us to be seen to support Phraates.'

'Word will have been carried to the four corners of the world of our recent victory over Mark Antony,' said Spartacus.

'And our visit to Sakastan will deter any aggression from these Kushans,' I added.

Gafarn studied the map. 'Perhaps if Phraates became aware of the dangers facing his eastern border he might be deterred from listening to the grievances of Queen Aliyeh.'

Silaces was unconvinced. 'Soon you will need a hammer and chisel to prise Phraates away from Ctesiphon. He likes intrigue and court life, and unlike his father views the idea of touring the kingdoms of his empire with distaste.'

'He is still young,' I said. 'He needs to grow into the role. I accept that he may not have the qualities of his father.'

'That's putting it mildly,' sniggered Silaces.

'Nevertheless,' I continued, 'he has defeated the Romans, which strengthens his position, which in turn is good for the stability of the empire.'

Spartacus was confused. 'Forgive me, uncle, but if you are such a staunch supporter of Phraates, why have you arranged a potential alliance against him?'

'He has a point,' grinned Gafarn.

'I have not formed an alliance against Phraates,' I insisted, 'I have merely taken measures to curb his youthful exuberance.'

Silaces held out his rhyton to be refilled. 'What if Phraates, realising he has potentially one hundred and thirty thousand soldiers to call upon, summons me to Ctesiphon to inform me he has decided to invade Syria or Armenia?'

Gafarn was laughing. 'Didn't think of that, Pacorus, did you?'

I had not.

'You will inform him that it will take at least six months to assemble such a force, perhaps longer,' I told Silaces, 'by which time we will have returned to our respective homelands, and then we will petition the high king, pleading for more time because we are experiencing logistical difficulties.'

'What difficulties?' Spartacus demanded to know.

I sighed deeply. 'Tell him your soldiers are deficient in weapons.'

Spartacus jumped up. 'No Gordyene soldier is deficient in weapons and equipment.'

I held my head in my hands. 'In the name of the gods, I know that, Spartacus.'

'Then why say it?' he scowled.

'It is just a ruse, a delaying tactic.'

He retook his seat. 'Ah, I see. I suppose I could tell him that, although if he thinks Gordyene's army is weak that might encourage Media to attack us.'

'We are just speaking in generalities, my son,' smiled Gafarn, 'I'm sure your uncle never intended to slight you or your army.'

Nergal leaned back and looked up at the intricately carved cedar wood ceiling. 'Of course, if Pacorus had accepted the high crown then all these plans and schemes would not be necessary.'

I shook my head at one of my oldest friends. 'Please don't, I feel a headache coming on.'

But the short time spent at Elymais refreshed our bodies and minds and ended all too quickly. We said our farewells to Silaces and continued our journey east, the cool mountain air giving way to the heat and dust as our great column skirted the Dasht-e Lut to the north. This desert was unlike anything in Syria or Mesopotamia where animals and people could eke out an existence and even prosper. Dasht-e Lut means 'emptiness desert' in Persian, a place of searing heat, strong winds and shifting dunes. Agbar and Talib scouted ahead as we wanted to avoid the main road used by the caravans carrying silk west to Egypt and Rome. Not that we intended any harm to those using the Silk Road from China; rather, we wished to avoid drawing attention to our column, which was venturing dangerously near to Carmania's northern border. So we entered the southern area of the Dasht-e Lut where travellers, if they had any sense, rarely ventured.

For two days we were blasted by howling sandstorms, forcing us to stop as clouds of sharp, golden sand particles engulfed us. Then the wind ceased and we re-commenced our journey, traversing a landscape seemingly devoid of life but possessing a wild beauty with its sand dunes the size of temples, white salt pans and pink sandstone hills sculptured by the winds. We carried on east through a horizonless expanse, the unrelenting heat sapping people and animals alike. We reduced the time we sat in the saddle to save the horses, their heads cast low during the hottest parts of the day and only reviving in the evening when they were relieved of their saddles and given water. We slept under the stars rather than pitch tents to save energy, which the squires were grateful for.

The days appeared endless but that was a deception. Shadows lengthened and the temperature dropped rapidly, the ever-blue sky overhead darkening quickly as we halted to make camp for the night. Stars filled the night sky to present a wonderful spectacle, which no one had the energy to appreciate after hours under a merciless sun traversing an energy sapping desert. So we slept like the dead and woke as dawn was breaking, the desert turning orange and purple as the sun rose above the eastern horizon. As the heat rose conversation invariably dried up as everyone focused on his or her individual journey. Patrols were posted to the flanks, vanguard and rear, but even they spent most of the time on foot rather than in the saddle. No one wanted to bear the shame of losing a horse to dehydration or exhaustion. Only the camels seemed immune from the harsh conditions.

On the sixth day of our ordeal in the Dasht-e Lut, the heat more intense than previously, if that was possible, my legs became like lead as I led a lethargic *Tegha* by the side of a huge star-shaped dune. My lips were blistered and I was regretting the decision to venture into this wasteland to mask our presence and cut a few days off our journey. Gallia, head covered by a floppy hat, her pale skin blotchy, walked ahead beside Zenobia with the Amazons. I turned to see Eszter alongside Isabella and, further back, Claudia walking beside another figure in black. Rasha probably. They seemed deep in conversation, Claudia's arms gesticulating, and the wife of Spartacus nodding. Hardy breed, the Agraci.

That night, as I lay exhausted staring up at the stars after a meal of hard biscuit and even harder cured meat, I questioned Claudia about her conversation with Rasha.

'I have not spoken to Rasha in days,' she told me.

'I saw you talking to her today,' I said, 'unless my eyes were deceiving me.'

'I was talking to a friend,' she replied.

I sat up and looked at her. 'What friend? We have been in this godless place for days.'

She gave me a withering look. 'No place is bereft of the gods, father.'

'Perhaps you could introduce her to me tomorrow,' I said.

'She is no longer with us,' she shot back.

I chuckled. 'She has taken herself off to her village, perhaps? Oh, wait, there aren't any settlements in this desert.'

'I will say no more on the matter,' replied Claudia.

On the seventh day of our journey we reached the city of Bam.

Located in a wide barren plain and surrounded by the Kaboudi and Baarez Mountains, the city of Bam was the gateway to Sakastan, a green oasis surrounded by dirt and sand. For over three thousand years people had come to Bam to trade, pray and refresh themselves in its cool waters.

Agbar accompanied the governor to welcome us to the Kingdom of Sakastan. A huge man with a shaven head, gold earrings and large belly, Governor Rogerio smiled a lot to reveal immaculate white teeth. He arrived in a large litter carried by a dozen slaves who looked clean, fresh and were dressed in fine white clothes, red sandals on their feet. We, in contrast, presented a sorry spectacle – unwashed, unshaven, our clothes dusty and our horses in need of a good brush and re-shoeing. I saw surprise in Rogerio's eyes when he alighted from his curtained litter to stand before us, but he was all smiles when Agbar introduced the kings and queens standing in front of him. He clicked his fingers to bring four slaves forward holding large umbrellas that they used as sunshades for Gallia, Diana, Praxima and Rasha. His eyes were filled with lust as he beheld my wife's blonde hair.

'We have all heard of Queen Gallia of Dura but the stories do not do you justice, majesty,' he bowed deeply, took her hand and kissed it. 'Such beauty is rare in this world.'

Gallia laughed. 'I fear days of being blasted by sandstorms and roasted under the hottest sun I have ever experienced have taken their toll, but I thank you for your kind words.'

Rogerio kissed her hand again. 'I have seen much of this world, majesty, but you are one of its wonders, truly.'

He continued to hold her hand, which Gallia gently removed from his grasp.

'We need water for our horses and men,' I told him.

'Of course, majesty, I have arranged for your army to be quartered north of the city where there is an abundance of water.'

We had arrived from the west, riding parallel to the great Silk Road running from the east through Bam and on to the west. Our thousands of horses and camels could not be accommodated within the various caravan parks around the city, so had to be quartered in a specially designated area beyond the extensive groves of date palms resembling a fat green serpent wrapped around the city. I was about to thank the governor when he barked orders to bring forward

61

another litter, this one with carved ivory decorations and pure white curtains on all four sides. Then he stepped forward and went down on one knee before Isabella.

'Welcome home, princess.'

Isabella grinned and held out her hand for Rogerio to kiss. This time there were no honeyed words or flashing smile, just a governor welcoming home a woman who would one day be his queen. Hopefully it would be many years before she wore Sakastan's crown.

'Your litter awaits, highness.'

Eszter giggled as Rogerio led Isabella to her waiting litter, clapping his hands when she was lying on the stuffed mattress and cushions, drawing the curtains to shield her from having to look at the city's common folk as she made her way to the palace. Agbar and his men, who like us were dishevelled and in need of fresh uniforms, surrounded the litter as the slaves carrying it sweated in the heat.

'My back aches like fury,' complained Gafarn, 'I could do with one of those.'

'Please take mine, majesty,' offered Rogerio.

'We will be riding to our quarters,' said Diana sternly.

But first Rogerio assigned officers from the garrison to escort the various contingents of our army to the camping area. I pulled Kalet to one side to emphasise the fact that we were guests in Sakastan and not part of a conquering army. He nodded earnestly as I stressed the need for him, the lords and their warriors to behave themselves and not cause any trouble. But even as the words were leaving my lips I could tell they were wasted. Bam was a rich city and wealthy cities are filled with brothels where those with money can indulge their fantasies, after first sating their thirst in one of the dozens of inns ranging from back-street gambling and fighting pits to establishments with their own stables and fine dining.

'Try not to get yourself killed,' were my parting words to a Kalet salivating at experiencing everything an eastern city had to offer.

Bam was an imposing place, surrounded by a high mud-brick wall with over thirty square towers along its extent. The defences were bolstered by a wide, deep moat filled with water, wooden causeways across it giving access to the city. Guards shoved curious onlookers aside when the kings and queens and their bodyguards rode through the teeming city to the citadel positioned on a hilltop at its centre. Faces of every race stared at our column, barefoot urchins ran up to us to beg for money and the scent of market stalls selling spices from China filled our nostrils. Bam was a dusty, crowded, busy city, a hive of commerce in the middle of a stony, barren plain.

'Watermelons!'

Eszter jumped from her horse and ran over to a stall piled high with large green oval balls. The column halted and Rasha joined my daughter, bartering with the scrawny stallholder who wielded a knife with dexterity when a price had been agreed. The two women squealed with delight as he cut up a pair of watermelons and they began feasting on the juicy red innards.

'I'll have one as well,' called Nergal, sliding off his horse.

Within half a minute we had all dismounted and the stallholder was clapping his hands together with delight as his goods were purchased. Even Claudia dismounted for the opportunity to gorge on a watermelon. We stood like naughty children, juices spilling on our dirty tunics and leggings, grinning like idiots as we devoured the sweet-tasting fruit.

'It is to your liking, highborn?' the stallholder asked me, his purse now bulging with coin.

'Immensely,' I replied, juice running down my neck.

Our yellow-uniformed escorts lowered their spears to keep a curious crowd at bay, their commander calling to us.

'We should get to the citadel, majesties, the city is full of thieves and beggars.'

We were beginning to attract a growing crowd of young children, all in filthy rags and rank in odour, each one holding out a hand in the expectation of money from a highborn. It was time to leave, I agreed.

We pushed our way through the throng to get back to our horses, Eszter and Rasha buying more watermelons that they tossed into the crowd by way of a diversion. I arrived at *Tegha* being held by soldier of our escort and felt a tug on my tunic. Fearing a thief, I spun and drew my *spatha*, to see a terrified boy no older than ten staring at me, wide eyes filled with alarm.

'What?' I grunted irritably.

He held out a small rolled parchment. 'For you, great one.'

I sheathed my sword, took the papyrus and tossed him a coin for his troubles.

'Don't sneak up on people, it might end badly.'

He gave me a wolfish grin. 'Thank you, king slayer.'

Hot, tired and now irritable, I shoved the scroll into my tunic and did not think of it again until Gallia and I were in a luxurious large stone bath sunk into the floor of our bedroom, slaves having filled it with fresh, cool water drawn from a nearby well.

'Qanats,' I said.

Gallia opposite opened her eyes. 'What?'

'The water that gives this city life comes from qanats, which are underground tunnels tapping into underground mountain lakes. They were built four hundred years ago by the Persians.'

'That would explain why the water is so cool,' she said, a slave girl rinsing the last sand particles from her blonde locks. The girl then began to massage my wife's skull with her fingers, making Gallia drowsy.

'What was in the letter?' she sighed.

'I had clean forgot. It will wait.'

After our bath our limbs were covered in oils and massaged to ease the stresses of the past few days from our bodies. It did not take long for both of us to slip into a deep sleep, the slaves absenting themselves to allow us to rest. When I awoke the light outside was fading and oil lamps were burning in our room. I picked up the unopened letter and broke the wax seal bearing the image of a peacock, the emblem of Carmania.

'Who is it from?' asked Gallia.

'Hamide, the mother of Phanes and Peroz.'

'What does she want?'

I tossed the letter on the bedside table. 'I have been summoned to a meeting with her.'

The next morning, when the steward allocated to attend to our every need arrived at our door, I requested that he fetch me clean goose feathers. He assured me that he already had an abundance of writing instruments and there was no need to fashion them myself. But I told him that I needed them for my helmet.

'You are not a soldier reporting for duty, Pacorus,' Gallia teased me as I pulled on a fresh pair of leggings.

'I might as well try to make a good impression on Peroz's mother,' I told her, 'Agbar has informed me she is a formidable figure.'

'I doubt she wants to welcome you to Sakastan,' said Gallia, 'more likely she is here to cause trouble.'

The steward, newly returned with a basket of white goose feathers, assisted me putting on my armour: a two-piece black leather cuirass. They were muscled pieces, the front embossed on the upper chest with a golden sun motif, two golden winged lions immediately below. Fringed strips of black leather, adorned with bees, protected my shoulders and thighs.

'Beautiful armour, majesty,' he said, 'the lion is the emblem of Dura?'

'No, the griffin. This armour was a gift from a friend and was taken from a dead enemy soldier.'

'Castus,' said Gallia.

I stared out of the window at the blue sky and thought of my long-dead German friend. Was it really thirty years ago?

'Good times.'

'Majesty?'

The steward was looking at me in expectation. I returned to the land of the living and picked up my helmet, a splendid steel piece with large hinged cheek plates and a brightly polished brass crest. For comfort it was padded on the inside.

'Place the feather in the crest.'

I strapped on my sword belt and examined my boots, which were spotless, slaves having removed them the previous evening and returned them gleaming. I had sent orders that Azad and Kewab were to escort me to the camp of Queen Hamide, which was located south of the city among the extensive date groves ringing Bam. With them were a hundred cataphracts in full armour, including full-face helmets. Their horses were covered in scale armour protecting their heads and necks, the eyes of the beasts shielded by metal grills. The men also wore light white cloaks that draped over the hindquarters of their horses. It took half an hour to ride from Bam's citadel to the outer gates, the press of people and carts slowing our progress to a crawl. Azad wanted to use his ukku sword on the hordes of beggars flocking around us, some of the children trying to prise away the metal scales on the horses' scale armour, earning them a slap round the face from the irritated horsemen. Finally, we reached the gates to leave the good citizens of Bam behind, and cantered to the camp of the Carmanians.

Away from the bustle of the city the queen's camp, sited to take advantage of the shade offered by date palms nearly all over seventy feet tall, was an oasis of calm and order. Guards armed with spears, swords and carrying large round shields painted red and bearing a golden peacock guarded the perimeter, a group of them halting our column until the commander of the queen's escort could vouch for us. He arrived with a group of mounted spearmen who also carried shields sporting a golden peacock, escorting me to the tent of Queen Hamide herself, situated on the edge of the expansive grove. I say tent but it was a large pavilion surrounded by wood and canvas stables, a wagon park and a corral filled with camels, which was mercifully downwind of the royal quarters.

Azad and the cataphracts were escorted to the stabling block where they would be at least be able to take off their helmets, and wait in the shade until my audience was over. I and Kewab, helmets in the crook of our arms, followed the commander of the queen's guard into the pavilion to an audience chamber where Hamide was sitting on a couch.

She was a small woman with white hair and a round face, her skin wrinkled, giving her an unattractive appearance. Her dark brown eyes looked at the handsome Kewab in his gleaming armour and then me.

'Which one is the king?'

I stepped forward and give a slight tilt of my head. 'I am.'

Her eyes narrowed. 'You are shorter than I expected and not as imposing as I had been told. But then, stories are always embellished and the further away the topic of conversation the greater the exaggeration.'

She pointed at Kewab. 'Who is this, your son?'

I smiled. 'Commander Kewab is one of my senior officers.'

'He will stand; you can sit.'

She pointed at a couch opposite the one she was lounging on, a low table piled high with dates, sweet meats and pastries between the two. A fawning slave took my helmet and requested that I unbuckle my sword belt. I asked why.

'Because everyone knows King Pacorus of Dura is quick to use his sword when provoked. My guards think it prudent to disarm you lest you try something.'

I unbuckled the belt and handed the slave my sword.

'I can assure you I have no intention of using it.'

Hamide chewed on a date. 'Another myth shattered. Today is threatening to become one of disappointments.'

I sat on the couch and Kewab also surrendered his weapon. Hamide clapped and two slaves came forward, one carrying a silver tray holding a gold cup, the other a silver jug. The cup was filled with a white liquid and offered to me. I eyed the liquid.

'It is called *kallu* ,' said Hamide, 'palm wine, if you will. It is quite safe.'

I sipped at the liquid, which had an agreeable, sweet taste.

'Does Governor Rogerio know you are here, lady?'

'Governor Rogerio is a fat sycophant who is best avoided,' she said. 'I specifically requested a place away from him and his city.'

'It is a magnificent city.'

'Bam is like all cities, King Pacorus, it stinks of shit and is full of detestable common folk. That is why rulers build citadels with high walls on hills, to keep them out of sight and mind. Unfortunately, high ramparts do not prevent noxious smells from permeating even the strongest of strongholds. I find the snakes and frogs of the date palm grove more to my liking.'

'I'm sure you did not summon me here to complain about Governor Rogerio.'

She clicked her fingers to prompt a slave to offer me a dish of pastries.

'You go to Sigal to attend the wedding of your daughter Isabella to my grandson Salar.'

I nodded. 'After we have recovered from our journey. I take it you will not be attending.'

'You suppose right. But if I was I would tell my son Peroz the same as I hope you will advise him.'

The pastry was delicious. 'Which is what?'

'To abdicate in favour of Salar who would become a regent until a suitable candidate for king can be found.'

I nearly choked on my food. 'Why would Peroz abdicate?'

'To prevent war,' she answered bluntly, 'war between Carmania and Sakastan. My late husband recognised the rivalry between Phanes and Peroz and knew that it might grow into hostility. My sons were never close but they are fast becoming bitter enemies, which will lead to war between their two kingdoms sooner or later.'

'What is that to do with me?' I enquired.

She smiled, an expression alien to her, I surmised.

'Do you know who the queen of Carmania is?'

I wracked my brains in vain. I turned to give Kewab a pleading look but he was likewise ignorant as to the name of Phanes' wife.'

'Her name is Arundhati,' she told us.

'I'm sure she is delightful,' I said.

Hamide rolled her eyes. 'She is a bland bore, but that is irrelevant. Her ancient family is known and respected not only throughout Carmania but on the other side of the Indus as well. She has produced a son and two daughters, all of whom have an excellent lineage. The son's right to the throne will not be challenged.

'Now, can you tell me the name of the Queen of Sakastan?'

'Roxanne,' I answered immediately.

'A whore from Dura,' she sneered, 'who is queen because my son was allowed to mix with whores during his stay in your city, King Pacorus.'

'Peroz was not my prisoner,' I said.

'More's the pity,' she spat, 'if he was then at least he would not have been free to mix with undesirables, though I have heard that morals in Dura are somewhat lax.'

I bristled at the insult. 'As you say, lady, stories become twisted and embellished with their telling.'

70

But Hamide had just begun. 'Whores are not supposed to become queens; it is against the natural order of things. You should have reminded my son of that when he was visiting the brothel she worked in. It is as well that High King Orodes gave Peroz the crown of Sakastan because otherwise my late husband would have been forced to banish him so outraged was Phanes.'

'So, things worked out in the end,' I said naively.

'My son's patience is fast running out and it is only a matter of time before he attacks Sakastan,' warned Hamide, 'both to remove the shame inflicted on his family name by the marriage of his brother to a whore, and to teach the insolent Sakas a lesson.'

I suddenly regretted not learning more about the peoples who inhabited the eastern kingdoms of the empire. Kewab cleared his throat. We looked at him.

'If I may throw some light on the topic, majesty?'

'Please do,' I told him.

'The Sakas are related to the Scythians, majesty, the nomads who inhabit the great steppes to the northeast of the Parthian Empire.'

'They are thieves and murderers who wormed their way into the empire,' added Hamide, 'and now dare to call themselves Parthian.'

I held up a finger. 'If I remember correctly, Sakastan has always paid its annual dues to Ctesiphon.'

'Nonsense,' snapped Hamide, 'they raid Carmania's northern border incessantly.'

I smiled; having heard the reverse was true. I wondered which side was telling the truth.

'Something amuses you, King Pacorus?' glowered the queen. 'I suppose I should thank you for killing King Porus, who was a tyrant with an insatiable appetite for whores and land.'

She clicked her fingers for her cup to be refilled.

'There must be something in the water at Sigal that makes its rulers predisposed to whores. But once again the Sakas are proving troublesome and High King Phraates has assured Phanes that he will be supported in any action he may take against Sakastan. You can now see my reasoning behind Peroz abdicating.'

I could see the machinations of Phraates that much was true.

'And the new king of Sakastan will be a candidate agreeable to both Phraates and your son, I suppose?'

'Why not?' she said forcefully. 'The alternative is war and none of us want that.'

'I agree,' I said.

She looked surprised. 'You do?'

I finished my *kallu* . 'No one wants war, lady. But neither will I ask Peroz to vacate his throne, certainly not for the ambitions of your son whom I suspect wishes to become ruler of Sakastan as well as Carmania. As for the idea of Salar being a temporary regent, it is nonsensical. I doubt your son would allow both Peroz and Salar to live if he had a say on who should sit on Sigal's throne, to say nothing of my daughter.'

I stood. 'If your son has grievances he should state them at the Council of Kings at Esfahan, which is designed to resolve disputes within the empire.'

'Tell me, King Pacorus,' she shot back, 'did you resolve your disputes at Esfahan? Of course you did not. You plunged the empire into civil war so do not lecture me concerning what my son should or should not do.'

I bowed my head. 'It has been an honour meeting with you, lady, thank you for your hospitality.'

'Do you know what they call you in these parts, King Pacorus? *Kingaleyar* – King Slayer. Let me think, there was Chosroes, Porus, Narses and Mithridates, who was actually high king.'

'Your point, lady?'

She regarded me with a haughty expression. 'If you do not advise Peroz to abdicate you may have his death on your hands. This is not Dura, king Pacorus.'

'On that we agree,' I said, taking my leave.

I was in a foul mood by the time *Tegha* was brought to me and I was in the saddle at the head of my escort leaving camp.

'A curious woman,' remarked Kewab.

'Curious! I am surprised that she has lived this long considering her poisonous tongue. It was just as well she relieved me of my sword before she began lecturing me.'

'Do you think the high king is encouraging her son to start a war with Sakastan, majesty?'

'Probably, but Phanes must feel that even with Phraates' support he is incapable of removing Peroz. So, he gets his mother to do his dirty work for him.'

I felt something hit my back plate and halted *Tegha* , turned in the saddle and saw a filthy boy in rags tossing something at me. Camel dung! He ran up, grinned and hurled a large piece of dried excrement hitting me in the face. He squealed with delight and retreated a few paces, lifting up his moth-eaten tunic to reveal his genitals to me. He then picked up another piece of dung and threw it, hitting my cuirass.

'Right!'

I tossed *Tegha*'s reins to Kewab and jumped down from his back. I could have ridden on, or ordered one of my men to apprehend the urchin, or even given the command to have him skewered. But Hamide had riled me and I wanted to vent my frustration and anger. Tanning the arse of this little demon would do nicely. He stuck his tongue out at me, hurled another piece of camel dung and ran into the date palms. I ran after him, following him as he darted left and right in an effort to outrun me. He was quick but my blood was up and I was within a couple of paces of him when he suddenly swung right behind a massive date palm that must have been over a hundred feet high. I followed and stopped in my tracks when a serpent rose up before me.

It stood at least six feet tall, an unblinking pair of bronze eyes staring at me, emitting a spine-tingling growl, its hood flared in anger. I had never seen such a snake before. I drew my *spatha* as it glided forward to attack, swinging the blade to chop of its head. It retreated to avoid the blow so I jabbed the point of my sword at its head. It lunged at me, avoiding the blade that I was forced to withdraw to fend away its fangs. Its movements were fast, too fast as I retreated, thinking that like most snakes it would seek an escape route if given the opportunity. It did not. If followed me, baring its fangs that resembled white scythes as it tried to bite me. I swung my blade again and again to kill the hooded monster before me, all my strikes missing its green scaly body. I was about to be defeated by a reptile.

I pulled my dagger from its sheath and jabbed it at the king cobra to hold its attention. It snapped and growled at the blade, giving me time to raise my sword to chop down at the snake's body. I stepped forward to hack down at the venom-filled monster, a sliver of sunlight shining into my eyes and blinding me for a split-second. My bladed chopped down but cut nothing and as I stepped back I saw nothing. The king cobra had disappeared. I spun round, worried it might be behind me. It was not. It had disappeared, as had the boy whom I had completely forgotten about.

I walked back to the waiting horsemen, Kewab passing me *Tegha*'s reins.

'Is everything all right, majesty?'

I hauled myself into the saddle. 'Fine.'

I said nothing about the strange incident to anyone, though that afternoon I sought out Claudia, who I was told was visiting the Fire Temple in Bam. It was dedicated to the god Ahura Mazda whose followers, the Zoroastrians, had been worshipping fire for five hundred years.

'Don't be ridiculous, father,' my daughter said dismissively, 'the Zoroastrians do not worship fire, they see it as representing their god's wisdom and light.'

She looked totally different today as she stood beside me in the temple, a grand mud-brick building sitting in the middle of a large garden surrounded by pine, cedar and cypress trees. A high wall that was guarded day and night by the governor's soldiers enclosed the garden. The temple comprised a portico with two pillars, behind which was a room giving access via a corridor to a square room housing the sacred fire, fed night and day by sandalwood and incense called loban.

'This is a great honour, father,' said Claudia, who unusually was in a deferent, servile mood.

Dressed in a long white gown, her head covered by a white headscarf, she looked slender and attractive, far from the fearsome black-clad woman that inhabited Dura. We both wore white, a strict requirement of the fire keepers staffing the temple. She nodded towards the fire burning in the huge white dish atop a great metal urn.

'That is the Atash Bahram, the "fire of victory", formed from the embers of a thousand other fires, each from a different section of society. Thus, there are embers from the fires of brick makers, potters, hunters, blacksmiths, bakers, herdsmen and on and on. It also includes fire started by lightning.'

'Looks like an ordinary fire to me.'

She rolled her eyes. 'To an unbeliever, it would. But there is great power here. Because you are a king you have been allowed into the temple, despite not being a follower of the faith.'

'Why did they let you in?' I joked.

'Because I am a member of the Scythian Sisterhood, which is revered throughout the empire and beyond.'

I told her about the earlier incident with the boy and king cobra. She smiled.

'She told me she would send you a sign.'

'Who?'

She looked at me and sighed. 'Who watches over us still?'

She was speaking of Dobbai, which comforted me somewhat. But as I relived the incident I could not fathom the sign.

'What has camel dung to do with anything?'

'Is has nothing to do with anything,' she said, 'the cobra was the sign, probably of a mighty foe that will appear unexpectedly. When are we leaving for Sigal?'

76

'Soon.'

We stayed at Bam for a week, though a score of Talib's men left earlier to reconnoitre the border between Carmania and Sakastan to discover who was raiding whom, if indeed there was any cross-border fighting. There were many Carmanians and Sakas in Bam itself, though Rogerio was a firm governor who clamped down on any trouble within the city's confines quickly and ruthlessly. A policy I became aware of when Gallia and I were asked to visit the governor's mansion.

Positioned within the citadel and raised to give views of the city below and the groves of date palms beyond, it was a place of bubbling fountains, exotic birds and calm. Rogerio rose and bowed when we were shown into his private garden, inviting us to sit on couches arranged beneath a large sunshade.

'I trust you have refreshed yourselves, majesties,' he smiled, clapping to bring wine and fruit.

'We have,' replied Gallia, 'you have been a most diligent host.'

We reclined on the couches, slaves serving us wine, dates, oranges, apricots and grapes. Rogerio whispered into the ear of a guard who bowed and disappeared.

'It gladdens me to see you both refreshed and invigorated. Alas, my heart is burdened by a distasteful affair.'

I raised an eyebrow. 'Oh?'

The guard reappeared, accompanied by two more yellow-uniform soldiers, between them the sorry shackled figure of Kalet. He caught Gallia's eye.

'Princess.'

'Silence!' barked the guard commander, striking Kalet with the back of his hand. The lord spat blood on the gravel.

'This man, this filthy wretch, claims to be Lord Kalet of Dura, majesty,' said Rogerio.

'I regret to say he is, governor.'

Rogerio was shocked. 'Him?'

'I assume he has broken one of Bam's laws.'

'One?' said Rogerio with incredulity. 'Brawling, inciting violence, committing violence, urinating in the street, vomiting in the street...'

'It's not my fault the food in this city is rotten,' pleaded Kalet.

Rogerio shook his head. 'The list goes on and on, majesty. I must ask you to confine this man's companions to camp with immediate effect. They are like a plague of locusts that have descended upon us.'

'I will do so immediately,' I promised.

Gallia batted her eyelids at Rogerio. 'Is there any way Lord Kalet can be released into our custody, governor?'

The commander of the guard was most unhappy but a seductive Queen of Hatra was difficult to resist.

'We would be eternally grateful,' she cooed.

Rogerio clapped his hands and beamed at her. 'It shall be as you wish, highness.'

He ordered the shackles to be removed. Kalet flexed his hands and rubbed the cheek that had been struck by the commander. I jumped from the couch and interjected myself between him and Kalet.

'We will be leaving now, governor,' I announced, grabbing Kalet by the arm and leading him away.

'We are forever in your debt, governor,' said Gallia softly, rising from the couch and following us.

I bundled Kalet from the mansion, the desert lord grinning in triumph and rubbing his hands together with glee.

'Clearly my words were wasted on you,' I fumed.

'You said try not to get yourself killed,' he stopped and opened his arms wide. 'Here I am, hale and whole.'

'What would your wife say, Lord Kalet?' asked Gallia.

Kalet winked at her. 'She's a thousand miles away, princess, and what happens in Bam stays in Bam.'

Two days later we left the city and continued our journey to Sigal.

Chapter 4

'Orodes' son? Here, in Sigal?'

Peroz nodded. 'Arrived two weeks ago, along with a companion.'

I looked at my friends who wore expressions of shock and surprise. We had arrived at Sigal after an uneventful journey through the arid and desolate terrain of western Sakastan to find the capital surrounded by fertile lands and forest. The city, which served as a guard post for the caravan route from eastern Parthia to India, was ideally positioned in a triangle formed by the confluence of the Erymanthus and Argandab rivers. The reunion between Isabella and Salar was touching and Peroz and Roxanne made all of us feel very welcome, but then the King of Sakastan announced that a young man had arrived in his kingdom claiming to be the son of the late high king and my friend Orodes.

'He is an imposter,' I stated firmly, 'Orodes only had one son and he sits on Ctesiphon's throne.'

We sat on wicker chairs stuffed with cushions taking in the stunning views of the lush valley below; Peroz's fortress enjoying a commanding position atop a rocky crag. The city of Sigal stretched before us, the mud-brick buildings protected by a high perimeter wall. The horsemen that had accompanied us were camped a few miles downstream alongside the caravan park, where they and merchants watered their beasts in the cool, clear Erymanthus.

'I knew Orodes for over thirty years,' I said, 'we all knew him.'

I looked at Gallia, Gafarn, Diana, Nergal and Praxima in turn.

'He had no other sons aside from Phraates.'

'Pacorus is right, Peroz,' said Diana. 'On none of his visits to Hatra did Orodes mention another son. He would have confided in us, of that I am sure.'

'Me too,' nodded Praxima, 'Orodes was a man of honour who would have faced up to fathering another child.'

'That is what we thought,' said Peroz, looking at his wife, 'but Cookum convinced me otherwise.'

I looked at Peroz. 'Who?'

'The boy's companion,' Roxanne told me.

The Queen of Sakastan was still the beauty that had worked in Dura all those years ago, her high cheekbones and narrow, delicate nose complementing her luscious lips. Now in her fortieth year her looks had not faded like many whores her age. But then she had left that life many years ago to become a queen in the east. What's more, she had escaped the curse of many whores whose bodies were damaged by hard usage and had managed to produce an heir for Peroz, a fine young man who was days away from becoming my son-in-law.

'What does this son of Orodes, so-called, want?' asked Nergal, his long legs resting on a footstool.

'He has sought sanctuary here,' Roxanne told us.

'When they arrived both had the appearance of hunted animals,' said Peroz. 'I said they could stay here.'

'That was a mistake,' I said harshly, 'you should get them out of your kingdom as quickly as possible.'

Gallia was shocked. 'If this, what is his name?'

'Vartan,' Roxanne told her.

'If this Vartan is the son of Orodes then he deserves our protection, Pacorus,' Gallia berated me.

' *If* being the operative word,' I replied. 'If Phraates gets wind of this he will demand him back.'

'Why?' asked Roxanne.

I smiled at her charming naivety.

'Because, dear lady, this Vartan represents a challenge to his position and Phraates is not the sort of man to take such things lightly.'

'Where did they come from?' enquired Gafarn.

'Susa,' replied Peroz.

Susa was the capital of Susiana, Orodes' homeland, a place he rarely visited during his reign as king of kings.

'Why did he leave it?' asked Diana.

'His identity was discovered,' said Peroz, 'and Cookum felt his life would be in danger if he remained in the city.'

I chuckled. 'He's right about that, at least. Even now I'll warrant that Phraates has despatched scouts to hunt for his half-brother. You might as well send him to Ctesiphon and save time and effort, and earn the gratitude of Phraates.'

'Seems a little harsh, Pacorus,' remarked Gafarn.

'My thoughts exactly,' said Gallia. 'Since when did you become so heartless?'

'Why don't you meet Vartan, lord?' suggested Peroz. 'You perhaps knew Orodes better than all of us.'

I reluctantly agreed, reticent not because I was particularly interested in the dubious claims of what would be a bastard. Rather, because my mind was still preoccupied with my duel with the king cobra in the date palm grove outside Bam. Claudia said it was a message from the gods and it seemed more than a coincidence that this Vartan had appeared at Sigal. The two were surely connected.

Vartan obviously represented danger and I wanted to be rid of him as quickly as possible.

The next day, escorted by Agbar and four of his men, I walked into the city to see for myself the youth who had caused a stir among the citizenry. Sigal was a pleasant city and my mood, which had been dark the day before, had lightened after a good night's sleep in the arms of my wife, a good breakfast and taking in the morning air. It might have been approaching summer but the cool breeze from the mountains in the north meant Sigal had a pleasant temperature and had the added bonus of blowing away the stench of a city filled to the brim.

'We are blessed that trade from the east and west passes through Sakastan, majesty,' remarked Agbar, 'make way, make way.'

A handcart of apricots had overturned in the narrow street and its owner and his young son were frantically trying to pick up the spilled contents.

'Come on, let's lend a hand.'

Agbar looked aghast. 'Majesty?'

'We can stand here and you can shout yourself hoarse, or we lend a hand and clear the blockage. Tell your men to keep the scavengers at bay.'

Already individuals were trying to steal the fruit, the owner shouting and threatening them. I began picking up apricots and placed them in the back of the handcart.

'Thank you, sir,' said the man.

'You are going to market?'

He nodded. 'I had hoped to sell them before midday, but now I am unsure. Too many are bruised.'

I picked up an apricot, examining its orange colour and feeling its distinctive skin.

'Take all of them to the palace and inform the guardroom that they are a special delivery for King Pacorus of Dura.'

I opened the pouch hanging from my belt and fished out two gold coins. The man's eyes lit up.

'Will this cover the cost?'

'Yes, sir, thank you, sir. Who should I say paid for the goods, sir?'

I handed him the coins and carried on down the street.

'King Pacorus of Dura.'

'That was very generous, majesty,' said Agbar, shoving a man aside who was begging for money.

'I am in a generous mood, Agbar, which is why I am meeting this Vartan. You have met him?'

He nodded. 'Seems agreeable enough.'

'Why wasn't he detained in the fortress?'

'The king thought he should be treated with respect until his identity could be established.'

'I suspect King Peroz likes him,' I probed.

'I'm a soldier, majesty,' he said diplomatically, 'my job is to obey orders.'

Vartan and his travelling companion had been established in a roomy house near the mansions of the city nobility in the western quarter of Sigal. It was accessed via a sturdy wooden gate and was surrounded by a high mud-brick wall. The gate was flanked by two city guards who came to attention as we approached. Agbar said nothing as one opened the gate and we entered the compound. The two-story house was set amid a neat garden of fruit trees, eucalyptus and miniature pines, with a small fountain positioned in front of the main entrance.

'Very pleasant,' I murmured as Agbar opened the front door and we entered a hallway, a slave immediately appearing and bowing his head.

'Where are the guests?' asked Agbar.

'Taking refreshment on the terrace, lord,' the slave continued to stare at the floor.

'We will join them,' I said.

We paced through the airy, bright corridor to a pair of open shuttered doors at the far end to emerge on to a wooden terrace giving excellent views of the rear garden. The walls were covered with vines framing the snow-capped mountains in the distance. A fountain a few paces from the terrace added the calming sound of bubbling water to the overall sense of peace and quiet. We halted between two individuals reclining on couches enjoying apricots, grapes and slices of watermelon. They stopped eating and rose, one a plump, middle-aged man with large jowls and a bald crown, the other a boy around sixteen years in age with pale skin and fair hair. I stared into his green eyes and looked for any similarities between him and Orodes. I could see none. Still....

'This is King Pacorus,' announced Agbar, 'close friend of High King Orodes.'

'May he rest in the company of the immortals,' said the individual I assumed was Cookum.

'Bring wine for our guests,' he shouted. He had clearly made himself at home at least. 'Please, be seated,' he requested.

'I prefer to stand,' I said sternly.

Agbar leaned against the wall as I stood facing Vartan, who looked decidedly nervous.

'High King Orodes spoke of you many times, majesty,' started Cookum, 'of your friendship, bravery and of how you had made Dura a mighty stronghold.'

I spun to look at him. 'And yet, in all the years I knew him he never mentioned that he had fathered two children, one of whom now sits on Ctesiphon's throne.'

Cookum looked at his couch. 'May I?'

I nodded; he sat on the rich upholstery and exhaled loudly.

'It is a story that I was sworn never to reveal, and would never have revealed it had it not been for an unfortunate sequence of events that revealed Vartan's true identity.'

'What events?' I demanded.

A slave brought cups of wine for myself and Agbar, after first refilling the drinking vessels of Vartan and Cookum.

'A simple burglary, majesty,' explained the latter. 'In the years after Vartan's birth High King Orodes was very careful in concealing his true identity. Only myself and an old slave woman were entrusted with the truth.'

'Which was?' I demanded.

Cookum looked at Vartan. 'That Vartan was the product of a liaison between High King Orodes and a slave girl.'

'Impossible,' I hissed.

'Hear me out, lord,' pleaded Cookum, 'I beg you. I grew up in the palace at Susa, my father being the personal slave of High King Phraates, the father of Orodes. When Queen Axsen died, Orodes was distraught.'

That much was true. Gallia and I feared he might take his own life when his beloved died giving birth to young Phraates.

'Orodes hated Ctesiphon and in the weeks and months afterwards he frequently visited Susa.'

I found myself nodding in agreement.

'He found solace and company in the arms of a slave, majesty, a simple kitchen slave who had worked in the palace at Susa for years. She was rather plain and plump but Orodes saw something in her that reminded him of his late wife. Nine months later she gave birth to a boy. But before that happened she and my father, her husband, were moved to one of the high king's properties on the outskirts of the city. High King Orodes had freed them both and provided for them so they could look after the infant. My father became a wine merchant and in this way the secret of the boy's true father was concealed.'

Cookum took a swig of wine. 'My father and his wife brought up the child as their own and I viewed him as a brother.'

'What about your own mother?' I asked.

'She died when I was four years old, majesty, and Vartan's mother passed away when he was seven.'

'I remember,' said the boy.

Cookum continued. 'Only on his deathbed did my father reveal Vartan's true identity and made me swear to care for Vartan and maintain the fiction that he was his son.'

It was all credible but unverifiable and I was beginning to think I was being toyed with.

'What proof do you have of what you have told me?' I asked.

'You remember, majesty, that I mentioned a burglary,' said Cookum. 'When Vartan was growing up, unaware of his lineage, the

87

high king rarely visited Susa, throwing himself into the affairs of the empire. But he did write to me on occasion, enquiring as to the wellbeing of his son. He gave strict instructions that his letters were to be destroyed.'

His head dropped. 'Alas I disobeyed the high king. Not all the letters were destroyed. I kept some so one day Vartan would know the truth. When the high king died, I was glad that I had done so.'

'Very noble,' I said, 'but again I say there is no evidence. It is all a story.'

Cookum nodded at Vartan. 'Show him.'

Vartan nervously reached into his tunic, Agbar's hand going to the hilt of his sword in case a dagger appeared, but I waved him back. Whatever this boy was he was no assassin, of that I was certain. Instead of a blade he pulled out two pieces of papyrus, which he handed to me. I took them and was surprised to see the handwriting of Orodes. Their contents were nothing to speak of, being general enquiries about his illegitimate son, his health, education and so forth. I experienced a mix of emotions as I read the words and saw the writing. I held the letters after I had finished, remembering my friend, his charitable nature, his loyalty and his honour. I saw the broken wax seals on the letters and could just make out the insignia that had been pressed into the wax all those years ago: an eagle with a snake in its talons. The symbol of Susiana, Orodes' homeland.

I clutched the letters and regret coursed through me. Regret that I had not spent more time with my friend in his final years and regret that he had not felt able to tell me of his bastard son. I handed the letters back to Vartan and studied him more closely. He did not look like Orodes, but then neither did Phraates. And yet the two brothers did have similarities. Vartan had a pale complexion like his older brother, though was plumper. I looked at his fair hair and green eyes and surmised that those were inherited from his mother.

'You are in danger here,' I told him. I glanced at Cookum. 'What burglary?'

'Not all slaves are loyal, majesty,' he told me. 'A Greek who tutored Vartan had the run of the house and discovered the letters…'

'That you were supposed to have destroyed,' I interrupted.

Cookum nodded. 'To my eternal regret. The tutor rushed to the city governor, a close ally of High King Phraates with a few letters signed by the late high king. I had no choice but to flee Susa with little money and even less idea where we would go.'

'Why here?' I probed. 'Why Sakastan?'

'My intention was to take Vartan to India, or even China, far from Ctesiphon and beyond the reach of High King Phraates.'

'Sensible,' I agreed.

I left the house convinced that Vartan was the son of Orodes and that he should be moved on from Sakastan as soon as possible, not only for his own safety but because Phraates would not forgive Peroz for harbouring a possible challenger to the high throne itself. I advised Agbar that he should double the number of guards protecting Vartan and Cookum but when I returned to the palace that became unnecessary. When I informed Peroz that my doubts had been banished he gave orders for Vartan to be moved into the fortress. Out of curiosity my friends and I gathered in the throne room when Peroz formally welcomed the son of Orodes into his residence.

'King Pacorus informs me that you intend to cross the Indus and seek sanctuary in India or China,' said Peroz to Vartan as the boy stood before the king and his queen.

'That is true, majesty,' replied Vartan in a faltering voice.

'Be assured that you are safe within these walls until you are ready to proceed with your journey. Avail yourself of our hospitality and may the gods protect you.'

In the days following, the excitement concerning the illegitimate son of Orodes subsided, to be replaced by delight over the approaching royal wedding. Neither Peroz nor Roxanne said anything about Phanes but I knew that he had been invited to the wedding and had sent no reply. The marriage of their only child was an important event, not only for themselves but also for Sakastan and the Parthian Empire, for stability in Sakastan would contribute towards keeping the barbarians east of the Indus at bay. For this reason, I decided to pay Phanes a visit, informing Gallia as we walked through the castle gardens, the air sweet with the scent of herbs and flowers.

'Marcus was telling me about the fortress' well,' I remarked. 'Apparently it is fifty yards deep and has a diameter of twenty feet, a spiral staircase carved into the rock shaft providing access to the small lake at the bottom. From this staircase three tiers of four circular chambers face the shaft through a succession of arches. The engineers of Alexander of Macedon built it over two hundred and fifty years ago. Fascinating.'

She looked bored. 'The citadel has a well, what is fascinating about that? You think paying a visit to Phanes is a good idea?'

I shrugged. 'Why not? I have already met his mother, unfortunately, but if I can meet him then perhaps I can convince him to put aside his animosity to attend his nephew's wedding.'

'You will be wasting your time. He wants his brother to abdicate, why should he bother to attend Isabella's wedding. He probably despises you.'

I was shocked. 'Why?'

'Even after all these years you can still be naïve, Pacorus. Even when their father was alive there was no love lost between the brothers. Phanes uses the excuse of Peroz's marriage to a former whore as a reason for his hostility, but that is a lie. Roxanne only increased the hatred that existed long before she came along.'

'What would you advise?'

'Stay away from Phanes and his mother. Any approach you make will be interpreted by them as weakness and may encourage them to strike at Sakastan.'

We walked past a bed of multi-coloured tulips.

'Phanes blusters and rages, certainly,' I said, 'but I suspect he lacks courage. Why else would he send his mother to warn me?'

'Do not underestimate fierce mothers, Pacorus, remember Queen Aruna.'

I laughed. 'Mithridates' mother. How could I forget?'

The gardens were mostly empty aside from the odd gardener trimming a bush or a slave sweeping leaves from a path. With views of the mountains and trees hiding the city below the layout gave the impression of being far away from Sigal. Lapwings and sandpipers flew around us and white storks looked for food in the ponds. We stopped to watch a pair of golden eagles sitting on the top branches of a tall pine, the birds staring down at us.

'It is said that a pair of golden eagles stays together for life.'

We turned to see a man peering up at the birds, a tall individual with lustrous black hair. He presented perfect white teeth when he smiled and bowed to us both.

'Forgive my interruption, majesties, I hope I did not disturb you.'

'Not at all,' I said, the eagles above suddenly spreading their wings to fly away.

He beamed at Gallia. 'It is an honour to meet the king and queen of Dura. My name is Vima, a merchant from India and a friend of King Peroz.'

My first impression of him was that he did not look like a merchant. His build was slim rather than portly and his narrow face, sharp nose and thin eyebrows gave him a martial appearance. But he carried no weapon and his demeanour was reflective.

'What do you trade, Lord Vima?' asked Gallia.

'Spices, majesty,' came the answer, 'mostly pepper, ginger, saffron and betel that my camels transport from India to Drangiana, Aria and Sakastan. Of the three my favourite is Sakastan. I have a house in the city and consider myself honoured to have earned the friendship of its king and queen.'

I looked around the garden. 'It is a beautiful city.'

'And its king and queen are kind hearted and generous, Salar is a fine young man and Isabella a beautiful princess.'

'You know much about the affairs of the city,' said Gallia.

He flashed a smile at her. 'A merchant must know the lands he intends to trade in, majesty, otherwise he might lose his goods and become destitute.'

I looked at his expensive boots, fine red leggings and white silk shirt. He was certainly not destitute.

'Let me give you an example,' enthused Vima. 'If I was an ignorant man I would not know that the polite, welcoming couple walking through the royal gardens is in fact the feared king and queen of Dura.'

I laughed. 'Feared? I think I am too old to strike fear into anyone. Perhaps twenty years ago.'

'When you destroyed the Romans at Carrhae? Such a famous victory. A man can live his whole life thirsting to be a part of such an event. And you killed Crassus as well.'

I looked at Gallia, who said nothing and remained straight faced. Her bow had killed Crassus, an action I regretted, though she did not.

'That was his punishment for invading Parthia,' she said flatly.

Vima's eyes lit up. 'The beautiful Queen Gallia, whose fame has travelled beyond the Indus to my homeland. If provoked young girls threaten their male tormentors with castration at the hands of Queen Gallia and her Amazons, and even noble women alarm their husbands by talking of giving up their wealth and station to ride with the Amazons.'

Gallia was delighted. 'All are welcome to join the Amazons, we are a sisterhood of equals.'

'Walk with us, Vima,' I said.

He was a charming man, quick witted and eager to learn all about Dura and its army. He said little about himself or his family and in truth we were more than willing to discuss the triumphs of Dura and its army. Diplomatically he never asked anything about Spartacus and our time in Italy, though I suspected he knew we were both slaves in our early twenties. All of Parthia knew, after all.

'One thing confuses me, majesty,' he said to me.

'Which is?'

'You hate the Romans?'

'I do not particularly like them but I would not say I hate them.'

'I hate them,' said Gallia.

'I have heard that Dura's army is half Roman,' said Vima. 'How can you have Romans fighting for you if the queen hates them so much?'

'Ah, I see. In fact, my foot soldiers are equipped and organised along Roman lines,' I told him. 'When I fought in the Romans' homeland I found their military organisation to be exemplary. So when I returned to Parthia I was determined to model my own foot soldiers on the Roman legion.'

He grinned. 'But there are no Romans in your army.'

'There are a few,' I replied, 'indeed, the army's commander was once a Roman. Lucius Domitus was his name.'

Vima was astounded. 'A Roman commanded your army?'

'He was a dear friend,' said Gallia.

'And you may be interested to know,' I added, 'that my chief engineer, who is here to attend the wedding, is also a Roman.'

Vima looked at us both. 'The rulers of Dura are truly an enigma, and perhaps that is why they have defeated their enemies for so long. I have enjoyed our meeting immensely and look forward to seeing you at the wedding.'

He bowed deeply. 'With your majesties' permission, I will take my leave.'

We watched him go, passing a slave with a look of concern on his face. I felt a knot tighten in the pit of my stomach. Over the years I had developed a sixth sense when it came to bad news and this slave had doom written all over his face. He bowed his head and stared at his feet.

'King Peroz requests your immediate presence in the palace, majesty.'

When we arrived at the palace we were directed to a small meeting room where Peroz conducted his day-to-day affairs. Large folding doors gave stupendous views of the Hindu Kush Mountains in the far north. Peroz sat at his desk, huddled over an opened letter resting on the polished teak. Behind him stood Agbar and his senior commanders, in front of the desk Gafarn, Malik, Spartacus and Nergal. To one side stood Rasha, Diana, Praxima and Jamal, the women smiling at Gallia who walked over to them.

'Has someone died?' I said in an attempt at levity. It failed dismally.

Peroz looked up. 'Phraates has made Phanes Lord High General in the East.'

'Which begs the question,' said Gafarn, 'who is the Lord High General in the West?'

'Darius, probably,' suggested Spartacus, 'no doubt on the advice of his mother, Queen Aliyeh.'

There had never been two lord high generals. During my three tenures in the post I once had a deputy, who happened to be King Phriapatius, the father of Peroz and Phanes. But that had been many years ago.

'My brother can use his new position to create an alliance against Sakastan,' said Peroz forlornly. He slammed his fist on the table. 'Why has Phraates done this?'

'To create mischief,' suggested Nergal.

'He has a devious nature,' agreed Gafarn.

'His father would have been so disappointed,' reflected Diana.

I looked at Gallia and was tempted to announce to her and everyone else that I would ride to Puta, the capital of Carmania, and threaten Phanes with war and destruction if he attempted to form an alliance against Peroz. I could, after all, assemble an army of over one hundred thousand men if required. An evil grin crept across my face.

'Something amuses you, Pacorus?' enquired Gafarn.

I cleared my throat. 'What? No. Cool heads are required at this juncture. Peroz, what are your relations with Aria and Drangiana?'

Peroz pursed his lips. 'Amicable enough, why?'

'Because if Phanes is forming an alliance, those two kingdoms, which lie on your northern border, present the greatest threat.'

'What about Carmania in the south?' asked Nergal.

I shook my head. 'Though I have never met Phanes, I can state with some certainty he is a cautious commander who will only attack Sakastan if he is certain of victory.'

'You mean he is a coward,' said Spartacus, earning him a beaming smile from Rasha.

'Cautious,' I emphasised. 'Furthermore, that he has not attacked Sakastan already indicates that he prefers others to fight his battles for him.'

'A coward, definitely,' agreed Malik.

I ignored the smirking laughter. 'Invite the rulers of Aria and Drangiana to the wedding,' I told Peroz, 'extend the hand of friendship to them and it will not matter if your brother is made lord high general of the whole empire.'

'You are certain of that, Pacorus?' Praxima asked me. 'There are other alternatives.'

A tingling dread crept down my spine. 'What alternatives?'

'We are here, all of us, together with thousands of soldiers,' she stated. 'We ride to Puta, sack the city, burn it to the ground and lay waste Carmania before returning to attend Isabella's wedding.'

Spartacus roared in support and Malik, arms folded across his chest, nodded enthusiastically. But Peroz was ashen, his mouth open in shock. Gallia was gripping her friend's arm.

'Ever the Amazon,' she proclaimed with pride.

I looked daggers at her. The last thing I wanted was a war, and by the look of horror on his face Peroz was of the same opinion.

'A last resort, lady, and one not entered into lightly,' I told Praxima. 'Wars are easy to start, harder to finish. In any case Phanes can only make idle threats. Of the eastern kingdoms of the empire, Hyrcania and Margiana are allies of Dura, which means they are your allies, Peroz. Their neighbours, Yueh-Chih and Anauon, are more interested in defending their borders against the barbarians of the northern steppes rather than getting involved in a squabble between brothers. So that leaves only Aria and Drangiana.'

Peroz tried to appear determined but he looked bitterly disappointed.

'I do not want war.'

'No one does,' I reassured him.

'But if war comes know we all stand with you,' promised Praxima.

She really was not helping.

'Don't forget to invite your brother as well,' I said.

Peroz was confused. 'Phanes?'

'Naturally,' I told him, 'he is hardly going to start a war if he is here, among potential enemies.'

'He will not come,' said Peroz.

'But the fact that you have extended the hand of friendship will not be lost on the rulers of Aria and Drangiana, who will be unwilling to support Phanes in any reckless action.'

'That is a lot of surmising, Pacorus,' said Gafarn.

'Or we could just burn Puta,' suggested Spartacus.

'I will not have my daughter's wedding ruined,' I said forcefully.

Peroz decided to do as I advised but the letter had soured the atmosphere at Sigal and the spectre of Phanes hung over the palace like a black cloud. Gallia and Praxima were seething and that never ended well, but I was cheered when a tired and dusty Talib reported to me that night, the scout having ridden hard from the south. He flopped down in a chair in our bedroom and drank greedily when offered water, Gallia pulling up a chair to listen to what he had to say.

'The only raiding is being undertaken by the Carmanians,' he told us, 'though it is light and designed, as far as I can tell, to provoke a response from the Sakas.'

'What form does it take?' I asked.

'Mostly burning isolated farmsteads and carrying off farmers and their families for slaves. As a result, a strip of land along the border around twenty miles in depth is empty of people.'

'Are there no Saka soldiers on the border?' asked Gallia.

Talib nodded. 'The problem is that the local commander wishes to retaliate against Carmania, which would mean pillaging its farms and villages.'

'Which Peroz has forbidden for fear of provoking a war,' I anticipated.

'A war that Phanes desires,' said Gallia. 'Praxima was right.'

Talib looked at her. 'The Queen of Mesene, majesty?'

'It is a long story,' I said. 'When you and your men have rested, I want you to ride north to Drangiana and Aria. Find out if any troops are gathering near the border and try to pick up any caravan gossip. Merchants have a nose for any trouble brewing.'

The next day I wrote a letter to Silaces, informing him about the Phanes' promotion and requested that he send immediate word of any ominous developments at Ctesiphon. The empire was fortunate to be served by post stations throughout its length and breadth where couriers could ride on fresh horses to the next station. Positioned thirty miles apart, a letter could leave one end of the empire and be in the hands of its recipient at the other in ten days. It would take five days to get a message to Elymais and a further five to get a reply. During the interim we occupied ourselves calming Peroz and focusing on the wedding.

Isabella was deliriously happy and oblivious to the gathering storm beyond Sakastan's borders. She was delighted that her sisters, parents and friends had travelled hundreds of miles to share her day of joy. All thoughts of the machinations of Phraates and Phanes disappeared from my mind as I walked alongside her by the side of the Erymanthus, behind us four of Agbar's guards keeping watch.

'I love the river, it reminds me of the Euphrates,' she sighed as she linked her arm in mine and rested her head on my shoulders.

'And just as busy,' I observed.

Like at Dura there were many irrigation channels leading off from the river to water extensive orchards of fruit trees, vineyards and date palm groves, others feeding the crops that grew on each side of the river – wheat, barley and beans. The river valley was truly a place of abundance where the arid earth became a fertile plain. Sigal and its environs was a jewel in a barren landscape.

Isabella pointed at the hills in the distance.

'The king has promised to build Salar and me a mansion there, a place where we can have some privacy.'

'Is not the palace private?'

She laughed. 'Palaces are always full of people, noise and activity. Dura is no different to Sigal. Even the private quarters are never fully empty, what with slaves coming and going.'

She cast me a sideways glance. 'I always treat them with respect, the way I was taught, father.'

I laid a hand on hers. 'We will never have slaves in Dura's Citadel, but our way is not the way of the empire, or indeed the world.'

'In our own home we will employ servants, not slaves,' she stated with conviction.

'What about Salar?'

'He does as he is told,' she giggled.

'You truly are your mother's daughter.'

Date pickers, ropes around their waists and baskets hanging from the tree in front of them, stopped and waved at Isabella from their vantage points above, my daughter smiling and waving back at them. I too smiled when I saw the warmth of their affection. It augured well for her future. I was startled when a thin, elderly man placed a basket before Isabella, the guards rushing forward to level their spears at him. The basket was full of snow trout that the fisherman had wanted to give to her. She waved the guards back and thanked the man.

'For you, highness. A wedding gift,' he beamed.

He was barefoot, his clothes old and filthy and most of his teeth missing.

'You are most kind,' smiled Isabella. 'What is your name?'

'Abeed, highness.'

'I am pleased to meet you, Abeed. How is your family, I hope they are well?'

We stood near the river for what seemed like an age as Abeed told us about his wife, his children, his sister, her children and his mother, who was still in rude health. The guards grinned and nudged each other as they saw me getting fidgety. At long last Abeed had finished his potted family history and the ailments that afflicted him and his relatives and I stepped forward, to be stopped by Isabella.

'And how is your family, highness? I pray that they are in good health?'

Isabella then proceeded to give a detailed account of the wellbeing of Gallia, her siblings and myself. She introduced me to Abeed, the fisherman bowing and enquiring if I had had a good journey to Sigal. It seemed to go on and on but eventually we managed to prise ourselves away from the poor fisherman, one of the guards carrying the basket of fish back to the palace.

'Remind me not to walk along this stretch of the river again,' I moaned.

'General pleasantries are an important part of everyday life here, father,' she told me. 'A simple and polite exchange of words can earn respect and trust, both of which are essential to future rulers.'

She had learned much during her time here. She and Salar would make good rulers. We began to walk back to the palace.

'Claudia told me that I alone of your daughters would marry.'

'Eszter still has time,' I said, 'if I can find anyone to take her on.'

She shook her head. 'It is not her destiny, Claudia told me.'

'What else did she tell you?'

101

For the first time this day she looked sad.

'She told me about Valak, about her ordeal and how she became one of the Scythian Sisters.'

'I should never have taken her north,' I lamented.

Isabella gripped my arm. 'It was meant to be, father, she knows that now. She has no regrets.'

We reached the gates of the fortress. Isabella told the guard holding the basket of fish to give them to the poor. She had a good heart, unlike Phraates who refused to be banished from our thoughts. After I had said goodbye to my daughter I was summoned to Peroz's meeting room once again. When I arrived, it was like walking into a doom-laden cave, a morose Peroz and an agitated Roxanne standing behind him barely able to raise a smile when I entered. The king said nothing but rather pushed a letter across the table top and nodded at it for me to read. It was from the high king himself. After the opening formalities Phraates got straight to the point.

It grieves me to learn that Sakastan currently harbours a man who claims to be the illegitimate son of my late father, King of Kings Orodes. This is not only a disgusting lie but also a personal insult to me and therefore the whole Parthian Empire. I demand that this traitor, this usurper, be returned to Ctesiphon immediately to face the consequences of his foul and untrue claims. You can either send him back to me or instruct the Lord High General in the East to collect him on my behalf.

I placed the letter back on the table and looked at Peroz.

'What is your advice?' he asked me.

Kill Vartan would be the simplest answer, though I would never advise that. Besides, I had the feeling that the issue of the 'usurper' was merely a pretext for Phanes to cause trouble. I was beginning to dislike the ruler of Carmania.

'I suspect your brother is behind this,' I said. 'A rumour of Vartan's presence here must have reached his ears and thus was he presented with a golden opportunity to further his own cause.'

He leaned back in his seat. 'To defy the high king is no small matter, but I am loathe to sanction what would be the death of Orodes' son. If I hand him over to Phanes he will be killed.'

'Eventually,' I agreed.

He stood and walked to the large window giving stunning views of the mountains in the distance.

'High King Orodes, Vartan's father, made me king of Sakastan. What sort of man would I be to send his son to his death? No, I will not do it. The wedding is in two days' time. I will delay replying to the high king until after Salar and Isabella are married, and then I will inform Phraates that Vartan has fled the city before I could apprehend him.'

'He won't believe you,' I cautioned, 'best to keep Vartan confined to the palace until after the wedding. At least no one will see him, which will lend your story some credence.'

'Do you think I should tell him?'

I laughed. 'That his half-brother, who happens to be high king of Parthia, wants him dead? That information can wait until he is on his way east.'

The day of the wedding dawned sunny and warm, an army of slaves and palace officials beginning work in the early hours to set up the enclosure where the wedding would take place. The spot was just outside the city walls, near the river, Peroz deciding that the palace gardens would be too cramped to accommodate the dozens of invited guests, which included the kings and queens that had travelled to Sakastan and their entourages. Each royal contingent would sit at a long table covered with a white cloth, though the kings and queens themselves would be seated at the top table with Peroz and Roxanne. A thick, high wooden fence surrounded the whole enclosure, with dozens of Agbar's spearmen patrolling the outside to keep undesirables away from Sigal's great and good. Inside the atmosphere was relaxed and convivial, guests chatting and exchanging pleasantries as they were served wine and *hauma* , a beverage unique to Sakastan. I frowned when I saw Kalet and his friends downing copious quantities of it. They would probably pass out before the day ended.

Around the perimeter fence were poles from which hung griffin and elephant banners, symbolising the union of Dura and Sakastan. The marriage ceremony itself was all about symbolism. Isabella, resplendent in a pure white silk dress, was transported from the fortress on an elephant, flanked by a score of yellow-clad guards. In front of the elephant, which had gold-painted tusks, walked Sigal's high priest, before him two priests holding incense burners from which the smoke of esfand emitted. In this way evil was warded off from the bride-to-be.

In the compound itself, a white-robed Salar waited nervously seated on an ivory chair, in front of him a low wooden platform covered with a white cloth. Called the *sofreyé aghd* , on it were laid the elements that encompassed imagery and symbolism relating to the union of the prince of Sakastan and princess of Dura. Pride of place was a mirror, a wondrous item of flattened metal, a mixture of tin and copper called speculum that had been polished to such an extent to create a reflective surface.

'I look old,' I remarked to Gallia when I saw my all-too lifelike reflection in it.

'You look distinguished,' said Gallia kindly.

Gafarn dug me in the ribs. 'That's another word for old.'

Other items on the *sofreyé aghd* included simple candles, symbolising light and fire, flatbread called *nooné sangak* , which represented prosperity, and a bowl of gold coins to also encourage future prosperity.

The air was heavy with the scent of burning esfand when I assisted Isabella from the elephant and escorted her into the compound, hundreds of Sigal's citizens shouting and waving at her. Though veiled, she waved back, eliciting more cheers. I also smiled and waved, people ignoring me as they chanted my daughter's name. Agbar shouted at his men to keep them back but there was no threat, just a desire to be close to their princess.

Inside the compound the atmosphere was more formal but no less cheering, Sigal's aristocratic lords and their ladies clapping politely as I led Isabella to where Salar waited. Claudia, Eszter, Gallia and Praxima held a green canopy over our heads, the colour symbolising that the earth is the mother of all of us. The high priest continued his chanting until we arrived at where Salar sat, at which point he stopped, took Isabella's hand and led her to sit beside her intended, lifting her veil before standing back.

'Stare into the mirror both of you,' he ordered, 'so you can see your future together.'

He raised his arms and looked to the heavens.

'Great Ahura Mazda, unchanging, creator of all life, the source of all goodness and happiness, smile upon these your two children and bless them for the life they are about to embark upon together.'

He clapped and two of his white-robed priests stepped forward, one swinging an incense burner and the other holding a simple jar of honey. The high priest nodded to Salar who took the jar, dipped his little finger into it and offered it to Isabella who licked it. Then Isabella dipped her own little finger in the honey and Salar licked it off her digit.

'Thus will both sustain each other throughout their lives together,' proclaimed the high priest.

Slaves laid flowers – brightly coloured tulips – around the couple.

'These flowers symbolise life and beauty,' stated the high priest.

More slaves placed baskets of pomegranates at their feet.

'Salar and Isabella will have a joyous and fruitful future,' said the high priest. 'They are now man and wife and go forward as one, safe in the knowledge that Ahura Mazda has smiled upon their union.'

The dozens of guests crowded round the newly-weds clapped politely and began to disperse to their waiting tables. The high priest bowed to Peroz and Roxanne and then Salar and Isabella before leaving with his assistants to take themselves off to the temple in the city to pray for the newly-weds. Slowly my daughter and new son-in-law made their way to the top table, friends and family congratulating Salar and embracing Isabella. Kalet gave Salar a great bear hug and roared his approval. He was already drunk.

It was getting hot but we were spared the worst ravages of the sun by huge awnings erected over the tables where guests were talking and laughing as slaves served an endless supply of food cooked by field kitchens adjacent to the compound. The newly-weds were first served with a delicacy called *jahaver polo* , a dish of rice mixed with orange peel, berries, almonds and pistachios. It was very colourful and signified jewels and thus the wealth the couple would hopefully enjoy in the future.

Claudia next to me rolled her eyes. 'One cannot even eat without the food having some sort of religious significance.'

'As a servant of the gods I would have thought you approve.'

She sniffed in disapproval. 'These Zoroastrians think there is only one god, like Aaron. Look around you, father, do you think one god is responsible for the world and everything that is in it?'

'How can Shamash direct the sun above us and administer affairs in the underworld?' she continued. 'The simple answer is, he cannot.'

'You look lovely today,' I complimented her, 'white suits you.'

She rolled her eyes. 'I agreed to wear this ridiculous dress out of respect for Isabella, nothing more. I feel like a harlot.'

I roared with laughter, Gallia next to me frowning and the others at the top table giving me quizzical looks. All the women – Gallia, Diana, Rasha, Jamal, Praxima, Roxanne, Isabella, Eszter and Claudia, – wore sleeveless white silk dresses and I had to say they all looked beautiful and regal. Only the scowl on Claudia's face ruined the ensemble.

The spicy aroma from the field kitchens filled the air as veiled female slaves carried large silver platters heaped with local delicacies. These included a plethora of stews, including *fesenjan* containing walnuts and pomegranates; *bademjan* , made from eggplant and tomatoes; *baghali polo* , a delicious concoction of rice mixed with dill and fava beans; and a thick green herb stew called *gormeh sabzi* . Meat eaters were not forgotten – whole roasted chickens and slabs of beef and mutton were served as kebabs, being presented on long, thick skewers. The Agraci warlords and Kalet's friends were grabbing the kebabs and eating greedily from them, in between guzzling wine and *hauma* , guests at other tables looking at them with slight disdain. But they responded by raising their meat and drink and toasting the fine ladies and gentlemen of Sakastan.

Peroz looked a happy man. It was true the rulers of Aria and Drangiana had declined to attend, but they had sent their ambassadors to convey their good wishes to the newly-weds. That was something at least. I looked at Claudia eating rice with her hands. Despite her ordeal and journey into the Scythian Sisterhood she was still a good-looking woman, apart from when she frowned. She was frowning now. Then her eyes narrowed and she jumped up.

'Defend the king,' she bellowed.

I spat out a piece of meat in response, the others at the table looking at her with furrowed brows. But Claudia was not thinking of them as she hitched up her dress to reveal a dagger in a sheath strapped to her leg. She drew the blade and threw it at a slave girl who had just refilled Peroz's silver cup with wine. I watched open-mouthed as the point of the dagger pierced the slave's side. She yelped in pain and collapsed, a dagger that she had been holding in her left hand falling on the grass. Roxanne screamed in grief as another veiled slave, who had appeared behind Peroz, drew a knife across his throat. If the king felt anything it must have been only for a split-second because he was already dead by the time his head fell into the bowl of stew he had been eating.

The slave who had killed the king spun and stabbed Agbar in the stomach repeatedly, the commander of the king's guard dying in a sea of his own blood that stained his yellow tunic. Isabella was frozen in fear when the assassin turned to face her, blood-covered dagger in her gore-encased hand. I jumped up to place myself before the veiled killer and Isabella but out of the corner of my eye saw a blurred movement, turning at the last moment to see another veiled assailant thrusting her dagger at me. My reflexes, honed by many years of war, took over. I grabbed a silver platter of rice and swung it sideways, the point of the dagger going into the metal and piercing it, though thankfully not me.

I yanked the platter back to wrest the dagger from the girl but she surrendered it easily. Claudia had grabbed a knife from the table and was repeatedly stabbing it into the girl's neck, blood sheeting over her, my daughter and me as my eldest child nearly decapitated the assassin.

The compound was filled with shrieking and screaming guests as more and more veiled assailants attacked us. Where were the guards? Who were these veiled attackers? My mind suddenly returned to Isabella who stood, frozen in fear, in front of her Kalet throttling the woman who had killed Peroz.

'To me,' I shouted, Malik ushering his wife to safety, his Agraci warlords closing around her. They all pulled knives with long, wicked blades from their robes.

Kalet's lords grabbed Isabella, Eszter, Byrd, Noora and Salar and bundled them towards me. I took the knife from the woman Claudia had killed and ran towards Gallia, who had armed herself with two kebab skewers as she and Praxima defended Diana.

'Roxanne,' screamed my wife, 'Roxanne, leave him.'

Roxanne was cradling the dead Peroz, tears streaming down her face as she rocked to and fro, oblivious to the death being meted out around her. Gallia killed an assassin as Praxima held the woman in a headlock, stabbing her belly furiously, blood spouting out of her body like a fountain. But she could do nothing to save Roxanne who was suddenly surrounded by four killers and stabbed repeatedly, the queen of Sakastan joining her husband in the afterlife.

Around us more veiled attackers were targeting and slaughtering guests, those who ran being hunted down and knifed in the back.

'Let's get these bastards,' shouted Kalet, his warlords drawing swords they should not have been wearing under their flowing robes but which I thanked the gods for. He and his half a dozen lords ran at a group of female murderers, slashing and hacking with their swords, killing two immediately and forcing the others to flee. Malik's men joined them, black-clad killers chasing white-veiled assassins. Around us was carnage, the king and queen of Sakastan lay dead, and lying around and on tables were the dead bodies of the kingdom's most important lords and officials.

I heard a gurgling sound and turned to see Praxima and Eszter each holding the arm of a woman I recognised. Indira! The sister of Spada who had fought my wife at Dura and whom I had released afterwards. How I regretted that now. Nearby were two of her comrades, both dead from knife wounds. Gallia had grabbed Indira's hair, yanked it back before slitting her throat, the woman from Persis dying as blood shot from her neck in a hideous but satisfying spectacle.

Prince Pacorus was standing defiantly in front of his shocked mother and father, bloody knife in hand and eyes filled with wrath.

'Get the women out of here,' I told him.

Gallia kicked the lifeless body of Indira to the ground.

'The women are going nowhere. Defend the king.'

110

Salar, ashen faced and shaking, was staring at the bodies of his parents, Isabella clinging to him for dear life. Rasha and Spartacus, having killed three assassins and armed themselves with their weapons, were beside the new rulers of Sakastan. Spartacus looked at me.

'We should go, uncle, back to the palace.'

'Where are the guards?' murmured Salar forlornly.

Where indeed? But there was no time to ponder that question so I ushered everyone towards the entrance to the compound, checking to see Gallia and my daughters were present. They were all covered in blood, thankfully not their own. But their appearance was fitting for the foul desecration that had taken place and which would be avenged. But not today.

The guests, those still living, had fled and an eerie quiet had descended on the scene of slaughter. Where before there had been laughter and joy, there was now death, gore and the sound of buzzing flies. No matter where I had fought there had always been swarms of flies after the killing to gorge on the dead.

I walked back with my head down, in front of me my wife, children and friends hastening to leave this place of dead flesh.

'My lord, beware.'

I heard the voice, spun and saw a hate-filled visage before me and a dagger being thrust at my face. I brought up my own knife to block the blow but there would not be time. The world seemed to slow as I beheld my death and then saw the body of the female assassin crumple before me, hit by a spear with such force that it flung her back, away from me. Everyone stopped and ran back to me as the assassin shuddered and then died, the blade of the spear having gone clean through her body and out through her back.

The athletic Vima appeared beside me. 'Are you hurt, lord?'

'That was some spear throw,' said Gafarn admiringly.

'We are in your debt, sir,' smiled Gallia, who looked like a demon just arisen from the underworld with her blood-splattered dress, arms and hair.

'I owe you my life,' I told him.

He smiled. 'We should get everyone out of here.'

We needed no second prompting and hurried from the compound, passing slaughtered guards when we had exited. Clearly the attack had been carefully planned and executed. I prayed that the assassins who still lived had been apprehended by Kalet and the Agraci. But when we reached the sanctuary of the palace, a phalanx of guards from the fortress having joined up with us beforehand, two questions filled my mind. Who had ordered the attack, and how did Vima, a spice trader, learn how to use a spear so expertly?

Chapter 5

We burned the bodies of Peroz and Roxanne side by side on a huge pyre outside the city, by the river, so the people of Sigal could pay their respects to their murdered rulers. I and the other kings brought their soldiers into the city to supplement the garrison, which had lost its king, commander and head of the kingdom's army. Sorrow mixed with dread infested the city, made worse by the knowledge that the most high-ranking officials in the kingdom had been slaughtered at the wedding, along with their wives. Now all eyes turned to the new rulers, who were both barely out of their teens. At the cremation Salar and Isabella clung to each other like frightened and overawed children.

Afterwards the city was placed under curfew and we organised patrols to quell any disturbances and reassure Sigal's inhabitants that their city was not about to be engulfed by veiled female assassins. For good measure, I got Salar to issue a decree forbidding the wearing of veils within Sigal's environs for the foreseeable future.

He sat on his father's throne in the fortress' great hall and fidgeted with the crown that for some reason he was reluctant to put on his head. Perhaps he thought he was not worthy to wear it. More likely he was still grieving and was not thinking clearly. But clear minds had to swing into action for I was certain the carnage at the wedding was just the precursor to more violence.

'Well. What now?'

Gafarn's voice echoed around the high-ceilinged chamber.

'We hunted down and killed all those murdering bitches,' said Kalet proudly.

113

Gallia gave him a warm smile. Like Praxima and Rasha she had discarded the dress she had worn for the wedding and was attired for war: boots, leggings, white tunic and a sword belt round her waist.

'Perhaps we should have taken one alive,' mused Malik. He saw Kalet's frowning face. 'To try to get information regarding who ordered the attack.'

'My uncle,' said Salar quietly, 'who else would want my father and mother dead?'

Spartacus clapped his hands together. 'Well, then, we march on Carmania. How many soldiers can you raise, Salar?'

The young king, not yet officially proclaimed as such, opened his mouth but no words came out. He looked at Isabella sitting next to him but she could offer no advice.

'Perhaps I might counsel caution at this juncture,' I interrupted. 'We do not yet know the full facts. There is no proof Phanes ordered this attack.'

'He did,' stated Salar flatly.

Spartacus pointed at him. 'That's all the confirmation I need.'

'I will castrate Phanes myself,' threatened Rasha, earning her a grin from Malik and Kalet.

'Well said,' shouted Praxima.

'Who commands Sakastan's army?' asked Nergal.

It was a good question and one to which Salar had no answer. Agbar was dead, as was the army's commander. Salar was physically wilting under the strain of it all.

'Who is the most senior commander left?' I asked him. 'Think!'

He jumped when I spat the last word at him but he at least focused on something and after half a minute gave me an answer.

'Shapur. He is the commander of the army's elephants.'

'Send for him,' I said, 'he at least will be able to give us an accurate account of your army's capabilities.'

The doors of the chamber had been closed but we all turned when raised voices were heard in the hall outside. One of the doors opened and an officer entered, ran up to the dais and bowed to Salar.

'Forgive me, highness, but there is a man outside by the name of Talib who is demanding to be admitted to the throne room.'

'He is my chief scout,' I said.

'Let him in,' ordered Salar. 'And send word to Lord Shapur that he is to attend us immediately.'

The officer bowed, scurried back to the door and left the chamber, a dust-covered Talib entering a few seconds later.

'Idiot,' he spat as the door was closed.

He sauntered over to me and bowed, but before he could speak I pointed at Salar on his throne.

'This is the hall of King Salar of Sakastan, Talib, make your report to him.'

Talib, used to being given a long leash in Dura's army, gave Salar a bemused look. But Byrd, who had been observing events in silence, nodded to his protégé. Talib shrugged and bowed to Salar.

'We reconnoitred to the north, majesty, the gossip we picked up from caravans and locals leading us towards the Dasht-I Nawar. There we discovered thousands of horsemen watering their horses, a great gathering of banners showing winged horses and deer.'

Salar closed his eyes. 'The combined armies of Aria and Drangiana.'

He opened them and looked at us. 'The Dasht-I Nawar is a great lake that is surrounded by smaller lakes and wetlands. The winged horse is the symbol of Drangiana and the deer is the symbol of Aria.'

'How far away?' I asked.

'Two hundred and fifty miles,' came the reply.

'They can be here in eight days,' said Gafarn, darkening the mood in the hall.

'What about Carmania?' asked Nergal.

A sense of dread enveloped me. With an army massed to the north and Phanes' kingdom to the south, Sakastan was in danger of being crushed between the two if both forces attacked.

'What is the state of your army?' I demanded of Salar.

He looked at me, at Isabella and at Gallia as he desperately racked his brains. He was about to speak when the doors of the chamber opened and an officer entered, helmet in the crook of his arm and sword dangling by his side. All eyes turned towards him, which might have overawed many, but he continued to march purposely towards the dais, snapping to attention before his king and queen. Salar looked mightily relieved.

'Lord Shapur, we are glad to see you.'

I walked over to Salar and stood by his side, the tall, stick-thin officer in a simple yellow tunic and leggings ignoring me as he waited for orders from his king.

'This is Lord Shapur,' Salar announced to everyone, 'the commander of the elephant corps.'

Kalet sniggered and Spartacus rolled his eyes. They had both heard of my rout of Porus' elephants in battle many years ago, a clash won by a swineherd thanks to the quick-thinking Lucius Domitus. They may have scoffed at the idea of elephants on the battlefield but

I knew that Sakastan and the kingdoms east of the Indus saw a use for the tusked giants in combat.

'You will be aware that the commander of the king's guard and head of Sakastan's army have been murdered,' I said to Shapur.

He continued to look at Salar, who nodded.

'I am aware, majesty. I live to avenge their deaths.'

'You won't have to wait long,' said Kalet.

I looked daggers at my seditious lord.

'The army needs a new commander,' I said.

'We have decided to appoint you to this position,' Salar said to Shapur.

The elephant commander opened his eyes in surprise but regained his composure in an instant.

'Thank you, majesty. When do we march?'

'That's the spirit,' applauded Kalet.

Salar appeared delighted by his commander's bullish attitude and gripped his new wife's hand. Isabella gave Shapur a beautiful smile.

'Perhaps you could give us a short summary of the state of Sakastan's army,' I suggested, 'as I and the other kings present are ignorant concerning its strengths and weaknesses.'

'It has no weaknesses,' Shapur shot back.

Even I had to smile. This man who looked like a strong wind could break him in two was not only bullish, he was positively arrogant. Even the dour Byrd allowed the semblance of a smile to crease his lips.

'Stand beside me, Lord Shapur,' said Salar, 'so you may address the kings more conveniently.'

He needed no second invitation, stepping onto the dais and regarding all of us with his dark brown eyes. His face and arms were almost black from exposure to the sun, unlike the more olive-skinned Salar and Isabella.

'The camel corps consists of a hundred elephants, each beast having a guard of twenty spearmen and slingers.'

'That many guards?' Gafarn was surprised.

Shapur cast me a glance. 'Several years ago, majesty, the kingdom's elephants were discomfited by pigs. The slingers were introduced to ensure that any pigs will be killed long before their squeals reach the ears of the elephants.'

'I remember that battle,' remarked Malik, 'the elephants turned and crashed into the ranks …'

Remembering that he was in the palace of the king whose army had been routed by my army, the King of the Agraci fell silent.

'It is the sign of a professional army that its commanders learn from past experiences,' I said.

'For immediate service,' continued Shapur, 'Sakastan can raise five thousand horsemen and ten thousand foot, not including the garrison of this city, which numbers a thousand men. The lords of the kingdom can raise perhaps another twenty thousand men, but they…'

'Would be farmers and town militias,' interrupted Gafarn.

Shapur nodded.

'How many horsemen are gathered at the lake?' I asked Talib.

'I estimate around forty thousand, lord,' came the reply.

An oppressive silence descended. By the look on everyone's faces each was weighing up the odds, which would be stacked against Sakastan even if it had not lost its king and chief of the army. But

Sigal was in state of shock, which would spread to the whole kingdom unless drastic action was taken. My eyes rested on the dagger in its sheath hanging from Praxima's hip. She was deep in thought, toying with its handle.

'Castration,' I said out loud.

'Are you revisiting the idea of a legion of eunuchs, Pacorus?' enquired Gafarn.

I frowned at him. 'I'm glad you can find some humour in this predicament. No, I was thinking of Praxima's idea of castrating Phanes.'

'An excellent idea,' agreed Gallia, 'but it does not counter the threat of forty thousand enemy soldiers gathered in the north.'

'It does, my sweet,' I grinned, 'because I intend to castrate those soldiers, figuratively speaking.'

'What's he carping on about?' said Kalet.

But Spartacus had grasped my idea. 'Hit them now and hit them hard.'

I pointed at him. 'Exactly.'

'What about Phanes, father?' asked Isabella. 'If you all march north, he will be free to attack from the south.'

'You have a keen military mind, my dear,' smiled Gafarn. 'What do you say to that, Pacorus?'

I looked at Malik and Kalet. 'We are fortunate to have among us warriors who have raiding in their blood. To save Kalet and his men from drinking themselves to death in the less salubrious fleshpots of Sigal, I shall take them north. I also ask my friend and ally Malik to join us, as the Agraci are also adept at arriving unseen at an enemy's door.'

'A bold plan,' admitted Gafarn, 'though three thousand against forty is long odds.'

'Nonsense,' said Kalet, 'I've fought longer odds.'

'I will ride with you, uncle,' announced Spartacus.

'No,' I told him, 'you and your men, and women, will be riding south Lord Shapur.'

Nergal was uncertain. 'You will divide our forces?'

I nodded. 'We have little choice. Phanes wants Sakastan and has entered into some sort of pact with Aria and Drangiana. But I'm gambling on him letting others do the fighting for him. That was my impression when I heard he was trying to acquire allies at the Council of Kings not so long ago.'

'Or we could march north with all our forces and engage the combined forces of Aria and Drangiana,' suggested Spartacus.

'We could,' I agreed, 'but for the fact those two kingdoms have not declared war on Sakastan.'

Gafarn chuckled. 'Though you are going to attack them anyway.'

'At night,' I said, 'when they are least expecting it and we will be carrying no banners or identification. The worst thing we can do is wait for a declaration of war.'

Spartacus was delighted. 'Then we can also burn Puta?'

'I suggest advancing to Carmania's border first,' I cautioned, 'Salar does not want to be seen as the aggressor. But if Phanes offers battle by all means accept.'

In all, twenty-six thousand soldiers would march south in the proceeding days, including all the squires of Hatra and Dura who would ride as cataphracts. It was a tactic I had used many times: place the squires in full armour in the battle line to more than double the number of heavy horsemen. They were all between the ages of fourteen and eighteen anyway and spent each and every day learning how to be a cataphract, in between cleaning their masters' armour and tending to their own and their masters' horses. Using such a ruse Dura suddenly trebled its number of cataphracts to three thousand and Hatra's Royal Bodyguard increased to fifteen hundred steel-clad horsemen. It was all for show because Phanes would not offer battle.

'Are you sure about that?

Gallia stood framed in the doorway leading to our bedroom's balcony, hands on hips. She was far from happy. I gave my *spatha* a final wipe with a cloth and replaced it in its scabbard.

'I've met individuals like him before. They like others to get their hands dirty.'

'I should be coming with you.'

I walked over to her and gripped her shoulders.

'This city is on the verge of panic and Salar is out of his depth.'

She raised an eyebrow. 'Harsh.'

'Harsh but true. You and the Amazons will stay here to fortify his courage and ensure he does not do anything rash. Ideally, he should be marching south with his army but if he left the city, the gods alone know what would happen.

'I'm leaving the horse archers here for you to command.'

A twinkle appeared in her eyes. 'A thousand men plus the Amazons. You must be worried. Have no fear, I will clamp down hard on any sedition.'

'Just try to reassure Salar that his kingdom is not about to fall. He needs time to get used to being a ruler, as does Isabella.'

There was a knock at the door.

'Enter,' I said.

In walked Azad, Marcus Sutonius and Kewab, all bowing before I indicated they should take a seat. A slave followed them in and also bowed.

'Should I bring refreshments, highness?'

I shook my head. The day was beginning to wane, the hills and mountains beyond the city bathed in early evening sunlight and turning pink and purple.

'As I will be rising before dawn, I will make this quick. Azad, you will command the cataphracts when you and they march south with the other kings and Shapur.'

'And his elephants,' grumbled Azad.

I nodded. 'And his elephants. Try to act as a restraint on Shapur and particularly Spartacus. My nephew fancies himself as a modern-day Alexander of Macedon.'

He looked surprised. 'A king does not take lightly to being told what to do, especially the King of Gordyene.'

'In tandem with the King of Hatra I'm sure you will both be able to make him see reason. We will need every man in the coming weeks.'

I smiled at Gallia. 'The queen will be the power behind the throne while we are away. She will command the garrison and Dura's horse archers left in the city.'

I looked at Marcus. 'And talking of the city, I want you to assess the state of its fortifications. Bring anything that concerns you to the attention of the queen, she will allocate working parties to deal with any problems.'

'Are you expecting a siege, majesty?' asked the Roman engineer.

'Possibly, it depends on how successful my raid is.'

Kewab looked perturbed.

'Is something wrong, commander?' I enquired.

'Forgive me, majesty, but do you not risk undermining the authority of King Salar whose city this is?'

I gave him a sly smile. 'That is where you come in. I want you to be his military adviser. Explain to him what our strategic options are.'

'Limited,' he shot back.

'And shield him from the harsh truth,' I advised. 'It will avail us nothing if we buy the king time only for Salar to be filled with doubts. We need him strong and confident.'

'What is our strategy, majesty?' asked Marcus.

'Kill Phanes, lay waste his kingdom and defeat the combined army of Aria and Drangiana,' said Azad.

I thought about Hamide's words about what people called me in these parts.

'We will endeavour to avoid killing any kings. If I have learned anything it is such actions breed strife and festering animosity. May the gods be with you all.'

It was dusk when I finally flopped down on the bed and closed my eyes. I was feeling my age and hardly relished a few days of hard riding in the saddle. But it had to be done. There was another knock at the door.

'Go away,' I shouted.

'Forgive me, highness,' came the muffled reply from the corridor outside, 'I have an urgent message for you.'

I opened my eyes. 'Enter.'

The palace steward was apologetic and avoided any eye contact as he spoke.

'Forgive me, highness, but there is a spice merchant called Vima outside the palace who is desirous to meet with you on a most urgent matter.'

'Tell him to go away or he will be imprisoned,' said Gallia.

I stretched out my arms. 'Wait. Show me where he is. Vima saved my life, the least I can do is thank him.'

The corridors of the palace, which should have been filled with wedding guests and laughter, were hushed and empty as I followed the steward into the courtyard to the closed gates on the southern side. One had a door cut into it and a grill to allow guards to see outside the fortress from ground level. A gruff officer informed me that Vima was outside. I peered through the grill to see the trader pacing up and down.

'Open the door,' I commanded.

The officer unbolted the lock and told two guards to accompany me outside.

I waved them back. 'That won't be necessary.'

The officer shrugged, opened the door and I stepped into the empty street outside the fortress. Vima smiled and bowed his head. The door slammed shut.

'Thank you for seeing me, majesty.'

'Thank you for saving my life. How may I help you?'

He looked around to ensure no one was within earshot.

'You ride north tomorrow?'

I was taken aback. 'How is it that a spice trader knows such things?'

He tapped his sharp nose. 'Any trader worth his salt keeps his ear to the ground, majesty, especially when the winds of war are blowing.'

'Are they blowing?'

He folded his arms across his chest. 'Word is that a great army is mustering in the north, around the Dasht-I Nawar. A warrior such as the King of Dura would not wait until it came to him, I think.'

I was intrigued. 'So, what would he do?'

'Strike first, when the enemy least expects it.'

There was something about this Vima that troubled me. I sensed no threat. If he wanted me dead he could have let that veiled assassin at the wedding do it. So, what did he want?

'I know this land, majesty, let me lead your men north tomorrow, through the mountains that will hide your approach.'

'I have my own scouts,' I told him.

'They will lead you north along the Erymanthus, but the enemy have their own scouts that will detect your approach long before you get near their main body.'

'Why would you wish to do that, to put yourself in unnecessary danger? You wish to win favour with the king?'

He spread his arms and gave a wicked grin. 'I have business interests in Sigal. If the city is burnt they will go up in smoke like everything else. My motives are purely selfish.'

'If we fail, you might die.'

'But I have heard that the King of Dura has never been defeated.'

'I'm not old yet,' I said, 'there is still time.'

For some strange reason I trusted him, this individual who I had met only twice before. Perhaps it was no coincidence that our paths had crossed; perhaps he was fated to help me, and Sakastan. But perhaps it was all an illusion and he would be leading us into a trap. But I kept returning to him saving me at the wedding. My sixth sense told me he could be trusted so I gave him the benefit of the doubt.

'We will be exiting these gates before dawn, Vima. We will not wait for you.'

He was waiting for us the next morning, mounted on a splendid grey stallion, sword strapped to his side and a spear in his right hand. The column of Agraci and desert lords and their retainers led by Malik and Kalet cantered from the fortress as I pulled up *Tegha* and nodded to the spice trader. I notice that like the rest of us he had bags of fodder hanging from his saddle.

'Fine horse,' I said.

He looked at my bow tucking into its quiver. 'The famous Parthian bow. I look forward to seeing it in action, majesty.'

We set a hard pace, following the river north, Talib and his men riding ahead to ensure we did not encounter any nasty surprises. After I had explained to my chief scout that Vima could lead us straight to the enemy unseen, Talib agreed that the trader could ride with them. It saddened my heart to see the road largely empty of traffic, the caravans now avoiding Sakastan for fear of being caught up in the coming war.

In two days we had covered over eighty miles and on the third we left the Erymanthus to strike east into the hills. But what if the enemy at the great lake was already moving south?

That thought tortured me as we made our way through a mixture of arid and flat plateaus and verdant hilly terrain. My first impression of Sakastan had been of a kingdom that was harsh and barren, but here in the mountains there was no shortage of water and an abundance of lush terrain, interspersed with naked rock and stone. The number of streams surprised me, but Vima informed me that when the snows melted every spring it fed a plethora of streams, lakes and rivers.

On the fourth day we dismounted and led our horses up a steep, rocky path that zigzagged up a narrow valley, the scree underfoot making the going slow and slippery. It was also conducted in the face of a biting northwesterly wind that smarted our eyes and made the horses drop their heads.

After a couple of hours every step became harder as I struggled to keep a grip on the small stones. Men cursed as they fell and their horses grunted in alarm as they slipped but eventually we crested the hill and descended into a small densely wooded ravine. The wind disappeared, the sun shone and everyone heaved a huge sigh of relief. We made camp among the conifers, sheltered from the wind and having access to crystal-clear, fast-running streams providing invigorating cool water. Agraci and Durans disrobed to take the opportunity to wash their bodies, though guards had been posted at both ends of the ravine and Talib and his men ascended the slopes to keep watch for any enemy patrols.

After I had unsaddled *Tegha* , watered him and rubbed him down, I too shed my clothes and immersed myself in an ice-cold stream. The dust and grime of the previous few days was literally blasted away and I felt much better for it.

'They are nasty scars, majesty, though old I think.'

I turned to see Vima, soaking wet, standing by the stream. His athletic frame did not have an ounce of fat on it and made him look even taller. His black hair was matted to his skull.

'They resemble scars from a flogging.'

I emerged from the stream and wrung out my hair.

'You are correct. They are mementos from my days as a slave.'

He threw me my leggings.

'I have heard you were a slave of the Romans.'

'It is an old story but true, nevertheless.'

'There are no Romans in these parts,' he said.

I pulled on my boots. 'I thank the gods for that at least.'

'And yet there is still war.'

I put on my silk vest, worn to lessen the effects of an arrow wound. An arrow spins in flight and if one went through my leather cuirass the silk would wrap itself around the turning arrowhead, making it easier to extract. That was the theory, at least, one that I had thankfully never put to the test.

'There is still war because the Parthian Empire consists of independent kingdoms, each ruled by a monarch who is supposed to adhere to the wishes of the high king.'

I strapped on my sword belt. 'But if the high king stokes rivalries and conflicts then the empire can soon find itself enmeshed in conflict.'

'You have no confidence in High King Phraates?'

'I have every confidence in him to behave like a high king,' I replied, 'but at the moment he is like a sword blade that is yet to be tempered. Rulers like Phanes seek to further their own ends by taking advantage of his immaturity.'

Vima appeared to be fascinated. 'I have heard that the kings of the east are not committed to Phraates, seeing him as too young to be high king.'

'He is young,' I agreed, 'but he is the legitimate heir. The only heir.'

His narrow, thin eyebrows rose but he said nothing more. He seemed to know much about Sakastan and I wondered if he had knowledge of Vartan. Perhaps it would have been better to have killed Vartan when he arrived in Sigal, but I enjoyed the benefit of hindsight. Alas for Peroz and Roxanne. It was all irrelevant now, anyway, Phanes would have to pay for the murder of my friends.

We rested a day in the ravine before moving out for the final leg of the journey. Vima rode ahead with Talib and his scouts, Malik questioning me about the spice trader.

'He does not look like a merchant,' remarked the King of the Agraci.

'He's right there, lord,' said Kalet, 'most of the merchants I know are fat, rich and lazy.'

'Do you actually know any merchants?' I asked him. 'Aside from the ones you have robbed.'

He did not dignify my remark with an answer but Malik was convinced Vima was no trader.

'He has the appearance and bearing of a warrior. Surely you must see this, Pacorus?'

'Perhaps he is,' I said, 'but he saved my life, has thus far has proved himself a valuable ally and will hopefully play a part in a crucial mission. If he chooses to disguise himself, what of it?'

'I don't trust him,' stated Kalet starkly. 'He might be leading us into a trap.'

But he was not and on the sixth day, the sun in our eyes, I lay on my belly beside Vima and Talib staring down at what appeared to be a thousand campfires around a huge glistening lake. My heart sank when I saw the number of horses and men present, though I was glad that we had arrived unseen.

'I am once again in your debt, Vima,' I said.

The trader peered at the horsemen and foot soldiers of Aria and Drangiana below.

'They will not stay here long, I think. We arrived just in time.'

'What are your tactics, lord?' asked Talib. 'Even with surprise the odds against us will be heavy.'

'The cover of night will even the odds,' I told him.

We had arrived by horse but they would be left behind in camp. It would be too dangerous to launch a mounted assault downhill in the dark, over terrain that was uneven and covered with grassy tufts.

The day had been warm and sunny but the night was cool and breezy. The lighting of campfires had been forbidden for fear of alerting our presence to the enemy that vastly outnumbered us. So, we groomed our horses, cleaned our weapons, chewed on cured meat, drank cold water and wrapped ourselves in blankets in an effort to keep warm.

I assembled Malik and his senior warlords and Kalet and his roguish commanders as the light faded fast. It was all a great lark for them, though I noticed that not one of them was drunk or had been drinking. Raiding and slitting throats was too serious a business to spoil with alcohol. They crouched in a circle around me and listened to my instructions, though I was careful to stress that Malik was in joint command. He too was a king.

'We wait until just before dawn and then we attack. We go to kill as many as possible because the more we slay here the less will be marching south to Sigal.'

I looked at Kalet and his comrades. 'Leave anything that might make a noise in camp. I don't want forty thousand men waiting for us.'

They grumbled in umbrage and a swarthy one with a facial scar that made mine look like a scratch took exception.

'We know how to creep up on an enemy, lord, we have been doing it for decades.'

'You should come with us on a raid against Syria,' said another. 'We are in and out before anyone notices.'

They and the Agraci laughed. I held up a hand.

'You have been raiding Syria?'

Kalet sought to soothe my concern. 'One stretch of desert looks very similar to another, lord, it's easy to stray over the border.'

'I will lay aside the fact that each and every one of you has a detailed knowledge of the Syrian desert,' I said, 'but here and now I expressly forbid any raiding of Roman Syria. Having just fought a hard campaign against the Romans I do not want to provoke them into another war over a few thieved goats.'

'I resent that, lord,' complained scar-face. 'I would never cross the border just for goats. Horses, yes.'

The others laughed. They were incorrigible.

'We will speak of this when we get back to Dura,' I said. 'In the meantime, may Shamash be with you all.'

Scar-face gave me an evil grin and Kalet rubbed his hands. Malik remained as the group dispersed, placing an arm around my shoulder.

'You know what they are like, Pacorus. Wild and untamed, like the land they inhabit. I have no doubt that some of my lords also raid the Romans.'

'And you do not mind?'

He shrugged. 'The Agraci have always raided, it is in our blood. And now that we have the friendship of Dura the Romans are

131

reluctant to launch reprisals against us. Besides, the trade route through Palmyra benefits Rome as well as Parthia. Why would they cut off their noses to spite their faces?'

'What if a delegation from Damascus arrived at Palmyra demanding restitution?'

'I would ask for proof that it was the Agraci who thieved the goods,' he replied. 'Anyway, they won't do that?'

'Oh, why not?'

He smiled. 'Byrd, acting on my behalf, is negotiating with the Romans concerning hiring their stonemasons to construct some buildings in Palmyra. It will be a lucrative contract. They will not want to jeopardise it.'

I shared his joy. Years ago, I had told his father, Haytham, that one day Palmyra would be a city of stone. He had dismissed the idea but his son was about to make the prophecy real. I prayed that I would live to see the day when the first stone was laid.

I was kneeling on the ground with my eyes closed, praying to Shamash while clutching the lock of Gallia's hair just before we moved out of camp. When I opened my eyes and stood, I was aware of someone behind me. I turned, squinted and recognised Vima holding his horse's reins.

'I will take my leave now, majesty.'

I offered him my hand. He was surprised but took it.

'I have never shaken the hand of a king before.'

His grip was firm, determined.

'I am a man thanking another man for saving his life and giving me a great gift.'

'Gift?'

'Victory,' I said, 'for the enemy below is like a helpless lamb and we are wolves.'

Every tenth man remained in camp to tend the horses and provide a small reserve should we need to retreat quickly. Only a few of Kalet's men carried bows, including myself, most being armed with swords and daggers. The Agraci also favoured daggers, wicked curved swords and small round shields painted black. They also dressed in black and brown hues, as did my lords, their clothes blending into the gloom and thus masking their approach to the enemy camp.

'You had better stick with us, lord,' suggested Kalet just before we left camp. 'Don't want you getting lost on the way down.'

'Us' comprised Kalet, his brother, brother-in-law, uncle and a nephew who looked too young to be carrying a sword. My chief lord noticed my reservation.

'Don't worry about him, lord, he's deadly with a knife.'

The bleak mountains were half-visible in the pre-dawn light as we crept down the slope towards the tent city below. Every sword was in its scabbard and every knife in its sheath as two and half thousand men walked briskly down the grassy hill, spread out in a long line as far as the eye could see. There was no joking, talking or peering around as each man focused on his task, which was to cover the ground to the camp in silence.

As we got closer the tension increased, my heart pounding in my chest at the thought we would be discovered. The temptation in such a situation is to start running but even as the dawn was breaking to do so risked losing one's footing on the uneven surface. When we reached the bottom of the hill the pace increased slightly. We were now only two hundred paces from the camp perimeter, a sea of tents filling our vision as we crouched low to make ourselves as small as possible. I shivered when I saw figures leaning against spear shafts – cold and hungry guards more interested in their own discomfort than keeping watch.

The transition from night to day always seemed to dull men's senses and now we took full advantage of the brief lethargy. I stopped, pulled an arrow from a quiver that had been tightly packed with missiles to prevent them making a noise during the advance, nocked it in my bowstring and focused on the guard. I inhaled as I drew back the sinew, exhaled and let the bowstring slip through my fingers. There was a sharp twang, the guard looked up and then collapsed when the arrow struck him.

'Move!' hissed Kalet.

We fast-paced across the stretch of ground between our starting position and the tents, men drawing weapons as they closed on the enemy camp. And then we were among the foe.

Men darted into tents to stab and hack with frenzy at sleeping men, the screams and cries of wounded and dying shattering the silence that had hung over the camp. I shot a man armed with a spear springing from a tent, and another following him carrying a sword. On we went, Durans shouting in triumph as they tossed firebrands into tents and released horses tethered to temporary stalls, the beasts scattering in all directions to sow further discord.

Trumpets and drums sounded. The enemy was now awake and attempting to rally. I sprinted forward, Kalet and his relations by my side. I spotted a man bellowing orders to a rapidly forming line of archers. I halted, aimed my bow and shot him in the chest. I reloaded and shot one of the stunned archers, then a second and a third before Kalet and his men were among them, slashing left and right with their swords to cut down the archers. He whooped with joy as he butchered the last bowman.

Tents erupted in flames around us as the camp became a maelstrom of sound and confusion. Arrows were now flying through the air as the enemy began to rally and isolated groups of dismounted horse archers formed themselves into units to battle us. It was light now and a northerly wind had picked up, fanning flames and sending sparks and burning embers into the air to ignite straw and other tents. This in turn terrified horses that broke free and scattered in all directions. One ran past on fire, Kalet throwing himself aside to avoid being trampled. When the horse had passed we faced half a dozen fully armed spearmen carrying shields and wearing helmets. The shields carried the emblems of a deer – men from Aria.

One jabbed his spear into the shoulder of Kalet's brother-in-law, another tried to stab his brother in the chest but his nephew was quicker and threw his knife to hit the spearman in the throat. He dropped his spear, clutched at his throat and fell to the ground. I released my bowstring and sent an arrow through the eye socket of the soldier on the end of the line, nocked another arrow and shot that one through a spearman's wicker shield to pierce his chest. Kalet cut down a fourth enemy whereupon the other two decided discretion was the better part of valour and retreated, keeping their shields up and their spears levelled.

'Time to go,' shouted Kalet, putting an arm around his brother-in-law.

I agreed, stringing another arrow and felling one of the two surviving spearmen.

Kalet's young nephew dashed forward, retrieved his knife and then joined us as we fell back through burning tents, carts, supplies and dead bodies. Kalet cuffed him round the ear.

'Sound the signal and stop pissing about.'

The youth pulled a bone horn from his black tunic and blew it.

'Again,' ordered Kalet.

He sounded the horn three more times as we picked up the pace to reach the eastern perimeter of the camp. The air was now filled with grey smoke that stung our eyes and choked our lungs, but at least it added to the chaos enveloping the enemy. Groups of Agraci and Durans gathered briefly at the perimeter before racing back to the hill, men looking back to see if there was any pursuit. There was none.

When we reached the crest of the hill my lungs were on fire. Kalet slapped me on the back.

'Feeling your age, lord?'

'I have not had the benefit of your rustling practice,' I shot back.

He grinned and peered back at the camp below, now wreathed in thick grey smoke that also masked a large part of the lake.

'Now that is a grand sight.'

I had to agree and once I caught my breath I walked among the lords and their family members and retainers to convey my thanks. They forgot I was a king and slapped me on the back, embraced me and offered me waterskins filled with wine! The way they could seemingly magic alcohol out of thin air was truly amazing. More good news awaited us back in camp where Malik, not a scratch on him, was waiting with his warlords. I embraced my friend and we stood like mischievous children, grinning at each other while around us Durans and Agraci swapped stories about how many enemy soldiers they had killed. They were ecstatic, I was ecstatic but Talib brought me back to reality.

'We must leave immediately, lord, the enemy will soon be despatching horsemen to hunt us down.'

The wounded were strapped to their horses no matter the seriousness of their injuries. Some had only gashes and cuts; others had belly wounds. But the best that could be done was to bind their wounds, help them into the saddle and give their reins to a colleague who would lead their horse. It was fortunate that Parthian saddles were constructed around a wooden frame with four horns: two at the front and two at the back, all of them wrapped with bronze plates and padded. Thus, when a rider sat in the leather saddle he or she was held firmly in place by the horns, allowing him or her to turn to shoot a bow without fear of falling off. At least the wounded would not topple from the saddle, even if they passed out, though they might expire from loss of blood during the journey.

We retraced our steps, Talib, his scouts and those men who had been left behind in camp to guard the horses forming a rearguard to keep watch for any pursuers. We set a cruel pace, pushing our horses hard to put as much distance between us and any enemy as possible. It was midday, the sun high above us in a clear blue sky, when we called the first halt. Tired, sweating men jumped down from their saddles to give their panting horses water from their waterskins before leading the beast on foot after a short break.

I walked beside Malik, specs of blood on his robes, though fortunately not his own.

'Where is the trader, dead?'

'Vima? He left before our attack.'

'To go back to Sigal?'

I did not know. 'Wherever he is I pray he is safe. He did us a great favour today.'

Malik said nothing.

'You disagree?'

'He saved your life and guided us to a place from where we could launch a devastating attack on an enemy. But something tells me our merchant friend is not all he appears. It is like an itch I cannot scratch.'

'If he had intended us ill he would have made his move by now, my friend. When I return to Sigal I will give thanks in the temple for his services.'

We made it back to Sigal unmolested by the enemy, Talib preceding us to spread word of our great success. He must have embellished the tale because we returned to wild rumours that we had butchered over forty thousand men at the great lake, which was now red on account of the volume of Arian and Drangianan blood that had been poured into it.

Our tired but jubilant column rode into Sigal to a rapturous reception, cheering crowds held back by the city garrison as we threaded our way through adulation to the fortress where a transformed Salar officially welcomed us back. A radiant Isabella stood on one side of the king and Gallia on the other in mail armour, Amazons forming a guard of honour in the courtyard. With my wife were Jamal, Eszter and Diana, visions of beauty and poise. The only one not beaming with delight was Claudia, who stood with a smug expression on her face. When I had left Sigal had been drenched in defeat and doom but now it bristled with defiance and certainty.

138

Salar's yellow-uniformed bodyguard snapped to attention as the king and queen descended the stone steps to receive us, slaves taking our horses to the stables.

'Welcome back, father,' said a beaming Salar. 'You are most welcome.'

He walked over to Malik. 'Great king, Sakastan is in your debt.'

Everyone seemed to be smiling, including Gallia who embraced me long and fondly.

'I must go away more often,' I teased.

'Yesterday we received news that Phanes refused battle in the south and has fled back to Puta with his tail between his legs.'

Now I beamed with delight. 'This day gets better and better.'

It was a happy reunion and the elixir of victory washed away exhaustion and eased tired limbs. Salar, now looking every inch a king, invited us all to a great banquet to celebrate the double success. Only Claudia seemed detached from the celebratory atmosphere.

'What's the matter with you?' I asked her.

'I need to speak to you about a most urgent matter, father.'

Chapter 6

The other kings and the army of Sakastan returned two days later, to a wild reception. The elephants led the procession into the city, their steel-encased tusks glinting in the sun and their foot guards carrying yellow and red flags. Several of the beasts raised their trunks and roared, though with anger or delight I could not tell. The cataphracts positively glistened in the sunlight and as ever Prince Pacorus and Hatra's Royal Bodyguard looked magnificent in their scale armour and white-plumed helmets. In a nice touch both Pacorus and Azad had allowed the squires to ride into Sigal in scale armour, following their participation in the 'great victory' over Phanes. In a magnanimous gesture, Nergal, Spartacus and Gafarn threw captured peacock banners at the feet of Salar and Isabella in the fortress' courtyard. The King of Sakastan wanted to hang them on the wall of one of the palace's corridors, no doubt thinking that he would add to his collection of captured standards in the years to come, but Claudia told him that to have enemy emblems hanging on his walls would bring bad luck and she told him to burn them forthwith.

My eldest daughter summoned me to the fortress battlements the day after the great feast to celebrate the twin victories derided by Claudia.

'Salar should concentrate on reinforcing his defences instead of inflating the pride of the kings and queens that have travelled to Sigal.'

'I hope you are not including me in that group.'

She turned from me and walked along the battlements. It was late and the night was cool and clear, the sky filled with twinkling stars. Guards kept watch in towers at either end of the rampart we

140

walked along but there was no one to disturb us. Below the walls was the sprawl of the city and beyond the great silver streak that was the River Erymanthus. Claudia was dressed entirely in black, her high cheekbones highlighted in the moonlight to give her a slightly savage appearance.

'What do you see, father?'

I looked around. 'A fortress, a city and beyond that a river.'

'Turn your gaze away from the realm of men.'

She was staring into the sparkling sky and at one star in particular, one brighter and larger than the rest.

'The evening star.'

She shot me a rebuking glare. 'The Goddess Ninsi-Anna, you mean, the holy torch who fills the heavens, the radiant goddess whose light fills heaven and earth. The goddess of certainty and true direction. Travellers have availed themselves of her services for centuries to find their way.'

'Indeed,' I said, somewhat humbled.

'While you were away the goddess disappeared from the heavens,' she told me, 'only to reappear after two days.'

She turned away from the star to look at me.

'A friend came to me and told me an ancient tale, *The Wrath of Erra* . Have you heard of it, father?'

I had not. 'No. What friend?'

She avoided eye contact. 'A mutual friend.'

'Is there a reason for all this mystery?'

She ignored my question and once again stared at the evening star.

'The tale is at least eight hundred years old, perhaps older. Erra, God of War, plagues and mayhem, had decided to attack Babylon.'

'Why?' I asked.

She tut-tutted under her breath. 'I am not privy to the gods' motivations. Why don't you ask them yourself? Please listen.

'Babylon was under the protection of mighty Marduk so Erra travelled there pretending it was a friendly visit and upon arriving, feigned shock at how poorly Marduk was dressed. He told Marduk that he should do something about his shabby appearance. Marduk, embarrassed, told Erra he had no time as the defence of Babylon absorbed all his energies. Erra offered to watch over the city while Marduk obtained clothes befitting his position as a mighty god. But once he was out of the city Erra unleashed his wrath on Babylon and tore down many buildings and killed thousands of people.'

'A chilling tale,' I said, 'but what has it to do with me?'

'You have been deceived, father, by a false friend. At first, I was unsure as to what the tale alluded to, but a casual conversation with another old friend removed the veil of mystery to reveal the truth.'

'What truth?' I demanded, eager to return to Gallia and a warm and comfortable bed.

Claudia nodded at someone behind me. I turned to see the limping figure of Byrd approaching.

'Thank you for coming.'

I was not amused. 'I apologise for my daughter dragging you here at this ungodly hour, my friend.'

'No hour is free of the gods,' insisted Claudia.

'I am tired, getting cold and wish to get some sleep.'

'Tell him,' Claudia said to Byrd.

'While you away, lord, I ask around about the spice trader who saved your life.'

'Vima?'

Byrd nodded. 'I have met many traders over the years and he was unlike any I have encountered. So I enquired at the association of merchants, the spice traders' association and at the *caravanserai* .'

The *caravanserai* were parks and inns where camel caravans rested, refreshed themselves, traded and swapped gossip. They were almost as effective at transmitting accurate information as the empire's post stations.

'None has heard of Vima,' said Byrd.

'Vima is a deceiver, father, who like Erra comes with false promises.'

'Not this again,' I moaned. 'If Vima wanted me dead he would not have saved my life at the wedding, to say nothing of the great assistance he provided during the recent action around Lake Nawar.'

'A man who lies is not to be trusted,' was Byrd's gruff comment.

'Vima does not wish you dead, father,' said Claudia, 'he wishes to use you for his own ends.'

'Which are?' I demanded.

'That has not been revealed to me. Yet.'

I had had enough. I turned to Byrd.

'Come, my friend, let us leave Claudia to walk these breezy battlements alone. I have a warm bed awaiting me. How is Noora?'

Byrd gave a rare smile. 'Well, lord, she pleased that Talib has proved a good scout.'

143

I walked beside him towards the stone steps leading down from the ramparts.

'Dura's best scout retired some years ago but Talib is doing an admirable job trying to fill his big boots.'

'Remember my warning,' Claudia called after me, 'and remember the king cobra. The two are linked.'

'She like Dobbai,' said Byrd.

I shook my head. 'Too true, my friend, too true.'

I forgot about Claudia's warning as other matters of more import occupied my days. A letter arrived from Silaces stating that 'bugger all' was happening elsewhere in the empire, specifically around Ctesiphon. I wrote to Phraates describing the atrocity at my daughter's wedding and demanding that Phanes be stripped of the title Lord High General in the East. I did not inform him that I had led an assault against the soldiers of Aria and Drangiana and nor did I mention the on-going problem of Vartan. The youth showed no signs of leaving Sigal and in truth everyone took a liking to him. He was an agreeable young man and Eszter in particular took a shine to him. They could be seen frequently walking together in the palace gardens, the ever-watchful Cookum walking a few paces behind and behind him a couple of guards assigned by Salar. Having seen his parents murdered in front of his eyes, the king took no chances when it came to palace security, which was stepped up significantly. But as the days passed and no word came from the governor in the north of incursions by Arians or Drangianans, I began to feel more confident. Among us only Claudia was full of forebodings and after a while we all avoided her. She was like a dark cloud drifting around a palace slowly returning to normality.

The kings and queens amused themselves hunting, feasting and visiting nearby towns, every trip accompanied by a large retinue of their soldiers to show everyone that the King of Sakastan had powerful allies. Salar himself devoted his time to planning a campaign against Carmania in the south, Kewab continuing to advise and caution him. He acted on my instructions – I did not want Salar embarking on a war until I learned more of Phraates' intentions. But no word came from Ctesiphon and so we extended our stay at Sigal.

I had come to the city to attend my daughter's wedding and relax, but it had turned out very differently from what the others and I had expected. Sakastan was now on a war footing and I spent my days liaising with Salar and Shapur and the other kings. Spartacus kept bending my son-in-law's ear about taking the newly returned army north to invade Aria while, after I had convinced him to do so, King Silaces would invade Drangiana from the west. Following the northern campaign, Spartacus advised turning south once more to invade and conquer Carmania. Fortunately, the wise counsel of Kewab acted as a counterweight to Spartacus' wild schemes and Salar for the moment concentrated his energies on readying his city for conflict. Or at least Marcus Sutonius did.

My chief engineer was in his element, inspecting the walls of the city and fortress and strengthening Sigal's defences. One day he requested my attendance at one of the towers on the city walls, eager to show me his new project. I rode down to the perimeter wall in the company of Salar, who was keen to see what Marcus had put together. Behind us rode a score of the king's bodyguard, around us thousands of waving and cheering citizens with women holding up their infants so they could see their king. City morale seemed to be improving.

'I have not forgotten the murder of my parents,' he told me, holding up an arm in recognition of the adulation. 'My brother will pay, that I promise.'

'There is no evidence King Phanes was complicit in the murder of your parents, Salar.'

'Then who?'

I had no answer and in truth I sensed that Phanes did have a hand in the outrage, but I was mindful that Phraates had created Salar's uncle lord high general in the east. There was also the matter of Vartan to be resolved.

'He can stay here as long as he wishes,' stated Salar defiantly, 'if Phanes wants him then he can come and get him.'

'I doubt Phanes will venture near Sigal without the assistance of Aria and Drangiana,' I said.

He flashed a smile. 'But they have been defeated.'

'They have been inconvenienced,' I cautioned, 'but they will recover.'

'You sound like Commander Kewab,' he teased.

That was the intention but I merely smiled at the crowds that grew thicker as we neared the city walls. The guards jumped down from their horses and shoved the civilians back as the captain of the guard of the tower walked forward and bowed his head at us.

'Lord Marcus is ready, highnesses.'

'Lord Marcus?' I said, 'Romans don't like noble titles.'

Salar turned to give the crowd a last salute before entering the tower.

'I'm going to give him a vineyard,' Salar told me, 'will he like that?'

I wondered how Marcus would benefit from a vineyard a thousand miles from his home but said nothing.

'And an elephant if he desires,' added Salar, bounding up the stone steps.

The top of the tower was crowded with senior officers, including Shapur, gathered around a wooden instrument, next to which was Marcus in large floppy hat, baggy tunic and leggings. He looked like an eccentric philosopher, though without the long beards favoured by the Greek thinkers. The officers snapped to attention when Salar appeared, making way so the king could stand beside Marcus' new toy.

It was simple enough: a large bamboo bow mounted transversely on a wooden stand. It was a solid, workmanlike machine that looked like a larger version of the scorpions employed by Dura's army.

'Gather round, please,' said Marcus.

I noticed two grooves cut into the top of the stock, which allowed two arrows to be shot at once.

'Two arrows?' I said.

'Most observant, lord,' said Marcus. 'As time is short I have endeavoured to produce a machine that is functional yet effective.'

He went on to explain how the machine was loaded by means of a rear-mounted winch that drew the thick bowstring back via a trigger mechanism using a metal claw and linear ratchet. When the trigger was pulled the claw flipped up, releasing the bowstring. Each iron-tipped missile was nearly six feet in length.

'I have employed the principles of the great engineers Philon and Ctesibius in its construction,' finished Marcus, 'and am confident that it will allow its users to shoot at an enemy for prolonged periods.'

No one had heard of Philon and Ctesibius, two military engineers from Byzantium and Alexandria, but they applauded politely when Marcus had finished and invited Salar to pull the trigger. The king did so and beamed with delight when the two missiles shot out from the stock and flew in a straight line for around two hundred paces before dropping but continuing to travel for a further three hundred paces. The observers gasped in astonishment.

'Equip each tower with one of these wondrous machines,' commanded Salar.

'There are thirty towers on the city walls, majesty,' said Shapur.

'And all shall have one of Marcus' machines,' proclaimed Salar.

'Actually, I have studied all the towers and there is room to accommodate two at the top of each tower.'

Salar was in raptures. 'Let it be so, Marcus.'

Shapur was concerned. 'Sixty machines?'

Salar ignored him as Marcus went on to explain the work that needed to be done in front of the walls.

'There is no time to dig a moat, unfortunately. However, the area immediately in front of the city walls can be planted with stakes and littered with caltrops.'

Again, the officers looked at each other with blank faces.

'What are caltrops?' asked Shapur.

'Four-pronged metal spikes crafted in such a way so that when they are laid on the ground one spike always points upwards. If stepped on they can inflict grievous wounds on both people and animals. I suggest the areas in which they are scattered be proclaimed out of bounds to civilians and their animals.'

148

Salar was shocked. 'Do the Romans employ such terrible devices?'

'Of course,' said Marcus. 'They are most efficient and relatively inexpensive.'

Salar thought caltrops uncivilised, revealing a typically Parthian attitude to war that included never fighting at night and retreating from the field of battle before darkness came. I too had been brought up to adhere to such principles, until I fought with Spartacus in Italy.

So work commenced on the manufacture of the caltrops and Marcus' machines, Salar expecting news to arrive from his northern outposts that the Arians and Drangianans were marching south. They did indeed make for Sigal, though in a capacity none of us expected.

The first inkling that something was awry was when a letter arrived for Salar from Ctesiphon, its mood conciliatory, even friendly. In it Phraates expressed outrage at the killings at the wedding and promised to leave no stone unturned to discover who was responsible. He also stated he was sad to hear of the animosity between Salar and Phanes and had written to the latter to order him to halt any aggression towards Sakastan. The final part of the letter was most strange, requesting that Salar aid Aria and Drangiana in 'their present difficulties'. At the bottom was scribbled a hasty addendum:

The matter of Vartan will be resolved after affairs in the east of the empire have been stabilised.

Salar was pleased that the high king appeared to have changed his attitude but had no idea what the 'difficulties' Phraates had alluded to were. None of us did. But we were fully appraised when ambassadors from Aria and Drangiana arrived two days after the letter from the high king. Word had spread that those two kingdoms had allied themselves with Phanes and they received a frosty reception from Sigal's citizens when they approached the city. Shapur had to despatch a sizeable number of guards to ensure they were not harmed as they made their way from the city gates to the palace.

Once in the citadel they were treated as befitting their rank and status, relief on their aged faces as Salar and Isabella greeted them in the throne room. The chamber was hot, the atmosphere oppressive. Kewab, who stood like a hawk next to Salar on his throne, had advised the king to pack it with his senior officers in their finest uniforms. The visiting kings and queens were also in attendance, this time Gallia, Praxima and Rasha in their full war gear. Salar himself wore a magnificent silver-scale cuirass that shimmered in the light flooding through the large windows cut high in the walls.

The ambassadors, thin and uncertain though clad in rich apparel, walked nervously through the throng of opulently dressed officers to stand and bow to the king and queen. A steward handed the king their letters of introduction.

'Welcome Ambassador Altan,' smiled Salar, 'I trust King Tiridates is well?'

Altan bowed his head. 'Well, majesty, thank you.'

'And welcome Ambassador Chingis,' said Salar, 'I hope King Antiochus prospers.'

'With your help he will, majesty, he will,' replied the ambassador of Drangiana.

Salar registered surprise. 'My assistance? I thought your two kingdoms had allied with my brother, the King of Carmania?'

Chingis was an old fox who was used to disarming men with his words and swatted away the accusation.

'Drangiana has always been loyal to the high king of the empire, majesty, but has been careful not to be drawn into family disputes.'

'As has Aria,' added Altan.

'But now,' said Chingis, 'our respective rulers appeal to Sakastan, Parthian to Parthian, for aid in order to repel the foreign invaders.'

'What invaders?' asked Salar.

'The Kushans,' stated Altan. 'They first attacked the combined army of King Tiridates and King Antiochus around Lake Nawar, and then Kujula sent his armies into our kingdoms.'

'If the barbarians overrun Drangiana and Aria, majesty,' said Chingis, 'then Sakastan will be next.'

'Kujula is the leader of the Kushans, majesty,' said Altan, 'a cruel, barbarous tyrant who wishes to conquer the whole world.'

Chingis bowed his head at me. 'And the whole world knows of King Pacorus of Dura and his mighty army. It is fortuitous that you and your friends are here at Sigal, majesty.'

'I am here on a family matter only,' I informed the ambassador, 'and my army is far away.'

But Chingis was not about to let the matter drop.

'And yet here you are with the other great kings of the empire, together with over ten thousand soldiers. Such a force added to the army of Sakastan and the armies of Drangiana and Aria would be more than sufficient to defeat Kujula and send him crawling back to his so-called empire.'

Kewab had been whispering in the ear of Salar, who now spoke.

'My scouts reported that the combined army that was worsted around Lake Nawar was poised to attack my kingdom.'

The ambassadors both shook their heads.

'No, majesty,' insisted Altan.

'Nothing could be further from the truth,' stated Chingis.

Again, Kewab whispered into the king's ear.

'Then what was it doing so close to my northern border?' asked Salar.

'A joint training exercise,' said Chingis, 'and the reason it was held so close to your border was because only Lake Nawar could provide the water to supply such a large gathering of men and horses.'

He was very good, this Chingis. He elevated lying to an art form. Kewab again spoke into the king's ear.

'May we know who this person is, majesty?' enquired Altan, frowning at Kewab.

'You may not,' replied Salar curtly. 'But I will enquire as to the position of my uncle, King Phanes. Have your masters petitioned him for aid?'

Altan and Chingis looked at each other before the latter smiled.

'King Antiochus feels that since the army of Carmania was repulsed by your own forces, majesty,' he looked at me, Nergal, Gafarn and Spartacus in turn, 'assisted by the fine soldiers of Dura, Mesene, Hatra and Gordyene, he believes the army of Sakastan alone is capable of tipping the scales of war in our favour.'

'A sentiment echoed by King Tiridates,' added Altan.

'So you have abandoned King Phanes?' I asked.

'In desperate circumstances, one must look for certainty, majesty,' smiled Chingis. 'Our lords believe that the King of Sakastan and his friends can restore order to the empire.'

'That's a yes, then,' said Gafarn loud enough for everyone to hear.

Nergal and Spartacus laughed and for an instant the mask of diplomacy slipped from Chingis' face, though it was quickly restored when he addressed the King of Gordyene.

'A warlord who has taken two Roman eagles will have little problem dealing with the Kushan barbarians, lord.'

Kewab continued his advice to Salar.

'We will have to think on the matter. This audience is at an end.'

He rose and took Isabella's hand. We all bowed our heads as he made his way from the dais accompanied by my commander. Chingis and Altan were left fuming but had little choice but to grit their teeth and retire from the throne room with dignity. At least that night they were treated to a sumptuous feast laid on in their honour, entertainers and musicians keeping them and us amused into the early hours.

The next day I and the other kings were summoned to Salar's private apartments to discuss the recent developments. The king was in a confident mood as he spoke to us in his office, his back to the splendid views of the mountains in the distance.

'I am thinking of aiding Aria and Drangiana. It would be better to fight the Kushans on their territory rather than my own.'

'Sensible,' I agreed.

'What do you know of these Kushans?' asked Nergal.

'Only that they occupy the lands of northern India and have until recently confined their aggression to the Satavahana Empire to the south. We know next to nothing about their leader, Kujula.'

'What about the size and strength of his army?' asked Nergal.

'Again, our knowledge is wanting,' admitted Salar.

'My advice would be to wait until the Arians and Drangianans have exhausted themselves fighting these Kushans,' said Malik, 'before committing yourself. Let them bleed rather than you.'

'You two are to be congratulated,' said Gafarn, looking at Malik and me.

'Us, why?' I said.

'You managed to convince the Arians and Drangianans that is was these Kushans who attacked their army at the great lake, whereas we all know it was you.'

'Malik is right,' said Spartacus suddenly. 'Wait until both sides have butchered each other before making a move. That way you will have Tiridates and Antiochus by the balls.'

Malik laughed but Gafarn shuddered. 'Remind me, son, who are the barbarians?'

Salar was shaking his head. 'No, to do so would earn the lasting enmity of those two kingdoms, whereas if I march to their aid I will earn their gratitude. That in turn will make it easier for me to convince them not to support my uncle's aggression towards Sakastan.'

'And in support of your policy,' I said, 'Dura will march with you.'

'As will Hatra,' promised Gafarn.

Nergal nodded. 'And Mesene.'

'The Agraci offer you their swords, lord king,' stated Malik solemnly.

We all looked at Spartacus.

'Of course I'm in, you think I am going to sit here while you win all the glory?'

Chingis and Altan were delighted by the decision and left Sigal that afternoon, the city's inhabitants glad to see the back of them. Shapur had them escorted all the way to the northern border to ensure their safety.

Salar's army, fresh from its 'triumph' in the south, was prepared for the march north, along with the contingents of the kings. Morale among the soldiery was very high and Salar temporarily put aside his animosity for Phanes as he focused on the north, undertook inspections of his soldiers and promised that this time he would lead them personally. This had an invigorating effect on his men, who strained at the leash for the opportunity to fight the Kushans. But in the meantime, I had my own battles to fight.

Isabella cornered me one morning after I had attended the morning report of my officers in camp outside the city. These briefings were routine affairs and usually involved nothing more that Azad reporting horses that had gone lame, squires that had fallen ill and the many complaints of cameleers. When I returned in the company of my cataphract commander I found a pacing Isabella waiting for me. She linked her arm in mine after I had dismounted and a stable hand had taken *Tegha* from me.

'This is a pleasant surprise,' I told her, 'is everything well?'

'Well,' she smiled, though I could tell from her agitated state that the opposite was true. 'Can you spare me some of your time?'

'Of course.'

We walked through the palace, guards snapping to attention and slaves stopping what they were doing to bow to us, but Isabella was oblivious to everything. She led me towards the royal gardens, stopping before we reached them.

'Do you promise to keep calm?'

'Why, what have you done?' I joked.

She was deeply troubled. 'Eszter has been sleeping with Vartan.'

I bubbled over in rage. 'What?!'

She gripped my arms and fixed her large brown eyes on mine.

'Calm down, father. You must promise me you will do nothing rash.'

'Like killing Vartan.'

'Exactly.'

'I promise I will not do that.'

She closed her eyes and sighed. 'Thank you.'

'I will get Azad to do it.'

'No,' she said firmly, 'this is my palace, not yours. You will respect my wishes and those of my husband, the king.'

I was appalled. 'Salar knows about this?'

She sighed again. 'Unfortunately the whole palace knows. A slave who is a notorious gossip discovered my sister and her lover. Salar wanted to have his tongue bored but I forbade it. The fault was Eszter's, not his.'

She turned and glided into the gardens, to a shaded area sweet with the smell of tulips and eucalyptus. Waiting for us was Gallia, Claudia and Eszter, the latter eating a pastry with not a care in the world. I confronted her immediately, slaves being ordered away by Isabella as I spat venom at her.

'Do you know what have done? You have disgraced yourself, your family and the Kingdom of Dura. You are supposed to be a princess not a whore.'

'Pacorus,' interrupted Gallia, 'that is enough.'

'It is far from enough,' I shouted, 'I am within my rights to have Vartan executed for his gross actions.'

Eszter jumped up from her wicker chair. 'For what? For obeying a princess of Dura? I am not betrothed to anyone, what harm is there in enjoying myself?'

I could not believe my ears. 'If you wanted to enjoy yourself you could have learned to dance or play a musical instrument. You will never erase the shame if you give birth to a bastard.'

'That won't happen,' insisted Eszter.

I pointed at her. 'Really, can you see into the future now?'

'I take precautions, father,' she said matter-of-factly.

'Very sensible,' agreed Isabella.

'Silence,' I hissed, forgetting she was Queen of Sakastan. 'Who is complicit in your outrageous behaviour?' I demanded of Eszter.

'Don't be so stiff, father,' said Claudia, 'I supplied Eszter with the means to prevent an unwanted birth.'

I spun to look at her. 'You?'

'It's quite simple. Raw papaya or silphium, a member of the fennel family that is an effective contraception when taken once a month as a tincture.'

I flopped down in a chair, stunned by my daughters' blasé attitudes. I held my head in my hands.

'You should be thanking me, father,' said Claudia, 'my simple potions have prevented a possible dynastic war in the empire. If Vartan is the true son of Orodes.'

'He is,' insisted Eszter.

Claudia brought her hands together. 'Let us for the moment say that he is. Any heir he produces will be a direct challenge to the legitimacy of Phraates' reign and might be used by some as a pretext for getting rid of the current high king. An event not entirely unwelcome, I think.'

I gave her a murderous look. 'I'm glad you think it is all very amusing. I do not.'

I looked at Gallia. 'You are unusually quiet on this matter.'

'I have informed Eszter that I disapprove of her actions, but what is done is done. I have also told her that if she intends to marry Vartan then she will have to desist her liaisons with him.'

I jumped up. 'Marry him! I will decide who she marries.'

Eszter confronted me. 'I thought we were free to make our own choices when it came to husbands, or were your words all lies?'

'How dare you,' I shouted. 'I am your father and you will treat me with respect.'

'But I deserve no respect, apparently,' she replied.

I was nearly speechless. 'You think you deserve respect for acting like a whore?'

She slapped my face, the blow hard and determined. I was momentarily taken aback but recovered to raise my arm. But in an instant Gallia was before me.

'We do not strike defenceless women in Dura, Pacorus.'

My cheek began to throb.

'Defenceless? Hardly.'

'You will show respect in my palace, father,' said Isabella sternly. 'Remember I am queen here.'

158

The sisters and Gallia stood side-by-side in a wall of feminine defiance. In that moment, I was proud to have raised three proud and fierce daughters and to have the queen of the Amazons by my side. But those sentiments did nothing to solve the predicament that Eszter had created. I turned to Isabella.

'Well, majesty, will you tolerate lewd behaviour in your palace? You said yourself that it is common gossip within these walls. How long before it becomes known throughout the city and beyond?'

Isabella's unblemished brow creased. 'I assume you have a solution? But I forbid any violence towards Vartan.'

I smiled at Eszter. 'Actually, I do. Vartan will accompany the army when it leaves the city to march north against the Kushans. Let him prove to me and the world that he has the qualities possessed by his father, and furthermore that he is worthy to court my daughter.'

'Vartan is not a soldier,' protested Eszter, 'you will be sending him to his death.'

'He can ride, he can shoot a bow,' I replied, 'for he has taken part in the archery contests organised by Gafarn. My decision is final.'

I stared, unblinking at Eszter, daring her to contradict me. I could see that Gallia and Isabella approved of my decision.

'He might die,' said Eszter, distress in her voice.

'He might,' I agreed, 'but consider that his head might have already been decorating Ctesiphon's walls had it not been for the good grace of King Peroz, may the gods love him. For that reason alone, Vartan should offer his bow to the family that saved his life.'

'Good point, father,' said Claudia, 'we will make a diplomat of you yet.'

I pointed at her. 'And don't think I have forgotten about your part in this sordid episode.'

'It gladdens me to know that I am always in your thoughts, father,' came the sarcastic reply.

But that same day I had Vartan escorted from the palace, where he had more than made himself at home, to the camp of Dura's cataphracts and horse archers outside the city. Cookum protested to Salar but the king had him temporarily arrested for allowing Vartan to corrupt Eszter. The thought of anyone corrupting my youngest daughter made me chuckle but I thanked the king for his consideration. In truth, the affair was a minor inconvenience because Salar and everyone else was fixated on marching against the Kushans. I learned later that Claudia had given Vartan a scorpion talisman as a defence against evil and to guard against enemies. With hindsight, she should have given us all one.

On the day Salar led his army from Sigal such an idea would have been ridiculed. Fifteen thousand Saka foot soldiers and horsemen marched from Salar's capital, accompanied by a hundred war elephants and over twelve thousand soldiers drawn from Dura, Hatra, Gordyene, Mesene and the lands of the Agraci. To add to the spectacle of Saka kettledrummers, drummers on foot, trumpeters on horseback and horn players on foot, the cataphracts of Dura and Hatra rode in their full armour, roasting under a fierce sun and a mere hint of breeze.

The banners of the kings hung limply as we trotted north alongside the Erymanthus, the river low and slow moving now the spring melt waters were a distant memory. But at least the thousands of horses and camels would not want for water on the march. Salar in his silver cuirass and burnished helmet had grown into his role of king and Shapur had the bearing of a man who had been born for high command. As I looked around and behind me I was very

160

satisfied about how things had turned out after the horror of the wedding. With the help of the kings Salar would defeat the Kushans, thus earning the gratitude of Drangiana and Aria. This in turn would neutralise Phanes' efforts to steal the crown of Sakastan and would hopefully lead to Phraates taking away his ridiculous title of Lord High General in the East. I began to hum to myself.

'What are you so happy about?' asked Gafarn.

'I was just thinking that it is better to be the master of events rather than their slave.'

'Most philosophical,' replied the King of Hatra, 'the aroma of horse and camel dung mixed with dust and heat has obviously had a stimulating effect on you. By the way, where is your son-in-law.'

I tipped my head at Salar. 'Is your eyesight deserting you in your dotage?'

'I was not referring to Salar,' said Gafarn smugly. 'No, word has reached my ears that Vartan has won the hand of Eszter.'

'Don't attempt levity when it comes to Vartan,' Gallia warned him, 'Pacorus has no sense of humour when it comes to Orodes' bastard.'

'Don't call him that,' I snapped.

'But that is what he is,' said Gafarn.

'He is with Kalet and my desert lords if you must know,' I told my brother, 'out of sight, though sadly not out of mind.'

'Pacorus hopes he will be killed on this campaign,' said Gallia.

'I'm sure Kalet would slit his throat for you,' said Malik.

'Good idea,' agreed Spartacus.

'I sent Eszter to Hatra to improve her education and curb her wild ways,' I said, changing the subject, 'perhaps I was wrong to do so.'

'Eszter is a charming, well-educated young woman,' Gafarn told me, 'but she is a child of the desert and no amount of tuition can change her personality.'

He looked at Gallia. 'Not that I would wish to.'

'Pacorus is worried that a union between Eszter and Vartan will lead to civil war in the empire.'

'How so?' asked Malik.

'Because any son that results from said union represents a challenge to Phraates' authority,' I explained.

'Phraates is the legitimate high king,' said Gafarn, 'and I stress the word "legitimate".'

I nodded. 'I agree, but Phraates is not a lawyer but a high king and high kings let any potential challengers to their position live at their peril.'

'It is a situation that is both delicate and complicated,' agreed Salar.

The horses were walking now, their tails swatting away flies as they plodded along across the arid plain. We had diverted away from the river to avoid trampling the many groves and fields littering the banks of the Erymanthus. But further from the waterway the vegetation became sparse, mostly desert grass and shrubs. The hard-packed earth was parched and cracked in the summer heat, objects in the distance indistinct and hard to identify in the summer haze.

A member of the vanguard, an officer of the king's guard, left the ranks to gallop back to Salar, pulling up his horse sharply. We all halted our mounts.

'Riders approaching, highness.'

Shapur turned to the horsemen behind us. 'Close up.'

The yellow-clad riders trotted forward to form a cordon around us, long lances lowered in readiness. Zenobia called to the Amazons to form a cordon around the lancers, nocking arrows in their bowstrings. As they did so the column of horsemen behind slowed their mounts.

The riders were at first watery figures but became more distinct as they approached, moving at speed towards us. They slowed when they were within two hundred paces, one of their number continuing on as the rest brought their horses to a halt.

'It is Talib,' I said.

'Stand down,' shouted Shapur.

His men turned their horses to return to their original position and the Amazons slid their bows back in their cases as Talib pulled up his horse and bowed his head to Salar and then me.

'The Kushans, majesty, are but five miles away.'

Chapter 7

Momentarily we were stunned and looked at each other, not believing the Kushans had reached this far south. If their army was here then Aria and Drangiana must have already fallen, or at least their main armies destroyed.

'Perhaps it is just a raiding force,' opined Gafarn.

'No, majesty,' said Talib, 'it numbers thousands of horsemen.'

'Go and find out how many,' I told him.

He bowed his head, turned his horse and galloped back to his men before the whole group rode back towards the north.

'What does it matter?' announced Spartacus, 'we were marching to fight them anyway.'

'We can defeat these Kushans and be back in the city before nightfall,' smiled Rasha.

Her words were to be prophetic. Salar looked at me, unsure what to do. I did not want to undermine his authority but the enemy was closing fast and his army was still in a long column behind us.

'May I suggest we deploy into a battle line, majesty?' said Shapur.

'Yes,' answered the king, 'give the order.'

'Fetch Kalet,' I ordered Azad, and gave the command for the cataphracts to deploy for battle.

Gafarn told Prince Pacorus to do the same with Hatra's heavy horsemen and suddenly officers were riding around like buzzing flies to relay orders to their men. We held an impromptu council of war in the midst of the chaos, soldiers holding the reins of our horses as we used small stones to organise our forces. Our deployment was dictated by the ten thousand Saka foot soldiers that marched with us.

164

They would have to be placed in the centre of the battle line with the horsemen on the wings to prevent them being outflanked and surrounded. Prince Pacorus suggested that all the cataphracts be placed to the right rear of the foot soldiers, ready to be unleashed when the time was right.

Kalet appeared with his warlords in a cloud of dust that made us all cough.

'So the enemy has shown his face?' he grinned.

I pointed to the north, 'I need you and your men to form a screen while the army is deploying. Get close to the enemy and annoy them.'

'Try not to get yourself killed,' Gallia told him.

He winked at her. 'Don't you worry about me, princess.'

Then he and his warlords were gone and moments later a thousand horsemen thundered past us, throwing up more dust covering us all in a fine layer of dirt. But at least they would buy us precious time to allow us to get our men into position. Salar insisted the elephants be placed in front of his foot swordsmen with his foot archers placed between the great lumbering beasts. They would walk forward beside the elephants, shooting volleys of arrows at the enemy before the steel-clad beasts smashed through the centre of the enemy line. On their immediate flanks would be Salar's lancers, ready to support the elephants, though not too close for horses dislike the behemoths. They are not the only ones. I remembered the beasts stampeding when we faced Porus all those years ago. For that reason we were glad to be on the flanks of the army.

In battle men, and women, like to die among their family are friends. So Dura's thousand horse archers and hundred Amazons would be deployed on the right flank, alongside Nergal and Praxima's two thousand horse archers. The left flank would comprise Gafarn's fifteen hundred Hatran horse archers, the horsemen of his son Spartacus – two thousand men – plus the two thousand Agraci commanded by Rasha's brother, Malik.

'The gods be with you all,' I said after we had decided on our dispositions.

I embraced Gafarn and Nergal, Gallia doing the same with Rasha and Praxima. I was not fearful for myself but minor worries gnawed at me like a toothache. We had come to Sakastan to attend a wedding and so had left the camels carrying ammunition behind, as had the other kings. This meant, notwithstanding some spare ammunition, we were short of arrows when it came to fighting a battle, each man carrying two quivers – a paltry sixty arrows per archer. But my biggest concern was Salar, as yet untested in battle and indeed untested as a king. When he had remounted his horse, I called Kewab over.

'Stay close to the king. If the battle goes against us make sure he gets back to Sigal. Sakastan cannot afford to lose another king so soon after Peroz's murder.'

'Yes, majesty.'

He saluted and returned to his horse. I stared at the stones arranged in a line on the ground and wondered if the Kushan commander was doing the same. I stepped over them and walked to *Tegha*, hauling myself into the saddle. The six horse archers acting as my bodyguard were relaxed and confident, though I still worried about the army's dire lack of arrows. Zenobia with my griffin banner sat with them, Gallia taking over the command of the Amazons. Perhaps I should have asked Salar to command his foot archers to surrender some of their missiles to the horsemen. But that would serve only to weaken our centre. I turned *Tegha* and directed him towards the fifteen hundred cataphracts arrayed in two blocks: a dragon of Durans and half a dragon of Hatrans. Prince Pacorus was deep in conversation with Azad, the latter with his full-face helmet shoved up on his head. Pacorus stopped and bowed his head to me.

'Uncle, are you joining us?'

'I am not dressed for the part,' I answered. 'Stay close to the Sakas. If they break, you will be our last hope.'

Pacorus was shocked. 'You have no faith in Salar?'

'Of course, but faith does not win battles and we have as yet no idea how large the enemy army is.'

Azad looked past me. 'We are about to find out.'

I turned in the saddle to see Talib galloping towards us. His face was beaded in sweat and his horse was panting heavily but my chief scout was ecstatic.

'We outnumber the Kushans by three to one, majesty, perhaps more. They have no foot soldiers and my men inform me their line is stretched thin.'

Relief surged through me. 'Well done, Talib. Ride with me to convey the news to King Salar. How far away are the Kushans?'

He turned to squint northwards. 'Two miles, perhaps more. Lord Kalet has slowed them down.'

I wished Pacorus and Azad good fortune in the battle to come and rode to where Salar was positioned in front of his huge elephant banner flanked by Shapur and Kewab. Immediately behind them was a company of the king's guard and behind them five thousand swordsmen on foot, attired in colourful yellow loose-fitting tunics, baggy red leggings, and leather caps on their heads. Their ox-hide shields all sported elephant emblems, as did the many standards among their ranks. Either side of them rode Salar's lancers, the sun glinting off the iron scales covering their leather cuirasses.

The five thousand archers with their long bamboo bows that required one end to be anchored on the ground when used, were interspersed among the elephants. When we reached Salar the great beasts all seemed to be depositing large piles of dung on the ground. So much for the grand spectacle of battle!

Talib conveyed the welcome news that the Kushans were substantially outnumbered, which dispelled any doubts he had about the coming clash. Salar told Shapur to convey the news to his senior officers and then wished me well as I took my leave to ride across to my wife on the right flank. I cantered across the front of the horse archers of Mesene, Nergal's men raising their bows in salute and cheering. I raised my hand in recognition and caught sight on my left of the return of Kalet and his men, ill-disciplined as usual as they galloped towards the army in their usual carefree fashion.

Kalet reported to me personally when I had reached Gallia, who was in the company of Nergal and Praxima and surrounded by Amazons. The whole army was now fully deployed and advancing steadily towards the Kushans, now filling the middle distance.

'They have elephants,' were Kalet's first words. 'It's bloody hot,' were his second. He grabbed his waterskin, uncorked it and took a swig.

'Your future son-in-law is still alive, by the way,' he said to me.

'How many men did you lose?' I asked, unconcerned about Vartan.

'A few dozen, perhaps, they have horse archers who know how to shoot a bow.'

I stared at the advancing Kushans, elephants in the centre and horsemen on either side. But their line was shorter compared to our own and I felt a tingle of excitement as I anticipated our two wings sweeping around their flanks to envelop them.

Kalet put my thoughts into words. 'Easy victory, then.'

'You have done sterling service,' I told him, 'get your men behind the cataphracts. Once you and they are rested there should be rich pickings after we have routed the Kushans.'

He raised a hand, tugged on his reins and nudged his horse back to his dust-covered men. The whole army was advancing slowly across the parched ground towards the Kushans, the centre a blaze of red and yellow uniforms and banners. The elephants raised their trunks and the kettledrummers and trumpeters filled the air with noise. A pre-battle surge of emotion gripped me as I suddenly felt young again, my senses heightened by the prospect of imminent battle. I saw the banners of the enemy hanging limply on their flagstaffs. Then there was a gust of wind that came from nowhere, the enemy banners unfurled and I was deflated. The wind must have been sent by the gods because suddenly there was a host of cobra standards dancing in the hot air. Cobras! My mind went back to the date palm grove and my tussle with the king cobra and it all suddenly made sense.

'They've stopped.'

I barely heard Gallia's voice beside me, muffled as it was by the large cheek guards of her helmet protecting her face. She was pointing to the left, towards Nergal's horse archers on our flank and the great mass of Salar's horsemen and foot soldiers in the centre, a mile distant, who had suddenly halted. She turned and ordered the Amazons and our own horse archers to stop. And in front of us the short Kushan line continued to advance slowly towards us, seemingly oblivious to the fact that they were greatly outnumbered. A creeping fear embraced me when I caught sight of a lone rider galloping towards us. And in that moment I knew we had lost the battle.

Talib drew up his horse and did not bother to salute.

'A great army is assaulting Sigal, majesty.'

'What?' Gallia was disbelieving but I knew he spoke the truth.

Talib was above all a professional, a man who left nothing to chance. He always ensured some of his scouts trailed in the rear of the army to guard against surprise attacks. His diligence and foresight had paid off because one of those scouts had nearly run his horse into the ground to bring news that a fresh army had appeared from the hills to the east of Sigal. That army was now fording the river to attack the city, a city defended by less than a thousand men.

'Take the Amazons and horse archers back to the city,' I told Gallia. 'I will ride to Nergal and ask him to follow you.'

Gallia looked at me in astonishment. 'Go!' I shouted, 'or our daughters and the city will be lost.'

I left her to ride across to Nergal and Praxima, telling them the dire news.

'I request that you ride south with Gallia, my friends, along with your men '

They needed no second promoting and within minutes two thousand horse archers had wheeled about and were following the Durans. The army's entire right wing had left the battlefield. I continued on to Salar, the king in the midst of his guard with an anxious Shapur beside him. He already knew what was happening, the knowledge weighing down heavily on him. He looked a pale shadow of the man who had marched from Sigal full of confidence earlier.

'I will ride south back to the city,' I told him, 'with the Durans, Mesenians and my lords.'

I looked at the Saka horsemen to my immediate right – twenty-five hundred lancers in helmets and scale armour cuirasses carrying shields and swords.

'I request half of your horsemen,' I said to Salar.

He blanched. 'Half?'

There was no time for politeness. 'Added to what was our right wing I might be able to hold off the enemy army before Sigal while you organise a withdrawal. If not, then your kingdom is lost.'

He nodded and Shapur sent a rider to the lancers' commander ordering him and them to follow King Pacorus of Dura back to the city.

'May the gods be with you,' I said, turning *Tegha* and directing him towards the mass of horse archers kicking up a dust cloud as they cantered south.

'Inform Lord Kalet that he is to follow me,' I commanded Talib.

It was fifteen miles back to Sigal and the temptation was to gallop the horses to cover the flat, parched terrain as quickly as possible. But it was just past midday and the sun was scorching everything below, the temperature rising alarmingly. It would be futile to arrive at the city with blown horses on the verge of collapse, and Kalet and his men had already been duelling with the Kushans. So we cantered south, intermittently reducing our speed to a trot for short periods. It was infuriatingly frustrating.

No one spoke during the journey.

Gallia and Praxima were livid, Nergal stern faced and Kalet stoic.

'Marcus is a calm head,' said Nergal eventually, 'he will not let the city fall.'

But my head was filled with image of hordes of Kushan soldiers equipped with scaling ladders swarming over the walls and putting everyone inside to the sword. I thought of my daughters, Byrd, Noora, Diana and Jamal and wanted to scream in frustration. We had been well and truly duped. As we neared Sigal apprehension filled my belly. What sight would greet us? Had the city already fallen?

We approached the city from the northwest, the barren dirt giving way to green vegetation as we approached the fields and vineyards irrigated by the Erymanthus. Ominously, there were no pickers or labourers, indicating they had fled into Sigal.

'Head straight for the river,' I said to those around me, 'once there we can swing right to strike the enemy in the flank.'

'If they are not already in the city,' said Nergal darkly.

We could see the citadel clearly now and there was no smoke coming from it or indeed around it, giving cause for optimism that the walls had not been breached. We picked up the pace, moving through the fields to trample crops ripe for harvesting. Then we were through to the river. I pulled up *Tegha* and stared in horror at the scene further downstream, where hundreds of men were fording the waterway.

They were light foot soldiers – skirmishers – each equipped with a wicker shield, two or three javelins and a sword. They wore nothing on their feet, no armour on their bodies and a blue turban sufficed for head protection. But there were thousands of them and many were carrying scaling ladders. The stretch of land between the city gates and the river was steadily filling with Kushan soldiers. Already a phalanx of foot longbowmen was shooting arrows into the city and at the defenders on the walls. Forming a cordon around them were spearmen carrying long, narrow shields comprising a wooden frame over which was stretched ox hide. These men were well protected by leather body armour and iron helmets. As well as his spear, each man was armed with a sword.

'We must scatter the skirmishers and drive them back across the river before they can get close to the walls,' I said out loud. 'Where's the commander of Salar's men.'

The wiry leader of the lancers reported to me and I told him to form his men into a wedge that would drive through the enemy.

'Our horse archers will follow,' I told him.

He saluted and went back to his soldiers, moments later trumpeters relaying orders to his men who deployed into their battle formation.

'I hope we have arrows enough,' said Nergal.

We had arrived with just over seven and a half thousand horsemen, five thousand of which had bows. With each horse archer carrying two quivers that equated to three hundred thousand arrows. On the training field against straw targets it would have been more than sufficient, but in the chaos of battle not even a Parthian could ensure every arrow he shot would find a target. And the enemy also had archers.

'Shamash be with you,' I said, pulling my bow from its case by my side and nocking an arrow in the bowstring.

Trumpets sounded to our front where Salar's lancers had formed into a wedge three ranks deep, signalling the advance. I shook the hand of Nergal and lent over to embrace Praxima as our horse archers deployed left and right to follow the Sakas.

We shot two volleys over the heads of Salar's lancers as they charged, the arrows landing a couple of hundred yards in front of them to hopefully spread disorder among the enemy foot soldiers. But the Kushans had anticipated our attack and had formed a defensive square around their longbowmen. This meant our charge struck empty space as those enemy troops near the river dashed towards the city where the square was forming, and the skirmishers retreated back into the shallow water of the river. So seven and a half thousand horsemen galloped alongside the river, having achieved nothing, the lancers pulling up when we had advanced around five hundred yards.

In the dust haze it was difficult to get an accurate estimation of the situation, but as I turned *Tegha* I saw the black square of the enemy near the city gates on my left, the clear stretch of ground that we had just covered in the centre, and on the right the river filled with blue turbans.

'That was a waste of time,' said Nergal, Praxima beside him.

'We should shoot at the men in the river,' she advised, 'we will never break that square.'

'At least the enemy are no longer shooting at the defenders on the walls,' said Gallia, pointing to the enemy square, which looked alarmingly like a Roman legion so disciplined did it appear.

'Agreed,' I said, 'those men in the river are carrying scaling ladders and have no armour protection.'

Within moments three thousand horse archers were lining the riverbank, shooting at thousands of enemy foot soldiers desperately trying to wade through the water to reach to opposite bank. It was satisfying to take careful aim from a stationary position and see my arrows strike flesh, figures collapsing in the muddy water and, more importantly, scaling ladders abandoned and drifting downstream.

'Just like old times, Pacorus,' grinned Nergal beside me.

His face froze in astonishment as two arrows thumped into his left leg. He dropped his bow and Praxima screamed. She was joined by others as iron-tipped cane arrows began falling like rain among us, striking unarmoured horse archers and their mounts, horses rearing up to throw their riders.

'Retreat.' I shouted, an order conveyed by horns as the horse archers of Dura and Mesene scattered to ride back to their starting positions.

All order was abandoned as we shouted at our horses to move faster, more arrows felling beasts and their riders as the Kushan longbowmen unleashed another volley. Praxima had grabbed Nergal to prevent him from falling from his saddle. I rode on the other side of his horse to steady the beast, all three of us managing to canter further upstream, away from the Kushan square. One of Nergal's officers had managed to retrieve his king's bow and handed it to me when we halted.

We laid him down in the shade of a date palm grove, dismounted horsemen forming a screen of archers to our front. Praxima ripped off her helmet and cradled her husband, whose leggings were now soaked in blood, the arrows still lodge in his leg. Gallia was beside her, handing over her leather belt that she had unbuckled.

'Strap it round his wounded leg to staunch the loss of blood.'

Kalet appeared, jumping from his horse to report to me. He looked at the ashen-faced Nergal.

'That looks bad.'

'Shut up. Report.'

He bristled at my tone but told me what was happening.

'Those lancers took the brunt of the enemy's arrows; we were hit by the ones that overshot. I reckon that around a quarter of Salar's men were dropped.'

'And yours?'

'We scarpered as soon as the first enemy arrows fell. We lost maybe fifty, maybe more. What now?'

I looked with concern at Nergal. 'Now we wait for the rest of the army to arrive.'

Praxima, still holding Nergal, turned to me. 'We need to get him into the city, to Alcaeus, quickly.'

'I agree,' said Gallia sternly.

I looked at the large enemy square now firmly anchored in front of the city gates, and at the skirmishers re-fording the river after we had been forced to retreat. Where was the army? I turned to Kalet.

'Ride like the wind and find the rest of the army. Tell Azad and Prince Pacorus we need their cataphracts. Go.'

He raised a hand, vaulted into his saddle and disappeared with a group of his warlords.

'When they arrive, we will join them to force a way into the city,' I told Praxima.

I knelt beside a now shaking Nergal. 'Hold on, my friend, we are with you.'

He nodded and tried to smile but he had lost a lot of blood, though at least the tourniquet was doing its job. The senior Mesenian officers gathered around their wounded king, worry etched on their faces.

'Prepare your companies,' Praxima told them, 'we will soon be attacking.'

They bowed their heads and returned to their men. Gallia was briefing Katana, the commander of Dura's horse archers in the absence of Kewab, concerning the plan to batter our way into the city. He was nodding, his eyes glancing at the injured Nergal.

'Are you paying attention?' growled Gallia.

'Yes, majesty, apologies.'

'Go, then.'

Time seemed to slow agonisingly as we waited and Nergal grew worse. I paced up and down as Praxima held her husband and Gallia comforted her friend. The dismounted Amazons were forming a guard around us and somewhere to the northwest was Salar's army, including fifteen hundred armoured horsemen that we needed badly.

A strange silence had descended over the battlefield as the main enemy army stood immobile in its square and skirmishers scurried around like ants to surround the city with their scaling ladders.

'Commander Kewab.'

I heard the call and turned to see Kewab pull up his horse, flanked by Kalet and his warlords. He jumped from his saddle and ran over to me.

'Majesty, Azad and Prince Pacorus are close behind.'

I pointed at the enemy square. 'We need to break that to get into the city.'

He studied the Kushan formation for a few seconds and shook his head.

'Even cataphracts might have trouble breaking a square, majesty.'

'I agree, but with horse archer support we stand a chance. Tell Azad and Pacorus to be wary of the fields of caltrops either side to the city gates.'

Kewab saluted and turned, stopping when he spotted the injured Nergal. He looked back at me.

'Time is of the essence,' I told him. 'Where is the rest of the army?'

'Close, majesty, though still shadowed by the Kushan horsemen and elephants.'

Elephants? It was all so ridiculous.

'Might I suggest that King Salar's elephants might aid us against the enemy square, majesty?'

I looked at him in surprise. 'They look big and impressive but are totally unreliable in battle. I routed them easily enough many years ago.'

'Agreed, majesty, but King Salar has a hundred of the beasts and even if they stampede they might trample on those in the square. Horsemen cannot break a disciplined square.'

I looked at the square in front of the city gates and knew he was right. All the army's horse archers might wear down the enemy to allow the cataphracts to affect an entry, but by that time Nergal might have bled to death.

'Very well,' I said to Kewab, 'we are in your hands. We need to get into Sigal sooner rather than later.'

We ignored the hundreds of skirmishers wading across the river to begin to rake the enemy square with arrows. The horse archers of Dura and Mesene were widely spaced when they made their attacks. I led the former, having first asked Gallia to remain with Praxima to give her friend support. We amended our tactics to minimise casualties, the Duran horse archers wearing no armour but those of Mesene attired in red kaftans called *saravanas*, over which they wore scale-armour cuirasses: short-sleeved garments that reached to the mid-thigh, slit at each side to facilitate riding, with attached horizontal rows of rectangular iron scales, each row partly overlapping the layer below. That said, their limbs and their unarmoured horses were vulnerable.

I was soaked in sweat when I made my first pass, riding hard towards the square to avoid the arrows shot from it as soon as the Kushans spotted our advance. Their bows were long and were shot by the archers resting one end on the ground before drawing back the bowstring. This gave them great range but meant they were useless for short-range work. So we got close to the locked Kushan shields to shoot our arrows, knowing the enemy bowmen could not hit us.

I slowed *Tegha* when I reached the square and turned him right to take me along one of its four sides, pulling arrows from my quiver to shoot them over the shields into the square. Those following did the same while other companies attacked the other sides of the square. No arrows were being shot from inside the square, giving me hope that our own missiles were having an effect. But then disaster struck.

I reached into my quiver and searched in vain for an arrow, then looked at the other quiver and saw it too was empty. I had no choice but to wheel *Tegha* away from the square and ride back to the date palm grove. Behind me, one by one the Durans ran out of arrows and withdrew, those of Mesene doing the same. And still the enemy square remained seemingly untouched.

But my spirits rose when a fanfare of trumpets announced the arrival of the elephants. Arrayed in a long line, the sun glinting off the polished bronze plates protecting their foreheads and the steel that encased their tusks, I began to believe that the lumbering beasts might just be able to break the enemy square. If not, then surely the thousands of Saka foot soldiers and horsemen of Hatra, Gordyene and Agraci that followed them would. I sat and watched with hundreds of horse archers now without arrows as the elephants commenced their charge.

It was a disaster.

The Kushan skirmishers, responding to horn calls, massed directly in front of the line of elephants and then did something no one could have anticipated – they charged. I watched, open mouthed, as thousands of lightly armed men ran towards the wall of grey meat, bronze and steel, seemingly charging to their own deaths. But how I and everyone else had underestimated these Kushans. Each skirmisher carried three javelins and when they neared the elephants and their bodyguards, they proceeded to hurl their missiles at them. The archers in boxes strapped to the backs of the elephants cut down many Kushans, as did the slingers, but thousands more launched their javelins, to cause chaos among the beasts.

Ironically it was not the javelins that bounced off the bronze plates covering the animals' foreheads that caused mayhem; rather, missiles that struck those spearmen guarding the beasts. The shrieks and screams of men being speared caused alarm among the elephants, compounded by a few of the beasts being struck on their legs. Two reared up on their hind legs – which was a wonder to behold – turned and ran away from the rain of javelins. Two collapsed from what can only be ascribed to heart failure, and more swerved left or right to trample their guards and career into the elephants next to them.

And still the Kushan skirmishers hurled their javelins.

The mahouts – the trainers who sat on the necks of the elephants – had seen enough. They used their voices and bull hooks to withdraw their charges, those that were not in the grip of fear and panic. These men had spent years with their animals and were not about to see their lives tossed away for no purpose. I had to admit they executed their withdrawal with some aplomb, steering their beasts away from the Kushans and also from the bulk of Salar's army behind them retreating from the northwest.

The Kushan skirmishers began cheering, whooping and beating the insides of their shields, but they soon stopped when a wall of iron and steel cantered towards them out of the dust. I clenched my fist in triumph as Prince Pacorus and Azad led the cataphracts of Dura and Hatra straight at them – fifteen hundred armour-clad riders lowering their long lances and making the earth tremble as they picked up speed. The men must have been roasting in their heavy scale armour suits, their horses similarly protected by thick hide and iron scales, but their discipline was impeccable as two lines of heavy horsemen broke into the charge less than a hundred paces from the skirmishers. The latter scattered in all directions but that did not save many from being skewered on the end of a *kontus*, hacked in two by an ukku blade or having their skulls reduced to bloody pulps by a mace or axe.

As the skirmishers scattered the first line of the cataphracts slowed to allow the second line to close on the Kushan square. The intermingling of the heavy horsemen and skirmishers had prevented the archers within the square from using their long-range bows and now the cataphracts were too close to the square for them to be employed. The second-line cataphracts slowed their horses as they neared the square to ram their lances into the spearmen forming the walls of the formation. The *kontus* is a long weapon – up to eighteen feet – longer than the spears of the Kushans, and so each cataphract was able to thrust his lance into an opponent, the momentum of moving man and horse making shields useless as points were driven through hide and wood and into flesh and bone.

I could not see but Azad told me afterwards that when seven hundred cataphracts hit the northern side of the square, the formation buckled and nearly broke. But he and Prince Pacorus had issued orders to their men that they were to stay in formation and so after the initial strike, the horsemen retired. But the commander of the square decided to take no chances and moments after the cataphract attack the entire formation began to retire south.

'Mount up,' I shouted, 'the way to the gates is clear.'

Nergal, pale and lapsing in and out of consciousness, was put back on his horse, Gallia and Praxima either side of him. Then we galloped for the gates, the Amazons, the only ones who had any arrows left, spearheading our charge. We crossed a ground littered with dead skirmishers, but the enemy did not harass us and so we reached the gates unimpeded. To find them shut.

'Open the gates,' I shouted at the top of my voice.

'Open the gates, open the gates,' pleaded those around us.

I glanced nervously over my left shoulder, towards the Kushan square that was still shuffling away from the city. Between it and us the cataphracts were reforming, their horses now blown, to form a defensive screen, albeit a tired one. I heard a loud groan and saw the gates slowly open inch by inch. There were now thousands of horsemen clustered outside the city entrance and enemy bowmen within the accursed Kushan square were still in range, though mercifully they did not unleash any volleys against us. They were either out of arrows or were saving their ammunition. I gave thanks to Shamash for either. Then the gates were finally opened.

'Get Nergal to the fortress,' I told Gallia and Praxima.

'Where are you going?' Gallia asked me.

'I will stay here to ensure the rest of the army gets into the city. Go!'

They needed no second prompting. The queens of Dura and Mesene led the procession of horsemen into the city towards the citadel. I dug my knees into *Tegha* and cantered towards where the cataphracts were standing, the Kushan square having now stopped around four hundred paces from the city gates. Behind me Zenobia held my griffin banner and behind her rode the Amazons, commanded by Gallia to remain with their king. Azad and Pacorus raised their hands when I halted beside him. Azad's face was flushed and sweat was pouring down his face, his helmet in the crook of his arm. He pointed to a mass of skirmishers reforming either side of the square.

'Whoever is in charge of those soldiers, he knows what he is doing.'

'The rest of the army will be arriving soon,' Gafarn's son assured us, 'all we have to do is keep the enemy away from the gates.'

'They appear to be rooted to the spot,' I said.

They were, until the rest of Salar's army arrived, together with the horsemen of Malik, Gafarn, Spartacus and the baggage train carrying arrows, weapons, food, fodder, tents, tools and spare armour. Salar remained with Shapur as his commander organised his foot soldiers. He deployed his swordsmen in a great semi-circle, the bowmen standing behind them, in front of the city gates to allow the horsemen, squires and camels to get into Sigal. But as they did so the Kushan square began to march back towards the city gates, to be joined by enemy horsemen who commenced a withering rain of arrows against the Saka foot.

Salar's archers shot back and for a while managed to keep the hundreds of enemy horse archers at bay. But then the enemy longbowmen inside the square began to use up their remaining ammunition, cane arrows arching into a vivid blue sky to fall among the Sakas. The swordsmen in their leather caps holding ox-hide shields began to fall. I sat on *Tegha* near the gates and admired their courage as they died where they stood, Salar riding up and down, sword in hand, shouting encouragement and defiance against the enemy. He knew as I did that as long as they did so the horsemen and supplies could get back into Sigal.

Azad pulled up his horse. 'Someone should get him back into the city before he is killed.'

An arrow thudded into the ground a few feet away. Another struck a camel carrying tents, the beast collapsing in a heap and refusing or being unable to get up despite the pleadings and threats of its thrown owner.

'Get your men into the city,' I commanded.

He saluted and left, more swordsmen falling but Salar's archers shooting volley after volley to keep the enemy horsemen away from the gates. And still camels were waiting to get into Sigal.

Gafarn and Spartacus were already in the city, dismounting their horse archers and deploying them on the city walls to lend weight to Salar's archers, who would soon be out of ammunition. They stood on the ramparts above the gates, bows in hand, Rasha alongside them. I looked up and raised my hand in recognition.

The Sakas, under withering volleys of arrows, were still standing in what remained of their ranks, Salar and Shapur urging them on. It was a magnificent display of courage in the face of adversity but now the last of the camels and horsemen had reached the sanctuary of Sigal and it was time to save them. I rode forward into the rain of arrows, which were fortunately being directed against the swordsmen and bowmen. The latter were still shooting back and had actually forced the Kushan square to withdraw for a second time. But the enemy's horse archers, who darted in to shoot their arrows against the thinning shield wall to fall back unharmed, were doing the real damage.

'The army is inside the city,' I called to Salar, 'it is time you and your men followed it.'

He spun in the saddle, his eyes full of fire. I had seen that look a thousand times on the battlefield. The fury and exhilaration of combat had possessed his every sinew and all he cared about was facing the foe, irrespective of the consequences. He would never show his back to the enemy, even if it meant the death of his foot soldiers and even his own demise.

'Salar!' I shouted, 'get your men inside the city. Now!'

He was shaken by my tone and for a moment fury flashed in his eyes and his sword moved a fraction.

'King Pacorus is right, majesty,' said Shapur, reining in his horse beside his liege lord.

185

Salar was fuming but rather than sit and debate I grabbed his reins and wheeled *Tegha* around.

'Get your men inside the city,' I said to Shapur.

I looked at an angry Salar. 'If you are going to kill me, do it now. Otherwise, get your arse inside your city. Your kingdom, queen and people need you.'

He yanked his reins back and screamed at his horse to move, which it did with gusto, taking the king through the gates and into the city. An arrow slammed into the ground a few inches from *Tegha*'s right front leg. I dug my knees into his flanks and he too sped back to the gates. I left him with a guard and raced up the steps to the battlements where the archers of Hatra and Gordyene waited.

'Nergal has been badly wounded,' I told Gafarn.

'How badly?'

He looked at my face and had his answer.

'I will kill this Kujula,' said Spartacus, more in frustration that in boast.

Horn calls sounded in front of the walls and the Saka foot soldiers, previously rock-like in their immobility, about-faced and withdrew back to the city, Shapur screaming at them to stay in their ranks. To their credit their withdrawal never turned into a rout but when they were inside the city and the gates had been shut, the scale of their losses became apparent. In front of the entrance to Sigal was a semi-circle of yellow-clad corpses.

Spartacus drew back his bowstring, aimed his arrow high and released the sinew cord. The arrow arched into the sky before falling harmlessly into the ground, the Kushan horse archers having withdrawn to a safe distance beyond the range of our arrows, not that I had any. Spartacus roared in rage and shook his bow at the enemy.

Gafarn laid a hand on his shoulder. 'Save your strength, you will need it.'

'Is that him?'

Rasha was pointing to a group of horsemen cantering towards the Kushan square, the formation that had caused us so much trouble earlier. It had suffered casualties but had performed admirably. Indeed, it compared well to the Durans and Exiles, and I reckoned those two formations to be the best ground troops in the whole Parthian Empire, perhaps the whole world. Among the horsemen was a huge red banner showing a gold cobra, its hood flared and its fangs bared.

'Kujula, I assume,' I said.

The group reached the square and after a few moments it broke apart, its units marching to the river to refresh themselves. Groups of skirmishers established camps around the city but there were no more aggressive moves by the enemy that day. Tents began to spring up near the river next to the date palm groves and campfires were lit as the enemy consolidated their positions.

Sigal was now under siege.

Chapter 8

I went straight to the fortress, to the palace where Alcaeus was tending to Nergal. The streets of the city were crowded with soldiers, horses, camels and frightened citizens, though I was strangely detached from the doom-laden scene. My only concern was for my friend. Other wounded lay in the fortress' courtyard, groaning with pain as slaves and too few physicians tried to bandage their wounds and give them water. The cobblestones appeared to be slowly turning red as the sun waned, though perhaps it was just my tired eyes and imagination that conjured up the scene. In the palace, worried stewards fussed around and slaves offered to relieve me of my armour, but I brushed them away. We did leave our weapons and helmets outside Nergal's bedroom, a distraught Praxima, her eyes red with tears, looked pale and wan as we entered.

Rasha rushed up to her and wrapped her arms around her, Spartacus kissing her cheek and Gafarn smiling kindly at her. I embraced her and glanced at the bed where Alcaeus was finishing tying off a large bandage that encased my friend's injured leg. Gallia was seated on a couch holding the hand of a distraught Diana. Our Greek friend sighed and examined his handiwork. I was surprised to see Claudia appear from the balcony carrying a silver bowl from which smoke was emanating. She brushed past me to place it on the table beside the unconscious Nergal.

'Is that necessary?' asked Alcaeus.

'Entirely necessary,' my daughter shot back. 'It is crushed tamarisk bark mixed with frankincense. A gift for Damu, God of Healing, who sleeps by rivers among tamarisks.'

'I thought Gula was the deity of healing,' said Alcaeus.

188

Claudia smiled. 'Very good, Alcaeus, it gladdens me to know you have taken an interest in the gods. And you are right, Gula is indeed the Goddess of Healing. But Damu is the intermediary between Gula and mortal physicians.'

Alcaeus did not bother to reply but merely observed Claudia as she stood over Nergal, mumbled a prayer that none of us could fathom and then walked over to Praxima, ignoring the rest of us.

'Have no fear, he will make a full recovery.'

She then walked from the room. We all looked for confirmation of her prognosis from Alcaeus. He puffed out his cheeks.

'I have managed to stop the bleeding and fortunately the arrows did not shatter the bone in the leg. So I am hopeful of a full recovery, though he may have a permanent limp.'

There was a collective sigh of relief and Diana burst into tears.

'But Nergal will have to stay here for a considerable amount of time,' warned Alcaeus, 'a few weeks at least.'

'Well, none of us are going anywhere in the near future,' said Gafarn, 'unless the Kushans decide to march away.'

It was late before I managed to grab a few hours' sleep, beforehand assisting Salar in organising the manning of the walls with his soldiers. We ordered every other horse archer to stand to arms on the walls in case the Kushans tried a night assault. But the enemy was content to ring the city with a myriad of campfires to emphasise that a hostile army now surrounded Sigal. Despite the threat of imminent assault, I slept like the dead that night, but awoke after what seemed liked a few minutes, my limbs aching from the exertions of the previous day. I opened my eyes to see Gallia staring at me.

'What are you going to do?'

189

I stretched out my arms and sat up in bed. 'Have some breakfast. I always think better with a full stomach.'

After I had washed, shaved and donned some fresh clothes I sat on the balcony with Gallia eating a meal of dates, grapes, cheese, bread and yoghurt, washed down by fruit juice. The city below appeared untroubled, though the tents in the distance, beyond the walls, were a stark reminder of the danger we all faced. I smeared yoghurt on a piece of bread and shoved it into my mouth.

'It won't take long to starve the city into surrender,' I said. 'Feeding the population alone would be taxing, but with an army within the city walls starvation will come sooner rather than later.'

'Unless relief comes.'

I filled her cup and mine with fruit juice. 'Who? Phanes? He is the nearest but I doubt he will lift a finger to help the son of his late brother. A brother that he probably had killed.'

She took a sip of juice. 'You think Phanes is responsible for the attack at the wedding?'

'Who else?'

She tipped her head towards the distance. 'What about this Kujula? Killing Peroz would serve his interests.'

I leaned back and looked at her. 'He seems to have done well enough without resorting to assassination, having seemingly overrun Aria and Drangiana. But I accept he could be responsible.'

'As lord high general Phanes should be marching to relieve Sigal,' she said, more in hope than conviction.

'He should,' I agreed, 'but he had reckoned on leading a coalition against Sakastan, not fighting a full-blown invasion of the empire. Perhaps his mother will march to relieve us as she has more backbone than the King of Carmania.'

We both laughed, a knock at the door interrupting our mirth. A slave entered after being told to do so and bowed his head to Gallia and me.

'The king urgently requests your presence in his private apartments, majesties.'

I sighed. 'Trying to keep Salar calm will be our first task, I think.'

We left our breakfast to follow the slave through the corridors of the palace, ordering him to slow down when he threatened to break into a run. Gallia looked at me and shook her head. Panic was infectious and could spread quicker than a pestilence if allowed to flourish. He bowed his head again when we reached the entrance to the king's private apartments, two guards flanking the door snapping to attention when we passed them.

When we entered the king's office Salar jumped up and bowed to us both.

'You are king here, not me,' I told him.

'I wanted to thank you for saving my life yesterday,' he blurted out.

'I did nothing of the sort.'

Gallia disarmed him with a smile. 'We are here to help you, Salar.'

'How may we be of assistance?' I asked.

'Fetch wine,' he ordered, extending his hand to a pair of plush, ornate chairs opposite his desk.

We seated ourselves and Salar faced his balcony that gave breath-taking views of the mountains in the distance.

'An emissary arrived from Kujula earlier. He desires a meeting.'

'He wishes to press his advantage, no doubt,' I said. 'It is to be expected.'

Salar turned. 'He has requested to meet you, not me.'

I was taken aback. 'Me? Why?'

'I was hoping you could provide an explanation,' said the king.

The wine was excellent, produced locally, the vineyard unfortunately now in the possession of the Kushans. As I sipped at it I racked my brains to solve the riddle of why the Kushan leader would want to see me.

'You must go,' urged Salar, 'if only to buy us time. I sent a courier over the walls before dawn with a message for my uncle.'

I looked at Gallia. Salar, clearly agitated, began toying with a bronze seal on his desk.

'You think I was wrong to do so?'

I finished my wine and stood. 'No. Hopefully, Phanes will have heard that Sakastan has been invaded and will already be on the march. More importantly, he will have informed Phraates that his empire is under threat.'

My words seemed to soothe Salar, who stopped fidgeting with the seal. But then fresh concern showed on his face.

'It might be a trap. Kujula might want to assassinate you just as he did my father and mother.'

I leaned over and grabbed his arm. 'Calm yourself. Attend to your duties and let me worry about Kujula's motives.'

On the way back to our bedroom Gallia also voiced her concern.

'We know nothing about this Kujula. He might be nothing more than a murderer with a crown.'

'I beg to differ, my love, we know a great deal about him. We know he has a well-trained professional army; we know that his strategic awareness has allowed him to overrun three of the empire's kingdoms; and we know he wishes to talk.'

She frowned. 'What does your last point have to do with anything?'

I kissed her on the cheek. 'Because it indicates to me he is a man of learning and manners. If he was a murdering barbarian only he would be already launching his army against Sigal's walls.'

Before I left I visited Nergal, an exhausted Praxima slumped in a chair beside his bed asleep, an Alcaeus suddenly looking very old stooped over the King of Mesene examining his patient. The room was heavy with the pungent aroma of frankincense and burnt wood but I was cheered to see that Nergal, though asleep, looked relaxed, his face restored of some colour. Alcaeus saw me enter and put a finger to his lips. He walked over to me.

'How is he?' I whispered.

'All things considered, not too bad. Perhaps Claudia's incense helped.'

I smiled. 'Spoken like a true non-believer. You should get some sleep, you look exhausted. Try to convince Praxima to get some rest too.'

I was relieved to see Nergal no longer looking like a man who was at death's door and felt confident he would recover from his wounds. I took Azad and four cataphracts with me as an escort when I rode from Sigal, the guards opening one of the gates just enough to allow us to exit before hastily slamming it shut when we were outside the city. A party of Kushan heavy horsemen, equipped in helmets and scale armour and carrying large, round wooden shields bearing a cobra insignia, was waiting for us around two hundred paces from the gates. Negotiations between the garrison commander on behalf of Salar and his Kushan equivalent regarding my safe passage to and from the Kushan camp meant the mood was surreally relaxed. The archers on the walls were leaning on the battlements observing us as the commander of the Kushan horsemen nudge his mount forward and bowed his head.

'King Pacorus, welcome. Emperor Kujula is eager to meet you,' he said in Greek.

'As I am him,' I replied.

It was no lie. I was keen to set eyes on the man who had run rings around us the day before. Azad wore a mask of indifference, though I noted he examined the weapons and equipment of our escort closely. In addition to a long lance, each Kushan was armed with a mace for close-quarters work. Unlike our own heavy horsemen their steeds wore no armour and I was certain in a clash between the two the cataphracts would prevail. Then again, yesterday there had been fifteen hundred cataphracts on the field and these Kushans had still bested us.

The commander of the escort was an agreeable individual who enquired after the health of my wife and daughters, seemingly oblivious to the fact that he was part of an army that might put everyone inside the city to the sword should Sigal's walls be breached. But I reciprocated his polite manner as we rode through a camp filled with soldiers, tents, camels and civilian camp followers. The emperor's tent was pitched near the river, away from the bustle and dirt of the common soldiery and near a grove of date palms that provided shelter for the dozens of horses of his bodyguard. There was a slight wind that barely ruffled the huge cobra banner flying outside the massive round red tent surrounded by a wall of scarlet cloth. We rode into the compound where we were relieved of our horses and led to a huge awning under which couches and low tables had been arranged. A tall man wearing a huge white turban bowed his head to me under the awning.

'The emperor will be with you shortly, majesty, but if I could ask you to surrender your sword before he arrives.'

Azad grumbled under his breath but I unbuckled my belt and handed him my *spatha*. The tall man looked at Azad and his men.

'Give him your swords,' I commanded.

'You are under the protection of the emperor,' the man assured us, which did little to reassure Azad.

Our weapons were taken from us. The commander of the Kushan escort asked Azad and his men if they would like to take refreshments with him. Azad said no but I told him to accept the offer, if only so he and his men could sit in the shade and drink some fluids.

'He is here,' said the tall man.

I saw a man in white approaching, his hair as black as night above his thin face. He flashed a smile at me.

'King Pacorus, welcome.'

I was lost for words as I beheld Vima the spice trader.

His thin moustache and beard were immaculately trimmed, a broad grin on his thin face.

'Please be seated, my friend,' he requested, 'take the weight off your feet.'

He clapped his hands and a small army of slaves rushed to me, bowing with their hands together in front of their chests. They relieved me of my helmet, cleaned the couch with small brushes and placed cushions behind me when I sat on it. Another slave behind me began gently cooling me with a huge feathered fan.

The spice trader-cum-emperor of the Kushans sat opposite me. He was wearing a long, loose white patterned silk shirt called a *kurta*, which ended just above the knees. A one-piece white cotton cloth called a *dhoti* tied around the waist and held in place by a white ornamental belt covered his legs. On his feet he wore a pair of white leather boots.

'It all makes sense now,' were the first words I spoke to him.

'To be fair, I did tell you that my reasons for helping you at Lake Nawar were purely selfish.'

His tone was light, jovial, as though he was discussing a hunting trip with an old friend. But I was far from amused.

'And my daughter's wedding, was that your doing?'

In an instant his mood changed. His thin eyebrows flared and he leaned towards me.

'I am the head of the Kushan Empire, an emperor who commands millions, do you really think I would soil my reputation with such a despicable act. What sort of man would seek to spill blood on a bride's most special day?'

I wanted to disbelieve him but my instincts told me he was a man of honour and integrity, notwithstanding the disguise he had adopted. And he had saved my life at the wedding.

'I believe you,' I said.

Once again, the smiling Kujula returned. More slaves arrived with refreshments that were laid on the low tables between us. There were triangular pastries called samosas filled with vegetables and flavoured with spices and herbs, chicken and lamb kebabs and wheat bread called *roti*. We were both served with a curious drink called *thandai*, which was made from milk and dried fruits. It was most palatable. I finished a delicious samosa and dipped my fingers in a bowl of warm water offered by a slave; another proffered a towel so I could dry my hands.

'I assume you did not invite me here to sample the delicacies of India,' I said, 'delicious though they are.'

'I wanted to apologise for deceiving you concerning my true identity and to assure you that if I could I would hunt down those responsible for the atrocity committed at your daughter's wedding.'

'That is kind of you to say so.'

He held out his silver cup to be refilled. 'How is Queen Isabella?'

'Bearing up well, considering there is a hostile army camped outside the walls of her city.'

'The Kushan Empire needs land to feed a growing population, King Pacorus,' he told me. 'For decades, the Indus has marked the boundary between Parthia and India but now Parthia is weak and divided. It has a boy for high king, its rulers squabble among themselves and its kingdoms are at each other's throats.'

'The Romans thought that not so long ago.'

He washed his hands and a slave dried them for him. 'Indeed, but then Parthia amassed a great army commanded by its greatest warlord, with High King Phraates being reduced to a figurehead only. You think that those who live east of the Indus do not take a keen interest in the affairs of King Pacorus of Dura?'

'You flatter me.'

'I do not underestimate you, King Pacorus, which the Romans seem to have done on numerous occasions. Aria and Drangiana have fallen, Sakastan is on the verge of falling and I think I can safely assume you do not believe that Parthia's Lord High General in the East will be able to save Sigal, even if he had the inclination to do so.'

He extended his arms. 'Who else can save Sakastan? Phraates, the boy king who concerns himself with the intrigues at Ctesiphon? Dura, Hatra, Mesene and Gordyene, whose armies are hundreds of miles away?'

He dipped a piece of bread in a dish of yoghurt.

'I have an offer for you.'

I knew what he was going to say but wanted to hear it anyway.

'I am intrigued.'

'Evacuate the city, King Pacorus, take your daughters and beautiful wife back to Dura. What is Sakastan to you? A far-flung kingdom hundreds of miles from your own lands. Even as we sit here more of my troops are marching to Sigal.

'The city will fall and I would prefer it to do so peacefully rather than by storm, and all the associated horrors that come with it.'

'What about King Salar?' I enquired. 'It is he that you should be addressing. I am merely a guest in his kingdom.'

He smiled and wagged a finger at me.

'Let us speak frankly, King Pacorus. We all know that I would already be dining in Sigal's palace had not you been here. Salar is another boy who has, through tragic circumstances, ascended to the throne before his time.'

He leaned back and stared at the city. 'The Kushans are a rising people whereas Parthia is weak and fragmented. I will give King Salar two days before I attack the city. During that time, I hope you can prevail upon him to submit to my authority. If he does then he can continue to rule Sakastan as a client king of the Kushan Empire.'

I looked up at the awning. 'You mean a Kushan slave.'

He laughed, a glint of mischief in his black eyes.

'A slave? If giving me allegiance and paying an annual tribute to my treasury constitutes slavery, then you yourself have been a slave of the king of kings of the Parthian Empire ever since you returned from Italy.'

I was shocked. 'You know of that?'

'Of your Italian adventures? Of course. We are not illiterate barbarians, King Pacorus. You may be interested to know that in my library I have a volume dedicated to the military campaigns of King Pacorus of Dura and the military organisation of the Kingdom of Dura.'

He was toying with me, surely. But I had to admit that I was both flattered and intrigued. This man who called himself emperor was charming, that much was true. In another life we might have been good friends.

'You think I lie, King Pacorus? You saw with your own eyes yesterday how my army performed in battle. Do you not recognise your own tactics? I will have a copy of the book sent to you after you have left Sakastan.'

'That is most kind, lord,' I replied, 'but I have to tell you that I am going nowhere.'

I rose, thanked him for his courtesy and hospitality and declared my intention to return to Sigal.

'You will convey my offer to King Salar?'

I nodded. 'I shall.'

He suddenly grasped my arm. 'Do not die in Sigal, King Pacorus. I give you my word that you, your family and friends will be given safe passage out of Sakastan. And I will personally guarantee

199

the safety of King Salar and Queen Isabella if they submit to my authority. And further I will support Salar against his uncle.'

I rode back to Sigal in the company of Azad, saying nothing as we trotted with our escort through the rapidly forming Kushan siege lines. As yet no stone- or missile-throwing engines had appeared and I hoped that Kushan military engineering was as backward as Parthia's, though that was wishful thinking. At the gates, the commander of the escort saluted and wished me good fortune, waving at the archers in the towers each side of the entrance. They waved back.

'Brotherly business, killing each other,' I remarked as the Kushans about-faced and trotted back to their camp.

One of the gates creaked open and we entered a Sigal dripping with apprehension. The streets were unusually quiet, adding to a creeping sense of dread stalking us as we rode back to the fortress. But less than half a mile from the citadel we encountered a procession of civilians making their way to one of the many temples in Sigal. Some women were raising their arms to the heavens, imploring the gods to save them, while others were clutching the hands of their children and wailing.

'Halt,' I ordered, 'we will let them pass.'

There were a few old men and young boys in the throng but it was mostly a gathering of women who, seemingly in a trance, ignored the others and me as they passed by. *Tegha* became agitated as individuals brushed past him, moaning and sobbing and pulling their shawls tighter around their heads. I felt someone shove something into my right hand.

'Give this to Princess Claudia,' a woman's voice told me.

I looked down but saw only a sea of black and brown robes.

'Have faith, son of Hatra.'

'Who said that?' I shouted, but no answer came from the wailing press, which had soon disappeared as quickly as it had appeared.

'Are you hurt, majesty?' asked Azad, hand on his sword hilt.

'What? No.'

The street was now empty and we continued our journey. I looked at what had been thrust into my hand. It was some sort of animal head made from copper, though unlike any animal I had ever seen. It had a beard and horns with grotesque bulging eyes and a snarling canine mouth. A feeling of unease possessed me when I reached the fortress but went straight to see Salar.

I relayed Kujula's offer to him, the young king acting predictably after I had done so. He had assembled the other kings and queens, minus the gravely ill Nergal and the doting Praxima, in the throne room, together with Shapur and his senior officers. To rousing applause from the latter he pledged his allegiance to Parthia and Phraates, even though as far as anyone knew the high king had not lifted so much as a finger to aid either him or the kings of Aria and Drangiana. The other kings applauded politely, though I noticed that even the fiery Spartacus was subdued. Like everyone he had seen with his own eyes the enemy army tightening its grip around the city. It did not make for a reassuring sight.

Salar invited us all to inspect the stocks of arrows and weapons in the royal armouries inside the citadel, an appeal that we all felt obliged to accept. On the way, however, Kewab and Marcus, the latter looking very concerned, accosted me. They stopped me following the royal entourage and talked in hushed tones. I watched

Gallia disappear around a corner in the corridor and then we were alone.

'Marcus has been compiling an inventory of the city's supplies, majesty,' said Kewab.

'The thousands of citizens, together with the soldiers and their horses and camels, will quickly exhaust Sigal's food supplies,' Marcus informed me.

'When?' I asked.

'Two weeks at the most,' my chief engineer told me.

'There is only one logical course of action,' said Kewab.

I looked at him. 'Which is?'

'To organise a flying column to break out of the city to head west to Bam, there to summon reinforcements from Elymais to organise a relief of the city.'

I was surprised. 'You are advocating abandoning Sigal?'

'A sizeable garrison can be left behind that will be able to mount a strong defence,' said Kewab.

'And hold out until your relief army arrives,' added Marcus.

' *My* army?' I said. 'You think I would abandon Salar?'

'You must,' insisted Kewab. 'Only you of the kings has the experience and skills to save Sigal, and Sakastan. But you must do it quickly, lord.'

'You must leave tomorrow,' Marcus told me, 'before the Kushans tighten their grip on the city. Time is of the essence.'

'Clearly,' I replied.

I looked at their stern visages and knew they were deadly serious. I wanted to argue with them and indeed could have ignored their advice, but they were the best brains in Dura's army. I was convinced they were right and utterly depressed that they were so.

202

'We cannot strip the garrison,' I told them. 'There is little point in trying to organise a relief attempt if the city has fallen.'

'The walls are high and thick,' said Marcus, 'and as yet the enemy has not revealed any siege engines, which leads me to believe the Kushans might not possess such instruments.'

Kewab took out a papyrus scroll from his tunic and handed it to me.

'I took the liberty of compiling the composition of your flying column, majesty.'

I unrolled it and gave it a cursory examination. I raised an eyebrow.

'All the cataphracts, all Salar's remaining lancers, Spartacus' horsemen and all the Agraci.'

'Cataphracts, lancers and Agraci are useless for defending walls,' stated Kewab harshly.

'You have only a few hours to make this happen, majesty,' Marcus told me, 'the alternatives are that the city is either yielded or put to the sword.'

'Very well,' I told them, 'I will assemble the kings.'

I hastened to catch up with the royal party on its way to the armouries, turning a corner to run into Claudia.

'You look flustered, father.'

'That is because I am. Have you been visiting Nergal?'

'No, why should I? As I told you he will recover. He does not need me hanging about him like some official mourner.'

I suddenly remembered the crowd in the city and the strange amulet that had been thrust into my hand. I retrieved it and handed it to Claudia.

'This is for you.'

She took it and examined the carved head.

'Who gave you this?'

I shrugged.

'Tell me,' she demanded.

'You would not believe me.'

She turned the amulet in her hand. 'There is only one who would give you this. You know, even though you do not speak her name.'

'What is it?' I asked.

She held up the carved head. 'It is Pazuzu, king of the wind demons, and it is a message.'

She pointed at the scroll. 'What is that?'

I told her about the plan Kewab and Marcus had hatched and that I had reluctantly agreed to it, though I had yet to broach the subject with Salar and the other kings.

'Assemble them at once,' she said, 'I'm coming with you.'

The inspection of the armouries was cancelled as I requested Salar attend me in the throne room, together with the other kings and queens. Isabella and Eszter were also present, together with Vartan who had performed well in battle and was now the apple of my youngest daughter's eye. She was openly defying me with her public display of affection for Orodes' bastard son but I had more important things to worry about.

The doors to the throne room were shut and all slaves were banished from the chamber as I explained to everyone Kewab's plan. It did not go down well.

Salar, seated on his throne, shook his head.

'If the King of Dura abandons the city so soon after meeting with Kujula it will be taken as a sign that he has also abandoned Sakastan.'

'That would be a lie, lord king,' I assured him. I looked at Marcus, who stepped forward and bowed his head.

'If I may speak, majesty?'

Salar nodded curtly at the portly Roman.

By my calculations there are eighteen and a half thousand soldiers in the city, plus three thousand squires and various non-combatants, such as cameleers, servants and so on. Then there are the horses and camels of those soldiers, which number many thousands, all of which will soon put an intolerable strain on food stocks inside the city. And I have omitted the many thousands of civilians that are also within Sigal's walls.'

'The answer is simple, then,' proclaimed Salar, 'we sally from the gates and give battle to the Kushans to drive them from before the walls.'

Silence greeted this proposal. Those of us who had experience of war knew that the Shapur's lancers had been badly shaken the day before, to say nothing of the dire lack of ammunition among our horse archers and the fact that Salar had lost half his foot soldiers during the battle with the Kushans. I looked at Gafarn, Malik and Spartacus and their faces told me that none of them had any confidence such a sally would succeed.

'I am afraid, lord king,' I said, 'that our forces are currently in a weak position whereas the enemy is strong and confident.'

'Then we are lost,' murmured Salar.

'Far from it.'

Claudia stepped forward and, ignoring all protocol, stepped onto the dais and stood beside the king. Shapur placed a hand on the hilt of his sword and walked menacingly towards her.

'Are you going to slay me, commander? Perhaps you should focus your efforts on defending your king and queen. Remind me, how many of your men did you lose yesterday?'

Shapur, enraged, was stopped from drawing his sword by Salar who shook his head at the general.

'Say what you have to say, Claudia,' he said, 'and be mindful that this is not Dura.'

Claudia regarded Shapur coolly as he backed away from the dais. I noticed she was holding the amulet of Pazuzu in her right hand and kept glancing at it.

'My father will leave the city in the early hours of tomorrow, after which he will ride to Bam and there organise a relief army. He will ride straight through the Kushans, who will be occupied with other things at the time.'

Salar looked at her. 'What other things?'

Claudia gave him a sly grin. 'A visit from some winged friends.'

Frowns greeted her words but she looked at her palm where the amulet rested. She was speaking of the aid of the king of the wind demons, though how she would summon him was a mystery.

'Ridiculous,' scoffed Shapur.

'We will see, general, we will see,' said Claudia. 'But I hear Commander Kewab has a task for you.'

I looked at Kewab who was staring at my daughter with an open mouth.

'How did you know?' he muttered.

'Enlighten us,' smiled Claudia.

Kewab, flustered, cleared his throat. 'Well, I was thinking that perhaps General Shapur might leave with King Pacorus but head for the hills with a small detachment of men. There to organise raiding parties against the Kushan army. In this way, the enemy will be deterred from launching a direct assault against the city.'

'Clever,' said Kalet loudly, 'but me and my men should be the ones who should do that.'

'No, my lord,' protested Kewab, 'you and your men are all expert archers and as such they should man the walls.'

Kalet was far from amused. 'Man the walls when there's raiding to be had?'

'You will do as requested, Lord Kalet,' I told him, 'and with the help of the gods we might yet make it back to Dura safely.'

Claudia turned to Salar. 'And now, lord king, you have a decision to make. Will you let me aid you so you may enjoy a long and fruitful reign?'

Salar found no answer in the faces around him so he turned to his wife, the sister of Claudia, and one well acquainted with her upbringing at the hands of Dobbai. She gave her husband a faint smile and a nod. The die was cast.

Salar stood and took his wife's hand. 'So be it, may the gods smile on us.'

'On you, lord king, they will,' Claudia assured him, 'of that you can be certain.'

I did not sleep that night as I organised the column that would leave Sigal in the early hours, though my task was aided enormously by Kewab having already alerted the various commanders that they might be called upon to lead their men from the city. Salar ordered a curfew on pain of death and commanded Shapur to lead a thousand

207

foot and five hundred horsemen to accompany us, who would leave us to head for the hills surrounding the city. But as the city slept I was faced with a personal crisis.

Gallia declared her intention to stay in the city with her daughters and Praxima. In addition, Diana told Gafarn that she too would remain in Sigal to support her friends. This prompted Rasha to announce she would also be staying, along with the Vipers. I did not have the energy to argue with the sisterhood, and in truth in many ways it made sense. I knew that Isabella would never abandon Salar and Sigal and with Nergal so ill it was unreasonable to expect Praxima to desert her husband. But it also meant that the seventeen hundred horse archers of Mesene would also be staying with their king and queen.

The hour was late when I left the fortress' stables to bid farewell to my wife. Cataphracts, horse archers and squires had turned the courtyard into a nest of activity, checking weapons and equipment and sharpening sword blades. In the city thousands of other soldiers were undergoing the same pre-battle rituals, and grumbling cameleers would be complaining about all and sundry as they prepared their beasts for the breakout. Claudia was loitering in the courtyard, speaking to squires and blessing their weapons. I watched her speaking to cataphracts, smiling and placing a hand on an arm or shoulder. For a second I thought I caught a glimpse of the carefree, vivacious daughter I had known before her ordeal. But then she saw me and the vision was gone. She walked over, a company commander bowing his head to her.

'The gods are with you,' she told him.

'I hope you are right. By the way, how do you summon a demon?'

'I don't, I ask him to come from the celestial world.'

I was surprised. 'Just like that?'

She tilted her head. 'There are a few incantations to be said, but for a skilled practitioner of sorcery it is straightforward enough. The trick, of course, is to ensure that he does not stay in this world but returns to his own when his task is complete. If the celestial door closes too soon ...'

She shuddered.

I was curious. 'Tell me.'

'Let's just say a demon trapped in this world would be mightily enraged and could spread great evil.'

'I thought demons *were* evil,' I said.

'What a simplistic notion you have of the immortals, father. Like men, gods and demons have the potential to be both good and evil, and as such can have both harmful or beneficial effects upon humanity.'

'I'm not sure I am reassured. I am relying on you to keep your mother, sisters and everyone else safe while I am away.'

She threw back her head and laughed, which turned into an ethereal growl that unnerved everyone within earshot.

'The gods like you, father, but they are not at your beck and call and nor are they at mine. If they are pleased with us then they may aid us, though only for a while.'

'Dobbai once told me that the gods are cruel.'

She shrugged. 'So are you, father.'

I was outraged. 'Me? I have always ruled fairly and according to the rule of law.'

She rolled her eyes. 'I was not talking about how you rule Dura, I was thinking of your decision to continue to fight Kujula, thereby consigning Sigal to a siege that may claim many lives, as well as sparking a war that will cost the lives of thousands.'

'It was not my decision to continue to fight,' I insisted.

'Really? You could have persuaded Salar to come to an accommodation with Kujula, convinced him that Sakastan would have been no worse off swearing its allegiance to the Kushan Empire rather than Parthia, but you did not.'

'Sakastan is Parthian,' I told her, 'and I will fight with every fibre of my body to keep it so.'

She leaned towards me and kissed me on the cheek. 'There you have it. Be ready with your men at the gates as dawn breaks tomorrow.'

And then she was gone, leaving me alone in the courtyard. I walked back into the palace, which despite the hour was full of officers holding briefings concerning the breakout that would take place in the next few hours. I found Gallia, in full war gear, in our bedroom, counting the arrows in her quiver.

'Are you about to go on guard duty?' I joked.

'When you lead the breakout tomorrow, it will not be lost on the Kushans that thousands of soldiers have left the city. If I was their leader I would launch an immediate assault on the city.'

I walked over and held her in my arms.

'If you were the Kushan leader I would already be dead, I think.'

She grinned. 'I was thinking earlier of the time when I was in command of Dura in your absence when it was besieged by that Roman oaf whom we first encountered in Italy.'

'Lucius Furious, I remember.'

She finished counting her arrows. 'We defeated him, we will defeat the Kushans.'

I sat on the bed and stared at the floor.

She sat beside me. 'What's the matter?'

'We came here for a wedding and yet here we are, once again fighting for our lives. We win one war and another seems to spring up from nowhere. There is no end to it.'

She threaded her arm in mine. 'Life is struggle, Pacorus. In your heart you know this. When you build something worthwhile there is always someone who wants to take it away from you. When they try, we meet force with force.'

That was Gallia: hard and unyielding. Tonight, her granite-like attitude comforted me. I wanted to share the remaining precious hours left alone with her but she declared her intention to visit Nergal. I joined her, our wounded friend still unconscious and still being tended by Alcaeus. We crept into the bedroom to find Gafarn and Diana sitting beside a very pale and tired Praxima. I embraced her first, Diana afterwards, shaking the hands of Gafarn and Alcaeus. The Greek physician would remain in Sigal to tend our friend, whom I had to admit looked remarkably peaceful.

'How is he?' I asked.

'The bleeding has stopped, his breathing is deep and strong and all that remains is for him to awaken,' replied Alcaeus

'You have done a splendid job.'

'Mm, I wonder. I have lost patients who had similar injuries and yet Nergal lives. Claudia helped, I think, though I would never tell her so.'

'Here we are, then,' said Gafarn, 'once again on the eve of battle. How long has it been since we first all fought together in Italy?'

'Too long,' said Diana, 'you are getting too old for such nonsense.'

We all laughed. Her husband frowned at her.

'Who's too old?'

We turned to see Nergal looking up at us with a quizzical expression. Praxima closed her eyes to give thanks to the gods and then lifted Nergal's hand from the bed and kissed it, rubbing it against her face. Tears were running down her cheeks.

'I thought I had lost you.'

Alcaeus felt Nergal's forehead. 'How do you feel?'

'Refreshed,' came the surprising answer. 'What's going on?'

He tried to sit up but Alcaeus stopped him. 'You must remain in your bed. You have been gravely wounded.'

'What do you remember?' I asked.

Nergal appeared confused. 'Very little. How long have I been asleep?'

'Days,' a delighted Praxima told him.

Nergal looked at each of us and saw me, Gallia and Gafarn in our armour.

'It is good that the Companions are together again,' I said, 'an auspicious omen, I think.'

The death of Alaric during the campaign against Mark Antony meant there were no Companions in Dura's army, aside from Alcaeus, the rest having either died or retired. An era was passing but the veterans of Italy, assembled in this room, still had a part to play in the empire's affairs.

I sat on *Tegha* in the half-light waiting for dawn to break. It was still, quiet and warm, sweat trickling down my neck as I waited. Waited for what? Claudia had told me to break out at dawn and so I awaited my time. Behind me thousands of men also waited. The city streets were deserted of civilians but the huge column of horses and camels filled the concourses from the city gates to the courtyard of the fortress on the hill. Flanking me Azad and Prince Pacorus sweated in their scale armour, their horses similarly attired. *Tegha* wore no armour and I was equipped in my Roman helmet and cuirass.

Behind me nearly ten and a half thousand soldiers sat on their horses, together with three and a half thousand squires and hundreds of camels. Gafarn waited at the head of the Hatrans; an angry Spartacus chafed at the bit with the horsemen of Gordyene; Malik and his Agraci were with him; and bringing up the rear were three thousand Saka lancers. I was fairly confident we could force our way through the Kushan siege lines anyway, but with Claudia's help we could hopefully be far away from the city before Kujula could organise a pursuit.

'What's that?'

Azad craned his neck as he heard something. We looked at him then I too heard it: a low scraping sound that turned into an ominous growl. Where before there had been absolute silence, standards now began to flutter as a wind picked up, a wind that grew in strength and intensity until it became a long howl. The cry of Pazuzu.

'Open the gates,' I shouted at the guards standing in front of the massive, thick wooden barriers.

A loud crack overhead frightened the horses and made them skittish. I looked up and saw lighting in the sky, a sky that was turning blood red as a mighty wall of sand and dust reared up outside the wall. More lightning bolts shot down from the heavens and an ear-splitting thunderclap filled the sky. Outside the walls was a terrible maelstrom but not a grain of sand appeared to have entered Sigal.

'We are going out into that?' asked Azad, looking up at the orange wall of dust towering over the city walls.

The gates were now open.

'We are,' I said.

I drew my sword, dug my knees into *Tegha* and he raced forward.

Into a corridor of calm. Azad slammed his helmet on his head and followed me, as did Prince Pacorus. And behind them Dura's cataphracts cantered from the city. I glanced left and right at the towering walls of dust and heard the raging wind and terrible screams that were like nothing I had ever heard before. But in front of me there was a stretch of undisturbed ground, like an avenue between two rows of tall trees.

'On, on,' I shouted at *Tegha* .

He sensed my nervousness and broke into a gallop as I sheathed my sword and tightened the grip on his reins. I focused my attention on the ground ahead, ignoring the raging storm either side of me and praying to Shamash that the tunnel would hold until all the horsemen were safely out of the city and well away from Sigal.

It felt as if time had stood still and I had been transported to another world as *Tegha* galloped like fury but seemingly did not cover any ground. A fear gripped my mind that I had left the earth and was damned to ride forever on ground that had no beginning and no end. But just as my mind was about to be overwhelmed by despair I was suddenly riding in clear air, around me dirt and rock but no sandstorm. I continued on for a few minutes, fearful of looking back in case I saw the leering face of Pazuzu pursuing me.

'Uncle,' Prince Pacorus' voice was faint, distant. 'Slow down, uncle.'

I tugged on *Tegha*'s reins; he needed no second prompting to reduce his speed. I could see sweat on his neck and knew I had pushed him hard, too hard. I pulled on the reins again to slow him to a trot as Pacorus sidled up to me. He wore an open-faced helmet and I could see his beard was soaking in sweat. Azad appeared on my other side, shoving up his helmet to reveal a red face. He was panting heavily and his horse must have been fit to drop.

'You must call a halt, majesty, otherwise we will lose hundreds of horses.'

I pulled up *Tegha* when I realised we were surrounded by silence. Absolute, blissful silence. On our left flank was the Erymanthus, its waters calm and gently flowing. I had no idea how far we had travelled but Azad gave a fair estimate.

'We must have covered twenty miles in less than an hour.'

'We rest for a while before continuing on,' I told him.

Grateful men dropped from their saddles and lay on the ground, gasping, then unsaddled their horses and led them to the water. I was one of them, afterwards rubbing down *Tegha* and feeding him a small amount of fodder. As I was doing so Gafarn, Malik and Spartacus came to me, all soaked in sweat but well.

'That was some ride,' said Gafarn.

'I felt a hot breath on my neck, as if a monster was chasing me,' said an unusually downcast Spartacus.

'We rest for two hours and then continue with our journey,' was all I said. 'We need to get to Bam as quickly as possible.'

'At least that sandstorm would have created havoc among the Kushans,' said Gafarn.

'It will take them days to recover,' added Malik, who had fear in his eyes. It was the first time I had seen such an emotion in his face. Then again, I was fearful for those inside Sigal as well as for Claudia. What price would the gods exact for their assistance?

When we re-commenced our journey, the pace was deliberately much slower, much to the frustration of Spartacus who annoyed me so much that I despatched him to the back of the column to organise and lead the rearguard. We had made an excellent start but I and everyone else was aware it was the height of summer, Sakastan was a dry, hot kingdom, and if we pushed the horses too much after the terror and exertion they had experienced earlier, then many would drop down dead before nightfall. So we only made an additional thirty miles that day before making camp fifty miles south of Sigal, our forces spread out along the Erymanthus.

We posted guards and Spartacus organised a timetable for when sentries should be replaced, which was extremely generous as everyone was fit to drop after what had been a most strenuous and unnerving day. We had brought no tents and little food, so men sat around campfires sourced from trees growing near the river and chewed strips of cured meat.

'So, what is your plan?' Gafarn quizzed me.

'When we passed the post station earlier,' I told him, 'I left a letter signed and sealed by Salar ordering the governor of Bam to

216

muster as many men as possible. It should reach him in three days. With it was another letter that our friend Rogerio is to forward to Silaces at Elymais, requesting he send men to Bam as quickly as possible.'

Gafarn, his head resting on his saddle, raised an eyebrow. 'You put much faith in our friend Rogerio.'

'He is fat because he is lazy,' said Malik, 'when we get to Bam, you may be disappointed.'

'In that case, my friend,' I smiled, 'you can kill him.'

'What of Phanes?' asked Gafarn.

I closed my tired eyes. 'What of him?'

'He is closer than Silaces and so is his army.'

I opened my eyes and looked at my brother. 'I suspect that Phanes will wait and see what happens before committing himself. Do not forget he was organising a coalition against Peroz, and for all we know he was behind his assassination. It serves his interests for the Kushans to capture Sakastan.'

'Though not Parthia's,' stated Malik.

Gafarn chuckled. 'The one thing I have learned sitting on Hatra's throne all these years, my friend, is that each of the empire's kings has a different view as to what are Parthia's interests. Suffice to say that they nearly always coincide with their own. Aside from Pacorus here, of course, who does actually put the empire's interests before his own. That is why so many find him disconcerting. Of course, he would have made an excellent king of kings.'

'Don't start all that again,' I groaned. 'Get some sleep.'

I was wrong about Phanes. On the third day, after we had covered fifty miles the day before and twenty more before we rested for three hours to give our horses some respite from the scorching

217

heat, Talib returned to inform us that the King of Carmania and his army were less than fifteen miles to the south. Because a large number of foot soldiers accompanied Phanes, his army moved slowly. I called an immediate council of war, unsure what to do. We had left the river now and were heading west towards Bam. The road, usually filled with caravans and local traffic, was deserted. We had scouted deserted villages, the inhabitants of which had fled when they had learned that thousands of horsemen were heading their way, taking to the hills and mountains before we arrived.

'Did they see you?' I asked Talib.

He shook his head. 'The Carmanians have no scouts, majesty.'

'Do they have any elephants?' asked Gafarn.

'No, majesty,' answered Talib.

Gafarn looked disappointed. 'Pity, I have grown quite fond of them.'

Talib gave him a confused look.

'Ignore him,' I said.

Gafarn rubbed his hands. 'Still, elephants or not, Phanes' appearance gives us an opportunity of relieving Sigal sooner rather than later.'

'Agreed,' said Spartacus, 'let us join our forces to his and march back to the city.'

I looked at Malik. 'That would be a logical course of action.'

'But Pacorus is not convinced,' observed Gafarn, 'are you?'

'No,' I answered bluntly. 'But as our route means we must meet Phanes we might as well continue our journey.'

'It would make more sense to wait until he arrives,' said Spartacus.

'I do not trust Phanes,' I told him.

218

We encountered the king and his army in an arid valley flanked by mountains devoid of vegetation and seemingly life, the odd lizard scampering between rocks the only indication that wildlife inhabited this sun-blasted patch of earth. The heat between the bare mountains towering up on either side the valley was stifling, but at least there was no wind to increase the temperature.

The Carmanians filled the western end of the valley, their horsemen riding left and right to prevent us outflanking them when they spotted us. I called a halt and urged *Tegha* forward, Gafarn, Malik and Spartacus joining me, Prince Pacorus providing an honour guard of cataphracts. He was disappointed that the absence of wind meant the banners hung limply. A party of Carmanian horsemen left Phanes' army to ascertain if we were friends or foe, returning to their king when we had halted to allow them to get a good look at us. Having discovered we were Parthians, Phanes himself rode forward to greet us, a huge banner being carried behind him, sadly not fluttering proudly. I thought it an ill omen.

I turned to Azad. 'Ride ahead and introduce us to King Phanes, if you will.'

The commander of my cataphracts trotted across the pebble-strewn ground and provided information as to who was present. I had hoped that Phanes would have responded positively to our presence, but when we were within conversing distance his tone was short and abrupt to the point of impoliteness.

It was the first time I had met the King of Carmania. He was perhaps two or three years older than his late brother and looked quite different, with a narrow face, pointed chin and a hooked nose. He dressed like a king, though, his magnificent red leather cuirass sporting an embossed golden peacock and his helmet adorned with huge peacock feathers. When he addressed us, he did so like a strutting peacock.

'As the representative of King of Kings Phraates, appointed his lord high general, I have authority to requisition your soldiers for his highness' service.'

I looked at Gafarn who closed his eyes and gave a slight shake of the head. I was going to reply when Phanes looked down his nose at Malik.

'Except the Agraci, of course, who have no business being within the empire's boundaries.'

'You should take a trip further north and see that the empire's boundaries are constricting by the day,' said Spartacus, 'the more so if it had not been for the valiant efforts of King Malik, whom I am honoured to call a friend and ally.'

Phanes regarded him coolly. 'King Spartacus, I have heard much about you and your Agraci wife, truth to tell..'

'Say one more word about my wife and I will kill you right here,' threatened Spartacus.

The officers with Phanes were shocked by such language and for a moment were frozen with indecision. I decided to try to lessen the building tension but Phanes was not be deterred.

'How dare you, the son of a slave, speak to me, a man descended from a long line of Parthian kings.'

'You forget your place, Phanes,' said Gafarn, 'your position as lord high general does not grant you the privilege of insulting the empire's kings. My son and I await your apology.'

'Apology,' spat Phanes, 'you expect an apology for aiding and abetting a traitor? Where is the usurper Vartan?'

'I think the empire has more important things to worry about than the life of one young man,' I said, 'the Kushan invasion being the top of the list. While we sit here, their emperor has overrun two kingdoms and threatens a third.'

'Your kingdom will be next if we fail in our mission,' Malik told Phanes.

'We are riding to Bam,' I told Phanes, 'there to join with reinforcements sent by King Silaces.'

Phanes was unimpressed. 'You flee in the face of the enemy? Is this the same King Pacorus who defeated the Romans at Phraaspa, who assisted King Surena in destroying the Romans at Carrhae?'

'What do mean assisted King Surena?' queried Gafarn. 'It was Pacorus' victory alone.'

'That is not what the scribes say.'

'They lie,' said Spartacus. 'I was there, they were not. Who is responsible for such mistruths?'

'That was long ago,' I said, 'but I would advise you to join us so we can muster a large enough army to defeat the Kushans.'

Phanes pointed behind him. 'I march with forty thousand men, sufficiently large to destroy the Kushans, I think. It is *you* who should join me, and as lord high general I am ordering you to do so.'

We sat immobile and in silence staring at him. Gafarn broke the impasse.

'Here is the problem, my lord. You have little military experience and as far as I know none when it comes to commanding armies made up of contingents drawn from different kingdoms. All of us, on the other hand, have much experience of war and cooperating during times of conflict. That being the case, you will understand that submitting to your will is problematic to say the least.'

He turned to glance at the riders behind us. 'The men behind me represent the cream of our kingdoms' armies. We are hesitant to place them under the command of a novice.'

'That's putting it mildly,' sneered Spartacus.

Phanes officers growled and murmured angrily but Carmania's king was unconcerned.

'I do not need you, Parthia does not need you. Before you all I pledged that I will defeat the Kushans, arrest Vartan and place the Kingdom of Sakastan under the rule of my son Babak, after which High King Phraates will decide its fate.'

Spartacus looked at his officers. 'Where is your son?'

'At Puta, he has a fever and is too ill to ride.'

'Just as well,' mocked Spartacus, 'at last Carmania will still have a king when the present one is killed by the Kushans.'

Uproar greeted his words as Phanes' officers threatened the King of Gordyene and challenged him to single combat, which he readily accepted. Phanes curled a lip at my nephew.

'All will be settled. We are done here. All of you will move your men aside to allow us to pass.'

He told his officers to hold their tongues, turned his horse and returned to his army, swinging in the saddle as we too withdrew.

'High King Phraates will hear of this.'

'Of that I have no doubt,' I replied.

So it was that two armies passed each other in a barren plain in southern Sakastan, testimony to the divisions infecting Parthia even as foreign invaders ran amok within it. The horsemen of Carmania were splendid troops. The dragon of cataphracts all wore scale armour and open-face helmets, though unlike my own their horses wore only half-armour covering their bodies but not their heads or necks. The five thousand mounted spearmen wore leather cuirasses, helmets and carried large, round wooden shields painted red with a yellow peacock motif. Their primary weapon was a long lance with a sword as secondary weapon. The ten thousand horse archers wore no armour or head protection, though would provide formidable missile power on the battlefield.

If Phanes' horsemen were an imposing force his foot soldiers left a lot to be desired. The best were the two thousand élite foot archers armed with a recurve bow, spear, shield and sword and protected by scale armour cuirasses and helmet with a mail veil. Their spears and shields meant they could defend themselves against enemy horse and foot, while their bows gave them formidable missile power. As did the primary weapon of the two thousand slingers that marched with Phanes. But it was his twenty thousand levy spearmen that was the weak link in the chain. Recruited from villagers and townsmen, they had little training or motivation and their weapons comprised a spear and knife. With no helmet or armour, their only protection was a crude wicker shield. I had little confidence any would return to Carmania.

Chapter 9

The mood of the column was subdued as we headed west to Bam, knowing in our hearts that we should have joined with Phanes to both relieve Sigal and defeat the Kushans. But his arrogance had made cooperation impossible and having already been roughly handled by Kujula's soldiers, none of us had a burning desire to repeat the experience alongside an unreliable 'ally'. So we maintained a hard pace and reached Sakastan's second city in two days. I comforted myself with the knowledge that Phanes' approach would force the Kushans to either break off the investment of Sigal or weaken the siege lines to give battle. Then I was cast into despair with the thought that if the siege was lifted Phanes would be in control of Sigal and might arrest Salar, to say nothing of our wives.

Gafarn put my mind at rest. 'If you really believe Phanes can defeat Kujula on his own you are suffering from sunstroke. But he is a useful idiot in that he will turn the attention of the Kushans away from Sigal, albeit only for a while.'

'The useful idiot Phanes will buy us time, uncle,' Spartacus assured me.

I turned to give him a reproachful look. 'You must be more diplomatic when dealing with other kings.'

He was unimpressed. 'Why? Do they respect me? No. They call me the son of a slave behind my back and now to my face, so why should I treat them with respect?'

I sighed. 'Do you think those same kings say kind words about me behind my back? Or your father? They do not. But my reply to you is that you too mock them.'

'You have just called Phanes an idiot,' Gafarn reminded Spartacus.

'That is not an insult,' said Malik, 'more an accurate assessment.'

He and Spartacus burst into laughter, much to the embarrassment of Prince Pacorus. His brother noticed his squirming and jerked a thumb at him.

'You will never hear my brother utter a bad word about the other kings of the empire, even Darius of Media, may serpents gorge on his entrails.'

'Media is our ally,' insisted Pacorus.

'You see, my brother is the perfect Parthian prince,' grinned Spartacus, 'one day he will sit on Ctesiphon's throne.'

'You should not wish such a thing on your brother,' I jested, 'besides, hopefully Phraates will enjoy a long reign.'

'Not if the Kushans overrun half his empire,' said Malik, 'men do not respect or tolerate weak leaders.'

'That is why we are mustering at Bam, my friend,' I said, 'to fight for the continued existence of the empire.'

I pulled up *Tegha* , causing the others to halt. Gafarn frowned. 'Is your horse lame?'

I looked at Malik. 'My friend, we have no right to ask you or your men to fight for an empire in which many of the inhabitants despise the Agraci. I apologise for embroiling you in this lamentable situation.'

Malik, fierce looking with his black face tattoos, was impassive.

'You are my friends; my sister is married to King Spartacus and is trapped in Sigal with your wives and daughters. This is not about Parthia; this is personal.'

'You are a man of honour, lord king,' said Prince Pacorus.

Malik looked bemused and Spartacus rolled his eyes but Gafarn agreed.

'Such men are sadly lacking in these turbulent times.'

Before we had seen Bam, Talib brought us news that boosted our spirits.

'A Caspian Tiger banner hangs from the citadel's gates, majesty.'

'Khosrou is in the city?'

He nodded. 'And thousands of his men are camped outside Bam's walls.'

I had a broad grin on my face as we rode the last twenty miles to the city, to see a tent city adjacent to the one of mud-brick walls and buildings. I thanked Shamash that he had sent the King of Margiana. Khosrou, the iron-hard ruler of the kingdom that held the barbarians of the northern steppes at bay. He was now in his late sixties and his hair, beard and thin moustache were white as snow. His flat face resembled an old saddlebag but his dark brown eyes sparkled with mischief when Rogerio ushered us into the old king's presence.

Khosrou gave me a bear hug that threatened to crack my ribs.

'It warms my heart to see you, lord, though my ribcage begs you to release me.'

'Ha,' exclaimed Khosrou, 'you are getting soft in your old age, Pacorus. Where's that pretty wife of yours?'

'In Sigal, lord.'

He stepped back, surprised. 'You left Gallia in a besieged city?'

'It's a long story,' I said.

'Well let's hear it,' roared Khosrou. 'Bring wine,' he instructed Rogerio.

The fat governor, unused to being treated like a servant, smiled and hesitated but did as he was told when the stern visage of Khosrou rounded on him.

'Idle fat bastard,' he said loudly as Rogerio was leaving, 'about as much use as a eunuch at an orgy. So, let's hear this woeful tale.'

We sat on plush couches in the governor's audience chamber and relayed the story of how we had travelled to Sakastan to attend the wedding of Salar and Isabella and how a day of happiness had turned rapidly into one of horror, quickly followed by the coalition against Sakastan, which was overwhelmed by the Kushan invasion that overran Aria and Drangiana and threatened Sakastan and Carmania. Khosrou drank wine, nodded, examined us all and told Rogerio to order more wine as he told us the news from the rest of the empire.

'Phraates has put his faith in Phanes to defeat the Kushans and restore order in his eastern kingdoms. Apparently, he is also gathering an army to march to our aid.' Khosrou belched. 'Not that I believe him.'

'How is it that you are here, lord?' enquired Prince Pacorus.

'I was wondering that,' I added.

'The ambassadors of Aria and Drangiana have shown more backbone than their kings,' Khosrou told us. 'As soon as their rulers were defeated they took it upon themselves to visit the courts of anyone who would listen to them, bleating like despoiled virgins that Parthia must respond quickly to throw our friend Kujula back across the Indus. Anauon and Yueh-Chih are currently mobilising and will strike south when they have done so.'

227

'Heartening news,' said Gafarn.

'And King Phanes is marching from the south to relieve Sigal,' said Spartacus, 'so perhaps the Kushans will be caught between a hammer and an anvil.'

Khosrou belched again. 'This wine is gut-rot. I commend your faith in human nature but even if the hammer and anvil succeed, and it is a big if, I doubt it will dislodge Kujula from Parthia.'

I took a sip of wine. It was indeed second-rate. Clearly Rogerio was denying Khosrou his finest vintage.

'You still have not revealed why you came to Bam,' I said.

'I ordered my two sons to guard the northern frontier,' Khosrou told us, 'and left them to march at the head of ten thousand men to reinforce poor old King Cinnamus of Anauon. His kingdom has been at peace for so long that he barely has an army.'

He looked at Gafarn. 'One reason I don't hold out much hope for the great northern alliance. Anyway, while at his capital we received news from Salar's general that King Pacorus was leading an army to Bam to organise a relief column and had sent out a general plea for help. So here I am. How many men are with you.'

'Ten and a half thousand,' I answered.

'Silaces is on his way?'

I nodded.

Khosrou ran a finger around the lip of his silver cup. He looked at Spartacus and Malik.

'It will take more than a battle and the relief of Sigal to remove the Kushans from Parthia. If we give them time they will fortify the towns they have taken, and then it will be all but impossible to prise them out of the empire.'

'What do you have in mind?' I asked.

'We split our forces. When Silaces arrives, he can join with your heavy horsemen and ride to the relief of Sigal. Meanwhile, we will strike east into the Kushan Empire and burn every hovel we come across. That should get Kujula's attention.'

'We?' I asked.

Khosrou nodded at Malik. 'I would esteem it an honour, my lord, if you and your warriors would accompany my own. Pacorus will come with me, of course, so he can learn what real war is.' He pointed at Spartacus. 'You too, young pup.'

The 'young pup' was now in his mid-thirties but Spartacus was delighted to be invited to ride beside the legendary King of Margiana so just smiled contentedly.

Gafarn frowned. 'You have omitted me, lord king.'

'Hatra's Royal Bodyguard goes where its king goes,' said Khosrou, 'and so must remain with the relief force, as must your cataphracts, Gafarn. On our mission we travel light and at speed.'

Gafarn seemed satisfied by the answer, which made perfect sense. Clearly Khosrou had been giving the matter much thought, though my namesake was far from pacified.

'How will burning villages and murdering innocents save Parthia?' queried Prince Pacorus.

Khosrou regarded the hero of Hatra for a few seconds, the grizzled old warrior who had held the northern barbarians at bay for over forty years twisting his thin lips into a half-smile. Pacorus, resembling a Greek god in looks and a priest in morals, did not quite know what to make of the fearsome ruler of Margiana in his shabby leggings and stained tunic.

'Not all war is glory and fame, boy,' Khosrou told him. 'We all heard how you covered yourself in glory against the Romans in the north. Before I answer your question, how would you defeat the Kushans?'

Pacorus remained stony faced. 'We defeat Kujula in battle and he will slink back across the Indus.'

'Just like that.'

'Just like that,' said Pacorus forcefully.

Khosrou took a great gulp of wine. 'No, he won't. He will retreat north into Aria or Drangiana where he will entrench himself and order more men to be sent from his homeland. Do you know much about Drangiana, young prince?'

'Aside from the fact that it is ruled by King Antiochus, I must confess that my knowledge of his kingdom is wanting,' came the honest reply.

'Allow me to enlighten you,' said Khosrou. 'Aside from mountains Drangiana is also rich in tin, which means Kujula is now rich in tin, which he can sell to finance his campaign. It also means he will be very reluctant to surrender what he has won. That is why we must give him an incentive to return home.'

'If we defeat and kill him then the Kushans will return home,' offered Pacorus.

Khosrou was impressed. 'Perhaps they will. Or perhaps another leader will take Kujula's place and seek to expand the territory he has won. I'm afraid my knowledge of the Kushan Empire is even worse that your knowledge of Drangiana.'

He pointed a finger at the prince. 'Why did you defeat the Romans?'

'Because they failed to capture Phraaspa,' came the reply.

Khosrou smashed his fist into his palm. 'Exactly. But the Kushans have already taken the capitals of Aria and Drangiana, so they already have strong bases from which to operate. Did you bring your siege engines, Pacorus?'

'I came to attend a wedding, not conduct a siege,' I told him.

'The sad fact is,' said Khosrou, 'that Dura has the only siege engines in the Parthian Empire, so retaking the cities the Kushans have captured will prove time-consuming. And time is a commodity we do not have.'

'So we raid, kill and burn,' smiled Malik.

'Sounds good to me,' stated Spartacus with relish.

Khosrou was delighted and emptied his cup. He was now slightly drunk and there was a mischievous glint in his eye. He put down the cup and rubbed his hands.

'Every cloud has a silver lining. After we have ejected the Kushans from the empire, there might be an opportunity to return the favour and seize some of Kujula's territory. Planning on staying in the east awhile, Pacorus?'

'Not really,' I told him.

There was a knock at the door and a beaming Rogerio entered, followed by slaves carrying full wine jugs. Khosrou held up his cup to be refilled and the fat governor bowed to me, proffering a silver tray, upon which was a tiny piece of rolled papyrus.

'For you, majesty. It has just arrived attached to a courier pigeon.'

I took the note and unwrapped it, recognising Claudia's writing, albeit small. Without thinking I read the words out loud.

'Sigal safe, Kushans in turmoil, Nergal well.'

'Extraordinary,' said Gafarn.

Spartacus slapped his brother on the back and Malik nodded at me.

'How is it that a courier pigeon can fly unharmed through mountains full of eagles, vultures and hawks?' asked Khosrou.

'Princess Claudia has special talents,' said Spartacus, 'she was trained by the sorceress Dobbai. She speaks to the dead, is that not true, uncle?'

I shrugged. 'I think your imagination is running away with you, nephew. But it is cheering to receive news that our family members are safe.'

'I remember Dobbai, saw her a few times at the court of Sinatruces,' reminisced Khosrou. 'Now he was a good king of kings. Liked to kill first and ask questions later.'

'So we are agreed on our strategy, then?' I asked.

'When do we leave?' said Spartacus with relish.

Khosrou held up his cup again. 'As soon as we have emptied the governor's wine cellars.'

We did not empty the royal wine cellar, though we did strip his armouries of arrows to replace the ones we had left behind in Sigal. I was worried that without a camel train carrying ammunition we would still be deficient in missile power, but Khosrou assured me we were not going to fight any battles against the Kushans. Rather burn, pillage and run. We would also be living off the land, thus reducing the amount of supplies we would be taking with us.

While we waited for Silaces I was invited to Khosrou's camp, the king eager for me to meet 'an old friend'. Intrigued. I left Rogerio and his irksome enquiries as to when the great number of men, horses and camels would be leaving Bam and rode to the Margianan camp. It was a great sprawling collection of tents and horses. I say horses but the beasts Khosrou's warriors rode were more like ponies with their short necks, short legs and stolid bodies. A casual observer would have derided such beasts that came in all variations of colours and were an alien species when compared to the thoroughbreds of Hatra and Dura. But such observations would be wrong. The ponies of the great steppes were sturdy, fearless and able to withstand extremes of temperatures.

The soldiers of Margiana presented a ragtag appearance but that too was deceptive. As I rode *Tegha* through their camp I saw men grooming horses dressed in kaftan-like coats with one breast crossed over the other and tied in place. They had long sleeves that could double up as hand warmers in winter, though because it was high summer they were rolled up. Some men were bare chested as they tipped fodder into wooden eating troughs. I had ridden from the city with an escort of horse archers, immaculate in their ankle boots, tan leggings and white tunics. At Khosrou's tent things were more formal, guards halting us before we got within a hundred paces of the king's residence where we dismounted before I was escorted to the royal tent. In front of the entrance was a flagpole from which flew the king's Caspian Tiger banner. Inside were two individuals: Khosrou and a wiry man with a squashed nose and narrow eyes that looked like a helmet's vision slits. I smiled when I remembered an old friend.

'Kuban, this is an unexpected pleasure.'

He snapped his head forward in a bow. 'Majesty. You look well.'

'I look and feel old,' I told him, 'but it warms my heart to see you.'

'General Kuban, here, insisted on joining me,' said Khosrou, 'though was disappointed to learn that you left Gallia at Sigal.'

'She is a great queen and warrior,' said Kuban admiringly. 'We will make the Kushans pay for what they have done.'

His black eyes reminded me of the king cobra I had tussled with not so long ago and sent a shiver down my spine. As well as a warrior, I remembered Kuban being an accomplished torturer, which made me realise the campaign I was about to take part in would be very different from the ones I had previously fought in.

Silaces arrived four days after the message from Claudia, which in truth had reduced the nervous tension in the city and allowed us all to focus on the task in hand. Khosrou and Kuban were full of admiration that we had left our women behind in a besieged city, with the latter promising to carve a swathe of destruction in the Kushan lands in retaliation when we arrived in Kujula's territory. For his part, the King of Elymais arrived at Bam at the head of ten thousand horse archers and spitting blood.

'Phraates sits on his arse at Ctesiphon and does nothing,' he complained as he sat in the governor's beautifully decorated large office.

We lounged on plush couches, drank wine and were surrounded by walls decorated with sun and lion motifs, the lion representing divinity, royalty and the lineage of kings, and the sun symbolising the ruler of heaven. On the governor's huge mahogany desk was a bronze statue of *Pahlavi Senmurv* , the great falcon that sits on top of the mythical mother of all trees, the *Saena* . Rogerio himself sat at his desk. Khosrou wanted him to be excluded because he was not a king but I suggested that for diplomatic reasons he be allowed to attend the meeting of rulers.

'I begged him to send me soldiers but all he sent me was a condescending note saying he had every faith in Phanes.'

'The only one who has,' smirked Gafarn.

Silaces looked at me. 'Your threatening note worked too well.'

'I did not send a threatening note,' I insisted.

'Yes you did. A veiled threat, I grant you, but a threat nevertheless. The boy king won't shift his arse when there are, what did you say, one hundred and thirty thousand men poised ready to strike.'

'We don't need Phraates,' said Spartacus, 'we have a plan to defeat the Kushans without him.'

As it was Khosrou's plan, the King of Margiana explained his idea for lunging across the Indus while Gafarn and Silaces would march to the relief of Sigal. In addition, a combined army drawn from Anauon and Yueh-Chih would be marching from the north to trap the Kushans in a giant vice, though Khosrou was vague about its numbers and when it would march.

'It's up to us, then,' stated Silaces bluntly.

Khosrou nodded. 'Yes. We alone can save the eastern half of the empire from being lost.'

Rogerio sat with his head down twiddling his thumbs, overwhelmed by the enormity of the events that had taken place in Sakastan. He desperately wanted to say something but was intimidated and so remained silent.

'If you have something to say, spit it out,' commanded Silaces.

'Forgive me, majesty,' said Rogerio, 'but there are only thirty thousand soldiers camped here. Is that enough to…'

A knock at the door interrupted his words.

'Come!' he ordered.

A slave entered, bowed his head and walked briskly over to Rogerio, handing him a note. The governor read it and tossed it on the table.

'An officer of Phanes' bodyguard is outside.'

I felt a tingle of dread dance down my spine.

'What does he want?' said Rogerio out loud.

'Nothing good, I'll warrant,' said Gafarn morosely.

'Let's hear what he has to say,' Khosrou told the governor.

My heart sank when the dirty, sweating officer with a torn tunic and battered breastplate presented himself, dented helmet in the crook of his arm. He looked as though he would pass out at any moment.

'Fetch water,' ordered Gafarn.

'Sit down, man,' I said, 'before you fall down.'

Spartacus used his feet to push a chair towards the wavering officer, who gladly accepted the offer. A slave arrived with a jug of water, filling and refilling a cup as he drank greedily. It took him a few minutes to catch his breath but finally he was ready to relay his sorry tale. He stood but was ordered to sit back down by Khosrou.

'Bad news sounds no better if it is told by someone standing, boy.'

'The army of his highness King Phanes engaged the Kushans twenty miles south of Sigal, near the Erymanthus River. At first our horsemen drove the enemy riders back, exposing their foot soldiers. The king ordered his own foot soldiers to attack the enemy spearmen who were drawn up in a great square.'

I looked at Gafarn who shook his head.

The officer was close to being distraught. 'But the enemy horsemen counterattacked and drove our own horsemen back, which meant the king's foot soldiers were suddenly surrounded. Then the enemy square broke apart and attacked. Many of our spearmen drowned in the river but more were surrounded and cut to pieces. Faced with the imminent destruction of his army, King Phanes took a strategic decision to withdraw to save the rest of his army.'

'And where is that army now?' I asked.

'Pulling back to Puta, majesty, where it will be reinforced prior to once again marching against Parthia's enemies.'

Khosrou chuckled. 'And pray where does Phanes intend to draw his reinforcements from.'

The officer stood and removed a crumpled piece of papyrus from his tunic.

'King Phanes penned this letter on the march, majesty.'

'You mean retreat?' said Silaces.

The officer nodded. He turned to me and bowed. 'It is addressed to you, highness.'

He extended his arm and I took the letter. I decided to read it aloud as I was but one among equals.

'To my dear friend, King Pacorus.'

'He's changed his tune,' smiled Gafarn.

'He is about to beg,' said Malik.

I continued reading the letter. 'As a former lord high general, you will understand the utmost importance of acting speedily to avert disaster. After inflicting high casualties on the Kushans...'

Khosrou guffawed and Spartacus' face twisted into a grimace as he desperately tried to stop himself laughing. I frowned at them both.

'After inflicting high casualties on the Kushans,' I said loudly, 'I was forced to retreat in the face of the overwhelming numerical superiority of the enemy. I intend to withdraw to Puta, there to await the forces you and the other kings have assembled at Bam. I am certain that our combined forces can not only defeat the Kushans but also relieve the city of Sigal, where your beloved wife and daughters are trapped. I remain your friend and ally…'

I tossed the letter on Rogerio's desk.

'The Kushans pursued you?' I asked the officer.

'Yes, highness.'

'In what numbers?' enquired Gafarn.

'Several thousand, all horsemen, majesty.'

'That is good news for Sigal,' mused Spartacus, 'having to fight Phanes means they probably lack the numbers to attempt a storm.'

Malik nodded. 'Agreed, and if the Kushans are now invading Carmania their forces will be spread thin.'

'This Kujula,' said Khosrou, 'I hear you have met him, Pacorus.'

'Met him and fought him,' I replied.

'What do you make of him?'

I thought for a moment. 'Brave, intelligent and very ambitious.'

'The last quality might just be his undoing,' said Khosrou.

'The plan stands, then?' asked Silaces.

Khosrou looked at each of us in turn. We all nodded our assent.

'It does,' said the King of Margiana. He pointed at the officer. 'Get some rest, get yourself a fresh horse and ride back to your king. He will need you.'

'What message should I convey to my king, majesty?'

238

'Tell him we go to defeat the Kushans and eject them from Parthia,' I told him.

'But we will not be riding to Puta,' added Gafarn.

'King Phanes is lord high general,' said the officer.

'Not for much longer,' Khosrou told him, 'you may leave us.'

He left the room with slouched shoulders and head down but Phanes' loss, which was not unexpected, was our gain. With Kushan troops now venturing south into Carmania, Kujula's strength was further diluted. I felt confident we could both relieve Sigal and cause our enemy to withdraw back across the Indus by a punitive campaign in the Kushan Empire itself. As did everyone else.

The Sigal relief force jointly commanded by Silaces and Gafarn numbered sixteen thousand men, the bulk of which were the ten thousand horse archers of Elymais. But the army also included fifteen hundred cataphracts, three thousand squires, Sakastan's lancers and Spartacus' medium horsemen. There was also a substantial camel train carrying supplies, tents, spare weapons and hundreds of thousands of arrows. The army kicked up a great dust cloud as it made its way east. I extended my arm to Gafarn and Silaces.

'The gods be with you, Pacorus,' said Silaces.

I clasped his forearm. 'And with you, too, my friend.'

He wheeled his horse away and trotted towards the great column of camels and horsemen, his escort and banner man carrying his four-pointed star standard following.

'Keep my son safe,' said Gafarn, clutching my forearm.

'Spartacus?' I grinned. 'He should be the one taking care of me.'

I turned to Prince Pacorus. 'Make sure you do not repeat the mistakes of King Phanes, nephew. Do not underestimate the Kushans.'

The prince, resplendent in his gleaming steel scale armour suit, nodded solemnly.

'Hatra will not fail you, uncle.'

I raised my hand to them both, turned *Tegha* and rode away to catch up with the second column that was leaving Bam, my griffin standard being held by a Duran horse archer fluttering behind me. Khosrou's column was smaller – fourteen thousand men – and accompanied by far fewer camels. To say we were campaigning light was an understatement. There was no camel train carrying spare arrows, no replacement weapons and the bare minimum of food and fodder. I joined Spartacus, Malik and Khosrou and their banners: the red griffin joining the black flag of the Agraci, the lion of Gordyene and the Caspian Tiger of Margiana.

General Kuban's soldiers, compared to the finest from Dura, Gordyene and even the black-clad Agraci, looked like bandits on their ponies. But each man was protected by a cuirass comprising bands of hardened leather laced together and a padded leather helmet with neck and ear flaps. Like all of us they carried a recurve bow, slightly smaller than our own with a body constructed using wood and horn laminated together using animal resin. When the resin dried the resulting bond between the horn and wood gave the body of the bow enough strength to withstand the immense pressures placed on it when the bowstring was drawn. To increase the power of the weapon further, sinews from animal tendons were laminated to the outside face of the bow.

Like us they carried bows in cases on their right side, with up to five quivers on the opposite side, each one carrying thirty arrows. Parthian arrows were bronze, three-winged and socketed so that shafts could be inserted into the head. Unlike our own arrows, those of Khosrou's warriors were fletched with feathers attached to the shaft in a slight spiral pattern so they spun when shot, thus increasing their accuracy. For close-quarter work the Margianans carried a two-edge straight sword, a dagger and a spear with a long metal point.

Led by Khosrou's scouts, Talib and his men accompanying Gafarn, we headed northeast to take us into the hills that delineated the border between Sakastan and Drangiana. We moved fast, covering up to fifty miles a day with a rest day when we reached the banks of the Indus, the boundary between the Parthian Empire and India. We had left the windswept hills and mountains behind to enter a land of fertile plains interspersed with bare knolls. The few villages we had encountered had been deserted and showed signs of being plundered, no doubt by Kujula's troops when they invaded Parthia.

'Looks quiet,' observed Khosrou, squinting in the sunlight as he scanned the river from north to south.

'It must be a mile wide,' said Spartacus.

'And fast flowing,' added Malik.

'We should send scouts over the Indus and wait until they return,' I advised, 'it's too quiet.'

Khosrou roared with laughter. 'You are getting too cautious in your old age, Pacorus. We go now.'

He shouted at his horse, which bolted forward down the gently sloping riverbank and into the clear water. Spartacus grinned and followed, behind him Khosrou's guard cantering forward to splash into the water. I too rode down the now churned-up bank and

Tegha entered the water. It was refreshingly cool and though the current was fast, the river itself was not deep, water lapping around my legs as my trusty mount headed for the eastern bank. Either side of me, stretching up and down the western bank for half a mile, thousands of horsemen forded the Indus and began the first Parthian invasion of India.

The crossing was straightforward but not without hazards. Some horses stumbled on the muddy river bottom and collapsed into the water, their riders clinging on as the beasts swam rapidly to the opposite bank, soaking them both. Within an hour all our men and supplies were across the river, plundering the villages near the riverbank of food and livestock, before using the reed roofs for firewood. The inhabitants had fled to the east before we crossed the river and as night came no patrols were despatched to hunt them down. Instead, we butchered the pigs and roasted their flesh. The smell of cooked pork filled the warm night air as I walked with Khosrou to the riverbank, the Indus black and calm under a moonlit sky.

'I never thought I would see this river,' I said, 'let alone cross it.'

'Neither did I, but here we are. As soon as we start burning towns and villages word will get back to Kujula that his lands are under attack. Then he will come running.'

'You are certain of that, lord?'

He gave me a mischievous grin. 'He is seeking to expand his empire and will not take kindly to thieves sneaking into his domain. Believe me.'

I did not hear the beast spring from the water but saw the blur of movement as the crocodile launched itself at us. I shoved Khosrou aside, which saved his life because the huge monster, turned silver by the moonlight, snapped down its huge jaws on the king's boots. Lured by the aroma of roasting flesh, it mattered little to the creature that it had seized a living being.

'Rally to the king I shouted,' drawing my sword and plunging it into the crocodile's scaly back.

The point of the *spatha* pierced the scales and bit deep into its flesh. It roared in rage, released Khosrou and spun to attack me. I withdrew my blade and slashed at its jaws, which snapped shut around the metal to wrench it from my grip. It tossed the sword angrily aside and ran at me, its short stumpy legs moving rapidly as its huge body lumbered forward. I tried to retreat but lost my footing and fell backwards on to the sandy bank. I froze in terror as the crocodile closed on me, its huge jaws opening to reveal rows of razor-sharp teeth that would snap my body in two. I could not move or make a sound as time stood still and I could contemplate my demise.

The spear blade being driven into the crocodile made no sound but made the beast arch its back and momentarily forget me, giving one of Khosrou's bodyguard a chance to grab me by the scruff of the neck and haul me away. Two more spear blades were driven into the crocodile's body, the three soldiers gripping their shafts with both hands as they pinned the beast to the ground. Now the reptile was thrashing around wildly, hissing and growling as it desperately tried to free itself. To no avail. More of Khosrou's bodyguard arrived to plunge their spears into the beast, which stopped floundering around as it was stabbed repeatedly.

'Finish the bastard off,' shouted Khosrou, the grizzled old king being held back by the commander of his bodyguard for fear he might venture too close to the crocodile's jaws.

The beast was killed by a single spear thrust into its brain, suddenly becoming silent and still as the soldiers withdrew their spear blades and stepped back. Khosrou came over to me.

'Are you all right, Pacorus?'

'Thanks to your men, lord. It took my sword.'

'Find King Pacorus' sword,' Khosrou commanded.

My *spatha* was retrieved and we issued orders that archers were to be posted all along the riverbank, a safe distance from the water's edge. All horses and camels were withdrawn from near the river in case more crocodiles were loitering with intent to seize a meal. The carcass of the huge reptile was hauled back to the camp of Khosrou's bodyguard where it was butchered and roasted. I was invited to partake of the feast but I had lost my appetite.

The next day we raided into the Kushan lands proper, our forces divided into hundred-man groups that roamed for miles over the huge plain criss-crossed with rivers, lakes and swamps. The monsoon was coming to an end but the daily deluges had created vast flooded areas filled with birds and other wildlife. This was a lush, fertile land where every village cultivated wheat, rice, mangoes, guavas, plums, oranges, pomegranates and lemons. Though it was hot and humid, the heavy rainfall that fell in short, intense bursts brought welcome relief and refreshed both men and horses. The only problem was unfastening our bowstrings and storing them in saddlebags to prevent them getting wet. Our own bowstrings were made from sinew but the Margianans also carried horsehair bowstrings that did not absorb moisture and thus did not stretch.

On the first day, we encountered mostly deserted villages, which we fired, but on the second our columns began to overtake fleeing people weighed down with livestock and children. The morning sky was already filled with the smoke of torched villages when we came across a settlement crammed full of refugees, women and children screaming when my horse archers surrounded the village and nocked arrows in their bowstrings. With me were two companies of Durans and by my side their commander, the lithe Katana who had been born and bred in the city of Dura. The villagers were wailing and babbling in their native tongue. The men among them armed with a variety of spears, knives and farming implements formed a cordon around their wives and children. In the oppressive humidity, my banner hung limply from its shaft and sweat was running down my neck. All the male villagers were dressed in white cotton *dhotis*, many were bare chested, while the women were clad in white or yellow saris. They held the hands of their children tightly, knowing that the men on horseback before them were armed with recurve bows that could easily pierce their flesh.

'What now, majesty?' asked Katana.

I had no time to answer as a tall man with white hair and eyes like a cobra walked forward to harangue us.

'Who are you? What do you want? We have nothing save the clothes on our backs and paltry food supplies.'

They may have been poor villagers but they looked healthy enough and their settlement was large, containing numerous animal pens.

'He speaks Parthian, majesty.'

'I am aware of that. State your name and rank,' I said to the old man.

He chuckled. 'My name is Jagat and as to my rank, it is many years since I carried a spear and now I am just an ordinary villager trying to feed my family.'

He looked at the lines of horse archers either side of me. 'I assume you are of high rank.'

'I am King Pacorus of Dura, one of the kingdoms of the Parthian Empire.'

'This, lord, is not Parthia.'

I smiled at him. 'No, indeed, Jagat, but your emperor has seen fit to invade my empire so I am here to repay the compliment.'

He looked past me, to the smoke stacks on the horizon. 'With fire and sword, I see.'

'We show the same mercy to the Kushans as Kujula has shown to my people, Jagat. But we are not murderers. Tell your people they will be allowed to leave the village unmolested. Their homes will be reduced to ashes to send a message to your emperor.'

Two more elderly men walked forward to converse with Jagat, who must have told them what I intended because they threw up their arms and jabbered something to the villagers. A collective groan came from the group, quickly followed by wailing and screaming as women began sobbing and some held up their infants to us. They implored us for mercy, or at least I surmised they did, as I had no idea what they were screeching.

'We will defend or homes,' pledged Jagat, turning and barking a command.

The middle-aged and elderly men – there appeared to be few young men capable of bearing arms present – shuffled forward with their pathetic weapons.

'Don't be foolish,' I warned.

Katana raised his arm and as one every horse archer raised his bow, though none drew back his bowstring. Not yet.

'Kill one of the cows,' suggested Katana.

This prompted Jagat to rush over to the nearest cow and place himself in front of it.

'Barbarians,' he shouted. The villagers, aware of the imminent danger to the cow, fell to their knees and clasped their hands together, a pleading expression in their eyes.

'Odd,' said Katana.

'Take my life instead,' Jagat implored me.

Katana and his officers burst out laughing but I could see the Indian was serious.

'Take his life and that of the cow, majesty,' advised Katana.

Jagat pointed a bony finger at me. 'Queen Rana will have her revenge on you, barbarian.'

I was intrigued. 'Who is Queen Rana?'

But Jagat sank into defiant silence, his eyes filled with rage. I could have ordered my men to shoot him and the others down. It would have been all over in a few minutes, after which we would torch the mud huts and ride to another village to repeat the ghastly ritual. But the truth was I had no stomach for slaughtering innocents, but I was eager to learn more about Queen Rana, whoever she may be.

'I make you this offer,' I said to Jagat, 'come with me now and I will spare your village and all those who live here. I will even spare your cows. Decide now.'

He was taken aback by the offer and for a moment was lost for words. But his rage disappeared and he turned to speak loudly to the villagers, presumably to convey my offer. A grey-haired woman rushed forward and flung her arms around him. His wife, I assumed. He kissed her, reassured her and the men armed with weapons relaxed, a sign I took confirming he had accepted my offer.

'I have no horse,' he told me impertinently.

'Fetch him a remount,' I told Katana.

My commander was disappointed. 'We are not going to burn the village, majesty?'

'We are not going to burn the village.'

He told his officers to stand down their men, who removed the arrows from their bowstrings and walked their horses behind my standard. A spare horse was brought forward for the Indian, who had to be assisted into the saddle.

'It's been a while,' he lamented. 'How long will I be away from my wife and grand children?'

'How far away is Queen Rana?' I asked.

'A day's ride.'

'Then you will be back in your home within a week,' I told him.

He tactfully said nothing about the burning villages whose smoke littered the sky as we continued to ride east. But I did question him on his curious reverence for cows.

'The answer is both religious and practical,' he replied. 'Because it supplies nourishment a cow is identified with Aditi herself.'

'Who?'

He grunted in disapproval. 'The mother of the gods. No sane person would voluntarily anger the gods. But allied to its sacredness are the products that it produces. Milk, browned butter for lamps and dried dung for fuel. Milk nourishes children as they grow up and dung is used for fuel throughout India. Thus the cow is a carer for the people and a symbol of the divine bounty of the earth.'

'When did you learn our language?'

'I was a soldier and then a trader in pottery before old age made long journeys torture. I travelled across the Indus regularly to visit Aria.'

'I assume many of your young men are also in that kingdom now, as part of your emperor's army.'

'Some,' he answered guardedly. 'Others are closer to home.'

As the day waned the various columns converged around a huge lake where a great herd of water buffalo was drinking. A hundred at least were killed by arrows to supplement the gazelle that had been hunted and killed in the periods between torching villages. When the kings gathered around a large fire cooking a whole wild pig, faint red glows could be discerned on the horizon. Everyone stared at the gaunt, morose figure of Jagat who sat on the ground, refusing chunks of cooked meat, though accepting the offer of oranges and plums.

'Who's that?' asked a jubilant Khosrou, meat juices from the pork joint he was chewing dripping onto his beard.

'His name is Jagat, lord,' I answered, 'from a village we came across.'

'Is he a man of importance, uncle?' asked Spartacus.

'He looks like a beggar,' observed Malik.

'He is a man of no importance,' I told them, 'though he does have intelligence concerning a potential threat.'

'Who?' asked Khosrou.

'Queen Rana, the ruler of a city within a day's ride of here.'

'What city?' enquired Malik.

I called Jagat over and asked him to refresh my memory as to the name of the city he had been telling me about.

'Indraprastha. Queen Rana will have learned of your presence, majesty. I would advise you to withdraw while you still can.'

'Withdraw?' mocked Khosrou, 'I will hand over this Rana to my men who will take turns raping her.'

I winced with embarrassment. 'We should take care not to spread our forces too widely tomorrow.'

But the next day there was no time to deploy our columns again because the scouts brought news before we had quitted camp that Queen Rana's army was approaching.

I stood with Khosrou, Spartacus and Malik to formulate a battle plan. Fortunately three of us had already faced the Kushans and had been given a bloody nose. Assuming that this queen would fight in the same manner as Kujula, I gave my opinion on the coming clash.

'As soon as battle is joined the Kushans will most probably form their foot soldiers into a square.'

'Like your legions,' said Khosrou.

I nodded. 'But unlike my foot soldiers this square will also contain archers equipped with long bamboo bows, which have great range. This means they can engage our horse archers at long range, so stress to your commanders that they should not venture too close to the enemy square.'

Khosrou scratched his head. 'Then how are we going to beat them, assuming we are going to give battle?'

'We should give battle, lord,' urged Spartacus, 'to defeat this queen and capture her city.'

'Then we can burn it to the ground,' said Malik with relish.

'We draw their horsemen away from the square,' I said. 'First we destroy their horsemen and then we can reduce their foot at our leisure.'

It would not be quite that simple, of course, and battles were always risky affairs. But I drew comfort from the fact that all our Parthian horsemen were battle-hardened veterans and the Agraci were the best of Malik's warriors. In addition, the terrain – a flat plain with few trees – was ideally suited to mobile warfare. It was time to pluck the cobra's fangs.

Khosrou looked at Spartacus and Malik. 'We are agreed, then?'

They nodded in unison.

'You are commander-in-chief,' the old king told me, 'try not to get yourself killed.'

The day was warm and humid, the afternoon rain a long way off, the sky big, blue and cloudless. The scouts brought news that the Kushans were moving slowly, at the pace of their foot soldiers. Their reports told of horse archers, light horsemen, skirmishers, spearmen and foot longbowmen, but no elephants or heavy horsemen, at least none they could see. For their part, the enemy despatched their light horsemen to chase the scouts away. After an hour, the Kushans could be seen on the eastern horizon, a narrow black line at first but then expanding as the enemy deployed from column into line.

The busiest men on what would be the battlefield were the scouts who were sent to gather intelligence on the enemy while the rest of our army checked their mounts, quivers, armour and saddlery. The mood was calm, relaxed, everyone knowing that if things turned against us we could withdraw speedily to the west, back to the Indus if necessary. We did not need to fight this battle, but the desire to inflict a defeat on the Kushans was hard to resist. Slowly our battle line formed, Khosrou's ten thousand horsemen forming our centre, Spartacus and his twelve hundred riders comprising the left wing and Katana's eight hundred Durans deployed on the right wing. I held Malik and his two thousand Agraci in reserve, much to his chagrin. But as he had few horse archers it made perfect sense: I wanted his men to deliver the final blow when the time came; either that or cover our retreat if it all went terribly wrong.

I sat with Malik and Khosrou in front of the Margianan horsemen and watched the enemy line lengthen and thicken, red flags dotted among the Kushan host, the sound of drums and horns filling the air. Our own men sat in silence and watched the enemy line form. Riders galloped towards us and pulled up their horses on the lush grass. I recognised the flat face of Kuban under his padded helmet.

'It is as King Pacorus stated, lord,' he said, swinging in the saddle to point at the Kushans, 'foot soldiers in the centre, men equipped with shields in two blocks, skirmishers in front of them, with horsemen on the wings. I saw no archers.'

'They are behind the spearmen,' I told him, 'waiting for their moment.'

I turned and waved forward Jagat mounted on a horse and guarded by two of my men. All three trotted forward.

I pointed to the Kushans. 'Is your queen there?'

He looked horrified. 'On the battlefield? No, majesty. Women do not fight.'

I looked at Malik but said nothing.

'Who commands the army?' demanded Malik.

'I do not know, lord,' came the answer.

'Well, whoever it is, he will be pissing his leggings in fear by this afternoon,' said Khosrou, 'let's get things started. Kuban, signal the advance.'

The distance between the two armies was upwards of a thousand paces, which diminished rapidly as the centre and two wings cantered towards the Kushans. The ground trembled as twelve thousand horsemen advanced across the grassy plain, every man with his reins wrapped around his left wrist and clutching his bow in his right hand.

'Get him back to a safe distance,' I said to the men guarding Jagat.

The air was suddenly filled with war cries and hollering as Khosrou's men closed on the enemy foot soldiers, the horse archers on the flanks also making a lot of noise as they approached the enemy horsemen. Khosrou and Kuban had already turned their companies before the Kushan bowmen behind the spearmen had the opportunity to shoot a volley. But I saw what appeared to be a flock of birds suddenly appear in the sky before falling to earth, Khosrou's men cantering towards us.

'Time to withdraw, my friend,' I said to Malik.

His black banner fluttered next to my griffin as we rode our horses back to the black mass of Agraci warriors waiting patiently. Malik issued a command and they began to turn their horses to retreat west. For seasoned killers eager to wash their sword blades in enemy blood, it stuck in the craw but was essential if our plan was to work. We pulled back perhaps eight hundred yards before about-facing to see Margianans slowly wheeling around to face the east. The flat terrain at first made it difficult to discern what was happening on the wings, but the fog of confusion soon cleared when I saw my

Durans retreating rapidly leaving Khosrou's men in the centre behind. I clench my fist and shouted in triumph. It could only mean one thing: enemy horsemen were pursuing them.

I could not see but knew that the rear ranks of the Durans would be shooting arrows at the enemy over the hindquarters of their horses to both inflict casualties and goad the enemy into continuing their pursuit. I heard a chorus of horn calls and saw the rear ranks of Khosrou's horsemen wheel right, to take them behind the Kushan horsemen pursuing my Durans. I craned my neck and peered over to the left where Spartacus and his men had also beat a hasty retreat, which had now halted as the King of Gordyene about-faced his companies to attack the Kushans who found themselves suddenly surrounded by his men and the horsemen of Margiana. Half of Khosrou's men had wheeled right, half had wheeled left and suddenly our army had no centre as a deadly struggle broke out on the wings. Between them was empty space and I could see the long line of enemy foot soldiers in the distance. I knew the enemy skirmishers would be running to support the Kushan horsemen engaged in the mêlée, behind them the spearmen and archers. The latter in particular would be able to wreak havoc if they got within range.

'Now is the time, my friend,' I said to Malik, 'we must ride forward to halt the enemy's foot.'

The Agraci needed no second prompting and within a couple of minutes two thousand men armed with lances and swords and carrying round black shields were cantering forward, the sounds of close-quarters battle coming from either side as Parthians battled Kushans. I nocked an arrow in my bowstring when I saw the swarm of skirmishers dashing towards us, lightly armed men wearing no body armour or helmets who were focused on supporting their own horsemen. Instead they were faced with a line of black-clad Agraci hollering war cries. Trained to fight widely spaced and fleet of foot, they had no defence against horsemen. There were thousands of them but their wicker shields were useless as Malik's warriors rode through them and scythed scores down.

Upwards of two thousand were killed or wounded in the initial clash, the rest turning tail and fleeing in a desperate attempt to reach the sanctuary of their spearmen who were already halting and forming a defensive square. I slowed *Tegha* , took aim with my bow and shot a Kushan in the back, strung another arrow and cut down another skirmisher, hitting him in the stomach. One man charged at me, holding his shield in front of him and raising his javelin to throw it at me. I released the bowstring and saw my arrow go straight through the wicker shield into his chest. He staggered and fell to the ground, looking up forlornly as an Agraci horse trampled on him.

Malik was in his element, his bodyguard around him as he hacked left and right to cut down Kushans. Other Agraci speared skirmishers with their lances before drawing their swords to cut down more. It was turning into a massacre and would have been a bloodbath had it not been interrupted by cane arrows falling like rain among horsemen and skirmishers alike.

'Sound retreat,' I shouted at Malik, around us friend and foe alike being struck by arrows.

Malik heard my plea and seeing the arrows thudding into the ground, men and horses, shouted at his signaller to sound withdrawal. It seemed to take an age for the order to be conveyed but, like the raiders they were, the Agraci needed no second prompting and were already disengaging from the enemy. The retreat was a mad gallop to take us beyond the range of the Kushan arrows that were now falling in dense volleys, cutting down more skirmishers than Agraci warriors. The Kushan commander had swatted the Agraci away but in doing do had destroyed his own skirmishers. Had he known what was happening on the flanks he would have ordered a speedy withdrawal back to his queen's city. But he was a man not an eagle and had no way of knowing that the majority of his light horsemen and horse archers were dead, the remnants fleeing for their lives.

'The enemy commander is a madman,' said Malik, his sword blade smeared with gore.

A courier arrived from Khosrou to inform us that our right wing had been victorious and the Kushan horsemen were fleeing.

'Now is your time, my friend,' I said to Malik, 'give pursuit to prevent them reforming and returning to the battlefield.

It was a gamble because fighting was raging on the left where Spartacus and his men were still involved in a mêlée with the Kushans, but now Khosrou could send reinforcements to tip the scales in favour of my nephew. Malik offered me his hand and I shook it, then he was riding among his men, steeling their resolve for more slaughter. They needed little encouragement but they did need steering away from the now immobile Kushan foot soldiers that had formed an impenetrable square. As groups of Khosrou's leather-armoured warriors began riding over to support our left wing, Malik and his Agraci skirted the enemy square to pursue the fleeing enemy horsemen.

The second phase of the battle was about to begin.

There was a pause as both sides drew breath. A red flag showing a silver lion fluttered in the humid air as the King of Gordyene rode to converse with the rest of us. Some of the iron scales on his scale armour were missing and he looked like he had been in a hard fight. He raised his hand to Khosrou and myself.

'These Kushan fight well. It was a close-run thing for a while.' He nodded at Khosrou. 'Your men were the decisive factor.'

'All that remains is the destruction of that square,' said Khosrou.

Already companies were being deployed to block off the Kushan line of retreat, though our horsemen were careful not to stray within range of their bowmen. I was suddenly aware that I was dripping with sweat and looked into the leaden sky.

'It's going to rain.'

Like mad men we removed our bowstrings and stored them in leather pouches in our saddlebags. Thousands of men around us were doing the same as a few spits of rain hit us. There was an ominous rumble of thunder above and then the heavens opened. Visibility, before so excellent, suddenly dropped to less than a hundred paces as we were enveloped by a deluge. The unceasing downpour was a welcome relief as I removed my helmet, extended my arms, looked up and closed my eyes to receive blessed relief. I was lost in my own world as the rain increased in intensity and began to soak the ground. Soon a small lake began to form around me as the soil became waterlogged, unable to drain the rain that was falling on it. *Tegha* moved back and forth as he began to be unnerved by the cracks of thunder overhead and the occasional flash of lighting.

Movement was all but impossible and as the minutes passed I reflected on the possibility that the Kushan foot soldiers might use the rainfall to attempt to walk past our horsemen. But that would mean breaking up their formation and just as we were stranded in the rain, it would be no easy matter for thousands of foot soldiers to trudge through water and mud. And then the rain suddenly stopped.

Just as it had appeared seemingly out of nowhere, the clouds parted and the sun beat down on the sodden ground. It became very warm very quickly, around me men wiping their lacquer-covered bows with cloths and restringing them. We were all drenched, but in a matter of minutes steam began to rise from our clothes and horses. I stared ahead and smiled when I saw the Kushan square still in place.

'Time to end this,' I said.

We plodded across the waterlogged grass, letting our horses thread their own way through the drenched ground. It was an agonisingly slow process but after half an hour our forces had established an unbroken ring around the square. A thin ring admittedly but one the Kushans would have to break if they intended to withdraw back to the east. I wondered how Malik and his Agraci were faring, especially after the downpour. Pray Shamash they were safe.

I called Jagat forward. 'I think we should try to entice the Kushans to lay down their weapons,' I said to Khosrou and Spartacus.

'What's the use of that?' snapped Khosrou. 'We let them go and we will only have to kill them another day.'

'I am of the same opinion,' said Spartacus.

Khosrou gave me a rueful smile. 'I understand. You get them to surrender and then we kill them. Clever, Pacorus, very clever.'

'I never developed the taste for slaughtering unarmed men,' I told him, 'and I do not intend to acquire it today.'

Jagat appeared with his guardians, his thinning hair matted to his scalp. I pointed at the Kushan square.

'I wish you to accompany me to act as a translator. I intend to demand their surrender.'

'They will refuse,' he said defiantly.

I beckoned Katana over. 'They might, but until we ask them we will never know.'

I jumped down from *Tegha* and indicated my commander should do the same. I walked with him for a few feet and spoke softly to him. He showed surprise.

'Take three companies,' I told him. 'Take care, there might be isolated groups of enemy horsemen in the area.'

He saluted, remounted his horse and trotted away. I retook my saddle and waved forward Jagat and his guards, walking *Tegha* forward towards the Kushans.

'If they cut you down, we will avenge your death,' grinned Khosrou, those of his men nearby raising their weapons and cheering.

'Your words are always a comfort to me, lord king.'

'Are you not afraid?' Jagat asked me as we neared the locked shields of the Kushans.

My bow was in its case, my sword was in its scabbard and Jagat was obviously carrying no weapons. There was always a possibility that the enemy, enraged at the defeat of their horsemen, might take revenge on me, but I presented no threat and having been in a similar situation to the Kushans on a number of occasions, I had always been curious to hear what the enemy wanted.

'No,' I answered.

When we were around fifty paces from the square a voice called out to us. I halted *Tegha* and looked at Jagat.

'He says that is close enough.'

'Tell him I am King Pacorus of Dura and I am here to avoid further bloodshed.'

Jagat did as instructed and laughed when a reply came.

'He says that if you wish to avoid bloodshed then withdraw.'

'Whom am I addressing?'

Jagat relayed my query and a name was given to me.

'General Kaniska.'

'Tell the general that his horsemen have been beaten, that there is no escape and that he has a simple choice – concede defeat and march back to Indraprastha with his men, or die on this waterlogged ground.'

Jagat relayed my offer but the general was defiant, knowing that even without his horsemen he still, judging by the frontage of the sides of the square, outnumbered us. We returned to an unhappy Khosrou, eager to restart the battle.

'Have patience, lord,' I said, 'we will not have to use up any more arrows today.'

Khosrou's patience began to wear thin as we waited for the return of Katana and his men, all the time the heat rising as the midpoint of the day approached. And still the Kushan square remained immobile. Spartacus received a visit from his commander enquiring as to the delay.

'I was wondering that,' snapped Khosrou. 'Let's attack and get it done with.' He looked at me. 'And don't tell me to have patience. We are here to kill the enemy not wait until he dies of old age.'

The arrival, finally, of Katana put an end to his grumblings, though he was spitting blood when he saw my men marshalling a herd of cattle towards us.

'What in the name of the gods is this?' he bellowed in exasperation.

Katana rode over to me and saluted.

'Apologies for the delay, majesty, it took more time than anticipated to round up enough cows.'

'Cows!' exclaimed Khosrou.

'My lord,' I said to him, 'indulge me a little longer. You are in for a pleasant surprise.'

I mounted *Tegha* and accompanied Katana as his men herded the cows in a line towards the Kushan square, the words of Jagat ringing in my ears.

'This is sacrilege, King Pacorus, the gods will have their revenge.'

They might but this encounter needed to be brought to a speedy conclusion. So three hundred Duran horse archers approached the enemy, safe in the knowledge that the Kushans would not shoot at us. Ropes around the cows' necks kept the animals close to our horses as we halted around fifty paces from the locked shields of the western side of the square. There was absolute silence among the enemy but I could feel the eyes of the front-rank spearmen on me.

'Jagat, you will be my interpreter again.'

'I will not.'

'Ready,' I shouted.

Three hundred bows were raised.

'Loose!'

Three hundred arrows shot forward into the shield wall, my men aiming above the top rims of shields to strike faces. Hideous high-pitched screams came from the spearmen as arrows went into eye sockets, shattered teeth to exit the back of throats and broke cheekbones. Not all the wounds were fatal but they fragmented the shield wall as men collapsed to reveal those standing behind. My men could shoot up to twelve arrows a minute and every arrow, shot from the stationary position, was finding its mark.

'Stop,' I commanded.

To their credit the Kushans, unable to retaliate for fear of harming the cows, pulled back the dead and wounded and replaced them with fresh men to present an unbroken wall of locked shields once more. The silence had been replaced by moans and screams from those Kushans who had been wounded, the sound unsettling the cows.

'You can act as my interpreter or see more men die, Jagat,' I said, 'the decision rests entirely in your hands.'

He came forward on his horse. 'Very well.'

'Convey this message for me.

'General Kaniska, you and your men have fought valiantly but there is no need for further bloodshed. If you yield and your men lay down their weapons, then I, King Pacorus of Dura, pledge that their lives will be spared and they will be allowed to go where they will. Or we can stay here and fight each other until only one of us is left alive. You have five minutes to decide.'

Jagat conveyed my offer and less than a minute after he had finished the shield wall opened and a burly brute wearing a cuirass of overlapping steel discs appeared to confront me. He had a thick neck, close-cropped raven-black hair and carried a large sword in his right hand. He said something to Jagat in a deep voice.

'This is General Kaniska, lord.'

I jumped down from *Tegha* and tilted my head at the general, who looked at the line of my horse archers and their bovine companions. Kaniska looked me up and down and pointed at the cows, speaking in his native tongue to me.

'The general demands that you take the cows out of danger.'

'He will agree to my terms?'

Kaniska squared up to me and the archers nearby raised their bows to point the arrowheads at the thickset Kushan.

'Stand down,' I ordered.

This seemed to please the general who cracked the semblance of a smile. He said something else to Jagat.

'The general will agree to march from the field if the cows are released now.'

'I agree.'

'I would advise against that, majesty,' said Katana, 'there is no guarantee if we do so they will not use their bowmen against us.'

'That is a chance I am prepared to take. Take the cows away and do not harm any. And do not let any of Khosrou's men near them; they might try to eat them.'

Katana and his men, with the cows in tow, departed to leave me in the company of General Kaniska, Jagat and his two guards. It would have been easy for the general to order his men to surge forward and cut me down but what benefit would he have reaped? The death of a foreign king and the certain destruction of him and his men. Instead he ordered his men to stand down and begin stacking their shields and weapons.

'Queen Rana will not tolerate an invasion of her lands,' Kaniska informed me through Jagat.

'As we do not tolerate an invasion of Parthia,' I replied.

'Queen Rana is a dangerous enemy to make for she is the sister of the emperor himself. My advice, Parthian, is to flee back across the Indus while you still can.'

I thanked him for his advice and wished him and his men safe passage back to the queen's city.

There was still six hours of daylight left, enough to oversee the destruction of the Kushan shields, bows and spears. Officers were allowed to keep their swords but the rest of Kaniska's men would surrender their blades, which would be thrown into the nearest lake.

I sat on *Tegha* beside Khosrou and Spartacus as great plumes of smoke rose into the warm afternoon air from the bonfire of Kushan weapons. The enemy soldiers were tramping away disconsolately to the east, heads down and shoulders slumped. The great column of defeated and demoralised men must have numbered nearly twenty thousand, all vanquished by a herd of cattle. For that reason, it had been one of the most unusual battles I had fought in.

Khosrou was still unhappy. 'They will march back to Indraprastha where they will be re-equipped.'

Parties of Agraci were now returning to the battlefield, their horses blown and lathered in sweat, their riders similarly tired. A drawn but happy Malik came to our stand of banners and reported he and his men had chased the Kushan horsemen for miles.

'We had to stop when the heavens opened but the plain is littered with Kushan dead.'

'You have done well,' Khosrou complimented him. 'Pacorus got the enemy to surrender and now we have to watch them march away.'

'But without their weapons,' said Spartacus.

'Weapons can be replaced,' Khosrou informed him.

'It does not matter,' I told them all, 'Indraprastha is only a day's ride from here and I intend to reach it before General Kaniska and his army of weaponless soldiers.'

'To what end?' asked Khosrou.

'There is a great treasure there,' I said, 'one that will compel Kujula to leave Parthia.'

Chapter 10

That night both armies rested; our own jubilant, flushed with victory and having suffered light losses, the Kushans beaten, defenceless and cast down into the pit of despair. It was a surreal situation, a red glow coming from the campfires of the Kushan camp perhaps five miles away and another diminishing red glow nearer – the dying embers of the bonfires of enemy weapons and shields. The stacks of weapons had become funeral pyres as we cremated our dead – three hundred slain, a remarkably light figure compared to the losses suffered by the Kushan horsemen who were left to the lions and wild pigs who roamed the plain. We suffered around the same number of wounded, a few of whom would die of their wounds in the days to come but most carried only broken arms and cut limbs. All would have no option but to ride east with the rest of us. We could not spare the men to escort them back across the Indus.

Khosrou and many of his Margianans were roaring drunk, their king listening to Malik relay how he and his Agraci left a trail of Kushan dead for miles. Spartacus was also consuming large quantities of alcohol plundered from nearby villages. I drank none.

'Why so morose, uncle?' he asked, sitting himself beside me by the campfire, laughter and cheering all around. 'We have won a great victory.'

'We have won nothing,' I told him. 'The purpose of invading the Kushan Empire was to draw Kujula away from Sigal and Parthia. Our task is only half-completed. You should order your men to cease their drinking.'

He smiled like an idiot. 'Are you mad? Claudia told us that the enemy flounders before Sigal so our loved ones are safe. The gods are with us.'

He stood and raised the waterskin filled with drink. 'The gods are with us!'

Those within earshot, drunk and some barely able to stand, cheered wildly before many collapsed into slumber. I left them to carry out an inspection of the perimeter, which was guarded by sentries that were fortunately sober. The night was pleasantly warm, the sound of crickets drowning out the revelries of thousands of men in camp. Sullen guards, who had earlier drawn lots to decide who would lose out on the festivities, challenged me rudely when I approached them. I raised my arms and declared my identity, to receive a gruff reply. I was pleased they were in a bad mood. It meant they would not fall asleep but would rather reflect on their misfortune.

I kept an eye on the glow coming from the Kushan camp in the distance and wondered if General Kaniska was tempted to try a surprise night attack. He still commanded upwards of twenty thousand men and outnumbered us. The thought irritated me like a stone in my boot. I was now completely alone, having wondered beyond the perimeter. Clouds overhead meant it was pitch black beyond the light cast by a hundred campfires. As I did not want to step on a snake or twist my ankle in a hole in the ground I retraced my tracks.

'Wandering around in the dark, son of Hatra?'

I spun, drew my sword, stumbled and fell flat on my back.

I heard tut-tutting but could not see anyone.

'Anyone could come along and slit your throat. What would the chronicles say? The King of Dura met his end on some unnamed plain in India after a bout of drinking.'

I scrambled to my feet. 'I am not drunk.'

I focused my attention on the source of the voice and could barely make out a dark shape a few paces away. It looked like a wraith from the underworld and I should have been chilled to the core, but instead felt reassured as I recognised the voice of an old friend.

'Khosrou was always a fool but I suppose he serves a purpose.'

'He is a stalwart ally.'

There was a cackle. 'Stalwart? He's good at butchering nomads but lacks the intelligence to be anything more than a mediocre king. It is no coincidence that he rules a land of endless, empty steppe. It is much like his brain.'

'How are you?'

Another cackle. 'The same as the last time you asked me. You are still a hopeless romantic.'

I was desperate to ask about my family trapped in Sigal. 'I worry that I have done the wrong thing.'

'Crossing the Indus was a bold move, Kujula will take your bait.'

I was elated. 'Then Sigal is safe?'

This time a chuckle. 'If you want to know about Sigal, then ask.'

'Are my family safe?'

'How should I know? I am here, not there.'

'Have you come to torment me?'

A sigh. 'Have you so little faith in Claudia? She grows in knowledge and power, son of Hatra. But there is a price to pay for what she has achieved. There is always a price. Just remember that you are responsible for what has come to pass.'

'Me? Was I responsible for Kujula invading Parthia or the machinations of Phanes, which prompted the Kushans into believing they could absorb the eastern half of the empire?'

A second sigh. 'Have it your own way. You still intend to keep Phraates on Ctesiphon's throne?'

'I do.'

She laughed mockingly. 'You don't need me to torment you when you are perfectly capable of doing that yourself. Take care, son of Hatra, keep Spartacus on a short leash for his ambitions will set the empire aflame.'

And then she was gone. I would have given a fortune in gold just to spend a few more minutes in conversation with her but there was only the sound of crickets and the muffled revelries of men living life to the full. I felt alone and apart from my friends and the soldiers I commanded, an outsider looking in. In that moment, all I desired was to be back at Dura with my wife and family.

The new day dawned warm and sunny, men retching and vomiting after they had been awoken from their drunken slumbers. Khosrou looked as white as his hair as he railed against his subordinates before clutching at his head and bending over. I laid a hand on his back.

'Are you ill?'

He threw up on the grass and snatched a water bottle off one of his officers.

'Why aren't you hung over?' he asked me, rinsing out his mouth and splashing water on his face. 'I feel like death warmed up.'

'You look like it. We must be on the move soon.'

'Where?'

'The city of Indraprastha, lord.'

It was just as well that all our soldiers were mounted because there were many among them who were nursing thick heads and churning stomachs as we rode east, skirting shallow lakes and leaving the Kushans far behind. Jagat estimated the city to be fifty or sixty miles distant, which meant we would reach it in two days whereas General Kaniska's men would take at least four days to get there. In the afternoon we were buffeted by more monsoon rains that forced us to halt to give both men and horses a blessed respite. But by the end of the day we had covered forty miles and made camp by a wide, impressive river that Jagat told me was called the Yamuna.

Khosrou's mood changed from one of feeling sorry for himself as a result of over-indulging to a burning desire to inflict damage on the Kushans. So as we headed towards the city he organised columns to ride far and wide, looting and burning villages, killing anyone they came across and hunting wild animals. But he was no fool and made sure his scouts were also ranging far from the army, providing us with intelligence on an almost hourly basis. They told of a fertile land dotted with villages that were easy pickings for Khosrou's warriors, with no sign of any Kushan soldiers. Far from being pleased by this news Khosrou rounded on me as we cantered by the side of the Yamuna.

'We should have butchered those Kushans instead of letting them go. You made a mistake, Pacorus, for surely we will have to fight them again.'

'They have no weapons, lord,' I replied, 'and if I had not persuaded them to surrender we would have had to fight them, with no guarantee we would have triumphed.'

'I saw how the Kushans fought at Sigal,' said Malik, 'they are good soldiers.'

'What about this city we are heading for,' grumbled Khosrou, 'will that yield rich pickings?'

'It holds the sister of Emperor Kujula,' I told him, 'though she may have fled the city already.'

'She will not flee,' said Jagat behind me.

Khosrou glanced behind at the gaunt Indian. 'You have met this woman?'

'No, lord, I only know her by reputation.'

'The army she sent has been destroyed,' said Spartacus, 'which leads me to believe the garrison of the city will be small or non-existent. If she has any sense she will flee before we arrive.'

But she did not flee. When we arrived at Indraprastha we found a sprawling city by the side of the Yamuna, with high walls and rectangular-shaped towers at regular intervals along their entire length. Around the walls was a mixture of wooden and sun-dried clay-brick homes that were very vulnerable to attack. Khosrou, who commanded the largest contingent of our army, immediately ordered his men to fan out and throw a cordon around the city. Our approach was greeted with panic as commoners fled to the sanctuary of the city, a great column of humanity swarming around the city gates. I led my horse archers into the suburbs, the Margianans having already fired the huts, grey smoke rising into the sky and adding to the overall panic of the Kushans. I issued orders there should be no unnecessary killing and so we moved slowly, encountering only wild dogs for opposition.

We halted and waited for the civilians to get inside the walled city, archers on the ramparts shooting a few arrows at us that fell short and hit some unfortunates at the rear of the civilian press. Katana estimated there to be less than fifty archers on the walls either side of the city gates, though there were other entrances to the city and those were also guarded. Eventually, the gates were closed when the civilians were all inside and silence descended on the suburbs.

'What now, majesty?' asked Katana.

It was a good question. Perhaps we could have rushed the gates to force our way into the city, but that would have meant hacking our way through unarmed civilians. But if we had done so before we reached the gates they would have been closed. So the gates to the city were slammed in our faces anyway and we settled down to lay siege to Indraprastha. While the horse archers requisitioned homes and yards for stables and quarters, I walked with Malik and Spartacus to get a closer look at the city walls. There were buildings directly below the ramparts, which could in theory be used to support scaling ladders, but the walls were around forty feet high and men on ladders making such an ascent would be very vulnerable. Spartacus must have been reading my thoughts.

'Archers on the walls will be able to pick off our men with ease making such a climb.'

'And not just archers,' added Malik. 'Anyone with a rock to hand could knock a man off a ladder. You still wish to capture this queen, Pacorus?'

'We came here to inflict damage on the Kushans, which we have done. But to place the sister of Kujula in danger will surely turn his gaze back towards his homeland.'

'How will he know?' asked Malik. 'It is a great distance from here to Sigal.'

'Jagat has told me the Kushans make use of courier pigeons and use them to send messages throughout their empire on a daily basis. The birds can cover up to seven hundred miles a day so I have no doubt Kujula knows we are here.'

'Perhaps he does not care about his sister,' suggested Spartacus.

I looked up at the impressive, well-dressed walls. 'He cares.'

After walking around the outside of the walls for an hour or so, the odd arrow shot in our direction falling harmlessly short, we made our way back to the city gates where a delegation was waiting for us.

His name was Tusha and I later discovered it meant 'cold'. It was entirely appropriate because he was aloof and totally oblivious to the fact he was at our mercy. Slim, dripping with gold and accompanied only by a frightened young male slave, he exuded arrogance, authority and royalty. Katana informed me that he and the slave had walked from the city gates with his hands clasped in front of his body. The Duran guards had been so surprised and intrigued by him they let him approach unmolested, whereupon he spoke to them in perfect Parthian, declaring he had been sent by Queen Rana to negotiate an honourable surrender. Khosrou was quickly summoned but he and Tusha had to wait until we arrived back from our travels before negotiations began.

We washed our faces and changed our tunics before Tusha was brought into our makeshift headquarters, which was actually a simple square home built of mud-bricks with a reed roof. Light flooded in through two open windows either side of the hide sheet acting as a door. We sat on stools and faced the Kushan as he introduced himself.

'I am Tusha, governor of the city and Queen Rana's chief adviser.'

'You have balls,' said Khosrou in admiration, 'you're lucky Pacorus' boys didn't put a few arrows in you.'

One of Tusha's bushy black eyebrows rose. 'Pacorus? You are King Pacorus of Dura?'

'I am,' I answered, 'allow me to introduce my fellow rulers.'

I acquainted the governor with Khosrou, Spartacus and Malik, the Kushan rising from his stool to bow after I had uttered each name. He was most perfunctory in his etiquette, much to the amusement of Khosrou who cut straight to the chase.

'What terms is your queen offering?'

'Perhaps we might have some refreshments first,' I suggested, 'though we can offer only what we have acquired.'

'You mean plundered,' smiled Tusha.

'Just like your emperor is plundering Parthia,' said Spartacus.

The governor changed the subject as one of my men served wine that had been 'requisitioned' from a nearby inn. It tasted bitter but to his credit Tusha did not wince as he politely sipped it.

'The queen would like you to withdraw your men from the suburbs so the population can return to their homes.'

'I bet she would,' said Khosrou.

Tusha smiled politely. 'In return, the queen will offer you gold if you pledge not to attack the city, withdraw from the suburbs prior to retreating back to Parthia.'

'How much gold?' asked Khosrou.

I put down my cup of wine. It really was dreadful.

'We came to the Kushan lands not for gold,' I said, 'but to get your emperor to withdraw from Parthia. Your queen must pledge to send courier pigeons to him to demand his immediate withdrawal from all Parthian lands.'

'Otherwise we will burn her city,' threatened Spartacus.

'My queen wishes to extend an invitation to you all to visit her in her palace,' said Tusha, 'where I am certain your conditions can be met.'

Khosrou screwed up his face as he tasted the wine. 'So we can all have our throats slit? No thank you.'

'The queen will guarantee your safety,' insisted Tusha.

Khosrou roared with laughter. 'I will stick with Spartacus' option. Talk is cheap, governor, and I have no desire to see my head decorating your queen's walls.'

'My sentiments exactly,' said Malik.

'Perhaps the queen would be prepared to accept certain conditions that would guarantee our safety,' I suggested.

'What did you have in mind, majesty?' asked Tusha.

'Our men will take possession of one of the entrances to the city, in addition to lining the route from the gates to the palace, but will remain outside the palace walls. I assume it has walls?'

He nodded to me but his face registered concern. 'What is to stop your army entering via the gates you control and sacking the city?'

'Nothing,' gloated Spartacus.

I frowned at my nephew. 'The army will withdraw from the suburbs, as an act of goodwill.'

'That's our best offer,' said Khosrou.

'I will convey it to the queen, majesties,' smiled Tusha.

To encourage the spirit of goodwill I persuaded Khosrou to order his men not to burn any more buildings, a command conveyed to the army's other contingents. But our men still occupied the suburbs and as night fell I saw few torches on the city walls, indicating that the garrison was small. We had to assume General Kaniska was still heading for Indraprastha, though he and his men would not arrive for three days.

'I will take my men and ambush them,' said Khosrou as we sat in our headquarters eating a tasty meal of chicken kebabs, rice and samosas.

'That would leave me with four thousand men,' I replied.

'The Kushans don't know that,' remarked Malik.

'I could take my men instead,' offered Spartacus, 'how much resistance can a column of unarmed, beaten men offer?'

'None,' I said, 'which is why we are not going to butcher the general's men.'

Scouts were despatched to the west, however, to keep watch on the general's men and report back on their progress. Having little knowledge of the towns and cities of the Kushan Empire, we all assumed they would be heading for Indraprastha, though they might have already diverted for another destination. Uppermost in my mind was the situation at Sigal, which I assumed was still under siege. Claudia's message brought temporary relief but that had been days ago. We needed to bring matters to a close here as speedily as possible, which Queen Rana was also eager to do because the next day a message arrived from Governor Tusha that she had agreed to our terms.

I rode in the company of Khosrou, Spartacus and Malik with two companies of Durans, who took possession of the gatehouse and the walls on either side for a length of a hundred paces, while two more companies of Khosrou's soldiers, including Kuban, accompanied us through the city to the palace. Behind us fluttered our banners, an escort of Kushan heavy horsemen in scale armour and carrying long lances flying pennants showing a cobra motif formed a vanguard and rear-guard. I brought Jagat along in case the queen did not speak our language, the old Kushan looking around in admiration at the city he had visited only a few times previously.

As soon as we entered the well-maintained roads I was aware that, like at Dura, there was a regular network of streets running from east to west and north to south, intersecting each other to form blocks of buildings. Jagat next to me informed us that each block was divided into two areas: one containing dwelling houses, the other shops. The latter were usually built in a row along each street and were rectangular in shape with a small room at the rear.

'You can purchase anything in this city,' he told me gleefully, 'fabrics, perfumes, silver and gold jewellery, herbs, meats and fish.'

As we rode from the gates through the city we saw no markets and streets that were empty, whether as a result of a royal edict or because people had locked themselves in their homes we did not know. But the clean streets and well-maintained buildings pointed to a prosperous city. The palace itself was surrounded by a mud-brick wall faced with white plaster and accessed by two red-painted gates that led to a place of peace, water gardens, gazebos on small islands and exotic birds. Tusha met us at the gates, dressed as usual in his white flowing gown and accompanied by similarly attired officials who I learned were the chief magistrates of the city. They were all polite and accommodating as our horses were taken from us and we were escorted to the palace itself.

It too was constructed of sun-dried clay-bricks that had been painted white, which gave the building a brilliant appearance in the sunlight. The portico had white marble columns and white marble tiles, as did the corridor that led to a throne room filled with sculptures, carvings and paintings of Indian myths. I stopped at one particularly striking painting, which showed a fierce half-human, half-horse creature armed with a round shield and curved sword, doing battle with a beautiful woman who had eight arms and was riding a lion.

'That is a representation of the Goddess Durga fighting Mahisha, the fierce demon buffalo,' said a female voice, 'note what the goddess is holding in her hands.'

I turned away from the painting to see a delicate, beautiful woman sitting on a white-painted thrown wearing a white silk sari, her hair a lustrous black. Striking pearl earrings complimented the silver necklace from which hung diamonds.

'Her majesty Queen Rana,' announced Tusha.

We walked to the dais and as one bowed to the slim young woman with an oval-shaped face, slightly rounded chin and full lips. She dazzled us with a smile.

'We welcome you to Indraprastha.'

She was tiny, childlike, and my first sentiment on seeing her was shame. Shame that we were threatening such a frail young woman, combined with anger directed against Kujula that he had exposed his sister to danger. Her brown eyes settled on me.

'Welcome King Pacorus, whose fame and exploits crossed the Indus long before your famed Durans.'

She dazzled Spartacus with a smile. 'Welcome to you, King Spartacus, husband of Queen Rasha of the Agraci, brother to the fearsome King Malik who now stands in my throne room.'

Malik smiled at her and bowed to her once more. Rana next addressed Khosrou.

'Welcome King Khosrou of Margiana, a man whose courage and fortitude have brought peace to Parthia's northern border for many years. How fortunate is High King Phraates to have such a warlord by his side.'

She stood and spread her arms, her diminutive frame made even smaller by the chamber's high ceilings.

'And here you all are, having defeated the army of General Kaniska, one of the Kushan Empire's most talented commanders. I thank you all for your restraint in not putting my city to the sword.'

She clapped her hands. Two stocky slaves struggled to carry a wooden chest from the side of the hall to place it in front of the dais, putting it down with a thud. Tusha waved them away and walked over to the container, opening the lid to reveal a horde of gold coins. Khosrou's eyes lit up.

'In gratitude for preserving my city, allow me to make a small gift by way of thanks.'

'You are most generous, majesty,' I said, 'but in truth we do not desire your gold but...'

'But my brother to quit the siege of Sigal and return home. Yes, Governor Tusha has acquainted me regarding the objective of your campaign,' she told me, returning to sit on her throne. 'To which end I have already despatched a courier pigeon pleading with him to withdraw from the walls of King Salar's city.'

I was impressed. She was obviously well informed when it came to the death of Peroz and the accession of Salar, which led me to believe that she and her brother were in regular contact.

'That is all we desire,' I said.

279

'But we will keep the gold,' added Khosrou.

'Who won the battle between the goddess and the demon?' I asked, desiring to change the subject.

The queen once more left her throne, jumped down from the dais and linked her arm in mine, gently ushering me towards the painting. Malik, Khosrou and Spartacus followed, two burly guards armed with wicked curved swords shadowing their queen. We all halted in front of the painting.

'It took the goddess ten days of fighting to slay the demon, eventually piercing his chest with a trident,' said Rana.

'Why does she have eight arms?' asked Malik.

'So she can hold the things that govern the lives of mortal men.' She pointed to each instrument in turn. 'The chakra in her upper right hand symbolises righteousness, indicating that we must perform our duties in life. In her upper left hand is a conch, which symbolises happiness and shows us we must perform our responsibilities cheerfully. The sword in her second lower right hand symbolises the eradication of vice. The bow and arrow in her second left lower hand symbolises character as Lord Rama, showing us that whatever difficulties we face in life we should never lose our values. In her third lower left hand is a lotus flower, informing us that we must live in the world but not become tainted by its wickedness. The club in her third right lower hand symbolises devotion and surrender, that whatever we do in life we should do with love and devotion. The trident in her fourth left lower hand symbolises courage, which means we must have the fortitude to eliminate evil qualities inside us. Finally, you will see that her fourth lower right hand is empty, which symbolises forgiveness and the goddess' blessings.'

Khosrou was bored but I found it fascinating. 'It is an impressive image, as are all inside this chamber.'

'They were painted by some of India's finest artists, lord,' she beamed, 'it would be a tragedy if the world lost such works of art.'

'It would,' I agreed.

The queen invited us to take refreshments in her private gazebo, which was sited on a small lake to the rear of the palace. She was like a small child in her desire to please the rough-hewn Parthians and single Agraci who had invaded her kingdom. She instructed the ever-present Tusha to convey the chest of gold to our camp and assured us she had sent instructions to General Kaniska that he was to disband his army and send the men back to their villages, a goodwill gesture that we all appreciated.

Slaves served us wine, fruit juice, pastries and fruit as we reclined on plush couches and were fanned by other slaves who stood with heads bowed. I noticed all the slaves performed their duties with their heads cast down to avoid any eye contact. Swans swam gracefully on the water, skirting water lilies, and pond herons perched on branches overhanging the water. It was an extremely pleasant setting and the conviviality of the queen made us forget we were her enemies.

The next day Rana took us to the keeper of the royal couriers, the title of the individual who cared for the pigeons that took messages to the far corners of the Kushan Empire and beyond. A fastidious man, he fussed over his birds and took a dim view of any who encroached upon his domain. He had a few slaves that he treated abysmally, beating them with a small whip for the slightest transgression. But he loved his birds, having a name for each one and conversing with them as though they were human. They were treated, fed and housed better than most of the slaves in the palace, a fact that the keeper emphasised to us as he entered the royal coop to retrieve one of his precious charges. His name was Fani, which means 'snake', though he looked more like an overweight cat with his facial hair and pointed ears.

'This is Canda,' he cooed, gently holding one of the pigeons that looked just like the others, 'and like her name she is fierce and passionate.'

I looked at Khosrou who rolled his eyes but Spartacus smiled as the bird pecked at Fani's hand.

'There, there,' he said softly, 'you are in the presence of royalty and should act accordingly.'

Queen Rana handed me a small piece of papyrus, upon which were the words:

Make haste back to Indraprastha, I am in danger, Rana

They were written in Greek, which Rana assured me Kujula spoke fluently. I showed it to Spartacus who nodded and passed it back to the queen. There was no point in showing Khosrou or Malik as neither had knowledge of the Greek language.

'Normally I would write to my brother in our own language,' said Rana, 'but out of courtesy it is in Greek so you can see there is no subterfuge.'

She looked at me pitifully with her brown eyes and my heart went out to her. She was so small and delicate I wished I had left my sword in camp to show her I offered no ill intent.

Spartacus iterated our collective thoughts. 'We wish you only good fortune, lady.'

'You are all very kind,' she sighed.

Fani rolled up the papyrus and slid it into a tiny metal tube attached to the pigeon's leg. The queen nodded at him and he took the bird outside the aviary into the royal gardens. We followed and watched as he released the bird that flew into the air, circled the palace twice and headed west.

'At least it's going in the right direction,' said Khosrou.

Fani gave a disapproving grunt.

'How far can a pigeon fly in a day?' asked Spartacus.

'It is not unknown for them to cover seven hundred miles in a day,' replied Fani with pride. 'Though Canda will only fly to the staging post on the western side of the Indus, from where another will be sent to the emperor.'

He had inadvertently revealed the Kushans had already established messaging posts in Parthian territory. This indicated to me that Kujula had long planned his invasion and was determined to consolidate and expand the territorial gains he had already made.

Rana then took us all by surprise. 'My brother raised his siege of Sigal two days ago.'

We all looked at each other. If true, then our mission had succeeded. Khosrou sounded a note of caution.

'Words are cheap, lady. I do not wish to be rude but we need to see proof.'

'I would not expect anything else,' said Rana, frowning at Fani who bowed and withdrew from the royal presence.

Rana reached into a small silk pouch that she had been carrying and pulled out a crumpled piece of papyrus. She handed it to me and I saw it was written in the Kushan language, a mixture of

Greek and Bactrian. I focused on the words and eventually managed to decipher them: 'have left Sigal and heading north, Kujula.'

'Why did you keep this from us?' demanded Malik.

The guards behind the queen moved menacingly towards us but Rana held up a hand to halt them.

'I did not know your intentions, lord. You had defeated my army and arrived outside my city with your own army. If you knew two days ago that my brother had abandoned his siege, you might have put this city to the sword. I did not know then you were men of honour. I hope you can forgive me.'

'There is nothing to forgive,' I said, 'our argument is with your brother, not you.'

The scrap of papyrus seemed genuine and it was difficult not to believe the queen. What would she benefit by lying? It was obvious she had few soldiers to oppose us and if we so desired we could slay her on the spot, not that I would countenance such an atrocious act. I was inclined to give Rana the benefit of the doubt, which meant we could depart Indraprastha and return to Parthia. But as soon as we did so Kujula, alerted by his sister, might turn back and recommence his siege. Therefore, it looked as though we would be guests of Queen Rana for a while longer.

Rana herself was more than accommodating, ordering that all the gates into the city were to be kept open and allowing our soldiers to man the western entrance at all times. She sent carts filled with food to our camp and organised hunts for our senior officers. But despite this the men, confined to camp, chafed at the bit to be away from the city and return to Parthia, either that or be allowed to raid and plunder the rich land they found themselves in.

Two days after our first meeting, after taking refreshments with the queen, we returned to the palace stables to retrieve our horses, the adjacent barracks largely empty as a result of General Kaniska emptying the city of most of its soldiers. But there was still a small army of male and female slaves to sweep the courtyard in front of the stables, muck out the stalls, fill the hay and water troughs and rub down the horses. There was also a forge where sweating, bare-chested slaves worked metal in a furnace and on anvils.

'Where's *Tegha*?' I demanded as the horses of the others were brought from the stables.

The head slave bowed his head. 'Apologies, highness, one of the farriers noticed that one of your horse's shoes was loose and is having it fixed.'

Khosrou was in the saddle. 'Everything all right, Pacorus?'

'My horse has a loose shoe,' I told him, 'I'll see you back in camp.'

The six Duran horse archers of my escort were waiting by their mounts so I did not fear for my life. Khosrou and the others also had their own escorts.

'We'll wait for you, uncle,' said Spartacus.

'There is no need,' I told him, 'you go ahead.'

The other kings raised their hands and trotted from the courtyard.

'Here he is, highness.'

The slave was smiling at me as a tall, clean-shaven man wearing a sleeveless white *kurta* led *Tegha* towards me.

'Hurry,' snapped his supervisor.

The man increased his pace, bowed and handed me the reins. The supervisor struck him with the bamboo cane he was carrying.

285

'On your knees, dog.'

The man fell to his knees and elbows to offer himself as a mounting block.

'It's fine,' I insisted, 'I can gain a saddle without assistance.'

The supervisor went to strike the slave again but I seized his cane.

'You may go.'

I released the cane, he bowed and withdrew. The slave rose to his feet and pointed to *Tegha*'s right rear foot.

'The shoe was loose on that foot, majesty.'

I took a couple of steps, straddled *Tegha*'s leg and lifted it to look at the shoe. I nodded in approval.

'Excellent work.'

The slave moved closer and looked around to ensure no one but me could hear.

'Do not trust the queen, majesty, you are all in danger.'

It was an incredible thing to say, not because it was true or false. But for a slave to speak about his mistress was a death sentence. I could have drawn my sword and slain him on the spot and no one would have batted an eyelid. I could have killed him anyway if I had a mind to. What was a slave but a commodity? Though Queen Rana would have had a right to demand compensation for the loss of her property. Instead I looked at him.

'Why would you say such a thing?'

'My name is Titus Rutilus, majesty, formerly a horseman serving under Publius Licinius Crassus. I was captured at Carrhae and have been a slave ever since, first in Parthia before being sold to the Kushans.'

I was taken aback and stunned. After all these years I had no idea those taken at Carrhae were still enslaved, or even alive. I heard Dobbai's mocking laughter.

'What a fool you are, son of Hatra, what did you think would happen to those you took at your greatest victory?'

Rutilus said nothing more, dropping his head as I hoisted myself into the saddle.

'I will send for you, Titus Rutilus, and we will speak some more.'

I sent a note to the queen's palace that I required the services of the farrier who had attended my own horse with such efficiency. Rutilus appeared that afternoon with a rope around his neck, his hands bounds, led by a soldier of the queen's guard. I waited until the guard had ridden out of sight before cutting the bonds around his wrist and tossing aside the rope the soldier had passed to me. After being given water and a stool to sit on, Rutilus expanded on his knowledge of the queen's affairs as the other kings, whom I had informed of my meeting with a Roman slave, listened.

'Emperor Kujula has abandoned the siege of Sigal.'

'We were told this earlier,' said Khosrou, annoyed that he had been recalled from a tiger hunt to listen to a low-born slave.

'The queen told us herself,' added Spartacus.

'But did you know that he left Sigal over three weeks ago,' said Rutilus, 'before you had even crossed the Indus?'

We did not.

'How do you know this?' I asked.

'Palaces are places of gossip, majesty, and Fani is a notorious gossip. As well as being a pompous fool he is a boaster and regales his slaves with stories of the feats of his pigeons. Even before your army had crossed the Indus the emperor was on his way back to his homeland.'

'Why?' queried Malik.

Rutilus looked at me. 'To defeat and capture the king who provided the inspiration for his army and its tactics – King Pacorus of Dura.'

'I hardly think so,' I said.

'The emperor has studied your military methods closely, majesty, which is why I ended up here. He learned I had fought at Carrhae and ordered me to dictate to his scribes everything I remembered about the battle.'

'You are a legend, Pacorus,' laughed Khosrou. 'Let's go and kill that duplicitous bitch Rana.'

'I would advise you to quit your camp and ride west to the Indus immediately,' said Rutilus.

'We are not slaves,' sneered Khosrou, 'we still have our balls and are not afraid of any woman.'

'We have scouts keeping watch all the way to the river,' said Spartacus.

'But do you know that an army is currently marching from Mathura, majesty, the capital of the Kushan Empire,' replied Rutilus, 'a mere hundred miles to the east?'

'Impossible,' snapped Khosrou.

But why would the Roman lie? We could send him back to the palace with news of his gossip, which would result in his death. He risked much, too much for it all to be false.

'What do you want?' I asked.

'To be allowed to ride back with you to Parthia,' came the answer, 'and then on to Rome.'

'Many years have passed since you were last there,' I told him.

A luck of utter desolation appeared on his face. 'It is my home, majesty.'

It was a heartfelt plea and whereas Khosrou and Malik thought him a pathetic creature they had not been slaves and knew nothing of the things that kept those in chains able to endure the unendurable. I did.

'I will make this bargain with you, Titus Rutilus. If what you say is the truth, then I will provide you with a horse and safe passage through Parthia so you can return home. But now you must return to the palace.'

He marched back to the city with his head held high, two of my horse archers accompanying him, a rope around his neck, though I had given orders he was not to be abused during the journey. Meanwhile, we sent parties of scouts east to search for an army supposedly on its way to Indraprastha.

They found it, a long column of elephants, foot soldiers and carts though few horsemen, which meant its speed of march was slow. But when they returned on sweating horses the scouts informed us it was a mere twenty miles from Queen Rana's city. The queen herself was all charm and hospitality, inviting us to a banquet to be held two days hence. The intention was clear: while we were being feasted our camp would be surrounded and attacked. Either that or the Kushan army would enter the city to secure it and there wait for Kujula to arrive. Either way we would be either captives or dead men.

It was time to leave Indraprastha.

Chapter 11

Nearly twelve thousand Parthians, two thousand Agraci and one Roman rode west back towards the Indus after we had accepted the invitation to Queen Rana's feast. Khosrou was like a bear with a sore head, Malik wanted to send his best assassin to slit the queen's throat and Spartacus told us that Rana reminded him of Rasha, which blackened Khosrou's mood further.

'At least the monsoon rains have stopped,' I offered by way of lightening the mood.

'I blame you for this, Pacorus,' said Khosrou, who then mimicked a whining female voice. 'You have nothing to fear from us, lady, let me lick your arse, lady.'

Malik and Spartacus were grinning fit to bust.

'Very droll,' I remarked. 'I take it you won't be returning your share of the gold the queen gave us?'

'What?' roared Khosrou, making his horse rear its head in alarm. 'Don't be a fool.'

He shot a glance at Titus Rutilus riding behind me. 'What are you so happy about?'

Rutilus stopped smiling and cast his head down. 'Nothing, highness, forgive me.'

'Leave him alone,' I said. 'If it wasn't for him we would all be preparing for the feast where we would all have been murdered, no doubt.'

Khosrou mumbled something under his breath and I reassured Rutilus.

'You are no longer a slave but a free man once more. I will assist you getting back to Rome but you may find it much changed after all these years.'

'I expect so, majesty,' he admitted, 'but I live in hope that I still have family left.'

'What family?' probed Spartacus.

'I had a wife and two small children, though they will be adults by now.'

'Your wife might have remarried,' said Khosrou harshly.

'She might,' admitted Rutilus. 'I would not blame her for doing so.'

To familiarise him with recent events I told him about the division in the Roman world between Mark Antony and Queen Cleopatra in the east and the followers of Octavian in the west, of Mark Antony's invasion of Parthia and his defeat at our hands.

'That was caused by a bitch of a queen,' said Khosrou, 'and like your queen she never got her hands dirty. How come Queen Rana has no husband?'

'She had a husband, majesty,' said Rutilus, 'a wealthy noble from the south, but the queen found his presence at Indraprastha too constricting. He wanted her to be subservient and Queen Rana is like a young cobra, fierce and independent.'

'What happened to him?' asked Malik.

'He was found dead in his bed one morning,' Rutilus told us, 'with not a mark on his body. He had gone to sleep and simply not woken up.'

Khosrou chuckled. 'Poison, then?'

'That was the rumour, majesty,' said Rutilus. 'Since then no more suitors have come forward for the queen's hand.'

'I can imagine,' remarked Khosrou dryly.

Despite the complaining of the King of Margiana the army was in high spirits. It had been saved a costly siege, it had been well fed and now it was returning home. It was common knowledge that a Kushan army was pursuing it from the east, but that force was mostly foot soldiers and elephants and our horsemen could easily outrun them. The weather was warm and sunny, there was an abundance of water and forage and no enemy barred our way.

Until we neared the Indus.

Our horsemen ranged far and wide to provide a screen on all sides of the army and also shoot game that was in abundance. Mostly parties returned with carcasses of gazelle, wild pigs and antelopes, though occasionally they brought back slain aurochs – huge cattle as tall as a man that provided enough meat to feast half a company. The rains had gone but the plain was still covered with lush grass that fed the horses and numerous small lakes and streams that provided drinking water for man and beast. We moved fast, covering up to fifty miles a day to put distance between us and the Kushans advancing from the east, but had given no thought to our passage back to Parthia being contested. But on the third day an advance party of Khosrou's men encountered a group of Kushan horsemen and, following a brisk skirmish in which his riders drove off the enemy, returned to report there were now Kushans to the west.

The initial alarm gave way to the conviction they were probably the remnants of General Kaniska's army that Malik's men had failed to eradicate. Interrogations of the scouts revealed that two parties of Kushans had been encountered, one numbering around a score, the other less than ten men. None of the hunting parties had noted the presence of enemy riders so we dismissed the idea of a large force of enemy soldiers anywhere near us.

On the third day, I diverted from the march to lead two companies of Duran horse archers to a village that had remained unmolested during our advance to Indraprastha. I took Jagat with me because it was his village we were returning to. We rode into the settlement to see villagers running for their lives, women grabbing children and wailing when they saw dozens of horsemen approaching their homes. Jagat called to them to remain calm and not flee, jumping down from his horse to announce his return. Gradually calm returned to the village, though men and women still hastened to their homes rather than stay and listen to the discourse between Jagat and the horseman with a scarred cheek.

I untied a leather pouch from one of the front horns of my saddle and tossed it to him. It contained gold coins, part of the treasure gifted to us by Queen Rana.

'For your services.'

He caught the pouch, opened it and his eyes lit up.

'I would advise you to use it to get out of the Kushan Empire. Your queen may not forgive you for acting as my translator.'

'I am old, King Pacorus. What use would killing me serve?'

'Tyrants rarely think rationally, Jagat.'

He looked around at faces peering out from doorways.

'Thank you for not burning my village. I know others among you were eager to visit death and destruction upon us.'

I turned *Tegha* . 'Shamash be with you, Jagat.'

I returned to the army to find it halted and looks of concern on the faces of the other kings.

'We have problems,' Khosrou told me, 'our scouts have encountered parties of Kushan horsemen to the north and south.'

'How far away?' I asked.

'Around thirty miles.'

'One of our parties came across a column of foot soldiers to the north, heading in our direction,' added Khosrou.

'We must assume it is the same to the south,' said Malik.

'It would appear that the Kushans have withdrawn their armies from Parthia, uncle,' said Spartacus.

'That is something, at least,' I admitted.

'We need to get across the river as quickly as possible,' urged Khosrou, 'before we are trapped by enemies marching from the north and south.'

'Not forgetting the foot soldiers following us,' added Malik.

We recommenced our journey, setting a hard pace to hopefully put as much distance between us and the Kushans approaching from the north and south as possible. I was comforted that those forces appeared to contain foot soldiers, which would reduce the distance they could cover each day. So, we rode west across a flat landscape littered with the residue of villages we had torched during our arrival in Kushan lands, their charred remains deserted apart from the odd scavenging vulture.

We covered thirty miles that day and by the late afternoon were confident we would be camping by the side of the Indus before nightfall. Scouts sent north and south returned to report seeing no enemy soldiers, either mounted or on foot, leading us to believe that we had outrun them. No Kushans had been spotted to the rear of the army at any time, and as we slid off the backs of our horses to take a well-earned break we congratulated ourselves that we had achieved what we had come to do. We had drawn Kujula away from Sigal and indeed Parthia, and it appeared that the forces that had occupied Drangiana and Aria had also been recalled, though that was mere conjecture. I walked over to Khosrou who had removed his helmet and was wiping his sweating face with a cloth.

'It will be good to reach the foothills of the mountains and breath some cool air; this humid atmosphere is no good for my chest.'

I laughed. 'Indeed, lord. I just wanted to personally congratulate you for thinking up this little enterprise. It has achieved more than I could have hoped for. May I suggest that when we return I lobby for you to be appointed lord high general of the empire?'

He spat on the ground. 'You can lobby all you want but the day I become Phraates' official arse licker is the day I slit my own wrists.'

I roared with laughter and slapped him on the back. 'You are ever the diplomat, lord.'

Then I spotted them, a small group of riders galloping towards us. They were some of Khosrou's men armed with long spears and wearing their distinctive leather armour and riding their hardy ponies. I don't know why their appearance unnerved me so but I could not take my eyes off them as they slowed and pulled up their mounts in front of Khosrou. The old king turned and accepted the salute of Kuban who removed his helmet and handed the reins of his horse to a subordinate. Malik and Spartacus had wandered over to hear what Khosrou's second-in-command had to say. Even before he did so a feeling of dread enveloped me.

'I have just returned from the river, lord, where a great army is camped along the western bank. A Kushan army.'

'How many?' asked Khosrou.

'Thousands,' answered Kuban.

'How many soldiers do these Kushans have?' exclaimed Spartacus in exasperation.

'It must be Kujula's army,' I said.

Khosrou screwed up his face in anger. 'That Roman slave was right. We should have killed that bastard pigeon keeper and all his birds.'

It was a cry of futile rage, a feeling that possessed us all as we realised we were like an animal herded towards a trap by an army of beaters, in our case three armies: one to the north, one to the south and one behind us.

'What is your plan, Pacorus?' asked Malik.

He and the others looked at me, expecting me to spirit up a masterstroke out of nowhere. I was, after all, the victor of Surkh, Susa, Carrhae and Phraaspa whose army had never been defeated in battle. I burst out laughing. What did it all matter now? We were outnumbered, far from home and in real danger of being trapped. How I wish Claudia was with us to conjure up a sandstorm to mask our escape across the Indus. First of all, though, I needed to see the army camped on the other side of the Indus.

'I desire to see the Kushan army myself before I can make any plan,' I told everyone.

'Good idea,' agreed Khosrou.

'I'm coming,' said Spartacus.

Malik nodded. 'Me too.'

We waited until our horses were rested before saddling them and riding them towards the river, a score of my horse archers acting as an escort. No one said anything as we traversed the lush green plain, a herd of water buffalo looking up as we passed them by the edge of a small lake. After an hour, we came across the Indus and halted. At this point the waterway was perhaps five hundred paces wide, the water blue and slow moving. We walked to the water's edge and I noticed that the level had dropped by two or three feet, which would make a crossing easier. The current also seemed to have eased.

We stood and studied the opposite bank, smoke from a hundred campfires or more weaving its way into the early evening air. There was no wind and an ominous stillness had descended. I felt a trickle of sweat run down my cheek. The Kushan camp extended north and south for a considerable distance. I could make out elephants at the water's edge and horses, beside them individuals resembling ants scurrying around.

'They have posted no guards on this side of the river,' observed Spartacus.

'They have no need,' I said, 'Kujula knows we have to cross the river here if we want to avoid fighting those of his soldiers that are on this side of the river. He also knows we won't be engaging those forces.'

Khosrou was surprised. 'We won't?'

'To do so would mean remaining on this side of the river,' I said, 'and we need to get across tomorrow. We cannot attempt to find a crossing place further up or downstream because that would mean coming into contact with either of the armies bearing down on us from the north and south. We cannot withdraw back to the east because another army is approaching from that direction.'

'Caught like rats in a trap,' fumed Khosrou.

'There must be a way out,' said Spartacus.

I pointed across the river. 'There is.'

Khosrou guffawed. 'Straight through them? I like it.'

'Our losses will be heavy, Pacorus,' cautioned Malik.

'They might be, my friend, but they will be heavier if we stay here.'

I looked at each of them. 'Just one man's opinion. If any of you has a better plan, I will gladly step aside.'

'What time do we attack?' asked Spartacus.

'Just before dawn,' I answered.

No campfires were lit that night to keep our location a secret from the enemy, men sitting with their friends near their horses and chatting about home and family as they cleaned their swords, checked their bows and ate fresh fruit plundered from abandoned farms. The night was clear with a full moon illuminating the landscape, though the temperature had not dropped significantly. I walked among the Durans with Katana and found them in good humour. They had full bellies and I had distributed Dura's part of the small fortune given to us by Queen Rana among them. This 'campaign bonus' had raised their morale considerably, though whether they would be able to spend their gold remained to be seen.

'What are our tactics tomorrow, majesty?' enquired Katana.

'Simple enough. Your men will be deployed behind the Agraci who will use their spears to break the enemy line, assisted by the arrows of your men. The other contingents will adopt the same tactics.'

He said nothing as we passed a squad of Durans guarding their company's horses. They stood to attention and he raised his hand in recognition. We walked on and still he said nothing.

'Speak freely, Katana, I would like to hear your opinion.'

298

'Moving though water, with no cover and under enemy arrows will mean high casualties. And there is no guarantee we will break the enemy, not without cataphracts.'

'You are right,' I admitted, 'but our options are very limited. We cannot stay on this side of the river.'

'It would be better to let the Kushans cross the river, majesty, so we can make use of our mobility.'

'I agree, Katana, but Kujula has no intention of moving. He knows we are the ones who must move, though I am hopeful that he will not expect us to assault his force. The element of surprise may yet give us a chance, albeit a small one admittedly.'

Katana was unhappy but resigned to crossing the river in a few hours to battle a much larger Kushan force. But if he had reservations Titus Rutilus was a man without a care in the world. I found him practising his sword strokes with a spare *spatha*, swinging it with abandon and stopping to admire the smooth blade and wooden handle. Though their role was not close-quarters combat, every Duran horse archer was equipped with a *spatha* and dagger and received training in swordsmanship. He stopped when he saw me and bowed his head.

'Please carry on, Titus.'

'I never thought I would handle one of these again, majesty.'

'If you wish you could ride out of camp this evening, rather than take your chances with us tomorrow. It looks as though we will face daunting odds. You are, after all, free to go where you will.'

He swung his sword in the night air. 'Then I am free to stay, majesty, which is what I choose to do.'

We quit camp an hour before dawn, beforehand watering, feeding and saddling the horses and grabbing a few mouthfuls of fruit and rice and then riding towards the Indus. We moved slowly, nearly fourteen thousand horsemen trotting across the grassy plain, wild animals scattering before us as the companies deployed from column into line.

Malik's men, who had no discipline and whose idea of warfare involved bellowing war cries and charging headlong at the enemy, were placed in front of my Duran horse archers, who would shoot over their heads to provide missile support. Ideally, I would have placed groups of horse archers among the front ranks of the Agraci, but such tactics relied upon high levels of training and discipline, qualities quite alien to the average Agraci warrior. I had begged Malik to impress upon his men the importance of silence during our approach and he had ordered his warlords to restrain their warriors. But I knew when his men saw the whites of the enemy's eyes they would not be able to ignore their instincts.

In the centre were Khosrou's ten thousand soldiers, divided into two lines, each one containing five thousand-man blocks. On the left were the twelve hundred horsemen of Gordyene, also arrayed in two lines. Out battle line had a length of two miles, moving slowly across the plain toward the Indus, which was around four feet at its deepest point.

Dawn breaks quickly in northern India and as the first rays of the sun peeked above the eastern horizon behind us my heart sank when I saw those rays reflecting off thousands of spear points – the enemy was waiting for us.

How the Kushans discovered we were coming I did not know, only that we were now faced not with charging through an enemy camp but breaking Kujula's battle line. There was no turning back; the only way was forward. True to form the Agraci increased their pace, breaking into a canter that we had no choice but to follow. As we neared the river the Margianans on our right also increased their speed, splashing into the water to enter the Indus beside us. I nocked an arrow in my bowstring as *Tegha* pushed his way through the gently flowing river. The Agraci were now hurling abuse at the enemy, raising their spears as they called the Kushans 'sons of whores', 'eunuchs', 'boy lovers' and 'women', all designed to rile the enemy and totally wasted as the Kushans did not understand what was being shouted at them.

I looked anxiously into the brightening sky, expecting it to be filled with arrows shot from the Kushan longbowmen. But instead the enemy sent his horse archers into the river to disrupt our attack that had already been slowed by having to wade through the water. The first I realised what was happening was when riders among the Agraci in front of us began to fall into the water, their horses shrieking and collapsing into the river as arrows hit them. Our response was immediate: loosing arrows over the heads of the Agraci. One, two, three, four and more. Volley after volley to strike unarmoured riders. I glanced right and saw the air filled with missiles as the Margianans copied our tactics. Through gaps in the Agraci line I could see Kushan horse archers tumbling from saddles into the water. I heard shrill horn calls and saw enemy riders turning their horses. No arrows were now coming from the Kushans in the water as they fell back to the right wing of Kujula's army.

'On, on.'

I heard Agraci warlords screaming at their men to move forward, having been halted by the horse archer attack. I glanced at Katana beside me who shook his head in frustration. He knew as well as I did that we were still in the water and had yet to reach the main enemy battle line, which we had to break through if we were to reach safety. We could not outflank the enemy because their unbroken line of spearmen extended beyond the end of our own left flank, and I assumed it was the same on Spartacus' flank. So we had to try to hack our way through their centre.

It was futile.

As arrows arched high into the sky to fall among us, shot by the longbowmen behind the ranks of Kushan spearmen, the Agraci tried to spear and slash their way through the enemy spearmen on the gently sloping riverbank. But the spears of the enemy were long and it was all but impossible for men on horseback to even reach the men who held them. Black-clad Agraci milled around at the line of unbroken Kushan shields, those armed with spears trying to stab at the faces of the soldiers in the front rank. But behind the shield wall were skirmishers who hurled javelins with deadly accuracy to spear Malik's men. My horse archers tried to lend a hand but it was difficult to shoot through the fleeting gaps that appeared among the Agraci and even harder to hit enemy soldiers crouched behind long, narrow shields that protected just about the whole of their bodies. We were forced to bunch up with the Agraci to escape the Kushan arrows falling into the water behind us.

Like sheep we had been herded against the impenetrable barrier of the Kushan shield wall, which was being assaulted with gusto by the Agraci, to no effect. The Durans and I were now at the water's edge, the shield wall entrenched fifty paces back from the river. We were now stationary and trying to shoot at the enemy when gaps appeared. We had abandoned trying to shoot holes in the shield wall and instead launched arrows over the spearmen to hopefully strike those standing behind them.

'They've stopped shooting arrows.'

Katana, ever alert, was looking into the sky, which was suddenly empty.

'I thank the gods for that at least.'

But the gods regarded bloodshed with relish and if they were at work it was entirely for their own amusement. Above the sound of men grunting, horses whinnying and the clatter of weapons clashing was heard the sound of horns coming from the left. They were sounding a charge, that much I knew, and craned my neck to peer towards our flank. Where suddenly hundreds of men on horseback appeared.

Cobra banners fluttered among them, the same motif decorating the rawhide stretched over their wicker shields. They were light horsemen wearing no armour and only a turban for headgear. But they carried javelins as well as swords and within minutes they were hurling their missiles to strike unarmoured horse archers.

'Wheel left, wheel left,' shouted Katana, the signaller next to him blowing his trumpet frantically to convey his commander's wishes to those out of earshot. I pulled back my bowstring and released it to shoot a Kushan readying his javelin to launch. I forgot about the Kushan shield wall and the Agraci to focus my efforts on the hundreds of light horsemen that were enveloping our flank, throwing javelins and drawing their swords as they closed on Duran horse archers. For a few minutes, the air was thick with javelins and arrows in a frantic exchange of missiles but then the Kushans were among us, hacking and thrusting with their swords. I slid my bow back into its case and drew my own sword when a rider closed on me, his shield tucked tight to his body. He slashed at me with a diagonal cut but I shouted at *Tegha* to retreat and he backed away, the

303

blade missing my torso. The Kushan came forward on his horse and thrust his sword forward towards my chest. I ducked to the right but the sword point bit into the top of my cuirass. I hacked down with my *spatha* to knock his sword away from my body and whipped it back to draw the side of the blade across his face, slicing deep into his nose.

It was not a mortal wound but serious enough for him to drop his sword and shield to clutch his face and withdraw, only for another Kushan on my right to attack me with an overhead downward sword strike. I managed to parry it with my *spatha* but out of the corner of my eye I saw a leering Kushan on my left raise his sword to deliver a strike that I could neither avoid or parry. Sounds disappeared and time slowed in my helplessness, to be rescued by a sword being driven into the Kushan's armpit. He collapsed from his saddle and I was free to concentrate on the enemy on my right, our swords locked above our heads. I drew my dagger from its sheath with my left hand and stabbed it repeatedly into the Kushan's unprotected belly, turning his tunic red. He winced in pain, dropped his sword and flopped forward in the saddle. I chopped my *spatha* down on the back of his neck to sever his spinal cord and saw his lifeless body move away on the back of his horse.

Titus Rutilus had saved my life with his timely intervention and I raised my *spatha* to him in salute. But nothing could save my men or the Agraci who were being slowly forced back by the Kushan light horsemen, whose attack had emptied many saddles. We were losing the battle and I heard a new sound that seemed to herald our defeat, a mad trumpeting, but not one made by any human.

They came crashing through the Kushan light horsemen, maddened by the arrows stuck in them. It was fortunate that we did not see them up close because a rampaging elephant is a formidable creature. I counted twenty in all though there may have been more, but they had a devastating effect on the Kushan light horsemen they trampled through, scattering them like dust to the wind and saving our hides. Those Kushans in our midst heard the elephants too and saw their comrades swept aside, horses rearing up to throw their riders onto the riverbank where they were crushed underfoot by elephants.

The spectacle was awe inspiring and grisly, but more importantly gave the Agraci and my horse archers a blessed respite, as well as denting the morale of the Kushan horsemen. I sheathed my sword, pulled my bow from its case, strung an arrow and shot the nearest Kushan rider in the belly. My Durans needed no instructions as their training took over and they began shooting in all directions, each arrow finding a target to cause the Kushans to withdraw. The Agraci, having abandoned their attempts to hack through the Kushan shield wall, withdrew from the fray. The last of the rampaging elephants splashed into the river, the wooden boxes on their backs filled with dead men. But who had killed them?

'I see a white horse's head,' shouted Katana in excitement.

I looked around at the companies of horse archers reforming now the Kushan horsemen had melted away, searching for a horse with a white head.

'It is Hatra's banner,' Katana exclaimed.

I turned my gaze to where he was pointing, beyond the end of the still immobile Kushan spearmen, to see a wondrous sight – horse archers riding from the south, among them the banner of Hatra and behind them the four-pointed star of Elymais – Silaces! They must have been the ones who had scattered the Kushan elephants and in the process shattered the enemy's right flank. We had been shown our escape route. I turned to Katana.

'Get word to Malik that he and his men should ride around the Kushan centre and link up with the Hatrans and Silaces' men. Send riders to Khosrou informing him to disengage and follow the Agraci.

I looked up into the sky, expecting to see arrows shot by Kushan longbowmen falling among us, but mercifully all I could see were puffy white clouds and blue. It could mean only one thing: the horse archers of Gafarn and Silaces must be assaulting the rear of the enemy's centre.

It took an age for Khosrou's men to desist their attacks on the enemy shield wall and withdraw back into the river where they could then wade south before riding to where our friends and allies were forming a battle line. The riverbanks and water were choked with dead and injured horses, dead bodies and wounded men trying to reach dry land. I thanked Shamash the enemy foot archers were occupied because otherwise we would have had to conduct our manoeuvre under volleys of arrows. As it was the horsemen of Dura, Margiana and Gordyene had a blessed respite from the bloodshed as they directed their tired mounts to safety.

Khosrou still lived but hundreds of his men had been killed and hundreds more wounded.

Spartacus had fared better, partly because he only had twelve hundred men to command, which made controlling them easier. As soon as the Kushan light horsemen attacked he turned his companies ninety degrees to face north, from where in the water they could shoot at the enemy riders. I wish I had thought of that, but had I done so I would have condemned the Agraci to even higher losses.

My nephew, unharmed but devoid of arrows, was beaming as he came to my side and spotted the banner of his father.

'My brother will give this Kujula some Parthian steel,' he grinned, urging his horse ahead. 'The gods are with us, uncle.'

I looked at the dead in the water and the corpses of horses, saw the waterway streaked with blood and knew the gods were indeed here, though only to enjoy the spectacle. Where before there had been thousands of men battling each other, there were now only the dead and wounded as the Kushan spearmen about-faced to move away from the Indus to form a square to protect their longbowmen. I nudged *Tegha* forward to follow the companies of Durans that were heading for the stand of banners to the south of Kujula's army.

It was a happy reunion, Khosrou roaring with triumph as he greeted Salar, Silaces and Gafarn, his tired men on their blown horses forming into their companies to the rear of the kings. I slid off *Tegha* and threw my arms around Gallia, the Amazons raising their bows in salute as man and wife were reunited.

'Our daughters are safe?' I asked.

'Safe and well.'

'And Sigal, Nergal, what about Marcus and Alcaeus?'

She put two fingers to my lips. 'All are well, Pacorus, I thank the gods you are unharmed.'

I cupped her face and kissed her lovingly on the lips.

'There's still a battle to fight,' said Silaces gruffly, rolling his eyes at the sight of Rasha and Spartacus locking lips.

I released Gallia who took her helmet from Zenobia and mounted her horse. I gained *Tegha*'s saddle and the irritable King of Elymais provided an update on the overall situation. I shook the hands of Gafarn and Salar as the kings and queens gathered around Silaces.

'As soon as the Kushans quit the siege of Sigal we made sure the city was safe and then followed our friend Kujula as he retraced his steps. Your man Talib and his scouts kept in contact with them, which meant we could maintain a safe distance just in case the bastard retraced his steps and ambushed us.'

'And did he?' asked Malik.

'No, he was in a hurry so we had a pleasant march through the mountains. Kujula did pick up reinforcements as he neared the Indus, though,' Silaces informed me.

'The forces that invaded Aria and Drangiana,' I said.

'It would appear so,' nodded Gafarn.

'We have drawn the poison from the empire,' I said in triumph.

'Not quite,' reported Silaces.

A cursory examination of the ground lying to the immediate west of the Indus revealed the Kushans to be a large force of horsemen and foot soldiers, the latter now manoeuvring to form a giant square as a defence against the thousands of Hatran and Elymais horse archers that had attacked the rear of Kujula's army, to devastating effect.

'Seems like you have them penned in nicely,' said Khosrou, taking a swig from a water skin. He handed it to me. I had a raging thirst and grabbed it eagerly.

'Except for the thousands of enemy horsemen mustering on the other side of that square,' reported Silaces.

I took a great gulp and realised it was wine. I choked on the bitter liquid.

'A belly full of wine greases the limbs for battle,' grinned Khosrou.

'Wine?' I blurted. 'It tastes like vinegar.'

Prince Pacorus rode up, all gleaming armour and white plumes in his helmet. He saw me and saluted.

'It is good to see you, uncle, I'm sure Lord Azad will be pleased to know you have returned safely to Parthia.'

'Where is Azad?'

'With the rest of our cataphracts,' Gallia told me, 'about to destroy the enemy horsemen so we can annihilate the Kushan square.'

Salar yanked his reins to turn his horse to the right.

'I will lead the charge to rid the empire of these foreign invaders.'

'Get me a fresh horse,' shouted Spartacus to anyone listening.

'Where are you going?' I said.

'To lead my lancers,' he told me, 'I assume they are here.'

'They are,' confirmed Rasha proudly, 'along with my Vipers.'

'Time is of the essence, my lord,' said Prince Pacorus to Salar.

I was tempted to join them but the old wound in my leg had flared up alarmingly and *Tegha* was blown, along with those of Katana and his horse archers, those who were still alive. Khosrou must have read my thoughts.

'Let the young bucks seal the victory, Pacorus, we have done our bit. Unless they foul it up, of course, then we'll have to clean up the mess. Have some more wine.'

He passed me his waterskin and I took a measured swig. To our front the horse archers were withdrawing, revealing an unbroken square and in the distance a long line of horsemen. Behind us the

309

horse archers of Hatra and Elymais were refreshing their ammunition from the camel train carrying spare arrows. A lull had descended over the battlefield as both sides drew breath following our failed attempt to break the Kushan line and the arrival of Silaces' army. He had been elected commander of the different contingents on account of him having the largest number of troops. But now all eyes were focused on the coming clash between the rival horsemen. It was ideal terrain for mounted warfare – flat and treeless.

'Your man Kewab is organising our heavy horsemen,' Gafarn told me, 'let's hope he is as good as everyone believes him to be.'

I smiled then winced as a pain shot through my leg. 'He is the best.'

Gafarn was surprised. 'Even better than you, three times lord high general of the empire?'

'That was not a reward or recognition for anything, more a punishment.'

'I'm sure High King Phraates would be hurt to hear you say such things,' Gafarn looked around. 'Where is our young protégé anyway?'

Gallia grinned but Silaces did not see the humour in our words.

'The little brat should be here, defending his empire, not enjoying the company of whores at Ctesiphon.'

Gafarn was going to goad him further but I shook my head.

'Where is Kalet?' I asked, fearing the worst.

'Salar asked him if he and his men would like to raid Carmania,' Gafarn told me, 'he was more than happy to oblige.'

'Salar was worried that in our absence,' said Gallia, 'Phanes might be tempted to attack his kingdom once more. So, he sent Kalet to keep him amused.'

'That is hardly going to encourage peace,' I lamented.

'You know what peace is, Pacorus?' said Khosrou. 'The interval between wars.'

A mass blast of trumpets brought our conversation to an end and all eyes turned to the two lines of horsemen advancing towards each other. From our position, we could see the Kushan square next to the riverbank and on the left the hind quarters of Parthian horses walking forward, lances and *kontus* shafts held vertically by their riders.

Fifteen hundred cataphracts trotted forward, comprising Hatra's Royal Bodyguard and a thousand Durans commanded by Kewab and Azad. They were arrayed in two ranks, as were the fifteen hundred of Salar's lancers on their right commanded by their king, and the same number of Saka lancers led by Shapur, who I was delighted to learn had been a thorn in the Kushans' side during their abortive siege of Sigal. I was also pleased he had left his elephants in Sakastan. I later learned that Kewab had placed Spartacus' five hundred medium horsemen on the left of the line, which meant the Parthian line had a frontage of nearly a mile.

The earth began to shake as five thousand riders broke into a canter and then a gallop to charge the Kushans.

'Break the bastards,' shouted Khosrou, as a horrible scraping sound reached our ears, signalling that the two sides had collided. *Kontus* points skewered Kushan riders to inflict hundreds of casualties on Kujula's horsemen, but the emperor had many more riders and soon a furious mêlée was raging in which Kushan numerical superiority at first began to tell. But the element that tipped the scales back in our favour was a thousand ukku blades. Every Duran cataphract carried a sword forged from the mysterious metal from southern India that I had purchased for a king's ransom many years before. Now those blades with swirling patterns along their blackened length repaid their enormous price as they cut through Kushan swords, armour and helmets.

All we could see was a maelstrom of horsemen and all we could hear was a mad clattering noise that resembled an army of rabid woodpeckers at work. We sat in silence, praying to the gods to grant our soldiers victory.

'Get the men ready,' barked Silaces to a subordinate, 'we may have to cover their retreat.'

'Bring the companies forward,' Gafarn ordered his commander of horse archers.

The spectre of defeat was etched on their faces and the longer the mêlée in front of us went on the more I became fearful.

'We will lend our support,' I told Katana, who saluted and rode back to where my horse archers were restocking their quivers.

As the mêlée continued we grew ever anxious. Hundreds of horse archers began to form in their companies, all in column formation, ready to ride forward to shoot volleys at the enemy horsemen should they prove victorious and put our own riders to flight. But we had foolishly underestimated the fighting abilities of our cataphracts, who slowly but surely and despite being outnumbered, began to cut down the enemy horsemen with their swords, maces and axes. The mad chopping sound suddenly stopped and we looked at each other. Gallia grinned at me and I grinned back.

We did not know what precisely was happening but we could see that our horsemen were getting smaller, meaning they were advancing.

'Get your men forward and rake that square with arrows,' Silaces commanded his subordinate.

'I will be joining them, Silaces,' said Gafarn, turning his horse and raising an arm to my wife and me.

'Amazons,' called Gallia, 'follow me.'

I wanted to stop her but knew it was futile. Rasha was already organising her Vipers to join the force that would number nearly twelve thousand horse archers. My own, Spartacus' and Khosrou's horse archers were riding animals that had had a hard morning already and would therefore be retained as a reserve. I doubted it would be needed – the enemy's horsemen had been put to flight and were being pursued, the Kushan foot soldiers were immobile in their square, and the enemy had lost a large number of their foot archers. All that remained was for the square to be showered by thousands of arrows to seal our victory.

And then it all changed.

'What in the name of the gods?'

I heard Silaces' voice and saw three columns of horsemen riding towards us at speed. They appeared from the other side of the Kushan square, presumably held in reserve by Kujula. They galloped towards us until they were perhaps five hundred paces away before halting and deploying into a long line, placing themselves between the square and us. From the latter came the sounds of drums and horns.

'They're retreating back across the river,' I said.

Silaces clenched his fist. 'We will see about that.'

He and Gafarn launched their horse archers, who ran into an arrow storm that decapitated the heads of the company columns that rode forward to battle their Kushan counterparts. So they changed tactics to send companies around the flanks of the Kushans, who extended their line to compensate. The Kushans were well trained but they were greatly outnumbered and soon their line was ragged as they tried in vain to maintain a screen to mask the retreat of the Kushan square, which was now entering the Indus. Parties of horse archers galloped towards the Kushan line, wheeling right and right again to withdraw from the enemy as the Kushans shot arrows at our riders. The arrows fell short and other companies approached the Kushan line to draw their arrows. The enemy line began to assume the shape of a vast curve as Kujula's men did their utmost to protect the thousands of foot soldiers who were now wading across the Indus. Kujula was sacrificing his horse archers to save the bulk of his army.

I turned to Khosrou, who was emptying his waterskin.

'Time to get our feet wet again, lord.'

While Gallia, Rasha, Silaces and Gafarn were whittling down the enemy's horse archers, a task that demanded patience, courage and a great quantity of arrows, Khosrou and I led our tired horsemen back into the corpse-choked river to shoot at the thousands of Kushan foot soldiers who were making for the eastern bank. It was a surreal experience, the water gently lapping around our horses as we rode them against the mild current until we were around three hundred paces from the enemy mass. Then we proceeded to halt our horses and shoot arrows at the foe, aiming high into the sky so our arrows would fall among the Kushans. Those of the enemy who had shields hoisted them above their heads but our arrows fell like rain during a thunderstorm, my Durans and Khosrou's warriors shooting up to twelve arrows a minute at the Kushans. The latter's cohesion and discipline collapsed as they began a mad rush towards the riverbank, falling head first into the water in a desperate effort to avoid the arrow storm. Those who fell were trampled underfoot by those following and drowned instead of being struck by arrows. Others, hit by more than one arrow, floated downstream towards us, their lifeless bodies bumping into horses that reared up in alarm or thrashed around in the water in a state of panic, throwing their riders.

The dozens of corpses that began to float towards us, the vast majority being Kushan skirmishers who wore no armour or headgear, measured our success. Hundreds of abandoned wicker shields also drifted by, along with the long bamboo bows that had caused us so much strife at Sigal.

In the space of perhaps a quarter of an hour the eight thousand horse archers in the water had loosed nearly a quarter of a million arrows, killing or wounding perhaps ten thousand Kushans, though there was no way of estimating the enemy dead accurately because the current took the majority of corpses downstream.

When our quivers were empty Khosrou directed his horse through the blood-laced water to where I sat on *Tegha* .

'We should ride to the eastern bank and finished them, Pacorus. My boys have their lances and your men are equipped with swords.'

Across the river, thousands of Kushans, grateful to have survived the battle and the river crossing, were collapsing on dry ground. They were exhausted but so were we. I saw fresh banners to the north – Kushan reinforcements. I pointed to them.

'The Kushans who were approaching from the north when we on the other side of the river have arrived, my lord. I fear our part in the battle is finally over.'

315

He grunted in recognition and looked around at the bodies still passing by.

'Still, not a bad day's work.'

We withdrew from the water at the same time as the remnants of the Kushan horse archers forded the Indus to join their comrades on the opposite bank. Both sides were but two hundred paces apart but passed each other without violence, Kushan and Parthian quivers being empty. We rejoined the other kings and thankfully found both Gallia and Rasha safe and unhurt. We slid off our horses and removed our helmets, our hair wet with sweat and matted to our skulls. It was now very warm and all we desired was water. The liquid in our water bottles was tepid and tasteless but at least it was wet. My leg was now painful to walk on and as a result I limped.

'Are you hurt?' asked Gallia in alarm, examining my legs for any injuries.

'It's just my old wound, which is reminding me I am too old to play at being a warrior.'

She cupped my face and kissed my lips. 'You will always be my warrior.'

'Horsemen approaching,' called Malik.

It was the return of Salar, Spartacus and Prince Pacorus, all flushed with victory and every one of them battered and exhausted. They too, along with their men, slid off their horses, removed their helmets and nearly collapsed as hours of exertions and tension finally caught up with them. Squires came forward to remove the scale armour from their near-expiring masters and the horses they rode. Thousands of horsemen filled their lungs with air with their scale armour littering the ground around them. Across the river a similar spectacle was unfolding I had no doubt, though the Kushans had the luxury of reinforcements to call upon.

For this reason, I made myself a figure of hate as I urged Azad and his men to regain their saddles in case the enemy re-crossed the river to take advantage of our debilitated state. Gafarn did the same and soon hundreds of cataphracts were back in the saddle, in various states of armour, though their horses were spared having to wear their scale armour suits.

Khosrou's men dismounted to form a screen along the riverbank, ready to form a wall of spears should the enemy launch an attack. The squires were sent back to the camp Silaces and the others had established – some ten miles away – to assist the civilian camp followers in taking down the tents and bringing them forward to the river. That night I was determined to stay awake but I slept like the dead in Gallia's arms, waking with limbs that were painful to move after the exertions of the day before. Guards had been posted through the night and patrols were sent out just after dawn to discover the whereabouts of the enemy. They returned with news that the Kushans were in the same place, though now significantly reinforced.

'How many men can we muster?' asked Khosrou, remarkably sprightly considering his participation in the battle.

Kewab had already compiled a roll call of the army's various contingents and now presented his findings to the gathering of kings and queens who sat in Silaces' vast circular pavilion.

'We suffered nearly three and a half thousand dead and two thousand wounded,' my commander reported.

'We should cremate our dead,' I said.

'With what?' asked Silaces. 'There is a distinct lack of trees in these parts.'

'If the enemy crosses the river, there will be more men to burn,' said Malik grimly.

'We must send word asking for reinforcements,' suggested Salar, 'we cannot allow the Kushans to cross the Indus again.'

I nodded. 'Agreed.'

A guard entered and walked to Kewab, whispering into the Egyptian's ear. My commander passed on the message.

'A courier has arrived from Kujula, majesty, requesting that you meet with him forthwith.'

'Perhaps he wants to surrender,' joked Khosrou.

'Or have you murdered,' said Spartacus.

I discounted the notion. 'If he had wanted me dead he could have stood idly by at Salar's wedding.'

'You are going to meet him?' asked Gallia.

I stood. 'Yes, at the very least while we are talking his army is not crossing the Indus.'

'In the event of your demise,' smiled Gafarn, 'do you want your ashes returned to Dura or scattered here?'

'Very droll,' was my only comment.

It was a beautiful autumn day, the sky filled with white clouds and a gentle easterly breeze ruffling my griffin standard and that of Kujula's cobra banner on the opposite side of the river. I rode with Kewab and Azad to where a party of Kushan heavy horsemen waited with a guard of Duran horse archers on our side of the river.

'The emperor invites you to have a late breakfast with him, majesty,' said the Kushan commander in Greek.

'I accept his kind offer.'

Once more *Tegha* waded into the Indus, now mercifully free of the ghastly flotsam that had been choking it yesterday. The water was clear, slow moving and cool. I wondered where the final resting place of the corpses of the slain would be. Perhaps the current would take them all the way to the ocean, to be eaten by fishes. More likely they would be food for crocodiles. I shuddered at the thought.

The two banners flew side by side as Kujula and I enjoyed a meal of pancakes cooked on a fire nearby and served with orange juice and yoghurt. We sat on cushioned wicker chairs under a white silk sunshade. Kewab and Azad were also being served food and drink. It was like a meeting of old friends as Kujula complimented my commanders on their conduct the previous day.

'It gladdens my heart to see you well, King Pacorus.'

The warm pancake I was eating melted on the tongue.

'It does?'

'Of course, my sister informs me you were charm itself during your brief stay at Indraprastha.'

It thought of Queen Rana's duplicity. 'I trust she is well.'

'She is.'

Kujula handed the silver plate back to a slave, another coming forward with a bowl of water for him to wash his hands, a third proffering a towel when he had done so.

'You have defeated my invasion, King Pacorus, my congratulations.'

'I share the victory with my fellow kings,' I corrected him.

He waved a dismissive hand. 'Who? Silaces, a man promoted above his talents? Salar, who has barely reached manhood? I will concede that in Prince Pacorus your brother has a rare talent, but

King Spartacus is too rash, Khosrou is too old and Malik. Well, Malik is an Agraci who has no place in Phraates' empire.'

Azad was devouring a pancake but Kewab was listening intently to this foreign emperor who knew much about Parthia and its rulers, too much.

'And yet here we are,' I said.

Kujula flashed a smile to reveal his pure white teeth.

'Here we are. I have ordered wood to be sent to the place of battle and would esteem it a great favour if you allowed us to cremate our dead, King Pacorus.'

'If you promise not to invade Parthia I will gladly agree.'

He laughed. 'The Kushan Empire is growing, King Pacorus, and like all growing things needs space to fulfil its potential.'

'But not at the expense of Parthia,' I stated firmly.

'I tell you what. I will agree to a two-year cessation of hostilities,' he said, 'in return for which your high king will agree to meet me to discuss the frontier between our two empires.'

'He will not yield an inch of ground,' I told him.

'We will see, my friend, we will see.'

Kujula was as good as his word regarding the wood, which arrived all through that day and the next, hauled to the Indus on carts. I had Kujula's pavilion dismantled and returned to its rightful owner, who sent me a beautiful curved dagger with an ivory handle and a cobra pommel encrusted with small diamonds to represent the creature's eyes. Satisfied the Kushans would not attack us, I convinced the other kings to allow parties of their slaves and labourers to cross the river to retrieve the bodies of those Indians who had fallen in battle. They also transported wood across the Indus to allow us to cremate our own dead.

The ghastly task of collecting the dead, stripping their bodies of weapons and armour and consigning them to funeral pyres took a whole day. In the evening fires raged on both sides of the Indus and the night air was filled with the nauseous smell of burning bodies. Any triumphant feelings were banished by the smell and awful sight, things that I had seen many times but had never grown accustomed to. Out of respect we stayed until every corpse had been reduced to ashes, standing in silence to pay our respects to the dead. The Kushans did the same and when the dawn broke to herald a new day both banks of the Indus were once again filled with soldiers facing each other.

'What now?' said Gallia, staring at the Kushan host a few hundred paces away.

'Now we go home.'

She looked at me. 'You trust this Kujula?'

'I do.'

She pointed at the thousands of men lining the opposite riverbank.

'He now greatly outnumbers us and could easily launch an attack.'

'He could,' I agreed, 'but he won't. He gave me his word he would not cross the Indus for two years.'

She laughed. 'Dobbai was right about you being a hopeless romantic. I was thinking about her last night, about how she shaped our lives and those of our daughters.'

'She still does.'

'Mmm?'

I turned away from the Kushans. 'Nothing. It is time to leave this place of dead flesh.'

Khosrou and Silaces were most reluctant to depart. They had sat in silence when I told them about Kujula's two-year truce and now they scoffed at the idea of the Kushan honouring it.

'As soon as we are gone he will cross the Indus once more,' insisted Khosrou. 'I've met his kind before.'

I doubted that. 'If he wanted to do so, his soldiers could already have been on this side of the Indus. I believe he is a man of honour.'

Silaces rolled his eyes. 'He saved your life, we understand that. He likes you, we all like you, Pacorus, but his admiration for you will not deter him from expanding his empire.'

'Silaces is right, uncle,' chipped in Spartacus.

They had joined Gallia and me as the dragons and companies were dismissed after our night-time vigil and sent back to camp, the pungent odour of burnt human flesh tickling the backs of our throats and infusing our clothes. It really was dreadful and I wished to be away. The Kushans had the same idea because their numbers on the opposite bank soon thinned to nothing.

'You see,' I announced in triumph, 'Kujula is as good as his word.'

'It would be good to get some fresh air in our lungs,' agreed Malik.

'Have it your own way, Pacorus,' said Khosrou grudgingly, 'but this is not the end of things, mark my words.'

'I agree.'

He was surprised. 'You do?'

'Of course, but the empire needs to organise a proper response to the Kushan threat. Perhaps a meeting of the council of kings.'

Khosrou and Silaces groaned.

'A better proposition would be creating you lord high general, Pacorus,' said Silaces.

'I second the motion,' stated Khosrou.

'As do I,' added Salar.

'Hatra also supports the election of Pacorus to be lord high general for the fourth time,' grinned Gafarn. 'It must be a record.'

I was far from amused. 'There is no way on this earth that I will be assuming high command again. Three times is more than enough. Any of you are more than qualified for the position.'

'No chance,' snapped Silaces.

'I would rather eat my own liver,' said Khosrou.

'Being manservant to Queen Aliyeh would be preferable to being Phraates' lapdog,' stated Gafarn.

We all stared at Spartacus, who looked like a cornered boar.

'I'm married to an Agraci,' he babbled.

I looked at Rasha. 'I don't think that will save you. Rasha is after all high in Phraates' esteem since she gifted him the two Roman eagles taken at Lake Urmia.'

'No!' shouted Spartacus. 'I will not be bullied into this.'

Laughing, I looked at Salar who was also grinning.

'But we are overlooking the obvious candidate, a man who has not only withstood the Kushan storm but defeated it. A man who forged an alliance that threw Kujula back across the Indus with his tail between his legs.'

Salar looked around, searching for the individual I was talking about.

'He's referring to you, Salar,' said Gafarn.

The young king was shocked. 'I am honoured, but…'

'But nothing,' roared Khosrou, 'It is an excellent idea.'

'I agree,' said Silaces.

'My brother will object strongly,' said Salar.

'He has lost all credibility,' Gafarn told him, 'Phraates may be many things but he is no fool and knows that defeat is infectious. I think you will find the high king has already washed his hands of Phanes.'

'No great loss,' sneered Khosrou.

We stayed in camp a further day, by which time Kujula and his Kushans had long gone. We in turn packed up our tents and departed, making our way west towards the mountain passes that would take us back to Sigal. On the way, we said a fond farewell to Khosrou and his redoubtable commander Kuban, the old fox trying to lure Gallia back to Merv with the promise that he would make her queen of the northern steppes. She embraced him warmly, kissed him on the cheek and reminded him he already had a queen. His repost was he was still young and desired more heirs so they could squabble and fight to win the right to win his crown when he was dead. I watched his doughty warriors on their hardy ponies follow their king and thanked Shamash that Parthia could call on the services of such men.

We were in high spirits during the journey back to Sigal but arrived to find a city wrapped in grief.

Chapter 12

An official delegation, which included Isabella, greeted Salar and the rest of us two miles from the city, my daughter mounted on an elephant draped in a vivid red cloth, its tusks covered with gold. It looked ridiculous but was at least docile and did not spook our horses. My oldest daughter looked pale and drawn but I put it down to her missing Salar and the stresses of the siege that both had endured. She was happy enough to see her husband, their reunion touching and heartfelt. She embraced me and Gallia and welcomed the other kings and Rasha back to Sigal, but when I enquired as to the whereabouts of Claudia and Eszter she answered evasively they had remained in the palace.

The trip to the royal residence was a sombre affair, glum-looking civilians cheering the return of their king half-heartedly and pointing at Gallia and myself accusingly. What we had done to deserve such hostility I did not know, but was soon enlightened by a delegation of city officials waiting in the palace courtyard. White-robed priests were chanting prayers at the palace gates, burning esfand to purify the palace and those within it.

A row of yellow-uniformed swordsmen snapped to attention when a line of trumpeters sounded a fanfare, Isabella's elephant kneeling on the cobblestones so the king and queen could alight from the ornate wooden compartment chained to its back. I nodded and smiled at Alcaeus and Marcus who stood beside the line of officials, the most senior of whom, wearing a gold chain around his long neck, walked forward and bowed to Salar.

'Welcome home, majesty, the people of Sakastan salute you for your victory over the barbarians. We hope and pray your return will banish the plague that has descended on your people.'

Salar was shocked, as were we all, though he was in no mood to hold a council meeting after being away from his new wife for so long. He told the official he would convene a council meeting in the morning, leading Isabella and the rest of us into the palace. I cornered Alcaeus as the officials, heads shaking and mumbling to each other, took their leave.

'It is good to see you again, Pacorus, hopefully your return will signal a change in the city's fortunes.'

'Thank you. What is this plague? I saw no evidence of it during our journey through the city.'

'A strange thing. A few days ago, I received reports of newborns dying.'

'That, alas, is not unusual,' said Gallia, 'many infants, and women, die in childbirth.'

'Not a few,' continued Alcaeus, 'but every newborn. Only hours after a birth the child would die. Not one enjoyed a day of life. I examined a few of the bodies but could find no evidence of ailments or deformities. The mothers were also mostly in good health, though obviously distraught over the loss of their children.'

'Poison?' I suggested.

He shook his head. 'If it was in the water supply young and old would have been struck down, though high- and lowborn babies have been affected equally. It is bizarre.'

'The city is on a knife edge,' said Marcus.

The euphoria that had greeted the departure of the Kushan siege army had given way to a lingering suspicion that Sigal had suffered significantly less than expected because of sorcery. Rumours quickly spread that the queen's sister Claudia, a known user of magic, had used sorcery to conjure up the sand storm that had allowed her father and a great number of horsemen to leave the city unmolested, in addition to wreaking havoc within the Kushan camp. Indeed, so great had been the disruption to Kujula's army that it had been unable to mount a single assault upon the city. Gratitude soon turned to fear, then anger when infants began to die. Dark forces were suspected to be at work and fingers began pointing in Claudia's direction. For her own safety Isabella had restricted her sister to the palace where she remained out of sight, though not out of mind.

Claudia and Eszter welcomed us inside the palace, the former aloof and haughty, the latter glad to see us, both seemingly carrying a great burden. I queried Eszter as to her health but she merely smiled and told me she was well. Claudia barely spoke but noticed I was carrying a slight limp. Both absented themselves from our visit to the King of Mesene.

'You will find Nergal fully healed,' Claudia informed me.

'It is true that Nergal has made a full recovery,' said Alcaeus.

He had indeed. We found the King of Mesene in rude health sitting on his balcony in the company of Praxima. She looked more drawn and tired than him, though both of their faces lit up during a happy reunion.

'You look well, my friend,' I told Nergal.

He rose, walked a few steps and took a bow.

'And no limp?' Malik, Jamal on his arm, was astounded.

We were all delighted and mystified as to how Alcaeus had cured a limb that had been pierced by two arrows.

'I am as dumfounded as the rest of you,' the Greek announced, 'but I have to say it is my best work.'

We sat with our friends, drank and ate too much and reminisced about past glories and present victories, forgetting for a while the dreadful events taking place in the city below. It was good to be in the company of Companions again, with Malik and Spartacus as honorary members. I slept well that night, in bed with my wife, surrounded by my family and friends and behind high walls. I stayed in bed until nearly midday until a slave arrived with a message from Isabella to attend her in the palace gardens.

She was dressed in a white silk dress, a beautiful silver belt around her waist, and wore shoes of soft leather with silver buckles. She looked every inch the queen she was. Two guards shadowed us as we strolled through flowerbeds teeming with yellow and red tulips and beside water fountains. Her large brown eyes were filled with concern.

'Vartan fled the fortress before you returned, father,' she told me, 'along with Cookum and enough gold to purchase them both fine lives.'

That explained Eszter's morose demeanour.

'Probably for the best,' was my initial thought.

'Their actions would seem to suggest Vartan was not Orodes' son, father.'

'What does Salar think?'

She sighed. 'He is glad they have left Sigal and he is rid of the problem. He also desires to be rid of another problem, as do I.'

'Oh?'

'Claudia must leave the city as soon as possible before her presence provokes violence. The magistrates and priests are reporting that the people blame her for the terrible infant deaths that are afflicting them.'

'I cannot believe Claudia is responsible for such horror.'

She shook her head, her thick curling hair shining in the sunlight. She took my hand.

'You know who raised her, who doted on her and who passed on her knowledge to her. It is no coincidence she has followed Dobbai into the Scythian Sisterhood, a sect that is both revered and feared in equal measure.

'I have talked with Salar and we both wish Claudia to leave our city and our kingdom. You must inform her, father.'

I found Claudia in her bedroom, a spacious chamber with a balcony providing spectacular views of the mountains to the north. She was sitting at a table on the balcony when she told me to enter, giving me a cursory nod before returning to writing on the papyrus in front of her.

'You look as if you have suffered a great defeat, father, rather than having saved the empire. Notwithstanding the city criers proclaiming it was Salar who defeated Kujula. My cousin really is shameless.'

'I have to speak with you.'

She pointed at a chair on the other side of the table. I sat in it and noticed a wicker basket with a lid next to it. She continued writing, using a reed pen that she dipped in the ink pot on the desk. I cleared my throat.

'I am quite capable of writing and listening at the same time, father. What is troubling you?'

'The king and queen desire you to leave Sigal immediately.'

She continued writing. 'Because of the on-going deaths of the Saka infants.'

'Yes. I told Isabella you were not responsible but she and Salar fear violence may break out at any moment.'

Claudia put down the pen and looked up at me, resting her elbows on the mahogany surface.

'I saved this miserable city and kingdom from destruction and now its inhabitants want rid of me. That's ingratitude for you.'

'Just to clarify, you are not responsible for the death of Sigal's infants, are you?'

'Have you seen Nergal, father?'

'Nergal?'

'Your friend, the King of Mesene.'

'Don't be clever,' I snapped, 'of course I have seen him.'

'Well, then, you will have noticed that he has made a full recovery and does not even have a limp, despite being grievously wounded.'

'Alcaeus is a skilled physician,' I said.

She gave a derisive chuckle. 'It was not only his skills that saved your friend, father. You remember your friend Atrax? He had a nasty limp for the rest of his life, despite a host of royal physicians. Nergal walks with the gait of a young man and you think it is due to a single Greek doctor? Healing Nergal and facilitating your escape from Sigal were no small things. There was a price to be paid.'

I was shocked. 'You mean the infant deaths are linked to what you did.'

'Naturally,' she replied casually, 'while Pazuzu was aiding you the demon-goddess Lamashtu was free to claim the lives of Sigal's newborns, for Pazuzu is the guardian of pregnant mothers.'

I put a fist to my mouth, appalled.

'The needs of the many outweigh the needs of the few, father. What are the lives of a few children compared to the welfare of the millions who live in the empire?'

I was angry. 'And you are the judge who decides who lives and who dies?'

She remained calm, unconcerned. 'No, you are, father. It was you who wished to enlist divine help; I was merely the vessel to enable you to do so. When do we leave?'

'As soon as possible,' I averted my eyes from hers to look at the wicker basket.

'At least we know Vartan is a fraud, an elaborate trick engineered by Phraates, I think.'

I toyed with the lid of the basket. 'There is no evidence of that.'

'Actions speak louder than words, father. That he fled Sigal indicates his role was at an end, that he stole gold proves he was no son of Orodes. The only riddle to be solved is where has he fled to?'

'Why would Phraates engineer such a project?'

'To wound you,' she said, 'to embarrass you and to remind you that Phraates is high king and has a long reach. He also has a malicious character. All very simple, I would have thought.'

I removed the lid and leapt back when a cobra reared up, its hood flared and lunged at me. I knocked over the chair, fell on the floor and shouted in alarm. The two guards that had been posted outside Claudia's room ran in, swords drawn.

'Get out,' commanded Claudia, 'there is no danger.'

The cobra raised itself up but she merely stood and hissed at it, the guards wide-eyed as she stared into its black, cold eyes and extended her right hand.

'Be careful,' I warned, scrambling to my feet and drawing my sword.

But Claudia continued to emit a low hiss and gently laid a hand on the cobra's head, still staring at it. The snake slowly descended back into the basket, she swiftly replaced the lid and returned to her seat.

'Please do not touch things that do not belong to you, father.'

She glared at the guards. 'Are you still here?'

Troubled by what they had just seen, they sheathed their swords, bowed and exited the room.

'Idiots,' she sneered.

I was going to ask why she had a live cobra in her bedroom but thought better of it. She was a law unto herself and her life had taken a very different path to the one that I had hoped. But perhaps Dobbai had come to Dura not only to aid Gallia and myself but also tutor Claudia in her ways. Those ways were responsible for the deaths of newborns currently afflicting Sigal and the knowledge weighed heavily upon me as I later tried to console Eszter.

'There will be others,' I told her.

'He left no letter or gave warning, he just vanished.'

Her voice was like that of a small child whose pet had just died. I cradled her in my arms.

'I loved him, father.'

She was bereft of hope and disconsolate. I did not tell her I was secretly delighted the spectre of Vartan no longer loomed over us. If Eszter had married him it would have created all sorts of difficulties, not least the accusation of Phraates that Dura was harbouring a usurper. But now the dilemma had been solved at the cost of some gold coins and my daughter's broken heart. If Vartan had been a fraud then Phraates had succeeded in wounding my youngest daughter rather than myself, though it did cast the high king in a new light.

'We can find you a Parthian prince to marry,' I said, 'you will soon forget Vartan.'

'I will never marry,' she told me, 'Claudia has told me. I'm glad.'

I dismissed the idea. 'Nonsense, when we get back to Dura you will think differently. Do you want me to find him?'

Her ears pricked up. 'Who?'

'Vartan, of course, I can send Talib and his scouts to scour the land for him and his fat friend.'

She pondered the offer and for a few seconds her expression changed as she thought about seeing her beloved again. But then the mask of sadness returned.

'No, I am not interested in vengeance.'

That was a pity because the idea of dragging Vartan to Dura and having him executed for betraying my daughter had a strong appeal.

'As you wish.'

I conveyed to Gallia everything Claudia had told me earlier as she sat at her bedroom table brushing her locks, using a mirror of burnished silver. The night was still and cool, the shuttered doors to the balcony closed, light provided by oil lamps mounted on the walls.

'I blame myself.'

She stopped brushing her hair and spun to face me. 'Why? We were trapped in Sigal, remember? Without Claudia's help things might have turned out very differently.'

'All those infants,' I lamented.

'Perhaps when we leave it will stop.'

We did so the next morning, Salar and Isabella standing on the palace steps to bid us farewell. The king had provided a mounted escort but there was no need. It was very early and the streets were as yet still mostly deserted. It was a strange send-off. Eszter was glad to be leaving a place that had promised so much, but in the end had proved a bitter disappointment; Claudia and Isabella eyed each other with a barely disguised disdain; and Salar was protocol itself, barely able to hide his relief that my eldest daughter was leaving his kingdom. Malik and Jamal were glad to be away from palaces and riding back to their Agraci tents, Spartacus and Rasha delighted to be back in each other's company, though Gafarn and Diana were genuinely sad to see discord among our family. I kept glancing at Nergal, spear-straight in the saddle and looking remarkably fit and refreshed. If only he knew the price of restoring his health. Silaces was in a bad mood after a night of heavy drinking with Kalet, who had returned from the south with his men.

We linked up with our respective contingents two miles south of Sigal, the horsemen already on the road after striking camp before dawn. Kewab arrived with Titus Rutilus in tow, the Roman wearing the uniform of a Duran horse archer.

'In a few weeks you will be home, Rutilus,' I said.

Gallia turned to glance at the Roman.

'Ah, I forgot to tell you, my dear, this is Titus Rutilus who did us a great service when we were in Kushan lands. We owe him a great debt.'

'You are too kind, majesty,' said Rutilus. He bowed his head at Gallia. 'It is an honour to meet you, majesty.'

'You were a slave?' she asked him. 'Where are you from?'

'A town called Longula, majesty, located just south of Rome.'

Claudia giggled and even Eszter managed a smile as Gallia spun in the saddle and glowered at him.

'You are a Roman.'

'Yes, majesty, I was captured at Carrhae, a battle near…'

'I know where Carrhae is,' Gallia said icily, 'I was there.'

Rutilus was surprised. 'You, majesty?'

Her eyes narrowed. 'That's right, Roman, I was the one who killed your leader, Marcus Licinius Crassus.'

There was an awkward silence as Rutilus digested the revelation.

'It was a long time ago,' I said.

'And yet only a short while ago the Romans invaded Parthian once again,' said Gallia, 'only to meet the same fate. Mark Antony will not be returning any time soon.'

'I knew him in Gaul,' exclaimed Rutilus, 'or at least served under him. He was Caesar's deputy then.'

'Julius Caesar?' asked Kewab.

'Yes, commander,' answered Rutilus. 'A great general.'

'He was murdered in Rome by a group of senators,' Kewab told him.

'You should visit Ctesiphon, Roman,' said Gallia, 'before your return home. You will find there six of the seven Roman eagles

335

captured at Carrhae and the two that were taken at Lake Urmia. There is another in the Great Temple at Hatra that was taken by my husband in his youth.'

'Where is the other eagle captured at Carrhae, majesty?' asked Rutilus.

I turned to look at Rasha riding beside Spartacus.

'It was traded for a great treasure,' I told him.

As it happened I decided Ctesiphon should be on our route home, though the primary purpose was not to show Titus Rutilus Phraates' collection of Roman eagles but to plan a response to the Kushan threat. As we made our way there our numbers were whittled down. Silaces and his men returned to Elymais, Nergal, Gafarn and Spartacus headed for Uruk, taking Malik and his Agraci with them. At the Tigris we bade them farewell, along with Kalet and his lords. Kewab persuaded me it would be diplomatic to send Azad, his cataphracts and the bulk of Katana's horse archers with them, retaining an escort of only two hundred riders, including the Amazons, to make the trip to the capital of the Parthian Empire. Much to Gallia's annoyance I asked Titus Rutilus to accompany us, along with Marcus and Alcaeus. The two Romans spent most of the journey north along the side of the waterway chatting about Rome and Parthia and their respective political systems.

We sent heralds ahead to the governor of Susa requesting permission to ride through Susiana, which Phraates ruled along with Babylon, receiving a delegation from the city with an invitation from said governor inviting us to dine with him. I politely declined, informing the commander of his horsemen bringing the missive that I had been away from Dura long enough and desired to get home as quickly as possible. So we continued on along the eastern bank of the

Tigris, passing by huge date palm groves, populous villages surrounded by fields irrigated by the river and dozens of fishing boats on the waterway. It was a picture of a land prospering, and at peace. It brought a smile to my face. It was the reason I had dedicated my life to the empire.

Around six miles south of Ctesiphon we ran into another party of horsemen, all dressed in dragon skin armour, comprising a leather vest with attached overlapping polished silver plates that protected the chest and back. Their burnished open-faced helmets glittered in the sunlight, as did their whetted lance points. Their purple leggings and tunics showed they were from Babylon, the city of Phraates' mother and dear to his heart. The standard bearer beside the party's commander carried a banner showing the horned bull of Babylon, the symbol of the city's strength, power and rage. The officer removed his helmet and bowed his head.

'Greetings King Pacorus, Queen Gallia. No party of soldiers larger than twenty is allowed within five miles of the royal palace, majesties. High King Phraates invites you to rest and refresh yourselves at Ctesiphon, highnesses.'

We took Claudia and Kewab; Eszter declaring she had no interest in seeing another palace and especially had no desire to see Phraates again. She was happy wallowing in her self-pity so she stayed in the camp pitched beside the Tigris, Katana assuring me he would take her hunting with him to keep her amused.

'There is nothing like blood sports to mend a broken heart, majesty,' he told me.

It had been nearly two years since we had attended the coronation of Phraates and in that time Ctesiphon had changed markedly. In the days of Sinatruces and his son Phraates, the grandfather of the current high king, and even Orodes, the sprawling palace-cum-small city complex had been a mixture of opulence and decay. But now it was becoming a place of splendour, its perimeter wall, which previously an army could have marched through its many gaps, had been repaired by the hundreds of slaves who toiled unceasingly beneath a burning sun. At the restored main entrance two huge banners flew from the gatehouse, one showing Babylon's bull, the other the symbol of Susiana, the kingdom of his father's birth – an eagle with a snake in its talons.

Inside the walls a vast army of artisans brought from the four corners of the empire worked to restore the temples and palace to their former glory. Behind the palace were the private houses of the nobles who were high in Phraates' favour, including High Priest Timo and Chief of Court Ashleen. It was the latter who met us at the entrance to the palace, his round face showing a fixed, insincere smile as he bowed in an ostentatious manner and welcomed us to Ctesiphon.

'Hail, King Pacorus, tamer of the Kushans and thrice lord high general of the empire. Welcome to you, Queen Gallia, mighty Amazon who strikes fear into the hearts of Parthia's enemies. And welcome to you, Princess Claudia, whose fame as a sorceress is known from the Euphrates to the Himalayas.'

He ignored Kewab who was standing behind me, but placed himself beside me and requested we accompany him into the palace. I say palace but in truth there was more than one. However, as a result of Phraates' grand construction project they had all been linked to create one vast royal residence.

I had never liked Ctesiphon. It was a place of court intrigue and politics. As I walked along the marble floored corridor, with the lower parts of the walls clad in coloured marble slabs and the upper sections covered in mosaics, I could hear the vicious tongue of Queen Aruna, the mother of Mithridates who had taken an instant dislike to me. Her son too for that matter. It seemed like yesterday.

'The high king is well?' I asked.

'Very well, majesty, the more so since he learned of the defeat of the eastern barbarians. We are all indebted to you.'

Loathsome creature! I had learned Ashleen had been a friend of the late, unlamented Mithridates, both of them hailing from Susiana. He had escaped the great cull of that high king's officials after Orodes had ascended the high throne, and had managed to worm his way into the affections of Phraates. When Orodes died he became a father figure to the young prince, much to many people's dismay. And yet I had to admit that under his guidance Ctesiphon had become a place that projected kingship, power and wealth and was finally a fitting residence of the king of kings.

Phraates himself rose from his gold-covered seat when we entered the throne room, extending his arms in a welcoming gesture as we walked from the red doors across white marble tiles to the dais behind which stood half a dozen guards. Courtiers and their wives, the latter dripping with gold and silver jewellery, bowed their heads as we passed them. I wondered if Gallia felt out of place in her boots, leggings and mail armour. Probably not. For her part Claudia was dressed like an Agraci warrior in her black leggings and tunic. We stood in a line before the dais and bowed our heads.

'Everybody out!' shouted Phraates.

Ashleen clapped his hands to signal the courtiers should depart, nobles and their wives dutifully filing out of the chamber. I asked Kewab to wait outside the throne room.

'Chairs and refreshments for our guests,' commanded Phraates, retaking his throne.

Slaves set down large cushioned wicker chairs and ornate footstools, others serving us fine wine and freshly baked pastries. Phraates, dressed in a purple silk robe, gold on his fingers and a crown of gold and diamonds on his head, drank from a gold rhyton. He toasted me.

'To your victory over the barbarians. King Salar has written extensively concerning the campaign against the Kushans, the two-year truce you brokered and the happy news of the usurper Vartan fleeing into the night. The gods smile on Parthia.'

'For a while, majesty,' said Claudia.

Phraates gave his cup to a slave and leaned forward.

'What do the gods reveal to you, princess?'

'You are high in their favour, majesty.'

Phraates leaned back and smiled to himself. He looked at my daughter.

'You should leave Dura and come to live at Ctesiphon. There is plenty of room in the palace for Parthia's most famous sorceress and you could have your own apothecary.'

'You are high in the gods' favour, majesty,' said Claudia, 'because you create the circumstances to allow the immortals to enjoy and indulge themselves.'

Phraates looked confused. 'Meaning what?'

'Meaning a weak frontier invites invasion, which means bloodshed and the gods adore bloodshed, majesty.'

'You forget yourself,' snapped Ashleen.

'I forget nothing,' was my daughter's icy reply.

340

Phraates was within his rights to banish her from Ctesiphon or even have her flogged for her insolence, but instead he chose to ignore her and pointed to a slave standing a few paces from the dais, beside one of the thick marble columns supporting the hall's cedar roof. Keeping his head down to avoid eye contact, the slave walked forward and handed Phraates a magnificent sword in a purple scabbard encrusted with jewels. He stood, stepped off the dais and held it out to me.

'I wish you to give this to King Malik, together with my gratitude and that of the empire for his service against the Kushans.'

I was astounded. Was this the same man who had trumpeted 'Parthian purity' two years before, or had looked down his nose at the Agraci? I had to admit I was impressed by what appeared to be his growing maturity and slightly smug that he was perhaps turning into the high king I always hoped he would be. I took the sword and bowed to him.

'A most generous gift, highness.'

Phraates returned to his throne. 'I am not a god, princess, and am mindful of my shortcomings. But neither do I have a magic crystal that allows me to see into the future. If I possessed one I would have sent you to unleash a demon to ravage the Kushan lands and kill their emperor. My one aim is to protect the empire and I will do anything necessary to achieve that aim.'

He looked at Claudia. 'You should consider my offer, princess. I would welcome such a ruthless servant of the empire. Let us hope Sakastan will soon recover from the loss of so many of its infants.'

'I will consider it,' she said without conviction.

'King Pacorus,' said Phraates, 'join me in the Hall of Victory tomorrow.'

341

With that he stood, stepped down from the dais, walked to Gallia, took her hands and kissed them. He did the same to Claudia before exiting the chamber via one of the doors to the rear of the dais, two guards accompanying him. Ashleen invited us to stay in the palace but Gallia and Claudia were eager to return to camp, having no appetite to attend a banquet attended by Ctesiphon's fawning nobility.

It was a slight but both my wife and daughter pleaded extreme tiredness after the long ride from Sakastan, that and the stress of the preceding siege. Phraates sent a letter to camp enquiring if they wanted the services of the court physician to administer calming concoctions.

'I have a greater knowledge of herbs for relieving stress than any court doctor,' sniffed Claudia.

'Phraates is learning kingship,' I said, 'his attitude has vastly improved compared to two years ago.'

'How easily fooled you are, father,' Claudia chided me. 'His nature remains the same but he has discovered that a cloak of civility can achieve wonders.'

'Did you ask him about Vartan?' asked Eszter, picking at her chicken kebab.

We were enjoying a rare thing: a family meal, albeit one sat around a table in a tent and being served rudimentary fare of roasted chicken and bread, both purchased earlier from a nearby village.

'He was happy he no longer resides at Sigal,' I told her.

'Of course the real question,' smiled Claudia, 'is whether Phraates engineered the deception.'

'I suspect Ashleen,' I said, 'a man who was a compatriot of Mithridates and would therefore hold a grudge against Dura.'

'Against Dura or against you, father?' queried Claudia.

'Against me,' I admitted. 'But unless I challenge the Chief of Court directly the truth will probably never be known.'

'And will you?' asked Eszter.

'You have been cruelly deceived,' I said, 'but I doubt the intention of sending Vartan to Sakastan was to break your heart.'

'That was just a bonus,' lamented Gallia.

I nearly broke a tooth on an over-cooked piece of chicken.

'My own theory is that Phanes petitioned Phraates about the unsuitability of his brother to occupy Sakastan's throne, which led to him being appointed lord high general in the east. The appearance of Vartan at Sigal gave Phanes a reason to move against his brother.'

'Which would suggest Phraates knew about the deception of Vartan being Orodes' son,' suggested Gallia.

'Possibly,' I admitted.

'Certainly,' insisted Claudia.

'I hate Phraates,' hissed Eszter.

'Do you think he also had a hand in the murders of Peroz and Roxanne?' asked Gallia.

I shook my head. 'Alas, I think that sorry episode was entirely of my making.'

Claudia raised an eyebrow. 'You?'

'I invaded Persis, which led to the death of Spada, which led to the appearance at Dura of Indira. I suspect, and it is no more than a suspicion, that Queen Hamide learned of Indira's skill with knives and hired her and other assassins to kill Roxanne and Peroz.'

Eszter was appalled. 'She ordered the murder of her own son?'

I puffed out her cheeks. 'Perhaps she intended for only Roxanne to die. Who knows the truth?'

'I killed Spada,' said Gallia firmly, 'so perhaps blame should be apportioned to me.'

'The actions we take have consequences that affect our lives like a spider spinning a web,' said Claudia. 'The question now, though, is what action will father take against Phraates.'

She knew the answer before I opened my mouth. I had lobbied hard to put Phraates on Ctesiphon's throne and I was not about to undo all my hard work. I knew that both Silaces and Khosrou would willingly support me if I decided to dethrone him. But then what? Civil war? A fresh Roman invasion against a weakened empire? And surely any internal strife within the empire would tempt Kujula to mount another invasion, notwithstanding the truce.

'Invasions from both east and west,' I said out loud. 'I will not be responsible for such a thing.'

Claudia was not surprised. 'It is the right decision, father.'

Eszter stood and glared at her. 'The needs of the many outweigh the needs of the few, sister, I'm sure the mothers of Sigal will take comfort from that.'

She stormed away into the night, Claudia flicking a dismissive hand in her direction.

'Poor Eszter,' reflected Gallia.

'She would have been far poorer if Vartan had stayed at Sigal, mother. Fake or no, Phraates would have demanded his removal one way or another. Things worked out for the best.'

She had a mischievous glint in her eyes and I wondered what sorcery she had used to entice Vartan to flee Parthia. Perhaps none. Perhaps he was just a thief and imposter who spotted an opportunity.

'Eszter will soon forget Vartan,' Claudia told us.

The next day I returned to Ctesiphon to visit the Hall of
Victory. It was a modest-sized limestone building constructed on a
stone plinth to the rear of the palace, surrounded by a beautifully
dressed stone wall and accessed via a single wooden gate. The wall
was high so no one could see into the hall's compound. Phraates,
dressed in a simple white silk tunic, escorted me through the gate to
the hall itself, which resembled a Greek temple. Rectangular in shape,
it was flanked by rows of white marble columns and accessed by a
vestibule. This led to the sanctuary where the eight captured Roman
eagles resided, each one mounted in its own sandstone plinth. In the
centre of the hall stood a bronze statue of the god Marduk, the deity
of Babylon. Around the walls stood Babylonian guards in their purple
leggings and tunics, above them hanging the Roman *vexillum*
standards taken during the campaign against Mark Antony. Fitted to
the walls were captured legionary standards: spears holding a number
of metal discs called *philarae* and topped with a human hand image
called a *manus* . Each *signum* also had a plate beneath the *manus*
bearing a unit title.

The collection had been laid out tastefully and took full
advantage of the sun's rays flooding through the windows
immediately below the roof of wooden beams and terracotta tiles.
The stone plinths had been positioned so they were bathed in
sunlight, the silver eagles glinting and seemingly moving to give the
impression of live birds as the sun traversed the sky.

'Of all the kings of the empire, you have the most right to be
here, King Pacorus.'

'You are most kind, majesty.'

'You approve of this hall?'

I stood in front of one of the eagles. 'I do.'

'So, what to do about these Kushans?'

I turned away from the eagles. 'Phanes is unfit to be your lord high general, majesty, and should be removed from that position forthwith.'

Phraates, as ever escorted by two huge Scythian axe men, nodded.

'But who to replace him? Would you consider accepting the role once more?'

The thought appalled me. 'You do me great honour, majesty, but I fear I am needed back in Dura so I can guard the empire's western frontier.'

Phraates suddenly looked alarmed. 'You suspect the Romans may attack again?'

Byrd had told me they were in disarray. 'I fear so, majesty. They are desperate to retrieve the eagles in this hall.'

He gave me a sly glance. 'Should the Romans invade, I assume the one hundred and thirty thousand soldiers you were eager to inform me about before you departed for Sakastan will be sufficient to defeat any Roman invasion.'

'More than enough, majesty.'

'Mm, so that just leaves the Kushan threat.'

'I have been thinking on that, majesty, and believe I may have a solution.'

'Go on.'

'Just as you have appointed a satrap to rule Persis, may I suggest you do the same to organise and lead a force to counter the Kushans. A fully professional force of horsemen that can respond to any threats launched across the Indus, and one that can reinforce the army of the king whose realm is directly threatened by the Kushans.'

Phraates weighed up my proposal for a few minutes, walking up and down the row of plinths before pointing at me.

'But who would lead such a force? It cannot be Phanes and if I appoint Salar then Phanes will devote his time undermining his brother. Khosrou is too old, Aschek too lame and Cinnamus and Monaeses both too useless.'

It was a fair assessment, though if I had a mind to I would argue that Khosrou still had a lot of fight left in him.

'I was thinking of someone else, majesty.'

He looked at me in exasperation. 'Then name him.'

'Kewab.'

'Your Egyptian?'

'I prefer to think of him as the man who engineered the defeat of Mark Antony, the man who organised the defence of Sigal and man who is the rising star of Dura's army.'

Phraates was unsure. 'Would the kings in the east accept such an individual?'

'They would with your authority behind him, majesty.'

I explained in some detail how only Dura, Hatra and Margiana in the empire had standing armies. Every king had a personal bodyguard and garrisons and in times of war would summon his lords and their retinues to form an army. This gave him thousands of horse archers that had only a rudimentary knowledge of tactics. And only Dura had foot soldiers of any worth.

'A slightly harsh assessment,' said Phraates.

'My foot soldiers have beaten everything thrown at them, majesty, even when they have been greatly outnumbered. Training, discipline and superior tactics and equipment will win every time, if professional soldiers are handled correctly.'

'And you feel this Kewab is the right man to command such a force.'

'I do, majesty.'

He pondered my opinion for a few moments.

'And would this force include foot soldiers?'

'No, sire. It would need to be mobile and therefore composed solely of horsemen, a mixture of cataphracts and horse archers.'

'How many?'

'A dragon of cataphracts and nine dragons of horse archers, with an accompanying camel train of ammunition.'

He bowed his head to the statue of Marduk.

'Ten thousand professional horsemen, plus squires and cameleers would cost a king's ransom.'

'A small price to secure your eastern frontier, majesty.'

'My only concern is the loyalty of your Egyptian. He owes everything to you rather than me, which make me query his allegiance.'

'He knows I am loyal to the high crown of the Parthian Empire, majesty, and thus will fight to preserve your rule, just as I have done. He is above all a professional. Besides, if you are paying the soldiers of his force their loyalty will be to Ctesiphon.'

He turned and walked towards the entrance, his guards following.

'Bring him to the palace this afternoon, King Pacorus, and tell him nothing of what we have discussed.'

We met in the office of the high king, the same office I had sat with his grandfather and my father when we were fighting Narses all those years ago. How the years had flown by since then and now. Phraates' grandfather had been a kind, fair man and those qualities

348

had doomed him. His grandson was made of different material. The two Scythian axe men stood behind him as he waited for slaves to serve us wine in gold chalices before speaking to Kewab.

'King Pacorus speaks very highly of you, commander.'

'He does me great honour, highness, as do you inviting me to your palace.'

'I will come straight to the point, commander, because time is short. I have decided to create a permanent force on my eastern frontier to deter the Kushans. It will consist entirely of professional horsemen financed by Ctesiphon's treasury. I envisage its composition to be a dragon of cataphracts and nine dragons of horse archers. I wish you to command this force, commander.'

Kewab was shocked. 'Me? I mean, it is a great honour, highness.'

Phraates brought his hands together. 'King Pacorus is in full agreement with my idea.'

I could only smile. 'I am. We have two years before the Kushan truce is over, Kewab, and in that time, you will need to recruit, organise and train this unit.'

'As well as liaising with the kings of the east, who will play host to your force,' added Phraates. 'You will be promoted to the rank of satrap with a commensurate salary and be answerable to me personally,' finished Phraates.

Kewab's mask of professionalism slipped momentarily as he beamed with delight before composing himself.

'You bestow a great honour on me, highness. I will do my utmost to repay the trust you have placed in me.'

Phraates was generous to his new satrap, gifting him a substantial sum of gold for the inconvenience of relocating his family to the east, to the city of Farah, the capital of Aria. It was Kewab's choice, being approximately the mid-point on the empire's eastern border. The cadre of his force comprised a hundred of Dura's cataphracts and five hundred horse archers, soldiers well versed in the kingdom's tactics who would provide company commanders for Phraates' flying column. With Ctesiphon providing funding it was relatively easy for Kewab to build up and equip his force, and Phraates was insistent that the bulk of his command should comprise men drawn from Susiana and Babylon. In this way, he ensured that the small army owed its loyalty to him first, Parthia second. But in the aftermath of the Kushan invasion he and the eastern kings were focused solely on preparing for the next enemy incursion once Kujula's truce expired, rather than politics.

Kewab accompanied us back to Dura, he and the rest of us emotional when we first caught sight of the Citadel sitting atop the escarpment looming over the Euphrates. Chrestus had the whole army drawn up on parade in front of the city gates to welcome us home, ten thousand legionaries, a thousand cataphracts and nearly five thousand horse archers were a sight for sore eyes and I spent a long time going among the soldiery to thank them for their loyalty and congratulate them on their smartness and discipline. Afterwards, while leaning against the stone griffin standing sentry night and day over my city, I spent hours watching camel caravans travelling east and west along the road leading to Palmyra. The traumas of the past few weeks were becoming a distant memory.

I was sad to see Kewab go but with his elevated rank and fresh commission he was chafing at the bit to get back to the east, so after a mere two weeks back at Dura we bid him, his wife and one-year-old boy a fond farewell on the palace steps.

'I hope you return to us, Kewab,' I said.

'Two years will pass in the blink of an eye, majesty,' he replied.

Gallia broke protocol and kissed him on the cheek.

'Just make sure you and your family come back to us.'

Behind him his officers sat on their horses waiting for him, his wife cradling his small son beside him. I smiled at the boy and stroked his black hair.

'You are going on a great adventure.'

He gawped at me and burst into tears.

We watched them leave the Citadel, outside the city a hundred cataphracts, two hundred squires, five hundred horse archers and five hundred camels were waiting to accompany Satrap Kewab east. Aaron had already billed Ctesiphon for the cost to Dura of replacing every soldier, squire, camel and arrow, the gold arriving by return of post. It all pointed to Phraates maturing into what his father would have wanted him to be.

'After all these years and so much war and bloodshed, you are still a dreamer at heart. Come and be with us.'

Gallia was sitting with Claudia and Eszter at a table beneath the awning providing shade from the sun. But the sun was fading fast in the west, a huge red fireball turning the sky purple. Below the palace terrace the Euphrates looked like a polished curved blade laid flat on the earth. I turned from its calm beauty and walked to the table, taking my seat next to my wife.

'I was in the camel park today,' said Eszter casually.

'Shovelling camel dung?' asked Claudia.

Eszter looked at her. 'A newly arrived caravan from Sakastan brought news of the death of Queen Hamide.'

Claudia feigned indifference.

351

'Dead, how?' I asked, picking up a date from the table.

Eszter continued to stare at her sister. 'The bite of a cobra, apparently.'

'How unfortunate,' said Claudia.

I looked at her and remembered the cobra in the basket in her bedroom at Sigal. Surely a coincidence? And yet.

'Without the malign influence of his mother Phanes might be more inclined to improve relations with Sakastan,' opined Gallia.

I put down the date and fixed Claudia with my eyes. 'Very convenient.'

'Are the dates not to your liking, father?'

Eszter took a large gulp of wine. 'We all know the answer, though none will say it. I will. Claudia killed Queen Hamide.'

Claudia mocked her with laughter. 'So I turned into a cobra and slithered all the way to Carmania to bite the old hag, before returning to Dura?'

'You know what I mean,' sniffed Eszter.

'It may come as a surprise to you, sister,' smiled Claudia, 'but I do not hold dominion over all the creatures that walk or crawl upon the earth.'

'Let us talk of Hamide no longer,' pleaded Gallia. 'Hopefully I will have a grandchild soon and you will be a grandfather, Pacorus.'

'You will,' said Claudia with certainty, 'it is foretold.'

That gave me a warm glow inside. I gripped Gallia's hand and she smiled in return. Life was good again. We received regular guests, including Byrd and Noora from Palmyra, the old scout informing me the Romans were focused on fighting each other rather than gazing east towards Parthia. All eyes in the Roman world were on the

coming final battle between Octavian and Mark Antony and
Cleopatra.

'Once that battle is fought, Romani leader who is left alive will
be looking for fresh conquests.'

'Parthia will be ready, Byrd.'

'Jamal pregnant,' he announced suddenly.

His words heralded a wave of expectant women. News came
from Salar that Isabella was pregnant, prompting Claudia to don an
air of smugness that was at first endearing and then intensely
irritating. And then Gafarn and Diana made a surprise visit to inform
us that the wife of Prince Pacorus had been safely delivered of her
first child. These were heart-warming gifts indeed.

Another, unexpected, gift arrived a year to the day after I had
sat down with Emperor Kujula after the dreadful Battle of the Indus.
It was a collection of papyrus scrolls bound in a beautiful ivory-inlaid
wooden box, each side of the box and the top bearing the ivory
image of a griffin. The note accompanying the box was in Kujula's
own handwriting.

'To my friend and gallant foe, King Pacorus.'

A small crowd gathered in the throne room to see the gift that
had been sent from the Kushan Empire, though Aaron was wary of
its contents.

'Careful, majesty, it might contain serpents who will spring out
when the box is opened.'

'Take the box outside and burn it,' an alarmed Rsan
commanded the guards.

'They will do no such thing,' I said, waving the legionaries
back.

A curious Claudia and Eszter had appeared, along with Chrestus, Alcaeus and Marcus, all eager to see what was inside the mysterious box, which had been placed on the floor in front of the dais.

'Chrestus,' I said, 'hand me the box.'

The burly commander of the army picked it up, gave it a little shake and looked alarmed.

'There's something in it, majesty.'

'In all that's holy,' I cried, 'pass me the wretched thing.'

He did so. I rested it on my lap, unlocked the lid and lifted it. To discover a book inside. The number of papyrus scrolls indicated it was a large tome and I eagerly picked up the first scroll, unrolling it to read the title aloud.

'An account of the campaigns of King Pacorus of Dura from the time of his return from Italy to the Battle of the Indus.'

They crowded round to admire the beautifully written scrolls, which were all in Parthian.

'I would like to read that, majesty,' said Rsan.

'As would I,' added Chrestus.

I spent the next few days reading about the wars I had taken part in. I marvelled at the wealth of detail the book contained, not least the account of the great civil war that had put my friend Orodes on the high throne. After I had finished I allowed others to read it, though on the condition they came to the Citadel to do so. On no account would I allow such a prize to leave the palace. I earnestly looked forward to meeting Kujula again, though as a friend sitting across a table or as an enemy across a battlefield I did not know.

Chapter 13

Titus Rutilus enjoyed his stay at Dura, especially visiting the legionary camp and the mud-brick forts north and south of the city. He spent much time in the royal stables and armouries, taking delight in riding from the Citadel each morning in the company of horse archers and cataphracts. He marvelled at the Amazons, who adopted him as a sort of mascot. This middle-aged Roman, who had fought at Carrhae, afterwards becoming a Parthian and then a Kushan slave. He could not shoot a bow to save his life but he wielded a *spatha* from the saddle with some aplomb, though now his targets were straw and wood rather than barbarians. I joined him whenever I could, two men past their prime sweating under a burning sun trying to keep pace with women in their teens and twenties. Gallia was also present too, of course, pushing herself as hard as her charges and refusing to accept she was now middle aged.

Afterwards, our tunics dripping with sweat, gulping down the contents of our water bottles, the Amazons gathered round to hear something quite unique: an account of Carrhae told from a Roman perspective. I too listened with relish, hearing the names of men I had respected; Crassus, his son and Surena, the man who had been my squire before rising high to become the King of Gordyene. How I regretted how his life had ended and for years afterwards I had tortured myself with thoughts of how I should have intervened to save him. Gallia, normally cold and aloof towards Romans, temporarily put aside her amity to hear his gripping story.

I desperately wanted him to stay with us and offered him the position of farrier in the Citadel, with his own salary and lodgings in the city should he accept. He refused.

'It is a generous offer, majesty, and as a former enemy and slave I thank you from the bottom of my heart. But I wish to return home.'

I understood. It was the burning desire of all who had been in bondage: to return to the place where they had been born and lived before being brutally wrenched away from all they held dear.

'I hope you still have some family left, Titus.'

He suddenly looked lost. 'The belief they still live has kept me alive all these years, majesty.'

I wondered how many of those taken at Carrhae were still slaves, or indeed still alive. If they were it was most unlikely they would be following in Titus Rutilus' footsteps. Before he left I attended the weekly meeting of the council in the Headquarters Building, Rsan entertaining us with matters pertaining to the smooth running of the city and kingdom: repairs to the sewage systems, the state of irrigation canals, the size of the date harvest and the administration of the caravan park. My eyelids felt like lead as I tried to stay awake.

Aaron was the next to speak, arranging the papyrus sheets in front of him with military precision. The two clerks recording the minutes sat poised at their desks, waiting for him to speak.

'I have received word from Ctesiphon regarding the annual tribute,' he began.

The annual tribute was paid by every kingdom in the empire to support the expenses of the king of kings, which included the running costs of the palace complex at Ctesiphon.

'This year all kingdoms are being charged a surcharge to pay for the raising, equipping and maintenance of Satrap Kewab's mobile army.'

'So much for Phraates paying for it himself,' remarked Gallia dryly.

'I thought it was your idea, majesty,' said Chrestus, sweat running down his thick neck.

I nodded. 'It was.'

Aaron immediately seized upon this. 'Perhaps I might lobby Ctesiphon for Dura to be exempt from the lobby seeing as you were the progenitor of the idea, majesty.'

'What does that mean?' asked Chrestus gruffly.

'It means the king gave birth to the idea,' Rsan told him.

'You've got fat chance,' said Chrestus dismissively.

'Succinct and accurate,' agreed Gallia.

'We have been reimbursed for our men,' I said, 'frankly I have neither the inclination nor the strength to argue with the high king. We will pay the surcharge.'

'High King Phraates has given us an object lesson in kingship,' Gallia stated. 'He steals my husband's idea, proclaims to the whole of Parthia that he thought of it and gets everyone else to pay for it.'

'At least the ukku blades remained at Dura,' grinned Chrestus.

One hundred Duran cataphracts might have ridden east but their expensive sword blades remained in my armoury. The newly promoted squires who filled their places were issued with the ukku swords instead. There were limits to my generosity, though Aaron might have disagreed. The last item the meeting had to address illustrated why I had appointed him as the kingdom's treasurer, and why he was frustrating to the point of distraction at times. He picked over his last piece of papyrus like a priest examining the entrails of a sacrifice.

'This concerns the Roman slave Titus Rutilus, majesty.'

'Marcus finds his company most agreeable,' said Rsan, 'and will miss him when he departs for Rome.'

'As will we all,' I added.

Aaron rapped his fingers on the table top. 'Indeed, and I must bring to your majesty's attention his travelling expenses.'

I sighed. 'What about them.'

He read from the papyrus. 'You have gifted him a horse, saddle, saddlery, a sword, a dagger, a change of clothes, cloak, tent and a pouch of money, a not inconsiderable amount, for his journey.'

'You waste your time, Aaron,' said Gallia, 'Pacorus likes this Roman and would see him journey to Rome like a returning hero.'

'He is a hero, of sorts,' I told her testily, 'and I owe my life to him. Me and thousands of other Parthians. He goes back to his homeland with my blessing, my gratitude and my gifts. *My* gifts, Aaron.'

The treasurer smiled, folded the papyrus and nodded. 'It is as you say, majesty.'

Sporaces and a score of his men accompanied Titus Rutilus and me on our journey to Dura's northern border. It was a leisurely progress, the final leg taking us to a four-sided stone base in which was set two weapons: a Parthian *kontus* and a Roman *gladius* . The eastern side of the base was inscribed with the words 'Kingdom of Dura' and the side facing west 'Romana Syria'.

'This was the spot where armies of Rome and Parthia faced each other,' I told him. 'The Roman commander, Pompey, decided that peace was preferable to war. I liked him.'

'He was murdered in Egypt, majesty.'

'So I heard.'

I offered him my hand, to his great surprise.

'I wish you good fortune, Titus Rutilus.'

He took my hand. 'Thank you for everything, majesty.'

'I have a request,' I said, 'if ever you get to the Silarus Valley in southern Italy, ask whatever gods you follow to look kindly on the souls of those who fell there. I lost a lot of good friends in that valley.'

'I swear it, majesty.'

The day was overcast with a cool easterly wind blowing. I pulled my cloak around me and watched him ride into Syria. I prayed he would find the peace that all of us look for but few of us ever find.

Epilogue

The riddle of Vartan was never solved. With his disappearance from the empire Phraates lost all interest in the young man who had claimed to be Orodes' illegitimate son, though I did not doubt he had despatched assassins to track him down and kill him. If he did and if they were successful I never heard. But I doubted they found him because knowing Phraates' personality he would have proclaimed his vengeance to the whole empire. Even if he had been a fake Phraates would have wanted him dead to tie up any loose ends. There were rumours Vartan and Cookum had fled east across the Kushan Empire to seek sanctuary in China, and for a while I enquired at Dura's caravan park if anyone had heard of Vartan and his fat companion. None had. For her part Eszter's morose demeanour gradually faded to be replaced by the proud and independent princess we all knew and loved. I broached the idea of finding her a suitor but she was lukewarm. No doubt the experience at Sigal had made her wary of a new romantic involvement and so I did not pursue the idea. In the weeks afterwards she spent much time among the Agraci at Palmyra where she had a number of dalliances with some of Malik's warlords.

In the immediate aftermath of our return to Dura my main focus was on the Kushan threat to the empire. The truce with Kujula held, which gave Kewab time to organise his mobile force and liaise with the eastern kings to build a rampart against the Kushan invasion everyone was certain would come. Kewab himself sent regular weekly reports from Farah, which I read at the council meetings in the Citadel. They told of a skilled organiser and diplomat who found time not only to supervise the raising and training of ten thousand horsemen but also soothe the fears of the eastern kings who were suspicious that his small army would become a tool of Phraates to browbeat his eastern kingdoms. He even managed to visit Phanes at Puta, though the King of Carmania became a reclusive figure following the death of his mother. Increasingly his son Prince Babak assumed more and more powers in his father's kingdom, and happily he was able to work with Kewab for the good of the empire. Unfortunately, Phanes refused to allow any of his soldiers to join Kewab's force.

The intermittent border warfare between Sakastan and Carmania ended with the deaths of Peroz and Hamide, the demise of the queen mother having reduced the previously poisonous relations between the two kingdoms. Phraates stripped Phanes of his title of Lord High General in the East, which demoralised the king even further and led to what Alcaeus informed me had been an attack of apoplexy. As a result, he was rarely seen in public and rumours told of slurred speech and the loss of the use of his right arm. His misfortune was Parthia's gain, though, with the first meeting between Salar and Babak going extremely well and paving the way for improving relations between Carmania and Sakastan.

Salar himself made extensive enquiries as to who was responsible for the murder of his parents at his wedding but discovered no answers. The satrap of Persis, Osrow, aware that the assassins had come from the region he supervised, undertook punitive raids against the hill tribes that inhabited Persis, sending Salar the heads of the chiefs his men captured. But the gesture was intended to save his own head due to his fear that the kings of Dura and Sakastan might demand his execution for the outrage of Indira and her followers. He was fortunate that neither Salar nor I were vengeful individuals and so he kept his position and his head.

Phraates and all of us were focused on the eastern frontier and the Kushan menace beyond the Indus, and I had forgotten Dobbai's warning concerning the ruler of Gordyene. Mark Antony's invasion had been defeated and the Roman world was at war with itself. As a result, things were very quiet on the Syrian border and so the kingdom of Dura and I relaxed. Just as Gordyene launched a full-scale war against Armenia.

Historical notes

Most histories of the Parthian Empire concentrate on its struggles against the Romans but the Parthians also faced other threats to their empire, especially in the east where rising powers threatened their trade and lands. The Kushans were originally from China but were driven out of that land by another group, the Xiongnu, around 170BC. They settled in northern India, though at this time they were a loose confederation of tribes rather than a united people. It was under the leadership of their first emperor, Kujula, that the Kushans united in the 1st Century BC and began to advance west. They gradually encroached upon the Parthian Empire, wresting control of lands in modern-day northern Afghanistan and Pakistan. In addition to their campaigns of conquest, the Kushans engaged in seagoing trade and in commerce along the Silk Road between China and the Mediterranean. In this way the Kushans rose in power and wealth, eventually becoming a world power to rival China and Rome in the 1st and 2nd Centuries AD (by which time Parthian power had greatly waned).

The location of Sigal, the capital of Parthian Sakastan, remains a mystery but many scholars believe it is sited in the Bost area in modern-day Afghanistan. Today there are only the remains of a fortress built there by Alexander the Great, but in antiquity Sigal was recorded as being a prosperous city located in the triangle formed by the confluence of the Erymanthus (Helmand) and Argandab rivers. There were well-irrigated orchards between the rivers and the waterways also supported the growing of crops, as well as providing water for sheep, goats, cows and chickens. We also know that Sigal served as a guard post for the caravan trade from eastern Parthia to

India. The city had a strong fortress constructed of mud-bricks, in the centre of which was a deep well with seven galleries encircling its shaft. The well is still extant today.

Ukku steel, later to be known as Damascus steel, was legendary for producing blades that were both harder and more flexible than wrought iron, features critical in the making of a long-bladed weapon. In ancient times producing such blades was incredibly expensive but resulted in swords that were of the highest quality. The metal was sourced from India, being provided as a 'cake' of cast high-carbon steel that was then elongated to produce a sword blade.

Readers may be interested to know that the demon Pazuzu featured in the 1973 film *The Exorcist*, appearing as a stone statue in the opening scenes where he faces the priest Father Merrin, who battles him later in the film following his possession of a teenage girl in Georgetown, Washington, D.C. Pazuzu was originally a Babylonian demon-god whose popularity reached its zenith in the 1st Century BC. Ancient Mesopotamians regarded him as capable of great wrongdoing, but he was also invoked as a defence against evil. For example, pregnant women wore Pazuzu talismans as a protection against the Goddess Lamashtu who preyed on unborn and newborn babies. So when he was not possessing American teenage girls, Pazuzu was scaring off lesser demons and ghosts on behalf of defenceless mortals.

Made in the USA
Lexington, KY
13 December 2017